THE RAVEN'S LADY

Anne Manning

Time Travel Romance

New Concepts   Georgia

The Raven's Lady is an original publication of NCP. This work has never before appeared in book form. This work is a novel. Any similarity to actual persons or events is purely coincidental.

New Concepts Publishing
5202 Humphreys Rd.
Lake Park, GA 31636

ISBN 1-58608-682-0
© copyright Betty Kasischke
Cover art by Eliza Black, © copyright

All rights reserved, which includes the right to reproduce this book or portions thereof in any form whatsoever except as provided by the U.S. Copyright Law.

If you purchased this book without a cover you should be aware this book is stolen property.

NCP books are available at special quantity discounts for bulk purchases for sales promotions, premiums, fund raising, or educational use. For details, write, email, or phone New Concepts Publishing, 5202Humphreys Rd., Lake Park, GA 31636, ncp@newconceptspublishing.com, Ph. 229-257-0367, Fax 229-219-1097.

First NCP Paperback Printing: 2004

Printed in the United States of America

Chapter One

"Damn all men to hell!"

On her knees on an Irish hillside, Eibhlin Fitzgerald jabbed the trowel into the emerald turf. In her mind, however, rather than digging up a specimen of Ladies' Mantle, the razor-edged tool was excising something more vital to the self-esteem of her lying, cheating ex-husband. Startled by the sudden urge to inflict hurt, long after she'd thought the pain and humiliation gone, she drew a deep breath and concentrated on relaxing. Then, much more tenderly than she'd begun, she scooped the specimen from the soil.

Her voice low, she chided herself in a broad imitation of her father's brogue. "After all, Evie, 'tis not the poor wee plant's fault."

Unable to speak her ex-husband's name without opening a wound only now beginning to heal, Eibhlin filled her brain with work pushing *Himself* aside, where he couldn't hurt her anymore. She wrapped the rootstock in cheesecloth, admiring the inconspicuous greenish flowers and the wide, flat leaves which inspired the plant's common name. Still holding the sample of Ladies' Mantle, she pulled her mini-cassette recorder out of the pouch at her side and began recording.

"*Alchemilla vulgaris*. June 21, 1998. Eleven forty five AM. East face of Craglea, in vicinity of Killaloe, County Clare. Elevation, approximately one hundred meters."

After clicking off the recorder and dropping it and the Ladies' Mantle into her pouch, Eibhlin sat, hugging her knees, on the hillside. Raising her eyes to the summit of Craglea, she felt a sense of unity with the land. The life that filled everything called to her, beckoning her to join in.

Maybe she did hear the call. It was the summer solstice, after all.

Maybe I'll get to see some druids lurking around the Crag, or perhaps a party of the Little People making their way to one of the sacred mounds. Four weeks in Ireland and no fairies. What a bummer, she thought with a laugh.

"Little People." Her whisper was tinged with fond dismissal.

Naturally, the ignorant primitives of a thousand or more years ago would have made up stories to explain what they couldn't understand. What was really amazing was the old superstitions still held sway, especially here in the western counties. Just this morning Eibhlin had been warned away from the Crag by the woman from whom she'd rented a room in Killaloe.

Even as she laughed, she understood. This was Ireland. If there *were* Little People, they'd live here.

Surrounded by surreal green, with the perfume of fresh earth and nectar scenting the air, she gazed down at the place where Kincora was said to have once stood. Where Brian Boru, the only real Irish High King--*Ard Ri*, she corrected herself--had dreamed of bringing unity and peace and the rule of law to this island.

Gazing down at the scattered remains of Boru's palace, she could almost hear the songs her Irish-born parents had taught her and, as she began to hum *The Pretty Maid Milking her Cow,* she wished she'd brought her little harp with her. What a waste for it to be gathering dust in her house in Oregon while she sat here with all this music crying to be played.

Closing her eyes, her mind rippled with the pipes carrying a melody high above the beat of the *bodhran* and a hundred memories clamored for recognition all at once. Memories of her mother's songs and the stories which had made Ireland as familiar to her as the land around her childhood home in southern California.

They were the tales of heroes, Cuchulainn, Conchobar, Finn MacCuill--warriors and the strong women they'd fought and died for.

Ah, those were the days, she thought, a momentary swell of self-pity picking at her heart.

"Nope, no way, Evie. Don't let him do this to you."

Once more resolving to push away the failure that was her marriage, Eibhlin stretched out on the cool grass and closed her eyes.

She may have lain there for hours before a thrumming, beginning deep within the earth beneath her, roused her to wakefulness. It became a vibration, its rhythm gentle and slow. It touched her ears, her skin. She tasted it on her tongue.

Her hands moved of their own accord up her thighs... to her belly... to her breasts--now grown unbearably sensitive. Her hips ground into the yielding grass beneath her.

An aching cry of yearning filled her ears. Seconds passed before she realized the cry had come from her own lips. Her eyes flew open and she sat up, cheeks burning.

"Oh, my God." She sprung to her feet, moving up the hillside. Eyes darting from side to side, making sure there were no witnesses to her bizarre behavior, Eibhlin searched the hill for an explanation--a herd of elephants, a Space Shuttle take-off, something, anything, that would make the ground shake enough to bring her to the point of....

"Oh, my God!" She'd never gotten this worked up by anything *Himself* had ever done. Eibhlin pressed one hand over her heart in an effort to calm its racing pace. Her gaze combed the valley, passing along the length of the Shannon.

"What happened to Killaloe?" she breathed, disbelieving.

Killaloe was gone. Only a single stone building surrounded by a low fence of the same material marked the place where the small village had sat at the mouth of Lough Derg.

Eibhlin turned back up to the lake... and her breathing stopped. Where only a pile of stones had stood....

"Kincora," she exhaled finally, the sense of recognition overwhelming as she looked at the imposing wood and stone castle and surrounding palisade wall--a ruin no longer.

"No." Eibhlin shut her eyes against the impossible. "I'm having a dream. I went to sleep thinking about warriors and castles and so I'm dreaming of them."

But this was a remarkably detailed dream, she thought, peeking from eyes that stubbornly refused to stay shut. People scurrying around the buildings and along the Shannon. Fishermen bringing their catch ashore and turning their coracles over on the banks for the night. Swineherds leading pigs to the pens. Farmers coming in from the fields. On the far bank of the Shannon, just ready to cross, a band of mounted riders. They were too far away for her to make out their clothing, but she knew they were warriors.

And somehow, she knew what she was seeing was real.

Self-preservation made her stoop over to reach down for her leather bag which held her collected samples.

"I've gotta get outta here," she said aloud.

"*Cad e seo?*"

Eibhlin stopped in mid-reach. The voice boomed around her like thunder, deep and powerful.

"*Ce thu fein?*"

She raised her eyes, hoping the speaker wasn't as god-like as his voice was.

And raised her eyes... and raised them... and raised....

He stood on the hillside before her, one leg cocked at an angle. Eibhlin felt her mouth drop open in astonishment.

"*Ce thu fein?*" he asked again. Who are you?

Her Irish was a bit rusty, but she understood a simple question like that one. However, her eyes had taken over her entire brain to process the sight before her.

A warrior, nearly seven feet tall, heavily muscled, long of arm and leg, smiled down at her, dimples creasing both broad cheeks. He wore a light pull-over garment that reached to mid-thigh. A sword hung from his belt in a leather sheath. Tucking one thumb into his belt, he bent over slightly.

"Are you lost, woman?" he asked in Irish.

"*Ni hea*," no, she answered before her senses snatched control of her brain again.

She began a conscious catalogue of his features. The olive tone of his skin was too dark for an Irishman, yet in every other detail he was every inch the Celt, from the thick warrior's mustache framing his full lips to the heavy golden torque he wore around his muscled neck. His heavy blue-black hair hung in a glossy fall to his shoulders, sweeping back from his high forehead, its sheen interrupted only by a streak of startling white, beginning at his hairline just to the left of center.

He strode toward her with a power that was both physical and sensual. Some part of her woman's soul shrank from him even as he attracted her.

Then she looked into his eyes. The color of jet, they sparkled with the humor that was reflected in his smile. The instinctive apprehension caused by his overwhelming masculinity dissipated like smoke and she was left with only one thought.

Wow.

"Are you all right?" His smile faded and his voice took on a note of concern.

"Yes, just a little confused," she managed to answer.

"Confused? Well, you had best come with me to Kincora. Like as not you are sun-stroked out here. It is unseasonable warm. The king's physician can make certain you are not injured." He reached for her hand.

Eibhlin raised her own to take his. It was the most natural thing in the world. His warm fingers, long and strong, closed with surprising gentleness over hers. As she used his strength to stand, she pulled him closer.

"Christ's Blood!" he exclaimed and snatched his hand back. Deprived of his help with no warning, Eibhlin fell on her rear.

The warrior stepped back, his hand already on the hilt of his sword. His black eyes narrowed and he squinted at the space between them.

"What's wrong?" she asked as she got to her feet under her own steam.

"Did you not feel that?" He shook his hand, then examined it, opening and closing his fingers. Turning his head nearly sideways, he cut his gaze out of the corner of his eye. "Do you not see it?"

He spread his fingers and leaned toward her. At a point right in front of her, his fingers stopped in mid-air. Then his balled fist headed straight for her head. Eibhlin ducked as the resounding thud of flesh and bone on some solid object echoed across the valley. Her warrior didn't even flinch, but dropped to one knee, eyes fixed. Eibhlin followed suit and they knelt there on the hillside, staring at nothing.

"It glitters like gossamer, yet I can not see it looking straight on." Once more he reached forward and touched the air.

A shimmer, like the ripples in a pond after a rock has been thrown in, spread out from the place where he touched. But he could pass no farther. Extending her hand, Eibhlin passed through the shimmering air with no trouble.

His eyes flew to hers and he stared at her. "Are you a fairy?"

Eibhlin choked out a laugh. "A fairy? Are you kidding?"

A frown creased his forehead and thinned his full lips. "What tongue is this?"

"Oh, sorry," she said as she switched back to Irish, "No, I'm not a fairy."

"Why do you laugh?" His frown had deepened as though he were personally affronted.

"Because the idea that I'm a fairy is ridiculous. Fairies were sprites, tiny things that lived under plants. Even if I believed in fairies, which I don't, I'm too big."

The warrior's eyes moved over her, lingering on her breasts that were pressed fully into the low neckline of her light cotton pullover. "You are but a mite of a thing."

Eibhlin bolted up and back, away from the heat of his gaze, trying not to be affected by his words, afraid to believe the obvious admiration she saw in his eyes. She supposed she would seem like a *mite* to him. He had to be at least a foot taller than she. But nevertheless, his assessment left her breathless. She'd always felt something of a cow--big and *full-figured*, as the bra commercial delicately put it. A *fairy*? At five-foot-eleven, she was hardly within the height requirements for the job.

He drew his sword and poked delicately at the air. His blade came toward her face. Instinctively, she stepped back, but the tip of the sword stopped. He pushed, but it would go no farther.

"It would seem that you can pass, but I cannot," he said with a smile. "Fitting, that. The lady should always have the choice." Offering his palm, he said, "Will you come with me?"

Eibhlin heard a voice in her soul urging her to reach for that huge, yet elegant, hand.

"Wait a minute," she said aloud in English, good sense returning. "This isn't happening. It's just a dream brought on by excessive heat. I'll have a drink and cool down a bit." She closed her eyes, blocking out the warrior who now looked at her like she was indeed one of the *Little People*, and reached for her bag and the little water bottle she kept inside. Even with her eyes tightly shut, she could feel his gaze on her.

She sipped her water. "At least I have good taste in hallucinations. He is gorgeous. Take that, you lying son-of-a-bitch. My fantasies are better than reality was with you."

"What are you saying? What tongue is this? I've never heard it, though it seems to resemble the Saxons' speech."

Eibhlin peeked at him. He was on his knees beside her, examining her like a bug under a jar. She noticed he was careful to stay away from the shimmering haze.

"With an imagination like this, maybe I should take up writing," she said aloud. In Irish she asked him, "Why aren't you gone? I don't believe in you."

Her warrior sat back on his heels, one raven-black eyebrow raised in amusement. "And I suppose this means I do not exist, then?"

She had to smile at his reaction. A body like that *and* a sense of humor. What a find.

"Oh, well, I might as well play along as long as it lasts. Mama will get a charge out of my Celtic he-man." She sipped again from her water bottle and slipped easily back into Irish. "So, warrior, what is your name?"

One corner of his full, delicious mouth raised in a smile. "My name is Brandubh mac Dougal. Kinsman to Brian mac Cennedi, *Ard Ri*."

A laugh bubbled from her. She looked at the plastic bottle in her hand and wondered if her landlady had slipped some Irish whiskey into it.

"Brandubh, huh?" Amusing little bit of fantasy scriptwriting. *Brandubh* meant *black raven*. Well, he was that--dark, sleek, beautiful.

"Well, Brandubh mac Dougal, I am Eibhlin ni Seamus." She carefully used the old form patronymic.

He rose and again extended his hand to her. "Come with me, Eibhlin?"

She knew from her mother's stories that in the Celtic tradition, the woman had the right to refuse any suit. Pretty enlightened for primitives, she thought.

"Okay, let's go." She looked away just for the two seconds it took to replace her bottle in her bag, but when she reached for his hand, she encountered only the empty air.

Brandubh had disappeared.

Chapter Two

She faded before his eyes, her lips moving, her voice dimming as she spoke more of her unintelligible words. But even as she evaporated into mist, she raised her hand to him.

Brandubh crouched on his haunches on the hillside, staring at the horizon, cursing his luck.

"God's bones. Just when I've all but paid the bride's price for Caoimhe." He looked back down where the grass preserved the outline of Eibhlin's rounded hips. "Where have you been? Why do you decide to show yourself now and then disappear?"

And why was he fool enough to be seduced by one glance of a woman of the *Danaan* who faded into the fairy mist as soon as he reached for her?

"Eibhlin." The name would not stay off his lips.

Brandubh stretched out a tentative hand and passed it through the air, but the barrier was gone. He hadn't really believed in the faerie realm before, but now he crossed himself to ward off the sin of inviting the old ways and old ones. Though a Christian from birth, he was also an Irishman.

As he knelt there on the hillside, he wondered why, if she were a fairy, did she look so very mortal? There was no otherworldly fragility to Eibhlin. Her body, tall and strong and full, had filled him with wanting from the first glimpse. Yet the manner of her disappearance gave him no other explanation but that she was one of the *Danaan*. But why would she appear to him?

Questions without answers infuriated him. With a yank on his belt, Brandubh started down the hill. He would go home and consult with his mother. Wise in the old ways, she would know more than he did.

Maybe she could even tell him how to command Eibhlin to return to him.

* * * *

"Brandubh? Where did you go, you big, hairy warrior, you?" Eibhlin pushed herself to her feet. Brushing blades of grass and dirt off her full skirt, she tried to hide from her disappointment. "Isn't that just like a man, though? Promises you medical attention, from the King's physician no less, then just disappears."

A quick glance toward the lake reassured her that she'd just awakened from a dream. The ruin of Kincora lay, barely one stone standing on another, by the west bank of the Shannon.

Disappointment settled over her. Only a dream.

Brandubh. Her black raven wasn't real.

Hours later, she sat alone in her rented room in Killaloe. A billowing froth of Irish lace framed the window where she gazed at the still sunlit sky. Try as she might to admire nature, it was Brandubh's face she saw. He was clear in her memory, every detail sharp and in focus.

A knock at the door shook her from her contemplation of the unfortunately imaginary Brandubh mac Dougal. After the second knock, she dragged herself out of her chair to answer.

"Mrs. Mahoney," Eibhlin said, trying to act happy to see her fifty-something Irish landlady standing in the hallway. The woman's perpetually smiling expression had been replaced by a look of concern.

"Have you had dinner, dear?"

Eibhlin shook her head. "Not yet."

"Why don't you join me?" Mrs. Mahoney raised her palm to fend off any possible refusal. "'Tis a fine lamb stew and I went to no small trouble bakin' fresh bread. Come." She took Eibhlin's hand. "Men like a woman with flesh on her bones."

Eibhlin knew that wasn't true. Not American men, anyway. But she hadn't eaten so she let her landlady drag her down to the homely kitchen. Puttering around gathering dishes and silver, Mrs. Mahoney maintained a nearly one-sided conversation.

"I knew your father, did you know?"

Eibhlin wasn't surprised. Everyone knew Seamus Fitzgerald.

"He was a fine lookin' man. You get your height from him. And such a wonderful voice. We all knew he'd be a famous singer one day." Mrs. Mahoney set a steaming bowl of stew before Eibhlin.

"Did you know my mother as well?" Eibhlin asked just before taking a spoonful of the stew. "Ummm, Mrs. Mahoney, this is heavenly."

Mrs. Mahoney pursed her lips in a modest smile of thanks and took her own place at the table. "No, I was not acquainted with your mother. She wasn't from here," she said. "'Twas said Seamus found her on the Crag."

"What?" Eibhlin's spoon clattered to the table, spattering gravy all over the linen tablecloth. Before today, such a statement would have only earned a laugh and invitation to continue. But Eibhlin didn't feel like laughing. "She's not from Killaloe?" she asked, dabbing frantically at the spots on the cloth with her napkin.

"No." The woman's simple answer and apparent lack of interest in continuing was irritating.

"So, you believe my father found my mother on Craglea?" Eibhlin prompted.

"Och, yes. Went up one Beltain morn and brought her home that night."

"Beltain?"

Mrs. Mahoney gave Eibhlin a look like she'd just indicated ignorance of St. Patrick.

"May Day. It's a feast day for the old ones, the druids and such." She blew on her spoonful of stew. "Like today, you understand."

"Today?" Eibhlin asked, even as she remembered.

"Midsummer's Day. The summer solstice. On such days, the fairy places are open to mortal folk to cross over."

Eibhlin sat back in her chair, suddenly realizing why Brandubh had asked if she were a fairy. Could her imagination possibly have created that question?

"Where did you gather today, dear?" Mrs. Mahoney asked as she took up her teacup and leaned back in her chair.

Eibhlin retrieved her spoon and tried to eat the creamy, thick lamb stew, though she was having trouble swallowing.

"On Craglea," she croaked.

"So, you went up to the Crag anyway, did you now? And it an old holy day." The older woman sipped her tea. "Did you see anything?"

"Of course not." Eibhlin heard the falsehood in her own voice. Clearly, so did Mrs. Mahoney. But Eibhlin was not in the mood to be grilled on her afternoon's hallucination. She guided the conversation to safer topics while she filled up on Mrs. Mahoney's fine cooking and finished her tea.

She suddenly had the most overwhelming urge to call her parents. Maybe it was just hearing about them from someone who knew them. Or maybe it was the strange story about her father *finding* her mother on the Crag, but she needed to talk to them both.

"Mrs. Mahoney, do you mind if I use your telephone?"

* * * *

The sun dropped into the Great Sea beyond the western shore as Brandubh kicked his horse to greater speed, always anxious to get home, yet this time urged by a greater need to arrive. The horse's hooves hit the water and Brandubh ignored the growing cold of his soaked leggings as they splashed across the ford of the Shannon that had given his father's holding its name--Ath Sionnain. Even before he was within the gates, he threw his right leg over the neck of his frothing mount and, sliding to the ground, tossed the reins to a stable boy.

"Boy, is Lady Sadbh about?"

"Yes, Brandubh. In the weaving room."

Naturally, his mother would be attending to her business. He strode toward the small stone building that housed the looms, shouting back over his shoulder, "Cool him well, lad. He's had a hard ride all the way from Kincora."

Brandubh had to nearly bend double to pass through the doorway. A building used by women, the weaving room had not been planned for the

THE RAVEN'S LADY 11

comfort of men. Even once inside, his head threatened to break through the thatched roof, but a lifetime of painful lumps had trained him to take care around low ceilings.

Another cross he had to bear--though not nearly so irksome, he thought with a smile--was apparent as soon as the door closed behind him. The women had stopped their work, staring at him, some in open invitation. Any other day, he'd have returned the smile of one of them, accepting what she offered. But today, he was interested in only one woman--and she was not here. He was not even sure she was real.

A young girl, tiny and pretty in her way as the wren she so resembled, sprang from her place and flew across the room. Brandubh felt a guilty flush. Caoimhe had not been on his mind at all this day, except as a problem to be solved.

"Brandubh." Caoimhe came toward him, smile bright and hands outstretched. "You've finally come home."

He took her hands and bent down to allow her to peck him on the cheek. She stood away, hurt. He knew she'd hoped for a more exuberant greeting.

"I came to speak with my mother, Caoimhe."

"Really? Does that mean you are ready to go to my father? Your father has talked to him."

Had her voice always been so piercing? And she was so small, barely reaching the middle of his breastbone. Though a grown woman at sixteen, she had a form more like a young boy, barely fleshed out as a woman ought to be.

As Eibhlin was--full and ripe and....

Brandubh pulled his attention back to Caoimhe. Her smile had turned to a pout and she was deep in the self-concern he had always excused before.

"I do not like being paid for with horses. Cattle are traditional, Brandubh. How do I know what ten horses are worth?"

"My horses are the finest in Ireland. Your father will be glad to get them."

He was immediately sorry for the words, because Caoimhe took them as agreement to the marriage and her face glowed. Even though he had not made any offer--and would make none now--he could not tell her that in the presence of the other women. He could not cause her to lose face. 'Twould be much better to let her put out the story that she had rejected him.

Immense was his gratitude when he saw his mother coming toward them.

"So, my son, you come in here after being away for months, just to disrupt my work?" Sadbh ni Mahon approached, long, flaming hair hanging in a thick braid down her back. With barely a glance at the girl, she said, "Are you finished, Caoimhe? I promised that length of wool to the abbot for Michaelmas."

Turning her back on the pouting Caoimhe, Sadbh linked her slender arm through Brandubh's and led him out of the house and down the path to the river before she spoke again.

"Caoimhe has been boasting about catching you. I am mightily tired of it. But I suppose you are fixed on her." Sadbh sighed and shrugged, not giving Brandubh a chance to get in a word before she went on. "Well, I was the same. When I saw my Dougal on the river bank, I could not be moved. Uncle Brian stormed and shouted, but I knew what I wanted. You are my son in this, my dear."

Brandubh nearly laughed as he listened to her. She had been against him choosing Caoimhe from the first. The only thing worse than having to tell Caoimhe he would not offer for her would be having to listen to his mother declare she had known all along it was not a suitable match.

"You are quiet, Brandubh."

He stopped their progress along the bank and helped her sit on the grass. Brandubh remained standing, knowing he'd be pacing before he was through. Asking for help of any kind was never easy for him.

"Mother, I need advice."

Sadbh's icy blue eyes widened in surprise, then narrowed. "Of course, my dear."

"It's about Caoimhe. I...."

One auburn eyebrow raised in a perfect bow. Brandubh pressed on. Best to get it over with.

"I am having second thoughts about offering for her."

"There is another woman." It was not a question.

"Yes... no... well, I don't know." He raked his hair away from his temple. "This is going to sound very strange...." And he told her about Eibhlin. Sadbh spoke not a single word, never interrupted, only raised her chin and nodded once or twice. When he finished his tale, she sat forward.

"She vanished from your sight?" she asked in an awed whisper, her usually cool expression openly excited.

"Yes."

"This was today?"

"Yes." He'd been hoping for something more helpful.

A teasing smile, one he knew well, curved her lips. "What do you want from me?"

"I want you to tell me how to get her back if it is possible. Do not pretend you know nothing of these things."

Sadbh shot up from her seat. "Lower your voice, Brandubh. I will not be branded a pagan and denied the sacraments simply for revering the old ways. Even the native priests are not as tolerant as they used to be." She linked her arm through his again and started them off, away from the palisade.

She was silent for a long while. When she took a deep breath, Brandubh recognized the story-teller in her.

"Tales abound, Brandubh, in which people disappear, never to be seen again. Some people return from the fairy realm only many years or even centuries later, aged and dying. These things occur around the fairy places--the dolmens, the mounds, the forts, sometimes just on places like Craglea where the old ones dwell. And they happen at certain times of the year, the old feast days.

"If your Eibhlin is of the *Danaan*, she will be there if she wishes to be found." Sadbh stopped and turned him to face her. A tall woman, she still had to raise her eyes to look into Brandubh's. "If she is mortal, and what you witnessed is a... doorway from one place to another, then you may have to wait for the next old holy day, which will be Samhain." She shrugged. "Then again, you may never see her again."

"I do not accept that."

Sadbh's rich laugh rang out. "My dear, you have no say in this. These things are beyond our ken. Even if you do see her again, say next Samhain, and what you have deduced about the curtain is true--that she can pass but you cannot--then you will still have no say. She will have to choose to cross over. If her choice is no, then *you* will have no choice but to accept it."

Brandubh bit his tongue to halt the curse that soured there. He despised helplessness more than anything. All his life he'd trained, worked, studied, to ensure that he would always have a choice, no matter the case. No one, not even his mother or father, knew why he had been so driven. And he'd never tell them.

"Then I will be there on Craglea at Samhain."

Sadbh nodded. "What about Caoimhe?"

Brandubh grimaced, but accepted his responsibility. "I will speak with her privately and tell her that I will not be offering for her."

"She will be shamed before the other women."

"I refuse to be guilty for that. She knew nothing was settled."

"She is a young girl, Brandubh, in love with you since she was a child."

"She still behaves as a child," he grumbled in reply.

Sadbh stood away and coolly studied his face.

"My son, I agree that Caoimhe is not the woman for you. I would have you find a woman with whom you can have what your father and I have. Such is not possible with a woman of the fairy mist. Keep a tight rein on your feelings until you know whether this Eibhlin will return to you. Do not become obsessed with her to the exclusion of flesh and blood women who can warm your bed in ways a vision cannot."

"I touched her. Her flesh is soft and her blood is as hot as mine."

Even while he spoke his ardent words, Brandubh considered his mother's. Had he not already admitted to himself that he did not know whether Eibhlin was real?

He tipped his head toward his mother and gave her a smile.

"I will be cautious, Mother. And you will have your grandchildren, Sadbh ni Mahon. You have my word on it."

"Good." She laid her hand on his arm. "I wish you good fortune, my son. Come, let us go in to see your father. He has missed you. Perhaps you will remain with us here for a time."

He set his hand on hers and walked her back inside the palisade, already anxious and impatient with waiting that had only begun.

Chapter Three

The phone rang four times before her mother answered.

"Hello," a voice, still tinged with the lilt of an Irish brogue, answered.

"*Dia duit*," Eibhlin said. "Hello, Mama."

"Ah, dear one, *dia duit*. What a pleasure to hear you speak the old tongue. You've been practicing, have you?"

"Yes, I certainly have."

"Are you having success in finding what you need?"

"Yes, I am." I sure am, she added silently. Unfortunately, he wasn't real. "The grant money's holding out and I'm going on to Scotland tomorrow."

"'Tis a wonderful thing you're trying to do, dear one." Her mother was silent for a beat. "I am so proud of you, though I do wish you wouldn't travel all alone. I barely got a wink of sleep while you were in China."

Eibhlin heard the unspoken words. You are all we have left, dear one. Take care.

So often while doing her work she thought of her older brother, now dead for nearly twenty years. She could only barely remember the brief happy time before her brother had gotten sick, though the memories of the two, long, agonizing years it had taken Conor to die were more than clear.

The words came out, unbidden. "Mama, I still miss him."

"So, do we, dear one."

"Mama," Eibhlin said, trying to stop herself, but it was like trying to hold back a flood using only your hands. "I know you only tried to protect me by hiding it all from me, by keeping me from the funeral. I understand, really. Can you understand that I'm doing this now so I can have my healing? If I can find a cure or at least a treatment that's not worse than the disease, if I can help make it easier for all the other children who have to go through that hell...." Her throat tightened on her. She would also do it for herself, and once and for all let go of the guilt of being the one who lived.

Her mother's sigh crackled over the phone line. "I suppose, in a way, I envy you. You are in a position to do something with your studies. That was the worst, watching wee Conor fight so hard and being unable to do anything to help him."

"I have you to thank for being able to do this, Mama."

Her mother was silent for a long moment. "It was always in you, dear one. You have always had the gift."

"But, Mama, you were the one who taught me about plants and what they can do." That her career should now be defined by a childhood hobby struck her as ironic. "Did you ever think, Mama, how strange life is?"

Her mother's laugh rang in her ears. "Dear one, you have no idea."

That's quite a reaction, Eibhlin thought.

"Moira, let me talk now," Seamus Fitzgerald came on the extension. His rich baritone, whether speaking or singing, thrilled the soul. "Hello, my angel."

"Hello, Dad. Hey, you won't believe what a small world it is. My landlady here in Killaloe is a friend of yours. Her name is Patsy Mahoney. You guys will get the biggest charge out of this. Mrs. Mahoney claims that you, Dad, went up to Craglea one Beltain morn and came back with Mama that night."

Both Moira and Seamus laughed softly.

"'Fraid I don't remember a Patsy Mahoney. Are ya believin' her, now, Miss? Think you I went up to get my woman from the Crag?"

"Seamus," Moira chided. "'Tis a most romantic tale, no? At least as good as that of Angus and Caer. 'Course, your ol' da here...."

"Old? Listen, woman...."

Moira cut back in. "...Never pined in illness for me."

"I would have, love, if I'd thought I could never have you."

Her parents chuckled and Eibhlin suddenly felt lost. Their love was so strong after so many years--forged in poverty and riches, joy and sorrow. She had basked in that circle of light all her life, but now it seemed too small to hold her, too.

"What is amiss, dearling? You're so quiet."

"Nothing, Dad. I guess I'm just feeling a little sorry for myself. You and Mama are still so much in love and I couldn't seem to keep my husband home."

"Now, Eibhlin, you stop that this instant." Moira's voice was stern. "You knew he was a philanderer when you married him."

"I don't really want to hear about *Himself* right now."

"You brought him up." Moira was merciless when Eibhlin needed to hear something. "You never felt for him what you will feel for another man one day."

"You have your crystal ball fired up there, Moira ni Conor?"

"Do not be impertinent." Moira's voice softened, "I promise you, one day you will know how wonderful it can be."

Craglea and her dark warrior crowded into Eibhlin's mind. Only momentarily considering how crazy it would sound, she blurted out, "Mama, you know a lot about Brian Boru, don't you?"

There was a silence on the other end of the phone. Eibhlin shivered with anticipation, both excited and fearful.

"Yes, Eibhlin, I do." There had never been any more explanation than that. Moira Fitzgerald just knew the old language, the old customs, the old songs and stories.

"Have you ever heard of a man called Brandubh mac Dougal?"

Silence.

"Mama?"

"Just a minute, dearling," her father's voice was the one that answered.

A sniff preceded her mother's return to the conversation.

"Yes, Brandubh was Brian's kinsman. His mother was the daughter of Mahon mac Cennedi, Brian's brother. Why do you ask about Brandubh?"

"I just ran across the name associated with Brian's and I wondered."

Silence. Eibhlin shrugged her shoulders to smooth the creeping unease.

"Are you two going to go mute on me every time I say something?"

Seamus laughed. "I'm sorry, dearling."

He paused and she could hear him thinking.

"Evie, Irish ways may seem strange to you, raised in America as you were, but remember, in every myth is a seed of truth. Discount nothing. Be open to anything. Make your decisions based on what your heart tells you to do."

Seamus paused. When he spoke, Eibhlin heard his voice tremble.

"And remember we love you, no matter where you are."

Moira came on, her voice wet with tears. "Your father is right. Every day of your life has been a preparation for the next. I love you. Never forget that." She sniffed loudly into the phone.

Eibhlin opened her mouth, then closed it as the creeping feeling down her back spread to tickle her ribs.

"And I will know you," Moira said, "no matter when we next see each other. Good luck, dear one."

Completely silent through the last part of this strange conversation, Eibhlin was now unable to stop them from ending the call. Her mother's sob of anguish tore at her heart just as the *click* of the disconnection sounded in her ear.

"Mama!" Her shout went unanswered.

She sat in Mrs. Mahoney's parlor, numb, receiver lying in her lap, overwhelmed by a startling confusion.

Shutting her mind against the feeling that they had just said good-bye to her forever, she grabbed the old-fashioned rotary phone and moved with maddening slowness through the twenty-plus digits of calling card number, access codes, country codes, area codes, finally her parents' phone number in California. The busy signal infuriated her. Over and over she dialed, dialed, dialed.

Finally after an hour of trying, she decided to go to bed and wait until she got to the airport the next morning. She had an eight o'clock plane to catch to Inverness. More Celts, she thought, with a sigh. More druids. More superstition.

* * * *

Brandubh returned to Kincora the next morning. He waited for her on Craglea all day until darkness fell, but she didn't appear. Every day for a week he haunted the Crag, every day becoming more sure she was only a wisp from the other realm.

Until he remembered the feeling of her hand in his.

She was real. Perhaps. If she was real and his mother's advice was correct, he had no choice but to wait until Samhain.

More than four months away. He gritted his teeth at the prospect of such a delay. Yet, there was nothing he could do about it. So, he returned to Ath Sionnain to wait.

As soon as he arrived, he wondered why he had not simply gone to his own lands. Lon Dubh required a master's hand. It was not right to leave the running of it to his steward, competent though Hauk was.

Of course, it did not require a great deal of thought to conclude that he had unfinished business here.

Caoimhe. He had to break with her once and for all, before he brought Eibhlin. Everyone in the tribe knew he had asked her father about her-- Caoimhe had made sure that was well-known. Even though it was not his doing, he would give her the chance to save face.

Yet, despite his good intentions of seeing to the matter immediately, for three days he avoided being alone with Caoimhe or speaking to any of her family. However, he couldn't avoid her anxious adoration across his father's great hall. He had to face her.

He found her after supper, standing apart with a few of her friends. Still with no idea of how to say what had to be said, he approached and groaned inwardly as her face lit up when she saw him. She would be hurt, for she was young and fancied herself in love with him. Yet, for her good he had to be honest.

Yes, she would get over him in time and transfer her affection to another, one who would return it in equal measure. He was doing the right thing.

That thought helped him overcome his cowardice.

"Caoimhe, will you walk with me?" he asked.

She blushed prettily and her friends tittered as she laid her hand on his arm and left the hall with him.

They walked in silence through the courtyard and passed through the high gates. Caoimhe didn't speak, but Brandubh could feel her questioning gaze on his face. Glancing at her expectant expression, he realized she thought he'd brought her here to ask her to marry him.

He'd faced death in battle with less dread.

When they were far from the ears of others, Brandubh cleared his throat and leapt into the fire.

"Caoimhe, I know you think we had an understanding, but I cannot marry you."

Damn, I had not meant to be that blunt, he thought as her eyes opened wide and a weak moan escaped her rounded mouth.

"Why?" Her voice scraped his ears raw. "You promised. Your father agreed with my father."

"Caoimhe, I am a man. I make my own agreements. Dougal merely asked if your father was interested and what the price would be. I haven't talked to Conor myself." He sat and pulled her down beside him. Trying to be gentle, he wanted her to understand his decision. "Caoimhe, you are a pretty girl and you will make a good wife, but for some other man, not me. My heart is pledged elsewhere and I cannot give you my whole self, as it is meant to be."

Caoimhe's shocked expression turned to a baleful glare. "You mean my family isn't rich enough for you."

"That is not the case at all. I...."

"Your mother is behind this, isn't she?" Her voice pierced his head like a spike. She jumped up and faced him, leaning into his face. "I will not put up with it, Brandubh. You have agreed to marry me and you will."

Brandubh gazed into Caoimhe's face, nearly on a level with his, though he was seated. This illumination of her character strengthened his resolve. His next words were plain and as honest as he could make them.

"No, Caoimhe. I will not. You'd best find someone more malleable, closer to your own age, whom you can bully."

"Just because we're not rich like you."

"No, little one. Wealth matters not at all. You could have ten thousand head of cattle and I still would not offer for you."

Caoimhe stood quietly, her arms hanging limp at her side.

"If you don't marry me, I will kill myself."

Brandubh squelched a wave of disgust. Her childish attempt to get her way was unmoving.

"Little one, I'm not worth throwing your life away for."

"I never wanted any other man." Her voice quivered and her shoulders slumped. "I only wanted you."

That piteous statement touched him in a way her threats had not, and he felt a rogue for hurting her. He reached for her, wanting to comfort her. She stepped back.

He dropped his hands back to his sides.

Her eyes glistened with unshed tears.

"I will haunt you, Brandubh. My family will avenge my death." She turned and ran into the night.

"Caoimhe," he called after her, but he didn't run after her. Let her go cry on her sister's shoulder. Moira was sensible and would talk her out of this madness. Caoimhe was a devout girl. She'd never kill herself.

However, he thought, it would also be prudent to let her father know of her threat.

Brandubh started off in the direction of Dougal's fine stone house, where he would likely find Conor mac Turlough among those sharing an ale and listening to Dougal's stories. Raucous laughter echoed down the path and he wondered which fantastic tale Dougal was recounting this time.

Only a few steps from the house, Brandubh stopped and turned toward the palisade gates as the sound of hoofbeats arrived on the night air. The rhythm was that of an exhausted horse. No Irishman ran his horse to exhaustion. A tired horse misstepped and broke necks. Moving beyond the dim light of the torches, he could make out the shadowy form of the horse coming closer.

"Brandubh! The *Ard Ri* summons you to Kincora."

Brandubh recognized the voice of the rider as that of his friend, Gadhra, and ran forward to meet him. The spent mount stumbled as Gadhra pulled the reins to stop him.

Grabbing the bridle and calming the animal, Brandubh turned his irritation onto his friend.

"What is wrong with you to ride a horse near to death?"

"Necessity, Brandubh," Gadhra said as he dismounted and threw the reins to the stable boys who scurried around. "Care for him, lads, he served Brian well this night."

"There is no necessity that requires killing a horse. Is it better to be left afoot?" Brandubh allowed Gadhra only a moment of time to get his feet set firmly on the ground. "What is amiss? The *Ard Ri* summons me tonight?"

"As soon as you can get to his side, Brandubh. He needs every strong sword arm he can find. The King of Leinster has got himself a pack of Viking wolves. They are sweeping through Offey and are on their way to Kincora. Word is the monastery at Clonmacnois is being threatened as well."

"Even such a renegade as Maelmordha would not defy the *Ard Ri*'s protection of the monasteries."

"Would he not? Brian is old, Brandubh. He is tired."

"Boru is ten times the man Maelmordha ever will be."

Gadhra sighed and shrugged. "Yes. But... the worst news is, the northern chieftains, Malachy and the others, are offering excuses instead of fighting men. If Maelmordha tastes victory, they may decide to wait longer, just to see if Brian will be able to hold on to his power."

Brandubh nodded and waved over a young boy. "Saddle my horse and prepare twenty more for travel. Brian will require fresh mounts. And walk that horse until he is properly cooled. Put him away wet and I will drown you in the river."

"Aye, Brandubh." The boy nodded, eyes wide, obviously believing the threat.

* * * *

Brandubh rode toward the gates at Ath Sionnain, bone-tired and bloodied, at the head of a column of men in much the same condition. Still under the lingering influence of the near intoxication some found in battle, his men--Dougal's men, in truth--were able to sing and laugh and enjoy their quick victory over the band of Viking mercenaries.

"Did you see Brandubh cut that Viking captain in two pieces? Just like...." The speaker's hand swept down with finality and he provided a slurpy sound mimicking that of a blade moving through a human body.

"Aye, a beautiful thing it was, too. Our Brandubh is a lad, indeed. I seen him shave the heads off two, drop his sword and jerk the jawbone off another. 'Tis said Brian did the same when he was a young'un."

Brandubh suppressed a shudder of horror, glancing down at his hands. If he had done such a thing, he did not remember it now. 'Twas often the case.

"Does it truly trouble you, Brandubh?"

Brandubh turned toward the sound of the voice and was surprised to see Caoimhe's brother, Uaid mac Conor, riding beside him.

With a shrug, Brandubh answered, "I do not remember it. How can it trouble me?"

"Too bad. 'Twas a glorious sight. Nothing like a good fight to get the juice flowing. Some woman will get a fine ride tonight, eh?"

Uaid wore a smug smile that Brandubh would have loved to wipe from his face. But he only shrugged again.

"I have never much found fighting an enjoyable drink, Uaid. I fight when I have to, or when I am commanded to. I would not change places with the men I have killed, but I regret every life I have taken. My prayers will be added to those of the holy monks that the conflict may be settled without further bloodshed."

"Come, Brandubh. You cannot convince me that you have no love of the fight in you. I have seen what comes over you in a battle. You become like Cuchulainn. Just as the legends tell of the battle rage, your face changes, you actually grow larger, man. 'Tis a frightening prospect, I will say. Thank the good God that you are with us and we do not have to face you across the field."

"What is all this foolish talk, Uaid?"

Gadhra had come alongside and Brandubh was glad for the company. All this talk of battle rage and pulling men's faces apart was distinctly uncomfortable.

"By the way, Uaid, why were you so late in arriving at the fight? Were you riding a different kind of mare when the call came?" Gadhra's voice rumbled from deep within his chest. Brandubh recognized the anger. "We lost a score of men before you bothered to show your face."

Uaid flushed, but kept his visible anger under control. "I was involved in some family business. Brandubh had a talk with my sister and she needed consoling."

That made Brandubh turn. "How is she, Uaid?"

"Broken-hearted."

The words had been delivered like a knife in the gut and Brandubh knew they had been meant to hurt. That was all right. He could take a bit of pain in exchange for that which he'd inflicted.

The soldiers' celebratory songs faded into silence as the wailing of women's voices drifted to them on the late summer air. Even Uaid assumed an appropriately respectful demeanor.

"How is it they got the news of the dead so quickly? Did you send messengers ahead, Brandubh?" Gadhra asked.

"No."

They rode through the gates and were confronted by a courtyard filled with Dougal's people, parting before them like the Red Sea before Moses, all eager for news of the battle. But Brandubh thought he saw another emotion written on their faces--sorrow, surely, but not the kind spent on soldiers.

Sadbh ran forward to meet him, Dougal right behind her. She opened her mouth as though to speak, but when she saw Caoimhe's brother, Uaid, riding by Brandubh's side, she snapped her lips shut. Dougal stepped in front of her and waved Brandubh off his horse. Caoimhe's father, Conor mac Turlough, did the same to his own son.

Dougal's olive-toned face was even more seamed than usual. He lay his hand on Brandubh's shoulder.

"My son, there is bad news. Caoimhe killed herself last evening. Took her eating knife and pierced her heart with it."

His father's words slammed into him with the force of a Viking's ax.

She could not have.

Yet, she'd told him she would.

"No!" Uaid's cry rent the air. He threw himself on his father's shoulders, Conor looking no better able to deal with the grief. "Why?" Uaid finally managed to ask.

Conor glanced over at Brandubh. His accusation was as clear as if he'd spoken the words.

Yet all he answered was, "I don't know, Uaid."

"Well, I do."

Every head turned at the sound of the voice of Caoimhe's older sister.

"Go home, Moira," Conor pleaded, his voice tired.

Moira ni Conor ignored her father. "What is more, *he*," she pointed at Brandubh, "knows as well. He broke her heart and left her in despair. He is guilty of my sister's blood."

Uaid roared and launched himself at Brandubh. Uaid was a large, strong man, but Brandubh was larger, stronger, and a more experienced fighter. He easily subdued the younger Uaid, pinning him flat on the ground, while their fathers stood by, ready to step between them. Powerless for the moment, Uaid stopped struggling. When his eyes caught Brandubh's, they were blazing with anger.

"I will kill you, Brandubh."

"Take care, man. Do not make rash promises. I never meant to hurt her."

Uaid said nothing more, but where before there had been admiration in his eyes for Brandubh, now there was only loathing and the promise of revenge.

The next day, the judges declared Caoimhe's death a suicide and, for that reason, no blood price was levied against Brandubh. Deep inside, though, he acknowledged he was partly to blame.

No one accused him openly, except for Moira and Uaid. Conor hid away in his house, seeing no one. Yet the lack of blame made it harder for him to remain at Ath Sionnain. There was no way he could purge himself of the guilt or try to make penance when no one held him accountable.

So, he left his father's lands and returned north to his own holding of Lon Dubh. There he worked like a man possessed, sweating and straining out the guilt and making his penance for his part in the tragedy of Caoimhe's death.

And as the days made weeks and the weeks months and Samhain approached, his mind turned toward the hope that Eibhlin would return.

* * * *

November 1

Eibhlin's plane arrived at Shannon airport right on time. Within fifteen minutes, she'd rented a car and was headed for Killaloe. With a little bit of luck, she'd be able to get to the Crag and still make her flight to New York at sundown.

The shipping crates containing all the samples she'd gathered in the British Isles were waiting in the cargo bay of the plane and her notes had already been transcribed and faxed to her co-workers back in Oregon. Her work was done here and it was time to return home.

She didn't allow herself to examine her reasons for flying out of Shannon when Heathrow had been so much closer to her final stop. But, since she was here, why not take a quick trip out to see the Crag one more time? The fact that Brandubh mac Dougal had not been much out of her mind since that day in June couldn't have anything to do with the intensity of the need.

"I'm visiting the old sod," she explained to herself. "Of course, I don't expect to see him. He was a dream after all. Just a dream."

Just a dream that wouldn't let her alone. Brandubh mac Dougal had become a good deal more real to her than her ex-husband was. She pictured Brandubh's face with no effort, right down to the exquisite white marking in his long black locks, while she had trouble remembering if *Himself* even had hair.

Eibhlin went around Killaloe. As much as she'd have liked to stop and visit with Mrs. Mahoney, she didn't dare spare the time. Her plane was leaving at five-fifty. She took the back roads, driving as fast as she dared, slowing only when she saw Craglea in the distance.

* * * *

After she did not return, he'd tried to convince himself that she was only a dream--a perfect woman who lived only in his imaginings. Yet he'd had no desire for any other woman since he'd seen her here so many weeks ago.

So, here he was, climbing Craglea, trying not to doubt his reason. When he reached the summit, he stopped short.

"What is this thing?" On top of Craglea was a bright red wagon. Like no conveyance he had ever seen, it was small, covered over, with seats visible through windows in the sides. There was no tongue for hitching a team that he could discern.

Intending to examine this strange thing, Brandubh approached it purposefully. He never got close enough. Crashing into an unseen barrier, Brandubh found himself seated on his arse. For a moment he was confused.

A shimmer of light twinkled at him, taunting him.

"The curtain," he whispered. If the shimmering curtain was here--which he still could not pass--then....

She was here. Voices crackled through the air. Brandubh stood and reached forward until his fingers touched the barrier. The wagon was the source of the crackling voices.

They faded and grew stronger along with a foreign-sounding music. Brandubh leaned down to examine the brilliant red color. On either side of a shining metal cage on the front--he thought it was the front since the seats faced that way--were two round globes. The wheels were smaller than wagon wheels, and they were not made of wood as far as he could tell, but of some black material. The hub appeared much larger if the cap covering it was a measure.

"Ummmm."

The sound of the sigh drew his eyes to the place where she lay on her on the brown grass, her long legs crossed at the ankles. She had put her hands behind her head, which caused her breasts to strain at the material of her clothing.

Brandubh felt a smile growing on his face. Eibhlin, he whispered her name in his mind, relishing the sound. Fingers still trailing the curtain, he came as close to her as he could and knelt on the grass. If the barrier had not been between them, he would have pulled her into his arms.

"So, you have returned," he said.

"Brandubh," she whispered, her eyes opening to meet his.

Brandubh had never known before what it was to truly desire a woman--not just mindless coupling to relieve the tension of sexual need, but to desire a particular woman, knowing he'd never tire of her. He knew now.

She reached for him. He waited for her hand to pass the barrier before threading his fingers with hers.

Chapter Four

"Are you really here?" Eibhlin asked, unsure she really wanted him to be. But when his long, strong fingers seized hers in an almost painful grip, an empty place filled in the middle of her chest.

She let him pull her to him. A tingle rippled through her as she passed through the shimmering curtain that had separated them. The tingle was replaced by the sensation of safety as his arms surrounded her. His large hands cupped her bottom and caressed before pressing her against his hard body.

"Ah, Brandubh," she whispered. His height, his breadth, his muscled bulk made her feel small. Her head came only to the bottom of his chin. Eibhlin turned her face up to his. When he tipped his head slightly to one side and lowered it toward her, her lips parted in anticipation.

His mouth captured hers, his hunger feeding hers and his heat weakening her knees. Her arms went around his waist and she held on. His tongue played across her lips, seeking entry. She opened to him, allowing him to sweep through her mouth, plunging deeper and deeper, again and again. When her head was light from lack of breath, Brandubh broke off the depth of the kiss and nibbled at her bottom lip, sucking it to plumpness before gently scraping his teeth across the tender skin.

Brandubh tightened his arms around her and plunged his face into her hair. "I feared you would not return," he whispered.

"I had to," she answered, knowing it was true. She'd been compelled to return here. Eibhlin pulled aside his mantle and touched his skin with fingertips and lips, becoming drunk with the taste of him.

Brandubh's large hands moved along her sides, then up under her loose sweater infusing her with warmth. They stood for a long time, touching and being touched, as though they had all the time in the world.

"What are those voices?" he whispered, his mouth opening against her neck.

"Hmmm?" Eibhlin was absorbed with the feel of him. He was so big, so hard. He even smelled good, all outdoors and horse and man.

"The voices in the air. Whence do they come?"

She listened. "Ah, it's just the car radio." The scratchy sound of the radio surrounded them as she applied herself to learning the taste and feel of him.

"World Air Flight 920 has crashed into the Atlantic just after take-off from Shannon airport. Rescuers are on the scene, but thus far, there are no survivors. We will have more details as they become available."

As the words jelled in her mind, she stiffened in his arms.

"What?"

Twisting away from him, Eibhlin ran to the car and slipped behind the wheel, waiting in vain for more details. Instead, U-2's latest hit started.

She stared at the radio, disbelieving. "It crashed? No survivors?"

"What is amiss?" Brandubh remained standing where they had embraced.

She would have been killed if she'd been on that plane.

"My plane crashed," she said, not bothering to switch to Irish.

"Are you going to speak so I can understand you?" His frown creased his forehead.

She should go to Killaloe right away and call her mother. Moira knew 920 was her flight number and would be frantic when she heard the news.

"What time is it?"

Brandubh looked up. "Near to Vespers."

"What *time*, Brandubh?"

"I told you."

The sun was disappearing under the horizon. She had to get to a phone.

Eibhlin jumped out of the car, intending to go to him and tell him good-bye. The curtain separating them, the curtain only she could cross, shimmered, its warning to keep her distance coming too late.

The pleasant tingle of passing changed to an electric shock.

Her skull suddenly felt as though it would explode.

"No!" she cried, slamming her hands against her head. "Leave me alone!"

Memories not her own filled her mind as millions upon millions of people passed through her, with their lives, deaths, joys, sorrows. She lived each one in the blink of an eye. Had Brandubh not caught her in his strong arms, she would have collapsed, exhausted, on the autumn-dried grass of Craglea. With a wordless cry she clung to him, the only solid thing in the universe.

"Here, sweetling," Brandubh said, his voice tender as he sat with her on the grass, pulling her onto his lap, holding her until she was done shaking. "What happened, love?"

"All those people...." She gulped a hiccup. "All those people...."

Brandubh held her as darkness fell around them. Her mind cleared and she became aware that his arms were gentle and he lay his cheek against her hair. He was so warm, so strong, so big, and she snuggled against him, letting him treat her like a treasure.

"Can you tell me what happened now?" His whisper caressed her ears.

"It was like moving through a crowd, except the people went through me. I heard them thinking--about what to cook for dinner, what they'd done at work, what they'd done with their lovers last night. There were so many.... and some...." She shook again. "Some were awful, Brandubh, cruel, evil...." Eibhlin struggled to push those things from her mind.

Brandubh's answer was to hold her closer, keeping her warm inside the cocoon of his arms. She let him protect her while she tried to make sense of it all.

The silence hanging over the Crag captured her attention, and she was grateful for the distraction.

"Where's the radio? Darn, the battery is probably dead. I *knew* I should have switched the ignition off."

Brandubh was frowning again. "You will cease speaking this strange tongue. Speak Irish."

"I'm sorry," Eibhlin replied testily. "I don't know the word for... *that* in Irish. Let me get up." She pushed against his shoulders and stood, shakily at first, to walk around the crest of Craglea, trying to get her bearings. She'd driven the little front-wheel drive car up the hill, probably in violation of all existing environmental laws, and parked it....

"Right here," she said in a chilled whisper.

The car was gone.

"Not again."

This was getting really tiresome. She was a scientist and scientists didn't do well in situations where there was no rational explanation for something like the disappearance of a thousand pounds of metal.

"Where the *hell* is my car?" she shouted to heaven.

When she turned and caught sight of Brandubh, he was frowning again. She switched back to Irish.

"I know, Brandubh, I know. My...." she sputtered, waving her arms wildly at the place where she'd parked the rented car.

"Your conveyance?" he offered.

"Thank you. Yes, my *conveyance*."

"It is gone."

"I *know*!" Eibhlin knew she was screeching and was completely unable to stop herself. She stalked around, hands on her hips, her mouth moving silently around a stream of invective too awful for a decent woman to know, much less give voice to.

"Love," Brandubh said, laying his hands on her shoulders and turning her to face him, "you are where you belong, now. You are with me."

Eibhlin stepped back. "No, I don't belong here."

Here. Eibhlin hadn't thought much about where *here* was. She turned and stared down at Lough Derg, where the Shannon flowed along toward the ocean. There on the banks, a huge structure protected a brood of smaller thatched houses scattered within the surrounding wooden palisade.

Kincora stood in its glory. Suddenly, *here* wasn't quite as important as *when*.

"Brandubh," she asked, fearful of the answer, "what year is it?" Eibhlin turned, forcing her eyes to meet Brandubh's.

His face bore an expression of understanding and sympathy.

"It is the Age of Christ, 1013."

Chapter Five

Eibhlin collapsed. Brandubh kept his distance, giving her room and time. Her reaction concerned him, though he did not know how he would have handled what she had just experienced.

He'd seen the curtain, its gossamer shimmer growing brighter as she approached from the other side. Then he'd watched the red wagon she'd called a *kawr*, fade away along with the curtain, leaving her here, with him, where he'd been convinced she belonged.

Now, he wasn't so certain.

"I don't want to be in 1013," she said, her voice soft and pleading.

Brandubh was suddenly sorry he had not warned her, that he'd not given her the chance to choose.

Then she looked at him and any sympathy he'd had dissipated like water on a smith's anvil.

"*You*, you barbarian! How dare you! I've got a life, a career. I was working on the biggest project in the history of pharmaceutical chemistry."

Brandubh frowned. "You are an alchemist?"

She slowly closed her eyes. "No. I am a *chemist*. I deal in science, not sorcery."

Her eyes, those stormy, dark gray-blue eyes which had not so long ago held a clouded passion, now were narrowed at him. He could feel his flesh bubbling under her singeing glare and was again almost sorry, though not for her sake this time.

Almost.

"You put me right back where you got me from, Brandubh. Right now. I want to go home."

"I did not get you, Eibhlin. You came to me. It is the will of God which brought you here."

There was no sign that she agreed.

"At any rate," Brandubh continued, "I know not how you came to be here, only that I wanted you to stay. If the shimmering curtain is gone, perhaps you are meant to be here, regardless of your desires. However, there may be someone who can help you."

"Who?"

Her eagerness to be gone from here and him cut deep.

"My mother. She knows something of the old ways and was the one to tell me how to find you again."

"Oh. So, there's someone else to thank for this disaster. Where is she? Take me to her." Her balled fists rode her hips and her chin thrust forward. "Now."

Brandubh reluctantly abandoned his hope that she might quickly accept being here.

"All right, Eibhlin. My mother happens to be at Kincora now. Come." He held out his hand to her.

Her eyes dropped to his hand, but she made no move to take it.

"Oh, no. You touched me once and I lost my head and missed my plane. Keep you hands to yourself, warrior."

She stepped around him and started down the hill toward Kincora. Brandubh watched her for a moment. Though her words had been angry, the gentle sway of her rounded, generous hips lured him to follow.

His body tightened with want.

Barbarian. Warrior. Is that what she thought he was? Was that *all* she thought he was? He chided himself for having started thinking of a life with her. Yet she fit so perfectly in his arms, against his body, her mouth to his, it was already inconceivable that she would leave him.

Her purposeful stride said louder than words that she could easily conceive it. Halfway down the hill, she stopped and turned.

"Well, are you coming?" she shouted to him before whirling back in her original direction.

A smile spread across Brandubh's face. If his mother's explanation was true, he had at little bit of time, until the winter solstice, to change her mind.

He loved a challenge.

* * * *

"Damned cocky barbarian," Eibhlin muttered, when she caught sight of his smile. She could only imagine what had brought such an expression to his too-handsome face. Continuing down the hill, she was careful of her footing. The last thing she wanted right now was to twist her ankle and have her he-man carry her. It was important to her, though she couldn't say why, that she enter this place under her own steam.

She had purposely kept her eyes on the ground, watching her path, trying to put off the confrontation with the looming reality ahead. But as she got closer to her goal, her eyes moved from the base up the high timbered palisade.

And she stopped. The gates were at least twenty feet high and made of the same solid logs that formed the palisade.

"Impressive, is it not?" Brandubh's warm breath swept across her neck, raising gooseflesh along both arms. "Let me escort you, my Lady." He offered his arm in a gesture so smoothly gallant that it had to be natural.

"Who taught you your manners, warrior?"

"My father and my mother. Who else educates a child?"

She laid her hand on his forearm, trying not to notice the warmth of his dark, olive-toned skin, trying not to feel the sinew underlying that skin, trying not to enjoy the sensation of that much controlled power beneath her fingers.

She didn't try too hard, though. *Himself* was so thin, so pale, and had he ever looked at her like Brandubh was doing now?

He led her through the gates into a courtyard filled with activity. Women moved as though floating toward the great house, their long skirts swaying with each step. Men laughed and talked and watched the women as they, too, headed for the supper tables in Brian's hall.

It was so foreign, yet so familiar. Each of her mother's tales rushed through her mind, the memories as fresh as new. She half-expected to see Moira crossing the yard, arms outstretched, welcoming her home at last.

Could I actually be dead? Had she made her plane and died along with all those other poor people? Was this some kind of Heaven?

No, she thought with a grimace and wrinkled nose, Heaven would smell better.

"What is this face you make?" Brandubh asked.

A warmth stole up her cheeks. "Nothing," she lied.

He smiled and the warmth reversed direction and moved straight down into her belly.

"Truly, it does not always stink so, but today the Viking merchants from Limerick have come to do some trading. They are not so fastidious as we might like. Brian does not normally tolerate slovenliness, especially here in Kincora."

Such a commonplace statement brought home to her in a way nothing else could that this was really happening. That she was in the year 1013. But how? Time-travel wasn't possible.

Yet, here she was, standing within the stronghold of the *Ard Ri*, the High King, and the only one who had actually gained some measure of obeisance from the contentious Irish petty kings and chieftains.

"Is he really here?" she asked Brandubh in a hushed whisper such as one would use in a museum.

"Who?"

"Brian Boru."

"Oh, aye. Brian does not much leave Kincora these days." At her questioning look, he explained, "Brian is seventy-two. For a fighting prince to attain such an age is an amazing thing. Of course, Brian is an amazing man." He continued toward the gates, guiding her steps so she could look her fill.

"Take care here," he warned as they stepped around some horse droppings. "Boy," he bellowed to a stable lad, "what are you about? The *Ard Ri* will skin you for a belt. Be quick."

"Aye, Lord Brandubh." The boy hopped to grab a wooden rake and scooped up the offensive pile.

Lord Brandubh? Was he an important man, then, her warrior?

Her curiosity about his rank here was forgotten as she felt the eyes that followed her progress through the courtyard. She hadn't realized that she might be as interesting to the locals as they were to her. The boy peeked at her over his shoulder as he hauled away the dung and she noticed many of the others did as well, though their curiosity was better hidden by the Irish sense of hospitality.

Her clothes, though not outlandish, were clearly not of this place. Her warm creamy white Irish fisherman sweater was baggy enough to hide the fact that she wore nothing underneath it, and her skirt fell nearly to mid-calf, but that was still shockingly short compared to those of the women around her.

Brandubh pulled her along through the ten-foot wide doorway and into the great hall where ranks of long trestle tables were arrayed before a dais on which a single table rested. Here, Brian would dine with the highest ranking members of his court arrayed around him.

She plainly gawked at the room. Lamps were built into the walls and their light reflected off the fresh whitewash and brass border that ran around the top of the wall. In a large central hearth a cheerful fire burned, its smoke rising toward the thatched roof where a small hole allowed it to escape. The posts supporting the roof boasted brass bands decorated with the interlocking curves distinctive of Celtic art.

Brandubh pulled her toward an alcove off the main hall.

"There is my mother. Come. We will speak to her. Perhaps she can obtain clothing for you that is not so conspicuous."

Eibhlin hadn't realized her hand was still resting on Brandubh's forearm. It occurred to her that was a fairly familiar gesture and someone, his mother maybe, might get the wrong idea and decide not to help her get back where she belonged.

Better not to upset the old girl right off.

As her fingers began to slide, Brandubh's huge mitt gently, but firmly, settled over them, holding them.

"Mother," he called.

A tall, willowy woman with softly burnished red hair turned at the sound of his voice. So did a lot of other heads belonging to women who were far too young to be his mother. By the daggers shot at her, she could only guess Brandubh was a valuable commodity in the local marriage market.

The red-haired woman, herself hardly seeming of an age to have a son Brandubh's age, sailed--actually sailed--across the floor to them. Up close, Eibhlin could see the gentle lines around the eyes and the wisps of pure white that softened what must have been the most glorious head of hair in Christendom. The woman's eyes, a glacier blue, were hardly cold when she looked upon her son. Then they settled on Eibhlin in intelligent perusal.

"This is my mother, Lady Sadbh ni Mahon. Mother, this is Eibhlin ni Seamus."

The blue eyes lit with pleasure.

"Ah, so this is your woman from Craglea. Welcome, my dear." Sadbh held out her hands and Eibhlin didn't even think before taking them. With a squeeze, Sadbh pulled her to her side. "Now, I think the first thing is to get you attired so you are not so conspicuous."

"My thoughts exactly, Mother." Brandubh made to follow them out of the hall.

"Where are you going?" Sadbh asked as she turned. "The women's hall is no place for you, young pup. Go find your father. If you are needed, I will seek you out." A hand wave indicated she was freeing him to do as she commanded.

Eibhlin stifled a smile.

"But, Mother...."

Sadbh had already turned and was dragging Eibhlin toward an alcove. "We are of a size, my dear. My clothing should fit you well."

Eibhlin tossed a glance over her shoulder to Brandubh who, wearing an expression of supreme irritation, turned on his heel, mantle spreading like wings around him, and headed off toward a group of men in the corner of the huge hall.

"Pay him no mind, child. Keep him besotted."

Eibhlin stiffened.

"Excuse me, Lady Sadbh, but I'm not interested in keeping Brandubh besotted." Eibhlin paused for a moment wondering if he really was besotted--and if she would really mind it all that much. Shaking that from her head, she said, "The only reason I'm here is to talk to you. He thought you might be able to help me get back...." She stopped, not knowing what she could say. Back *where* I belong? Back *when* I belong?

"Back?" Sadbh spoke only the one word and waited.

"I don't belong here." Eibhlin heard the misery in her own voice.

Sadbh apparently did, too. "Where do you belong, my dear?" she asked gently.

The words on her tongue were fantastic, unbelievable, impossible.

Even though she'd nearly accepted the events of the last few hours, she couldn't bring herself to speak of them.

Sadbh saved her the trouble, offering her own explanation.

"Could it be your place is," she paused, clearly weighing her words. "...Outside of ours?"

Eibhlin froze in her tracks and stared at Brandubh's mother.

"Come, child. Let us not draw undue attention to ourselves. Here is my chamber." Sadbh pushed open a heavy wooden door, revealing a large room sparsely, but comfortably, furnished. Clean rushes covered the floor like a carpet and a huge bed sat kitty-cornered in the far corner. On that bed, a huge man lay, one arm thrown over his eyes.

"Is that you, *cara mia*?" He sat up, rubbing his eyes with the tips of his fingers. "Sometimes, I wish you'd let me take you back to Italy. Things were so much simpler there. The Medicis could take lessons in conniving from Brian. I vow, Sadbh, I will kill your uncle if the Danes do not do it first. He is demanding Brandubh's service for another year. Can you believe it? The boy should be...." His now-opened eyes stared with obvious admiration at Eibhlin.

One thing about these barbarians, she had to admit, they knew how to make a girl feel good.

"Ah, who is this ravishing creature?" The man, most definitely Brandubh's father, rose with masculine grace and crossed the room toward her.

"Eibhlin ni Seamus," Sadbh made the introductions, "My husband, Dougal O Daghda."

Eibhlin was a bit surprised at the name. *Daghda* was the name of the chief god of the Celtic pantheon. He was the king of the *Tuatha de Danaan*, the "People of Dana", who had dominated this island before the coming of the Celts. They had refused to be vanquished and merely set up a realm co-existent with mortal man's. They were the fairies of Irish myth.

And this man claimed to be one of their descendants.

"Enchanted," he whispered over her hand before brushing the back with his breath. "So this is my Brandubh's Eibhlin."

The father's love in his voice touched her heart, setting her at ease in his presence.

Dougal was certainly handsome enough to be one of the *Danaan*. She could see where Brandubh had gotten his coloring--olive skin, raven black hair, even the white blaze at the hairline.

"Out with you, Dougal." Sadbh wrapped both hands around the powerful forearm and pulled. Dougal grinned at her inability to budge him.

"*Cara mia*, would it not be impolite to leave our guest so abruptly?"

"Out," Sadbh repeated, pulling once more.

This time Dougal turned to Eibhlin and with a continental shrug allowed himself to be tossed from the room.

"Tell Uncle it is not necessary to hold dinner. We will not be long."

Sadbh softened her command with a smile and a kiss blown after him.

His laughter lingered after he'd gone.

Sadbh shook her head. "Maddening man. Yet I could not live without him."

She crossed the room, stopping by a large chest sitting under the window. Raising the lid and reaching inside, she said, "Here we are. I'm afraid it is a bit old, but still in good repair. Will it do, my dear?"

Eibhlin took the heavy woolen gown, marveling at the rich russet that rivaled the color of autumn leaves.

"This will go well with it." Sadbh had also pulled out a long length of wool dyed in a deep blue. "And a brooch to pin it with. Here, now, let me help you."

The first bit of culture shock was immediate. Eibhlin pulled her sweater over her head, forgetting to be embarrassed at her lack of a bra or anything else beneath.

"My dear, where is your shift?" Sadbh hurried over to the trunk again, returning with something of yellowed linen. "Do all your people go without underclothing? Your gowns must get... smelly so quickly."

Eibhlin nearly laughed, but settled for a smile. "Most women wear, ah, supporting garments and maybe a..." She decided to keep things simple. A slip by any other name.... "Shift with a dress, ah, gown."

"Ah," Sadbh said, as if she understood everything. Maybe she did. "Irish is not your native tongue, is it?"

"How can you tell? My mother and father spoke Irish to me from my childhood. I've spoken it all my life."

Sadbh returned Eibhlin's gaze. "You speak well, yet there is a difference. My Dougal sometimes says things strangely."

"Dougal isn't Irish?" realizing even as she asked that he wasn't. He'd called his wife *cara mia*. "He's Italian."

"Yes. Though he is now more Irish than most Irishmen."

"Is that why he took an Irish name?"

With a nod, Sadbh said, "He felt it would be better for us all. At the time he came, there was an uneasiness about foreigners, especially Italians. Everyone worried about spies from Rome, poking about in our business." She arranged the woolen wrap around Eibhlin and pinned it to her shoulder. "There. Two colors, one of the tribe Dal Cais. That should be enough for now."

"What do you mean?"

Sadbh shook out the pleats until they lay to her satisfaction.

"It is the old code. Bondmen are permitted only one color, freemen two, warriors three, and so on according to rank. The *Ard Ri* may wear seven, though Uncle rarely becomes quite that much the peacock." Raising the hem of Eibhlin's gown, Sadbh said, "At least your shoes look close enough to our own, they won't be noticed. Though I suppose feet are the same everywhere."

Eibhlin found herself liking Brandubh's mother very much. So much so, that she felt comfortable enough to ask, "How did an Italian come to

Ireland and marry the daughter of the king of Munster?"

With a look of pleased surprise, Sadbh said, "You recognize my father's name? So few do. It all happened so long ago."

"He was a great man, I have heard," Eibhlin said.

"He was a very good man. Probably too good to be a king. I do not remember him. I was but an infant when he died." Sadbh sighed and busied herself with a final primp to Eibhlin's costume. Then she stood away for the final inspection. "I believe you will do," she pronounced with a smile before linking her arm through Eibhlin's and shepherding her out of the chamber and back out along the path they had taken before.

Now that Eibhlin knew she wasn't the only one who didn't belong here, she felt compelled to ask about Dougal's appearance.

"How did Dougal come here? Did he appear on Craglea?"

"Oh, no, my dear. I've never heard of a man being taken like that. It's only women in the tales, you know. No, Dougal was a sailor. Though he has many other talents besides seafaring. I found him one fine morning washed up on the bank of the Shannon. He was near death and I took him home and tended him. After he recovered, I told him he owed me his life and I would take him for husband."

"And he married you? Just like that?"

Sadbh's laughter was filled with memory. "Not quite. He fought it until I convinced him he was meant for me."

That comment froze Eibhlin in her tracks. It was too close to Brandubh's assertion that she was now where she belonged to let it lie.

"Is that what Brandubh thinks about me? Because if it is, he can just forget it. I have to get back where I belong."

"And you think I can help you?" Sadbh had taken Eibhlin's arm again and they continued on their way toward the main hall.

"Brandubh said perhaps." It was all she dared say. The possibility of being stranded here, in this primitive time, wasn't something she could contemplate now.

Sadbh sighed deeply. "Yes, perhaps. Though I cannot claim to understanding. I can only tell you that I have heard tales and that there seems to be some rhythm to these sorts of things."

Rhythm. It was such a pagan concept. Not the will of God, not the interference of Satan in the affairs of men, but a rhythm, a natural, predictable, beneficent cycle of life.

"I have to go home, Lady Sadbh."

"Perhaps you *are* home, Lady Eibhlin."

Eibhlin was stricken speechless.

They entered the main hall where dinner was still being served. Sadbh led her up to the dais which bore the main table. Eibhlin's eyes sought for Brandubh. This was his fault.

Even as she sharpened a few choice words and tried translating more from English, her eyes were drawn to the man sitting in the middle of the main table. His robe of royal blue, trimmed in gold, covered a body wide and strong. He lounged, like a lion after a kill, one arm resting on the back of the chair Brandubh occupied on his left side, Dougal on the other.

"Brian," Eibhlin whispered.

"Yes," Sadbh replied, the one word full of pride. "Uncle," she said louder as they stopped before the Ard Ri, Sadbh dropping into a deep curtsy and Eibhlin awkwardly following suit, "may I present to you, Lady Eibhlin ni Seamus."

Brian stood, true to his legend, the tallest man in Ireland. He had to be nearly seven feet, and in spite of his seventy-two years, his back was straight, his arms still fully muscled and powerful. The mane of red-gold was still thick and hung to his shoulders. Very few strands of gray marred its perfection. The eyes of sky blue were clear and devoid of the weakness of age.

Merciful heavens, had there ever been such a threesome as this? One by one, she met their eyes. Brian returned her admiration. Dougal winked at her and gave her a devastating smile. Brandubh scowled.

He's jealous of the way Brian's looking at me, she thought, and the idea pleased her right down to her toes. She pushed it aside. It wasn't something that she ought to encourage.

"Your majesty."

"So, this is Brandubh's prize from Craglea? Please, Lady, rise. Come and sit at my table." Brian whacked Brandubh in the shoulder, actually moving Brandubh's substantial bulk, and waved him aside. "I would have the lady sit by my side."

Chapter Six

Brandubh knew he was scowling and he knew the reason.

The old lion had given Eibhlin his trencher and was now selecting meat from the platter and vegetables from the common bowl with his own hand, doing his best to seduce her with food.

Dougal--my own father! Brandubh growled silently--sat with a fool's grin and a knowing look, observing Brian's solicitude.

And there was nothing Brandubh could do about it.

"Your accent, my dear, is different, though your Irish is very good. Where did you learn our tongue?" Brian kept her goblet full of the rich Italian wine he favored. Eibhlin kept drinking.

She gave the *Ard Ri* a resplendent smile. "My mother taught me, my Lord."

Brandubh drained his goblet and poured it full again, though the wine had no taste tonight.

Dougal laughed out loud.

Brian listened only to Eibhlin and plied her with questions and wine.

Brandubh heard Eibhlin tell Brian everything, things she hadn't told him. He tried not to dwell on what they had been doing instead of conversing earlier on the hillside.

Her parents were Irish but they lived somewhere called *Kaliffornya*. Was that in Wales? he wondered. She explained her task of collecting medicinal plants and proving they were efficacious.

"What more proof is needed? Is it not enough that they cure ills?" Brian set some boiled vegetable before her on their shared trencher.

Brandubh poured more wine, drained it, and started to refill. Then he noticed that Brian was sipping his own. Brandubh replaced the flagon, leaving his goblet empty. He knew the old king's capacity. At the rate he was draining his cup, he'd be long under the table before Brian was-- probably Brian's aim.

So, he sat back in his chair and wished it were permissible for a son to wipe a foolish grin from his father's face. Dougal truly had a bizarre sense of humor. By his expression it was clear that he found this situation humorous in the extreme.

"It isn't the whole plant which cures, only substances within the plant. The kind of proof I'm talking about would involve isolating those substances and testing them in a controlled environment," Eibhlin said just before accepting a hunk of meat from Brian's knife.

His own eyes narrowing, Brandubh saw how Brian watched her lips close around the blade of his knife and then smiled the smile he saved for women whom he wished to bed.

The old fart wouldn't dare.

"How very interesting and how esoteric. And how very exhilarating to meet a beautiful woman of such intellect. We must continue our discussions at more length. But the hour grows late and we must decide what we are going to do with you while you are our guest. I would have you remain here at Kincora. I know of several practitioners of the old religion who might be able to assist you." Brian refilled her goblet--how many times was that?--and with unbelievable nonchalance laid his hand on the back of her chair and leaned toward her. His voice dropped to an intimate whisper. "Meanwhile, your company would greatly brighten an old man's day."

Brandubh would wager every horse he owned that it wasn't his *days* Brian was hoping Eibhlin would brighten.

"How kind of you to offer, my Lord."

"If we are to become friends, you must call me Brian."

She actually blushed, Brandubh noted, rolling his eyes toward the ceiling in disgust, disgust heightened by the sound of Dougal's smothered snort of laughter.

"Thank you, Brian." Eibhlin's awestruck whisper was sufficient to sicken a lesser man.

Enough. Brandubh opened his mouth to object to the proposed sleeping arrangements.

"Uncle, Dougal and I have already offered Lady Eibhlin our hospitality." Sadbh looked pointedly at the king. "Considering the circumstances of her appearance, the *Ard Ri* should remain aloof, do you not agree? Elsewise all your contributions to the Church might be discounted in the face of charges of dealing with the old ones." Setting a dainty piece of meat between her teeth and chewing slowly, she added, her voice thoughtful, "The Abbot is rather, well, strict about the influence of the old religion."

Brian didn't look pleased at the reminder. "Yes, niece. However, if no one tells the Abbot, he will not know, will he?"

Brandubh was ready to smash the oaken table into kindling at the turn of events. From the moment he brought Eibhlin into this house, he had lost control of the situation, first to his mother--no surprise, that--and now to Brian.

It was well past time to get it back.

Jerking forward, planting one elbow on the edge of the table, he attempted, unsuccessfully, to get Brian's eye. Damn, it was worse than being a child, the way they were ignoring him.

"Uncle, I believe I am responsible for her, since I am the one who found her."

"Found? I wasn't lost, you great lout!" Eibhlin's eyes flashed fire, warming him and making him ache to take her into his arms and carry her away to a more private place.

Brian's face said he was thinking the same thing.

Perhaps it is a good thing my King is not looking into my eyes right now, Brandubh thought, knowing he could hide none of his frustrated anger.

Eibhlin wasn't finished basting him with blame for her situation.

"You're right about being responsible, though. You did drag me here. But I think I will accept Brian's kind invitation." She turned toward the king with a sweet smile.

Brian slammed his hands together. "Excellent. Let me arrange a chamber for you."

Brandubh was about to argue until he saw a small gesture from his mother. Wait, she was saying. And he realized there was nothing he could do now. Brian's word was final.

All right, he thought, raising his goblet and sipping. *I can wait. But Eibhlin is mine and, if necessary, I will fight even the High King for her.*

* * * *

Brian himself showed Eibhlin to her chamber. She could scarcely believe she was walking beside this near-mythical man. He pushed open a heavy wooden door with the tips of his fingers.

"Here, my dear, I hope you will find it comfortable. If there is anything you require, simply call a servant."

Raising her hand to the level of his waist, Brian bent low and gently brushed the back, his lips just touching her skin.

"Good night, my dear."

"Good night, Brian. Thank you." She passed through the doorway and turned with a smile to gently close the door in the face of the *Ard Ri*. His deep rumbling chuckle passed clearly through the thick wood.

Eibhlin laughed softly with him. No untried girl, she knew perfectly well what Brian wanted from her and she would have been tempted to give it, in spite of his age, except for the fact that she'd already been entranced by another huge Irishman.

Remember how angry you are with him, Evie. Hold on to that and keep your distance. Brandubh is dangerous. Like a narcotic. You could easily become addicted.

Turning away from the door and her musings of Brandubh mac Dougal, she inspected her accommodations. No larger than her own bedroom in her small house in Oregon, the room was beautiful. To her left, a large tapestry hung on the one uninterrupted wall. A smaller one, bearing the three lions which were Brian's coat of arms, hung by the left side of the door. Off to the right, two chairs waited before the wide, high fireplace, where a cheery blaze glowed. The skin of a wolf rested between them, eyes forever glowering in a glassy stare.

"Nice doggie," she said, slightly uncomfortable under the examination of those eyes.

Crossing the room, she peered out the only window, which was no more than a slit between two stones of the wall--wide enough for an archer to shoot an arrow through, wide enough for fresh air, but not wide enough for a person to slip out.

As if she'd planned on it. There was no where for her to go.

Finally, she turned toward the large bed sitting in the far corner, so inviting with its warm covers and fluffy pillows. A canopy in the colors she'd learned were those of Brian's Dal Cais--blue and gold--hung over it. When she began to picture Brandubh in it, she turned away quickly.

As she unpinned the brooch holding the mantle over her shoulder, she acknowledged the twinge of guilt she felt for her treatment of Brandubh. It wasn't exactly as though he hadn't had a reason to think she might *want* to be here. He *had* waited until she'd reached for him.

Eibhlin blew out the fat candle on the small table by the bed and stripped off her gown, laying it across the foot of the bed. As she climbed under the heavy covers, she caught a whiff of lavender and coriander added to the mattress to repel insects.

Much more pleasant than Black Flag, she thought.

Wiggling down into the softness, she stretched all the way to her toes, pointing them, wincing as her leg muscles strained, then relaxed.

As soon as her eyes closed, there he was again.

She couldn't get him out of her mind. Ever since that day in June when she'd first seen Brandubh on Craglea, she'd tried to relegate him to her imagination, but his hard muscled body, the fire he ignited in her were too real to be denied. And the look of desire in his eyes....

If she were trapped here, would it really be so bad?

"Stop that!" she said, startling herself. Acquiescence would only ensure she wouldn't pursue every possible escape. She didn't belong here.

It might even be dangerous for her to remain. After all, she knew the future, including the heartbreaking destiny of the Irish, who would be subjugated by the Norman kings in just over a century. Once the English had a foothold here, it would be eight hundred years before even part of this green country would be truly free again. And then it wouldn't be *this* Ireland.

The Ireland of the twentieth century would be a place where only a small fraction of the people spoke the Irish language. Even the proud past of the Irish would be relegated to the trash heap. Kincora itself would be wiped from the face of the earth. The bloody English would see to that, she fumed with the furor of a true patriot.

"Damn. Now I've got myself all worked up over something I can't change anyway." Her divorce counselor had warned her about the futility of trying to change the immutable.

But was there such a thing as destiny? Or could the future be changed?

That was a really scary thought, and reason enough to get back where she belonged.

She laughed softly in self-derision.

"Oh, this is nuts. I'm a scientist. Time-traveling is fantasy, a swell premise for TV shows and books...." With another chuckle, she pulled the heavy woolen blanket up to her chin, closed her eyes and breathed deeply. "Either I'm dreaming or hallucinating or it's real. Tomorrow," she whispered with a wide yawn, "I'll figure it out tomorrow."

The only empirical evidence that mattered would come with the morning. If she woke up here tomorrow, she'd probably have to admit Sadbh had been right.

She *was* home.

* * * *

Brandubh paced the great hall long after Brian and Eibhlin had left, his anger growing with every step. If he didn't get some indication she was sleeping alone tonight, he was going to go up there and interrupt the *Ard Ri's* exhilarating evening.

"Come, lad," Dougal called to him from an arched entry way. "Brian requires your presence."

"Good thing for him that he does," Brandubh ground out, squashing the twinge of guilt at the treasonous thoughts he'd entertained. Besides, Brian was not a man to cross, nor to threaten, without serious consideration being given the matter. Maelmordha, king of Leinster and until recently Brian's brother-in-law, had learned this. Malachy, former *Ard Ri*, had as well. When Brian had a goal, he attained it. If Eibhlin was his goal, he'd not be likely to give her up simply for family loyalty.

Brandubh again swore he'd do whatever was necessary to keep her, then was stopped by his own arrogance. Was it a matter of *keeping*? She might have a word to say on that score.

He followed his father into the king's chamber. Brian had shed his mantle and sat, wine goblet in hand, in his favorite chair by the fire. His harp, the one he played for small gatherings of friends and family, sat on the hearth. Brandubh had always loved hearing his uncle play.

"Come, Brandubh, sit. Will you take some wine?" Brian waved one big hand toward another chair. Dougal, he waved to the other pair of chairs beyond the fire, where Sadbh already sat.

"I think I drank enough at dinner." Brandubh took the indicated seat. "While you were entertaining the lady."

Brian's face was lit by the slightest of smiles.

"Sadbh has told me what she knows. Now you, boy. Where did our Lady Eibhlin come from?"

"*Our*, Uncle?" Brandubh allowed some of his irritation to slip out. "As I said, I found her on Craglea. Last solstice I saw her there. I would have brought her then, but she faded from my sight."

"Faded?" Brian raised an eyebrow before sipping his wine.

"There was a shimmering curtain around her. It could not be seen head-on, but I was unable to pass through it. Eibhlin had no such difficulty. However, she and the curtain faded before she came across. Mother suggested that I return to Craglea on Samhain. Indeed, Eibhlin was there. I kept her here this time."

Brian sat up. "You forced her? She did not choose?"

"She had been about to come on Midsummer Day. Even this time she crossed over voluntarily. However, she did not see the curtain was fading. I did not warn her. So, I suppose, no, she did not choose." He leaned forward, knowing but not caring that his whole body presented his king with a challenge. "Uncle, I saw your interest. She is mine, however, and I will not leave without her."

"You forget yourself, boy," Brian's deep, rumbling whisper warned.

Brandubh gazed directly into the old man's still steely eyes, knowing he was one of the few men in Ireland who would.

"Forget not, Uncle, on whom you call when you need a sword. I am no boy, but a man, and I need not prove that to you. Eibhlin leaves with me tomorrow morning."

Sadbh's gasp followed him as he did the unspeakable. He rose and left the king's chamber without permission. She looked for her uncle's reaction to her son's insubordination.

Brian merely cocked an eyebrow at the slam of the door.

"Well, well. Our pup is serious, is he not, Dougal?"

"Indeed, Brian." Dougal went to the sideboard to refill his wine, then turned and leaned against the table. "He is indeed. He will not leave without her. He will not let you have her. And, Brian, you need Brandubh far more than you need a bedfellow."

Brian laughed, his deep bass ringing off the walls and through the hall.

"It was amusing to see him so irritated."

"You did all that just to irritate him?" Sadbh was amazed.

The king shrugged.

"Not entirely. If the lady had shown an inclination, she would be here, niece, not you. However, you can see how the matter stands." His smile soothed Sadbh's protective anger somewhat.

"Then you will put her under Brandubh's protection?"

"No." Brian forestalled her argument with one upraised hand. "She will be under Dougal's protection, and yours. If Brandubh wants her, he can offer a suitable bride's price."

"Who will decide what is suitable?" Sadbh asked.

"I will." Brian drained his wine. "You are correct, Dougal. Brandubh's good sword arm and his horses are more important to me than a woman's body. Even such a body as that one. And I would have my nephew happy and beholden to me. Since she is without family or property, I think three head of cattle or five horses should be a fair price." He looked to Dougal.

"Aye. Sounds fair."

Sadbh couldn't argue, though she didn't know how Eibhlin herself would react to having a price named for her when she did not intend to stay. From what she'd observed of the woman so far, it would be more difficult to convince her to remain willingly if she felt manipulated.

But it was near two months until the next solstice. Perhaps Brandubh would be able to convince her.

Sadbh wondered what she could do to help matters along. Her son wasn't getting any younger and she wanted grandchildren while there was time to enjoy them.

Chapter Seven

"Lady." A young girl's voice broke through the dreamy haze in which Eibhlin was surrounded by arms banded with muscle. Hair, black as a raven's wing, long and flowing, its ebony purity broken only by a blaze of white, rested on shoulders wide and bronzed.

"Brandubh," she whispered, reaching for the hands shaking her shoulders.

"Lady," the voice spoke with a trace of a giggle. "Lady Eibhlin, wake up."

Eibhlin sat up with a start. A young girl, her long blond hair tied back with a yellow ribbon, stepped away from the bed.

"Good morn, Lady. My name is Blanaid. I have you a basin of warm water." She was no more than thirteen, just barely beginning to blossom. A pretty girl, like her name, with a sweet smile.

"Good morning, Blanaid." Self-conscious, she asked, "Ah, was I talking?"

The girl smiled again. "'Tis no matter, Lady. My mother trained me to keep to myself what my betters do before me. Lord Brandubh is the stuff of many ladies' dreams. Maids' as well, for that matter. He is a handsome one. And very rich, too."

"Is he now?" Eibhlin sat up. Before her feet hit the floor, Blanaid was there with a pair of slippers.

"Let me help you, Lady." Blanaid's quick hands slipped the light leather shoes onto Eibhlin's feet. She then picked up her narrative as though no interruption had taken place. "Indeed, many head of cattle, even more horses. He breeds horses, all sorts, for racing and war and farming. He even has some of the tiny Scots ponies he breeds for children's mounts."

Eibhlin washed her face, thinking that for someone who'd been taught to keep things to herself, Blanaid talked an awful lot. But since the subject was Brandubh mac Dougal, she found herself fascinated. Blanaid prattled on about Brandubh and his wonderful physique, his extraordinary prowess with horses, his enormous strength, the identities of those maids who had enjoyed his attention, and the number of ladies who held out the hope he would soon be looking for a wife.

Blanaid handed her a linen square which she assumed was to be used as a towel. As she dried her face, Blanaid proceeded to the events of the last twenty-four hours.

"There was much distress when Lord Brandubh brought you into the great hall. Though it was relieved somewhat when the *Ard Ri* showed such interest in you. It was thought by some that the king would take you and Lord Brandubh would still be free."

"The king would what?" Eibhlin's voice ripped from her throat. She felt her breath start to come faster with the rising tide of her irritation.

"Did I say something wrong, Lady?" Blanaid's eyes widened with apprehension and she stepped back, her hands tangled at her waist.

Sorry she'd so frightened the girl, Eibhlin lay a gentle hand on her shoulder.

"I'm sorry, Blanaid. I didn't mean to shout. It's just that I'm not used to being talked about like that."

"Like what?"

"It's no matter." Eibhlin sighed. It appeared that women were as much sex objects here, for all the vaunted Celtic equality, as they were in the twentieth century. The only difference appeared to be that the standard of desirability now included the extra-tall, non-anorexic types.

Blanaid helped Eibhlin pull on the heavy woolen gown, then arranged the mantle, pinning it with Sadbh's brooch.

"Lady Sadbh sent these. You are to keep them if they please you." Blanaid held out a set of ivory combs.

With a gasp, Eibhlin took them from Blanaid's hand.

"They're lovely."

Blanaid smiled her sweet smile, once more relaxed. "Let me comb your hair. My mother says I have a way with a lady's hair."

Eibhlin let her have her way. While she combed, Blanaid's earlier assertion that she kept to herself what her betters did was further tested.

"You know, Lady Eibhlin, there was much consternation in the solar this morning when the Lady Sadbh brought these combs for you. She made very sure everyone heard her instructions. It is clear she favors you. Why, two ladies started crying to their mothers straight away."

Eibhlin wondered at that. Sadbh had as much as given her blessing last night. So, for that matter, had Dougal. But why would they favor her, with no family, no property, no past?

"There. You have such beautiful hair, so like a seal's coat. I've oft wished for dark hair."

"Where I am from, Blanaid, your color is preferred."

"Really? 'Tis a pity I cannot go there to find a husband."

Eibhlin smiled. "You are much too sweet for any man there."

"My mother says there is not a man in the world as deserves any of its women. But, what can we do?"

Eibhlin laughed as Blanaid pulled her long, heavy hair back from her temples, then loosened a lock at either side, which she twined around her thin fingers. The resulting cascade framed Eibhlin's face, softening her jawline. Staring at herself in a small hand mirror, turning her head from side to side, she scarcely believed the change just letting her hair down made in her appearance.

"Blanaid, thank you."

The girl blushed. "You are very beautiful, Lady. I only did a bit of arranging. Come now, they are breaking the fast in the great hall. You will make an entrance."

It sounded like a fine idea until she actually arrived at the entryway. The hum of conversation stopped and Eibhlin felt every pair of eyes fix on her, some decidedly unfriendly. But the audience was forgotten when Brandubh rose from his place at the main table and strode down the aisle between the two rows of tables on the floor. His eyes were locked onto hers.

"My Lady Eibhlin, please allow me to escort you to your place."

Familiarity and rightness filled her as she set her hand upon his offered arm.

"Thank you, Lord Brandubh."

He smiled then, a full warm expression of pleasure beginning in the ebony depths of his eyes. She realized then she hadn't seen him smile since his mother had taken her off to dress her properly last evening. It was a more welcome sight than she would fully admit to herself.

He led her up to the main table, where the men rose to greet her. Brandubh, making a point of it, sat her between Brian and himself. This morning Brian was cordial, but his attentiveness from last night was nowhere to be seen.

"I trust you rested well, my Lady?" he asked between bites of cheese.

"Yes, thank you, my Lord." Since he didn't repeat his request that she call him by name, she knew she was correct to believe the familiarity was no longer appropriate.

But she did catch Brian looking at her as Brandubh assisted her with her meal, his eyes smiling and a little wink telling her he wasn't angry she'd spurned, albeit gently, his advances. He actually seemed well pleased by developments.

The same could not be said for the many ladies who eyed her with outright hostility as Brandubh made sure her tankard was filled with ale.

He selected the choicest pieces of meat and cheese. He broke a small loaf of crusty brown bread and offered her half.

"I meant to give you this last even," he said as he pulled a bundle from behind his back. It was wrapped in a short length of velvet of Dal Cais blue.

"Thank you," she whispered and unwrapped the gift--a dinner knife of gold, with a jeweled hilt, protected in a delicate scabbard of calf-hide threaded with gold. "Oh, Brandubh. It's exquisite."

"'Tis but a small thing. And a necessary one if you are not to starve to death. I cannot always be present to feed you."

She returned the smile that followed his little joke and tried out the knife on the cheese laying on her napkin.

"It works." Popping the small cube of creamy cheese into her mouth, she let it melt before she said, "Thank you again."

He tipped his head in acknowledgment and they ate in a silence at once comfortable and pleasantly tense.

Breakfast progressed peacefully until a commotion rose at one of the lower tables. Several people jumped from the vicinity, even as several others jockeyed around to get a better view. Eibhlin followed the general chaos centering on a woman seated at a lower table, her colorful clothing proclaiming her a person of some station. Her hands clawed at her neck and she gasped and growled in distress.

"She's choking," a man's shouted above the tumult.

Besides one huge warrior-type slamming one ham-sized hand against the poor woman's spine trying to dislodge whatever had got caught in her throat, no one was trying to do anything. With one more struggling shudder, the woman jerked and fell over backward, hitting the floor with a thud, still ripping at her throat.

Eibhlin didn't even think. She jumped up and sailed over the table, a path opening for her. Grabbing the woman's hands, Eibhlin jerked her to her feet and got behind her. She stretched her arms around the woman's torso and, gripping her hands together, applied quick pressure just under the base of the sternum.

Nothing. The woman's body grew limp even as her skin turned a frightening blue.

"What are you doing?" A man, probably the woman's husband started to pull Eibhlin's arms away.

Eibhlin held on for the woman's dear life and heaved once more.

A shout went up from the spectators as a grayish brown projectile erupted from the woman's mouth. A young woman across the table caught it--and promptly screamed as she tossed it in the air.

After helping the woman sit down, Eibhlin knelt beside her.

"Are you all right now?" she asked, relieved, now that the woman's color was returning and her breathing, though labored, was again free.

"Yes, thank you, Lady," the woman answered in a hoarse gasp.

"Aye, Lady. You have saved my wife's life." The man who'd tried to intervene knelt on the woman's other side. "I am Padraig mac Finn. My wife here, is Orla ni Donald. We are ever in your debt."

"No thanks are necessary. I'm glad I could help."

"Lord Brandubh, is this lady under your protection?" the man asked Brandubh, now standing by Eibhlin's side.

"I am in no need of protection, sir," Eibhlin interrupted, irritated the men were going on as though she wasn't there.

Brandubh ignored her, much to her aggravation.

"She is under the *Ard Ri*'s protection until he delegates the duty to another," he said.

"I *said*, I am in no need...."

"Eibhlin, please." He cupped her elbow and helped her up. "Padraig, Lady Orla."

"Thank you, again, Lady," Padraig said, sinking to the bench beside his wife, his arm draped protectively over her stocky shoulders.

Brandubh dragged her away from the curious stares. She glanced back at the crowd that had gathered around Orla to listen to her tell of her experience, which included hand gestures.

"What was that you did?" Brian asked as she stepped back on the dais.

"I used the air in her lungs to push the food out of her throat. I can show you later, if you wish, my Lord."

"You'll have to do it quickly, Lady. I have decided to allow Dougal to assume your protection. You will accompany them back to Ath Sionnain."

"What?"

It was a moment before she realized that both she and Brandubh had spoken together.

"Uncle, she was to be with me."

"Lady Eibhlin needs the company of women, Brandubh, which I do not believe she will find in abundance at Lon Dubh." Brian raised one red-gold eyebrow. "At least not women of any virtue."

What did he mean by that? she wondered, throwing Brandubh a narrowed glance, which he chose to ignore.

"But, Uncle, I think...." Brandubh began.

Dougal interrupted, his face concerned. "I have had word from Sean that my presence is required at home. The tone of the message was sufficiently urgent that I feel the need to return as soon as it can be arranged."

Wherever Dougal's lands were, Eibhlin knew she couldn't go. Her only hope of returning to her own time was here, on Craglea.

"Lady," she stepped over by Sadbh's side, appealing, "I can't leave here. You surely understand."

Sadbh took her hand and squeezed it. "My dear, you will return to the Crag when the time comes again. Until then, enjoy our hospitality. I swear you will not be kept at Ath Sionnain against your will."

"It's not your intentions I distrust, Lady." As she spoke the words, Eibhlin's eyes were on Brandubh, whose expression indicated his own dissatisfaction with the arrangement.

Sadbh's smile was a knowing one. "Come along and help me pack our belongings."

Under Sadbh's supervision--her command skills were worthy of a Marine Corps Drill Instructor--they were mounted and moving within the hour. As the caravan of horses and wagons made its way northward, following the east bank of the Shannon, Eibhlin turned back to stare as Kincora--and beyond it Craglea--grew smaller and eventually disappeared as they topped a hill.

The Shannon drifted along, as it had for thousands of years, and as it would continue to for at least a thousand more. How little the countryside had changed, Eibhlin thought, gazing over the softly rolling land. Even after absorbing all the hurt coming her way, Ireland would remain. It was a comforting thought.

Brandubh appeared at her side on a tall horse. He sat straight and relaxed, barely moving the reins he held in one hand. His mount skittered in a nervous dance, but Brandubh never seemed to be unsure of his seat.

"There, now, lad." Leaning forward, he stroked the thick neck and spoke quietly. "Be easy, boy."

Whether it was the sound of Brandubh's voice or the touch of his hand, the horse quieted and walked, nice as you please, beside Eibhlin's mount. Brandubh rested his left hand on his thigh. She turned her eyes away from the sight of his hand... and his leg... and tried to remember she was here because of his interference in her life. She tried to remember she was angry.

"Are you enjoying the trip?" His voice clearly enough said he wasn't.

"The country is beautiful. The horse is gentle. The company, for the most part," she allowed irritation to grind her voice a bit, "is pleasant. Why shouldn't I be enjoying myself?"

"Because we were both manipulated."

"You're only getting a taste of your own medicine."

Brandubh's brow furrowed, as it did every time she said something he didn't quite understand, usually a literal translation of an Americanism. He was learning not to take it personally, though.

"If you mean that I manipulated you...." His dark eyes ran over her, a smile grew on his lips. "I suppose I did. I would like to again, my Lady. 'Twas quite a pleasant exercise."

Eibhlin forced her eyes to his and tried to keep her voice as light as his had been.

"My dear Brandubh, there has been quite enough *manipulation* of that kind."

He laughed, a deep, inviting sound. To hear that every day of her life....

More to take her own mind from the path it was following than to keep any conversation going with him, she asked, "Where exactly are we going?"

"To Ath Sionnain. Dougal's holding on the northern frontier of Munster." He looked behind them, then ahead. "'Twill only be another few hours at this pace."

"What was that other place Brian spoke of?"

"You mean Lon Dubh?" At her nod, he said, "Lon Dubh is mine. It sits at the convergence of Munster, Connaught, and Ulster. I would like to show it to you sometime. The sweetest grass in all Ireland is on Lon Dubh."

The mention of grass tapped a memory. "Is it true you breed horses?"

"Well, all Irishmen breed horses to one extent or another, my Lady. However, I can say I am rather better at it than most."

"And you take out time from fighting your wars to check on the horses?"

Something like a cloud passed over his face.

"I would rather think it the other way 'round."

Eibhlin wondered at the shortness of his tone. Had she said something wrong? The silence this time bothered her.

"How long have you had Lon Dubh?"

Brandubh glanced over at her. "Since my sixteenth birthday. It was a present from Uncle Brian."

"Do you live there?" A vision of those loose women Brian was so worried about flashed through her mind. She didn't like the picture.

"I am there probably half the time. Unfortunately, the *Ard Ri* has had need for my services much of late."

He didn't sound happy about that. And he didn't elaborate.

Darn it all, she thought, *am I going to have to drag every bit of information out of him?*

"Why have you never married, Brandubh?"

The corner of his mouth raised. "I have never found the woman I would wed." He stopped and turned toward her. "I assumed you were not married," he said, leaving the question unasked.

Maybe this would convince him to leave her alone and let her leave as soon as she could. "I am divorced."

Brandubh shrugged the continental shrug he probably unconsciously copied from his father. "Was he unfaithful?"

"Yes," she whispered, wondering why he would guess that right away.

"Then you had every right to divorce him."

"Doesn't the Church frown on that?"

"I suppose it does. Rightly so, since it is not a thing to be done frivolously. However, when a vow is already broken...."

She hadn't thought of it that way.

"Our legal system is still much like it was before the coming of Patrick," he continued. "Divorce is actually a rather simple matter. Life is too short to waste suffering needlessly."

That seemed an awfully easy view. What happened to making your bed and sleeping in it?

Oooh, bad cliché to pick in this situation, she cringed.

They rode on, neither speaking, nor much feeling a need to, so companionable was the silence.

After a time, Eibhlin shifted on her saddle.

"My rear is starting to feel like it's made of lead."

"Careful, my Lady. Let me call to my father and we will stop...."

Too late, Eibhlin realized her foot had slipped from the stirrup and she was leaning too far to the right and....

"Oooo... ooops."

Brandubh's strong arm came around her, lifting her back into her saddle with no more effort than he'd use to pick up a cat. Reminders of his strength were as potent as the tenderness she remembered only too well.

"Thanks." Eibhlin shifted, trying to get settled as well as her aching bottom would allow.

"My Lady, are you comfortable?" Brandubh asked.

She wasn't, but she'd never admit to him that she hadn't ridden a horse in at least fifteen years.

"I'm just a little out of practice."

"You could ride with me." His eyes narrowed and he patted his thigh. "Perhaps you would find the seating more comfortable."

Those dark Latin lover looks, able to turn an unsuspecting girl's tummy to mush.

Lucky for her she was neither unsuspecting nor a girl. She had to put a damper on this. It could go nowhere, not if she was to leave here with her heart.

"Lord Brandubh," she said with insulting precision, "I do not require any assistance."

He let a second pass before he leaned slightly toward her.

"Do not let your pride hold you away from that which would bring you joy, Lady."

Eibhlin laughed. "Is that supposed to be subtle?"

"I was not attempting subtlety. My intention is ever to be plain." He leaned closer and whispered, "No woman has ever fit my arms so perfectly, Eibhlin."

"So this is just about sex?"

He raised an eyebrow. "I will not deny what you already know. I hope I was plain enough that I want you in my bed. However, it is not a dalliance which I would have from you. You and I have been brought together. We belong together."

His words frightened her. Like her first day at school. Like the feeling of failure and the fear of being alone when she'd filed for divorce. Like the lingering sense of inevitability her parents left with her every time she'd talked to them since that summer day--was it only a little over four months ago?--as they hinted at great cosmic secrets and fate and destiny.

Eibhlin hated the fear that her life was not her own to control.

It pushed her to say the words that now came from her lips.

"No, Brandubh. We were not brought together. I was in Ireland to perform a task. I did it and I am going home, as soon as possible. There can be nothing between us. I am not interested in you for anything, not *even* a dalliance."

He narrowed his onyx black eyes and studied her.

Focusing on the purplish bumps of the mountains on the northern horizon, she refused to meet his eyes, though her skin burned under his gaze. Just about to loose her cool and turn on him, ready to tell him to go away, he gave her what she had claimed in her mind she wanted.

"My Lady." He tipped his head in a bow and rode away.

Her lips opened to call to him. Already she missed his company. But she only clamped her mouth shut and concentrated on staying in the damned saddle.

Chapter Eight

Ath Sionnain, literally the ford of the Shannon, wasn't as great a place as Brian's Kincora, but then, Dougal O Daghda wasn't High King. All the same, the timbered palisaded wall and earthen embankment gave Ath Sionnain the look of an impregnable fortress. They rode through the high gates into a courtyard as neatly planned and well-ordered as Brian's own.

It was cleaner, though. That was Sadbh's doing, Eibhlin had no doubt. In her short acquaintance with Brandubh's mother, she'd learned Sadbh had exacting standards and tolerated little foolishness where work was concerned.

An older man, snowy white hair sticking out of his head like feathers, hobbled from the large stone house that was obviously the Lord and Lady's own.

"Dougal," he called, "Thank God you got my message."

"What is amiss, Sean?" Dougal dismounted, then came over to help his wife. He set her gently on her feet and his arm came around her shoulders in a gesture at once proprietary and protective.

"May I help you down, Lady?"

Eibhlin's attention was diverted from the scene of Dougal and Sadbh, arms around one another as they listened to Sean. Brandubh stood beside her horse, looking up at her, but his eyes held none of the warmth she'd come to associate with his gaze.

And she couldn't help notice she wasn't *My* Lady to him anymore.

"Thank you, Lord Brandubh." Since leaving Kincora their communication had become painfully formal. She felt the loss of his smile and his touch as sharply as a missing limb.

His huge, incongruously elegant hands fit nearly around her waist, made her feel precious. Eibhlin set her hands on his shoulders, though he needed no help bearing her weight. The bunching muscles in his arms lifted her as though she were no more than a wisp.

As her feet touched the ground, he removed his hands from her waist and left her there, her own hands still up in the air where they had rested on his shoulders. Brandubh went to join his parents in front of the house.

It's better this way, Eibhlin thought. If he doesn't chase after me, I won't

THE RAVEN'S LADY

have to find the strength to push him away.

As if, she added bitterly. But the big jerk hadn't had to give up quite so easily.

Left alone in the courtyard, she looked over her temporary home. All along the palisade wall were small buildings, the purpose of some was obvious--stable, smith. There were smaller buildings inside the walled enclosure that were clearly houses. Small stools sat beside the doors and children ran in and out.

The house that dominated was three stories tall and built of stone and wood, framed with a symmetry and grace that pleased the eye. Small windows, shutters turned back, lined all three stories. Smaller additions were tucked against the sides.

Not so pleasing was the sight at the main door of Dougal's beautiful house. There they were, the gaggle of young ladies seeking out the handsome and oh-so-unattached Lord Brandubh Of-the-Many-Horses. They lingered at the entry to the house, their eyes making invitation which no healthy man could resist without divine assistance.

Better to be unfettered to a man like that, Evie, she thought. You'll end up sharing your husband again.

Husband? The thought made her eyes widen. Where in the world had she ever gotten the idea of Brandubh as a husband? Surely, he'd never said anything about marriage. He'd said he wanted more that a dalliance, which could mean nothing more than a prolonged affair, after which he would express how much she'd meant to him and how it was now time for them both to move on.

No, thank you, she thought, watching the women watching her. She'd been dumped once.

It wouldn't happen to this girl again, she promised herself.

What was wrong with her? It didn't matter whether he said anything about marriage or not. She wasn't staying here.

Sadbh came toward her. "Come, Eibhlin. The men have some business to attend to, so I will get you settled." She linked her arm through Eibhlin's in her characteristic protective, comforting gesture. "Don't let that swarm of honeybees worry you," she whispered. "You have the right of first refusal."

Eibhlin almost gave that refusal right there. But she knew it would sound petty. She was still hurt enough at his easy acquiescence to her demand to be left alone that she knew it would be coming out of a need to protect herself.

Instead, she half-turned to Sadbh and smiled. "I'll think about it."

Sadbh laughed. "If you decide to stay with us, my dear, poor Brandubh will have his hands full, I vow. Let's run the gauntlet and get it done with." She tipped her head toward the crowd of women--tall, short, thin, fat, blonde, brunette, and redhead. All with eyes fastened on Eibhlin with varying degrees of antipathy.

They mounted the steps, Sadbh's arm through hers.

"What are you doing here, ladies? Is there not enough to keep your hands busy? If not, I can surely find more for you to do."

Eibhlin could have laughed at the scurry Sadbh's words caused. All but one of the women scattered.

She stood at the door, her head high, her eyes burning. Eibhlin stared at her, an uneasy sense of familiarity fluttering in her stomach.

"Don't you have something to do, Moira?" Sadbh asked.

Moira. The sound of her mother's name stabbed Eibhlin in the heart with a sharp surge of longing. The physical resemblance between the mother Eibhlin had left behind a thousand years in the future and this girl with the angry eyes was amazing. The same height, the same warm brown curls framing a face of angel purity. The same softly rounded chin, the same small upturned nose. Her own mother must have looked much like this girl when she'd been young.

All except the eyes. There was too much bitterness in them.

Moira. The name meant *bitter*. This Moira fit the name.

"Is this the one? Is this the whore who stole Brandubh?"

"Shut your mouth and get out of my sight, now!"

Eibhlin was nearly as shocked by Sadbh's tone as she was by being called a whore by a woman who resembled her mother.

With a look meant to kill, Moira did leave.

"Eibhlin, my dear. Do not allow her to injure your feelings. She is still grieving and takes her bitterness out on any convenient target."

"Why does she grieve?" Eibhlin couldn't help feeling sorry for her. Moira must have had hopes of capturing Brandubh for herself.

Sadbh didn't answer. "Not now. Let's get you inside and settled. There will be time for this later."

Even as Sadbh pulled her up and urged her inside, Eibhlin's eyes were drawn back to the young girl who walked, slow and solitary, across the courtyard.

* * * *

Dougal handed Brandubh a cup. Gratefully accepting something so his hands didn't feel quite so empty, Brandubh drank deeply of the wine. His father took a seat in his chair by the fireplace and indicated that Brandubh and Sean should sit as well.

"Now, Sean, start over. I must admit I don't travel as well as I used to," Dougal said with a smile. "Now that I have my wine and can sit and attend you, perhaps I will grasp your news. What has been going on here in my absence?"

Brandubh hid his own smile behind his drink. Dougal was being generous because he loved the old man, but Sean had been more incoherent than usual. The only information he'd been able to convey was there had been a raid on Dougal's herds. Now it remained to extract the rest of the story.

Surely no more than an inconvenience. Cattle raiding was a venerated Irish custom, though Brian had stopped most of it, thinking it a disgraceful waste of energy when common enemies--Vikings and traitorous Irishmen--remained to be vanquished.

A small matter, Brandubh was sure, easily seen to.

So far they had deduced from Sean's somewhat disjointed telling that Dougal had lost around twenty head, all from the lands adjoining Lon Dubh. Sweeping back his feathery white hair, Sean started counting Brandubh's losses.

Brandubh took the news of thirty head with only a grimace. Slightly more than an inconvenience. He was not near so wealthy as his father.

"Well, son, we'll need every man you have." Dougal was already planning the retaliatory raid.

"There is more." Sean drained his wine, his hands shaking.

Brandubh had never seen the old man this nervous.

Sean set his cup on the table beside his chair. "They took Conchobar and Deirdre, Brandubh."

"What!" Brandubh shot out of his chair. He took hold of the old man's cloak and pulled him to his feet. "When? Who?"

"Please, Brandubh, release him," Dougal's quiet rumble penetrated Brandubh's burning rage.

Conchobar and Deirdre were the breeding pair that he'd planned to found a whole new line of horses with. Conchobar was a fiery black, big through the chest, with wind enough to last all day at a dead run. Deirdre was white as a dove's breast and tall for a mare, yet her lines were sleek and graceful.

He'd been breeding for them for twenty years, since he was a boy and had received his first pair at the age of ten.

Now they were gone.

"Brandubh." At his father's repeated call, Brandubh let Sean go as gently as he was able, considering he felt able to tear apart the whole of Ireland.

Full of shame, Brandubh said, "Please forgive me, Sean."

"It is no matter, my boy," the old man said. "I understand what they mean to you."

"Who was it, Sean? Do you know?" Dougal's voice was soft and he asked his question gently.

Sean shook his head, sending his hair flying like a snowstorm.

"Who, I do not know." The old man turned back to Brandubh. "When is simple. Samhain evening. Your men kept the raiders from setting fire to your house, but the horses were out to pasture. Deirdre had come into season unexpectedly and Conchobar could not be contained. Rather than see him injure himself, the stablemen turned him out with her, knowing you intended him to cover her in any event. The raiders came just as the barn doors were opened. They swept Deirdre into the herd of cattle and Conchobar followed her."

"Ah, *amore*. Our Conchobar will rescue his lady, no?"

Dougal's attempt at humor was not appreciated and Brandubh tried to let him know with a black look. Dougal was not intimidated.

"Come, son, let us go to our supper. We will rest tonight, then we will go to Lon Dubh tomorrow and try to deduce where our raiders came from." He raised his hand to cut off Brandubh's disagreement. "You are a man grown, son, and if you desire to go tonight, tired as you are, not knowing even where to begin, be my guest. I, however, will spend one night in my own bed with my woman. When I go out to retrieve what is mine, I shall be prepared to give even Satan a fight he will not soon forget."

Without another word, Dougal laid his arm around Sean's shoulders and led him out of the chamber.

Irritating as he sometimes was, Brandubh knew his father was also wise in the ways of fighting and, especially, retrieving what was his.

But, if anything had happened to Conchobar or Deirdre, Brandubh swore he would personally flay the flesh from whomever was responsible and make bridles of it.

* * * *

If one more simpering female draped her breasts across Brandubh's shoulders and told him how very glad she was that he had returned, Eibhlin was going to stick her in the belly with the beautiful little dinner knife Brandubh had given her.

The blatant displays of availability were embarrassing. That he'd allow it with her sitting right beside him was infuriating. Sadbh, on Dougal's right side, more than once rolled her eyes to the ceiling. She and Eibhlin had shared a disgusted sneer.

She was really starting to love Sadbh.

"Will you *please* go to your places and eat your supper?" Sadbh finally bellowed to the whole lot of them. "Blessed Mother, doesn't he have enough to worry about?"

Brandubh arched one ebony brow, in exact imitation of Sadbh's habit.

"Mother, I believe I am capable of shouldering the burden."

He reached up and seized the wrist of one of the more well-endowed beauties, a serving girl this time, and pulled her down so her full bosom rested on his broad right shoulder, raising a roar of approving laughter from the assembly.

Eibhlin knew--she just *knew*--he was doing it to make her jealous.

As if.

Once the female flies had left off buzzing around Brandubh --For cryin' out loud, she was starting to think like they talked--Sadbh laid down her knife and turned toward Dougal.

"I think we need to find something to keep Eibhlin busy while she is with us."

"Indeed, *cara mia*?" Dougal sat back with his cup.

Eibhlin opened her mouth to say, again, she had no intention of becoming comfortable here and she was going home at the first opportunity. She never got the chance.

Sadbh turned her whole attention to her, looking around Dougal's substantial frame.

"You see, my dear, since our healer died, we haven't had anyone really tending the herb garden nor making medicines. None of my ladies is gifted with plants. The kitchen garden is well-tended, but it is the spices and medicinal herbs that require attention. Didn't I hear you say something to the *Ard Ri* at dinner the other night about working with medical herbs?"

Sadbh knew perfectly well what Eibhlin had told the Ard Ri. In fact she'd pitched this very idea on the ride up here from Kincora. Eibhlin had thanked her and refused. She intended to stay locked in her room. Her feelings for these people were already more than she needed to try to put behind her when it was time to go.

"I know some things, Lady," Eibhlin answered with as little commitment as possible.

"Do not be so modest. I would be grateful if you could leave us with some of your knowledge when you go."

Eibhlin noticed the stress Sadbh put on the last words and the smile as she got the reaction from her son that she'd obviously desired. Glimpsing him from the corner of her eye, Eibhlin saw Brandubh release the maid's wrist and wave her away.

"It really would be a great help to us, my dear." Sadbh wasn't giving up and Eibhlin had heard enough to know that she usually got her way. Might as well let Sadbh have this round and save strength for the big fight when it was time to return to Craglea and go home.

"Of course, Lady Sadbh, if I can be of help."

Sadbh's smile grew broader. "Good. Tomorrow, we will begin."

Dougal turned to Eibhlin and lay his hand over hers. With a grin, he whispered, "You don't have a chance, you know." He tipped his head toward Brandubh, who was wearing an exact duplicate of his mother's satisfied smile. "Not against them both."

We'll see, Eibhlin accepted the challenge silently.

Chapter Nine

Pleading fatigue, Eibhlin escaped to her chamber well before the evening's entertainments began. Now lying cold and lonely in her bed, she tried to fall asleep as the poet's harp reverberated through the floor. The sweet music honed the edge of her pain as she remembered... things that hadn't even happened yet.

Then the singing started, raising the hairs on the back of her neck.

It was a very Irish voice, haunting, floating, now alto, now sailing soprano. So much like the voice Eibhlin remembered, the voice of Moira Fitzgerald ni Conor, as she'd billed herself when she'd cut solo albums in the mid-sixties. The nineteen sixties. As in nearly a thousand years from now.

Eibhlin sat up and got out of bed. Throwing the blue mantle around her shoulders, she pulled the door open and stepped out into the hallway, the voice enchanting her with its magic and making her ignore the cold floor beneath her bare feet.

She stopped at the top of the stairs.

It was the girl, Moira, singing a song Eibhlin knew well. It was the story of the abduction of the girl, Deirdre, whom the old king Conchobar had decided to marry. She'd run off with a beautiful boy, but Conchobar lured them back with deception and killed her lover.

As Moira got to the part where Deirdre, heartsick for her dead lover, throws herself from a racing chariot to her death, Eibhlin let her eyes seek out Brandubh. He sat on a pile of cushions at the side of the hall, to all appearances, not well-pleased with the musical selection. No doubt he was still plagued by the abduction of his four-legged Deirdre.

Then his eyes met hers. She didn't try to evade him.

You're mine. You are meant to be here with me.

His claims, though unspoken, were loud and clear and welcome to her aching heart.

Moira stopped singing. Eibhlin knew she wasn't finished. The poet playing accompaniment kept on for a few measures, but when it became clear Moira wouldn't continue, he stopped, as well.

The buzz of conversation in the hall grew louder and she could feel the gaze of the crowd on her and Brandubh. Still she couldn't break her eyes away from his. At that moment, if someone had told her returning to her own time was impossible, she'd accept her fate and go to him.

Then another pair of eyes claimed hers, eyes overflowing with anger. The knowledge that her presence here hurt this Moira, who reminded her so strongly of her mother, made Eibhlin turn away and run back into her room.

She threw herself under her covers, but she didn't sleep.

* * * *

He walked out into the night air and cursed himself for being a fool. There were a hundred women in his father's household who would give a year of their lives to spend one night with him.

Yet, here he was alone, his body hard, his blood hot.

"So, you do want her." The soft voice came out of the dark.

"What do you want, Moira?" Brandubh turned his back to her and walked on toward the stables. When he realized she was following, he ground his teeth together to hold his temper from erupting over her.

"Is she the one? I don't really require an answer. It was clear enough the way you practically took her with your eyes."

"Leave it, Moira."

"Tell me, Brandubh, what does she have that you couldn't find with my sister? Is she worth the price you'll have to pay in hell? Was she worth killing my sister over?"

At the doorway of the stable, Brandubh turned on one heel. Moira nearly collided with him. He stared hard into her face.

"Listen well to me, for I will not say this again. Caoimhe took her own life. I did not kill her."

Moira didn't back down. "Did she not tell you she would?"

It was Brandubh who took a step back, over the threshold. "She did. But I did not believe her."

"And you did not bother to tell anyone? You knew how passionate she was. No, Brandubh, you are not blameless."

"I never said I was."

Her eyes widened in surprise. She'd evidently not thought him willing to admit any guilt.

Brandubh turned and entered the dark stable.

He half-expected her to follow, but she only stood outside, watching. Waiting, perhaps?

For what? he wondered for an instant before the weight of a full-grown man landed on his back. He groaned under the burden and backed into a support post. Again and again like an unbroken stallion trying to rid itself of an unwelcome rider. He reached around, trying to pull his attacker off.

Then a leather thong looped his neck. Tightening, cutting off his breath. Brandubh grabbed the thong. He struggled to loosen it.

"Run, Moira." The voice whispered roughly from above him.

Brandubh saw her glance up, her face frozen in surprise. She whipped around and ran toward the house.

He gasped for breath. His fingers ripped at the hands that held the thong.

The man on his back slid off, pulling the leather, jerking Brandubh's head backward. Exposing his throat. Brandubh waited for the blade.

Too quick an end probably. Instead, a tall man came from the shadows and landed first one, then another, and another huge blows to Brandubh's stomach.

The air rushed from his chest and he fell to his knees.

A heavy foot collided with his chin. He flew into the wall. The wood splintered under his head. A flash of pain blinded him. His eyes shut against it.

Footsteps crunched through the straw. Coming toward him. He forced his eyes open in time to see a blade coming. He rolled toward the door.

Hands pulled him back into the darkness. A third man, bigger than the others, swept the back of his closed fist across the face of the swordwielder.

"I don't want him dead, yet," he said in the same harsh whispered voice that had warned Moira. "Put the sword away."

Two men held Brandubh. He didn't try to escape again. He was spoiling for a fight. He needed a fight. Fortuitous it was he'd been offered one. A meaty fist struck a blow.

The sound of the smashing flesh against his face was strangely satisfying. Brandubh felt his lower lip split. There was a sharp sting, but the pain was nothing. He felt the blood flow down his chin. The second blow closed his right eye.

He took the punishment. Giving some of his blood cleansed him of some of the guilt.

"Tell me now you aren't to blame, Brandubh," the man said.

The voice was no longer a disguised whisper. Brandubh wasn't surprised at the identity of his attacker. He'd only wondered how long it would be.

"Uaid, let me go," he managed to spit out, along with a mouthful of blood. "Let me have a fair chance against you."

"What chance did Caoimhe have?" The relentless fist fell again, this time against Brandubh's breastbone. "That's where she stuck her little knife."

Brandubh fell forward, unable to breathe, unable to speak, unable to even think about standing. Yet the hands picked him up, again making him a target.

Again Uaid's fists met Brandubh's face. Brandubh let his head go with the force of the blow, wasting most of Uaid's power. He gathered his strength.

"As you wish, Uaid."

Using the two men holding his arms as support, Brandubh brought his knees up to his aching chest and kicked outward. He caught Uaid under the chin and sent him flying into the partition between two stalls.

Uaid's eyes rolled back in his head, then closed. He slid down to his backside on the floor.

Before Uaid's two friends could decide to try to finish the job, Brandubh snapped his head into the nose of the one on his right. That one dropped his hold. Brandubh brought his right fist around into the face of the other.

The anger and frustration flowed out through his arms. He pounded first one, then the other, until two strong hands seized him.

"Enough, lad. Enough. You're upsetting my horses." Dougal pulled Brandubh off the bloody men on the ground and turned to a stableman. "Get them out of here and bring me Conor."

"No." Brandubh swiped the back of his fist across his mouth. "There is no need for Conor to know of this. I've caused him enough pain."

Slipping out of Dougal's hands, he went out into the dark alone.

* * * *

"Let's see. We have primroses." Eibhlin bent over and pulled a dried stalk from the earth. "Burnet saxifrage." She fingered the dried flowers where the seed pods had formed. "Ah, plantain, still with some flowers. Good."

The medicinal herb garden was a work of art. She wandered along the rows, marveled at the variety. There must be much more trade with the Mediterranean than she'd thought, for there was gentian, roman chamomile, and oregano. With the plants in here she could treat anything from flatulence to lung congestion. All she had to do was clean it out a little, maybe transplant some garlic along the wall to repel insects and rodents.

She pulled her mantle around her to hold out the chill of this early November morning and prowled her domain. Morning chores were well underway so she didn't pay much attention to the passers-by who paused in their comings and goings to gawk at the strange woman who'd come home with their lord and lady.

"Good morning, Lady."

She nearly jumped over the radishes at the sound of Brandubh's voice. Carefully drawing her dignity around herself, she turned to greet him.

"Good morning, Lord.... God almighty, what happened to you?"

He tried to smile. She could tell because one corner of his luscious lips, now swollen beyond kissable and bruised and cut, raised just a bit.

"I had a bit of trouble finding a light last night."

"It looks like somebody had no trouble finding you." She stepped over the remains of savory that had been left to go to seed. "Why didn't you come to me? I could have helped with the bruising." Gently brushing the tips of her fingers across the already yellowing skin of his cheeks, past the right eye still swollen shut she asked, her voice a whisper, "What happened?"

"It is a personal matter, Lady."

"Ah." She dropped her hand. "Are you in pain? I can give you something to help."

"No. It is not necessary. I just came to say goodbye."

"Goodbye?" A vise closed around her heart. "Where are you going?"

"We leave within the hour for Lon Dubh. Dougal believes we will find a better trail from there to follow the raiders." He tipped his head and regarded her with his one open eye. "Will you miss me, Lady?"

Should she tell the truth? "I would hate you to be injured, Lord Brandubh." She stepped back across the savory.

As he followed her over the row, he bent and broke off a stem. Crushing a leaf between his long fingers, he waved it beneath his nose. "Is it true, healer, that savory is a love drug?"

"It supposedly has that property." Eibhlin backed away from him. "It is also good for bleeding and for the stomach. Perhaps I should make you an infusion?"

He smiled a little, coming too close. "Perhaps you should. Would you now?"

"Now? But you're leaving. I don't think I have time. I'd need to boil water and then it would have to steep for a bit."

"Ah," he nodded. "I've also heard, Lady, the kiss of a beautiful woman is also efficacious. Such healing would send this warrior off to slay the thieves and recover his property. Would you be willing to give me such treatment?"

He was so close, she could feel his breath brush across her cheek. So close she could see herself in the reflection of his burning black eye. So close she could feel the heat of his body. It was so warm she longed to be wrapped within his arms. Her tongue slipped out to moisten her lips. They remained parted for the kiss she knew was to come.

His bruised mouth was more tender in its taking, but no less masterful. The bold stroke of his tongue, daring hers to come to him, the nibbling and tasting weakened her knees. She rested her hands on his shoulders, then her arms moved around his neck. Such a steady, immovable rock he was, her raven.

Brandubh's hands moved around her waist and down. She felt herself lifted and pressed against the evidence of his urgent need.

Still his lips possessed, his hands held, his tongue enticed her.

"Brandubh, you should not wear the healer out. Likely we will need her to care for real wounds after we meet the miscreants who have robbed us." Dougal's voice interrupted the moment, yet Eibhlin didn't remove her arms right away.

Damnation, but he kissed good.

"Will you care for my wounds, Lady?" Brandubh murmured huskily.

Feeling some of their earlier camaraderie returning, she gave him a smile. "I would not turn any wounded man away, warrior."

"Ah, good. For I have this pain I would have you tend to." He pressed her against the source of that pain and raised his eyebrow. That look was one she saw in her dreams. "Think you able to cure this?"

"I don't believe there is a permanent cure for this particular ache. Perhaps it can be treated, though."

Brandubh laughed, deep and shaking her throughout. "I look forward to it, Lady. 'Twill give me good reason to hasten this business." He dropped his lips to hers in a quick brushing kiss before he added, "I am glad for this, Lady. I would not care to lose you."

It sounded so much like a declaration of love she was left speechless.

* * * *

After the noontime meal, Eibhlin was taking inventory of Oona's medicines and found her predecessor to have been a clean and methodical chemist of no small talents. Each container was well-sealed and even dated. She had to throw out some of the infusions which were old, but she found the healer's room to be an acceptable place to earn her keep while she was here.

"Here you are," Sadbh stuck her head around the doorframe before entering. "Is it to your liking?"

"Yes, thank you. Oona was a gifted woman."

"Indeed she was. We miss her." Sadbh glanced around. "I wonder how this compares to what you're accustomed to."

"What do you mean?" Eibhlin asked.

Sadbh shook her head. "I'm not sure. I listened to your discussion with Uncle Brian concerning your work. Eibhlin, I am not a stupid woman. In fact, I am quite well-educated, but, I found your discourse to be difficult to follow. It seemed to me that your ideas were far beyond what has been thought before."

Eibhlin was amazed at the woman's insight.

"I've wondered about you," Sadbh continued, "ever since Brandubh first told me of you last summer. Your appearing on the Crag was so... strange." As though ordering her thoughts, she paused. "I will admit, at first, I was concerned he was yearning for a woman of the faerie mist. A

woman who could not satisfy the needs of a flesh-and-blood man."
Sadbh smiled. "I am relieved, you see, that you are not faerie after all."
Eibhlin smiled with her. "So what do you think of me now?"
The cool gaze settled on Eibhlin for a moment before Sadbh spoke again.
"I believe you are as mortal as I. Where you are from is not important to me. Yet, you are here with us against your will." Sadbh paused, her discerning blue eyes studying Eibhlin again. "If it is impossible for you to return, will you remain?"
Eibhlin laughed, a little bitterly, "What choice will I have?"
"I mean here, with us. With Brandubh."
"Lady, anything I say means nothing. I have no idea whether it *is* possible."
"Do you care for my son?"
My, but she was direct. Eibhlin had nowhere to go but right back up the direct route. No use lying to her.
"Lady, I want him, but I don't know whether that constitutes caring. My experience with men has not been good."
Sadbh sat on a low stool. "Tell me."
Eibhlin was dumbstruck at having such intimate information commanded so plainly.
"Now, my dear, don't think me a nosy old woman. Brandubh is my only living child and I would have him content." She raised her expressive auburn eyebrow. "I would have grandchildren. And yes, I am direct. There is no time in life for anything else."
Brandubh was the same way, Eibhlin thought. Well, why not? Somebody around here had to care that she was a divorced woman.
"All right. There isn't much to tell, really. I was married. My husband was unfaithful to me. I divorced him."
Sadbh nodded. "And?"
"That's all."
"That's all? So, when did this happen?"
In about a thousand years, was the answer on Eibhlin's tongue.
"About a year ago," she said, answering relatively.
"A *year*? My dear, you've been without a man for a whole year?" Sadbh jumped off her stool. "Have you lost your desire for men? No, of course you haven't. After all, I just saw you this morn with Brandubh in the garden. So, why are you putting him off?"
"I just met him. I don't know him well enough for... anything."
"I wasn't talking about *anything*. I was talking about a marriage."
"I thought so. Lady, I can't go through that again."
"If you mean a wandering husband, I can guarantee that will be up to you. If he gets what he needs in your bed, Brandubh will not stray far."
"I don't want him to stray at all."
Sadbh laughed. "That too, is up to your diligence in keeping your husband happy. Listen to me, my dear, Dougal's eye roams, but I know where he lies at night. From what I've seen in Brandubh's eyes when he

looks at you, I know he is like his father in this."

"This has been your goal all along?"

"Naturally. From the first, he spoke of you like no other. He was there when you came back, was he not? I have been watching him. He has taken no woman to his bed since the first time he saw you."

Eibhlin didn't know if she believed that. "Is he in the habit of reporting his bed-mates to you?"

Sadbh shrugged. "Of course not, but he is enough like his father that I can tell when he has been without. There are no women at Lon Dubh. Well, except for Ita, who keeps house for him, and... well, nevermind who else. He would not take a woman at Lon Dubh." Sadbh smiled. "Brandubh does not enjoy conflict in his household. Favoring one woman over another is a recipe for just that, as he has learned to his discomfort." This last was said with a laugh and she shook her head. "No, he would come here. Any number of the women here would be ecstatic to lie with him. He never tried to hide his favorites, the rascal, leaving me to deal with the cat-fighting."

"Favorites?" Now Eibhlin felt her eyebrow rising at this news. Being around these people was giving her all sorts of bad new habits.

"Did you love your husband?" Sadbh asked, the question coming out of nowhere.

It was a simple one. Why couldn't she answer it?

Because she couldn't truthfully say, yes? Because she truthfully hadn't? At least, she truthfully didn't know anymore.

"Lady Sadbh," one of the young maids yelled in the garden, "Lady Sadbh!"

"Right here, Marsali. Cease that shrieking. What is it?"

"You and the Lady Eibhlin must come to the front gate quickly."

The girl ran off before she could be questioned, leaving Eibhlin and Sadbh nothing to do but follow. At least Eibhlin was saved the necessity of answering of Sadbh's question. As they rounded the big house and came into the front courtyard, they both skidded to a halt.

Cows, more than Eibhlin had ever seen in once place at one time, milled around the courtyard, their low voices joining in a chorus of complaint. Surprise moved her feet and she waded into them. They kicked up dust that mixed with the earthy barnyard smell.

"Ah, Lady, 'tis a pleasure to see you again." The call came from a bandy-legged red-haired man strutting toward her. She started to stand aside, to permit the man to greet Sadbh as befitted the lady of the house. However, it was Eibhlin's hand he reached for. "Do you not remember me, Lady?"

Eibhlin looked the man in the eye. "No, I'm sorry...."

"You saved my wife from choking down at Kincora."

The name and face came to her and she smiled with pleasure.

"Padraig mac Finn. How is your wife?"

Padraig grinned. "She is chewing her food more carefully."

Eibhlin had to laugh out loud. "I'm glad to hear it."

"Where shall we put the beasties, Lady?"
"What beasties?"
"Your cattle."
Sadbh choked back a laugh.
"My cattle?" Eibhlin repeated, somewhat stupidly, she thought. "I don't have any cattle."
"You do now, Lady. Fifty of my finest stock for my Orla's life."
"Fifty?"
"Padraig," Sadbh cut in, "Lady Eibhlin is speechless with gratitude for this generous gift and I am sure when she regains her capacity for sensible speech, she will thank you appropriately. For now, take the cattle to the pen on the downwind side of the house."
Padraig bowed and grinned, apparently pleased that his gift had so rendered the Lady insensible.
Sadbh put her arm around Eibhlin's waist. "Congratulations, my dear. You are now a woman of property."
Eibhlin wrinkled her nose at the smell of what *her* property was doing in the yard. Fertilizer for her garden. How nice.
"Sadbh, what am I going to do with fifty head of cattle?"

Chapter Ten

"Here, my dear." Sadbh held out the heavy earthenware mug full of the apple-scented tea, prepared to Eibhlin's instructions.
Eibhlin took it gratefully and sipped the chamomile. She needed something soothing and chamomile was the first thing she thought of. Part of her problem might be she was still coming off caffeine. Since coffee would be unknown here until at least sixteen-fifty-something, she definitely had to find a substitute.
As she calmed down, she noticed that Sadbh had closed the doors to the solar, after clearing out the women who did their sewing in this light, comfortable room.
"Are you all right?" Sadbh took a seat next to Eibhlin on the chaise by the window. "Surely you expected that Padraig might do something like this."
"No, I didn't."
"You saved Orla's life."
"But fifty cows! Sadbh, I don't know about keeping cattle."
"Tosh. Cattle keep themselves. There is plenty of pasture and water here."
A wonderful idea presented itself. "You and Dougal take them, as payment for my keep."
Sadbh's eyes widened in horror. "Mother in Heaven, no. Hospitality cannot be paid for."

Pangs of embarrassment shot through her. Of course, Eibhlin had known that. She'd only forgotten in her urgency to find something to do with those cursed cows.

"I apologize, Sadbh, I didn't mean to give offense."

Sadbh patted her knee. "Of course not, my dear."

In spite of her own discomfiture, Eibhlin could not help but notice Sadbh's expression of concern.

"What's wrong?" she asked.

"Hmmh? Oh, nothing." But Sadbh was not a dissembler and couldn't hide her disquiet. "To be honest, I am concerned, Eibhlin. You are a woman of some property now. There will be choices open to you that you did not have before."

"Property? Fifty cows?" Eibhlin almost laughed. But Sadbh's distress was real. She took a sip of her tea before asking, "Are fifty cows a lot?"

"Yes, it is a respectable amount of wealth. This means your bride price will rise, of course. And there will be more difficulty in preparing the documents."

"Wait a minute. My bride price? What bride price?"

"Oooh. I have been clumsy. Now, do not become angry. I will explain. It is the *brehons*, the judges, not the priests, who conduct marriages in Ireland. Naturally, we also wed before the priest as well, but...."

If her pause meant she was waiting for a reaction from Eibhlin, she wasn't going to get one.

"When a man wants to marry a woman, he must offer her family something to make up for her loss--usually cattle," Sadbh continued. "If her family is poor, few cattle are offered. If they are rich, many cattle will be required. For her first marriage, the cattle go to her father and are added to the family's herd. If she is remarrying, she gets a part of the bride price for her own. The more times she gets married, the more she gets to keep of the bride price. It's all specified in the law."

Eibhlin was confused. "If I am wealthy now, why are you concerned? Won't I be a more fitting bride for a kinsman of the *Ard Ri*?"

"Indeed, and because you are being sponsored by the *Ard Ri*, it is conceivable that many more men will offer for you, running the price up."

Supply and demand. Capitalism. What a wonderful thing.

"So, Sadbh, are you going to be tight-fisted with your cows?" Eibhlin asked with a smile.

Sadbh frowned. "I am not sure, but I think you are asking if I resent having Brandubh pay more for you?" At Eibhlin's nod, she answered. "Of course not, my dear. It matters not to me how many cattle he offers for you, since they will remain with the Dal Cais tribe. But you are an even more attractive potential mate now. When it is known that you are also a healer, your price will increase even more. Men who cannot afford your price may decide to do it the old-fashioned way."

Eibhlin was bug-eyed. *This* wasn't old-fashioned?

"What might that mean?"

"Someone might abduct you and use you, then make whatever offer they are able. If he has lain with you, the offer will most likely be accepted by the *Ard Ri* and you would be declared married by the brehons."

"What! Marriage by rape?"

"Exactly."

Eibhlin thought of Brandubh's words on the Crag, which echoed what she already knew. A woman could refuse any offer.

"But, Sadbh, I still can refuse any husband the Ard Ri selects. Is this not correct?"

Sadbh sighed. "Yes, my dear. However, it is not an easy thing for a woman so used to find another willing to take her."

"I'm already a divorced woman. Isn't that bad enough?"

Surprising Eibhlin with her laugh, Sadbh shook her head.

"If your husband was truly adulterous, our law would permit you to divorce him and take all you had brought to the marriage and to keep the entire bride price. In the same way, you will be pressured to accept even a poor offer from a man who has already possessed you." Sadbh put a slender hand to her forehead. "I know it seems contradictory, but there you are. It is even more important that you decide now whether you will accept Brandubh. He will offer for you and no one will be able to match him."

"Why are you so sure?"

"Because Dougal and I will not permit it. Our herd and all other property will be available to Brandubh does he need it."

That was quite a declaration. Sadbh's determination to have her as a daughter-in-law was flattering, but would that determination, and the protectiveness she felt for her son, keep her from helping Eibhlin return home?

"I still want to return to my own place, Sadbh."

The older woman nodded. "I understand how you feel, Eibhlin, truly I do. However, you must consider something. Why did you come here? What brought you here?"

"Your son brought me here!"

"Did he?"

Eibhlin's bluster left her as quickly as it came. "All right, not exactly. But I am not here of my own free will."

"Then I don't know what to tell you. I have heard tales from some of the ones with the old knowledge that women are able to come if they want to. They cannot be forced nor coerced. I have never heard of a woman going back. Though, perhaps if they wanted to come, they had no desire to try." Sadbh sighed. "On the next solstice, I will take you to Craglea. If you wish to leave, I pledge to you your chance."

"I'm grateful, Sadbh."

"I wonder if my son will be as generous." Sadbh appeared to consider that for a moment before she said, "Well, I must ask your pardon, my dear. I have work to attend to."

Eibhlin watched Sadbh sweep across the rush-covered floor to go about her business, then wondered how to fill her own afternoon, envious of how the lady managed her household.

"I'd better get to work too," Eibhlin said to herself, since there was no one else around, "before she sets me to weaving."

She left the solar, stepping out into the great hall. There was still some cleaning she wanted to do in the herb room and now was as good a time as any. Passing the dais where the Lord and Lady presided over meals, she stopped.

"Oh," she whispered, kneeling by the corner of the platform where the poet's harp rested.

The harp was crafted of aged rowan wood, sleek and black, and was much like her own. With trembling fingers, she stroked the brass strings. The bell-like tone sent a rush of pleasure through her. Glancing around, seeing herself alone in the hall, she sat down beside the harp. Closing her eyes as her mother had instructed her, she lay her hands on the strings, seeking the songs that lived within them. Then she curved her fingers and, with only the tips of her fingernails, began to play.

"Oh, lovely."

Eibhlin's eyes flew open at the girl's voice. She guiltily took her hands from the harp and sat away from it.

"Please, don't stop. It will be pleasant to have such beautiful music to listen to while I work." A plain girl made her way down the big table on the dais. She wiped the surface of the table clean with long, efficient strokes. Without missing a place, she turned her face toward Eibhlin and said, "My name is Cera, Lady."

"I shouldn't have touched it." Eibhlin stood and meant to leave.

"Nonsense. Teague, leaves his harp here for any to try. He says he's found many fine poets that way. He will want to hear you."

Eibhlin walked away from the harp, avoiding the temptation of touching it again. She intended to leave the hall and get to her herbroom, but Cera spoke again, even as she dropped her cloth into a basket and picked up a rake.

"Is it true, Lady, that your are going to marry Brandubh?"

"Ah, well...."

"Has he kissed you?" Cera's face lit up with expectation. "He has a beautiful mouth. Well, he did before Uaid smashed it."

"Who?"

Cera explained while she swept old rushes from the dais into a pile on the side.

"Uaid. His sister is the one who killed herself over Brandubh. Everyone knew he never cared for her. Don't know why she just didn't go find another. Surely she was pretty enough."

"Killed herself?" Eibhlin asked.

"That's a lie, Cera."

Eibhlin tensed at the sound of Moira's voice.

Cera wasn't intimidated, but kept sweeping. "No, it's not, Moira. Your sister was spoiled and she thought she could have anything she wanted, including Brandubh."

Cera's words seemed unusually harsh. "Cera...." Eibhlin started, then made the mental connection. Moira's sister had killed herself over Brandubh.

Moira's words greeting Eibhlin's arrival at Ath Sionnain echoed.

Is this the whore who stole Brandubh?

Moira wasn't jealous. She was angry. She hated Eibhlin because of her sister.

"Brandubh also beat up your brother and *two* of his friends. Does your father know about that, Moira?"

"My brother did what he did for Caoimhe's sake. If not for this one, Brandubh would have honored his offer."

Eibhlin felt the words hammering in her head. *His offer.* He'd offered for Moira's sister.

"Phfft." Cera leaned on the wooden rake she'd used on the rushes. "You used to be my friend, and you could be yet, but until you let go of this anger you have toward Brandubh, I do not want to talk to you again, Moira ni Conor."

Eibhlin had kept her eyes off Moira until Cera called her by name.

"Moira ni Conor?" Eibhlin repeated the name.

"Yes. What of it?" Moira's eyes flashed like firelight through a brandy glass.

Her mother had explained the *ni Conor* part of her professional name as a tribute to her Irish ancestors. Eibhlin wondered if this Moira could be one of those ancestors? Could that be the explanation for the staggering feeling of familiarity? Yet, even if it were true, the thought brought no pleasure. This Moira clearly despised her.

"I'm sorry," she murmured, practically running from the hall.

* * * *

Moira watched her flee, wondering why she should feel anything for the woman who'd ruined her sister's plans for a happy life? Why the feeling of recognition?

Tossing the unrepentant Cera a glare, Moira left the great hall, though she was supposed to help Cera change the rushes. Lady Sadbh would punish her, but she didn't dare stay longer. Cera's offer of renewed friendship was weakening her resolve to exact revenge on Brandubh and his woman.

She stepped out into the yard and let her feet take her where they would.

Since Brandubh's admission that he felt some guilt over Caoimhe's death, Moira's anger had cooled. It was difficult for her to pile misery upon misery. Maybe part of her problem was a sense that she shared some of the guilt as well. She'd not been able to talk Caoimhe out of her infatuation, nor had she tried after Brandubh had made his lack of interest known. Faced with Caoimhe's tears, Moira wrapped the poor girl in her arms and assured her everything would be all right.

What she should have done was tell her exactly how things were. It was no kindness being kind when truth needed telling.

Of course, Caoimhe wouldn't have listened, but Moira could see Brandubh had no real intentions of offering. As time passed, and Brandubh's attentions continued to be spent on serving women, only a lovesick fool would hold on. In fact, Brandubh had been restless for weeks before going to Kincora last summer and had barely spoken to Caoimhe at all.

He had found the woman on Craglea. The story had swept through Ath Sionnain within minutes of their arrival. She was sent to him. Caoimhe could not compete with that.

Moira closed her eyes and set her hands to her temples. This was making her head ache. If old Oona had still been alive, she'd go for something to soothe the pain.

Her feet stopped. What would happen if she actually....

The woman had been afraid of her. Moira had seen it in her eyes. Though she didn't know where the fear had come from, perhaps if it were great enough, she would just go away. How fitting. And no one would really be hurt.

Deprive him of his lover, as Caoimhe had been deprived.

Fitting, indeed, she thought, as she headed toward the herb room.

Chapter Eleven

The knock at the door startled Eibhlin from her concentration.

"Come in."

The last person she expected to seek her out came through the door.

"Lady Eibhlin, may I speak with you?"

"Yes, Moira, of course," Eibhlin answered, her voice scratchy.

The girl came in and stood at the far end of the battered table that served the herb room.

"What can I do for you, Moira?"

"First, I want to ask your forgiveness for the way I spoke to you. What occurred before you arrived is not your responsibility."

Wasn't it? Eibhlin wondered. Would he have spurned that poor dead girl if.... She shrugged.

"There is nothing to forgive," she said.

Moira's lips stretched thin. Then she nodded. "And I'd like to ask if you would let me help you."

"Why?" Eibhlin asked, on her guard, even more so since her heart begged her to trust the girl whose dislike of her had been more than obvious.

Moira sighed. "I understand why you are suspicious of my motives. It is really no more than I have heard it said you mean to leave soon. We need a healer and I have an interest. I cannot say I have the talent, but perhaps I can learn enough to help, at least." Moira tilted her head, her angel-sweet face lacking any sign of a hidden motive. "Is it true you will leave?"

"My plans are my affair."

"Of course. However, it would not hurt to teach another, would it?" Moira paused, then added, "I wish to learn a useful vocation."

"Is that all?"

"What else could there be?"

What else, indeed? Well, Sadbh had asked Eibhlin to teach them about healing plants. It was technically part of her bargain. There was really no good reason to refuse.

"All right, Moira. You can start now." Eibhlin tossed her a bunch of savory. "Chop this for tea."

And so Moira's education began.

* * * *

"What the devil!" Dougal dismounted and stalked over to the pen where Eibhlin's herd milled and mooed.

"Hello, husband," Sadbh called as she came out of the big house. "Did you have success?"

"Yes," he answered. "Sadbh, where did these cattle come from?"

"They are Eibhlin's. So, tell me, what did you find?

"Eibhlin's? Where did she get cattle?"

Sadbh frowned. "Dougal, are you going to tell me about *our* cattle?"

He put his fists to his hips and hovered over her. "Not until you tell *me* where our guest got near to, what, forty head?"

"Fifty. Padraig brought them several days ago in payment for Eibhlin saving Orla's life."

As though that was all the information Dougal needed, she raised an eyebrow in anticipation of getting answers from him now. He decided the easiest course was to answer her.

"We found some of the cattle near Clonmacnois. Brandubh is bringing them."

"Conchobar and Deirdre?"

Dougal shook his head. "We lost the tracks just east of the monastery. Brandubh will set out again when he has fresh horses." He leaned against the fence confining the cattle. "Our Lady is a rich woman, now, eh?"

"'Twill make her more valuable. Three head will not be sufficient." Sadbh wrapped her arms around his waist. "Now, my husband, if you do not kiss me, I will invite you to find another place to sleep tonight."

Dougal took his wife in his arms and pulled her tight against him.

"Hah! You would seek me out before the moon is completely risen. Yet, I will humor you, wife." He lowered his head and took her mouth with a passion the years had only made stronger.

Riding in behind the seventeen head of cattle, Brandubh grinned at the spectacle of his parents presented in the yard. By Patrick's bones, they had been barely four days apart, but Dougal could have been months at sea if one judged by the reception his wife was giving him.

To have such a reception myself, Brandubh thought, never missing a wife of his own more than this moment. Missing Eibhlin, if he would be truthful with himself.

"Ah, Dougal, I see you have found that which you missed most. Here, now," he yelled at a wayward heifer and flicked a rope at her.

Dougal broke free of Sadbh's lips. "In truth, boy, it was your mother who could not contain her desire for my kisses."

"Such a conceited man. I will see to you later." Sadbh pushed him away with a teasing smile and turned to her son. "I am sorry, Brandubh, you have not found your horses."

"I have not lost all hope, yet, Mother. Conchobar was special shod and I think I can find him when I have more light. As long as it does not rain too hard." He leaned down to push the gate closed behind the last of the cattle he'd added to the pen. "Whence are these animals? I do not recognize the markings."

"They are Eibhlin's," Sadbh said and explained the reason for their presence here.

"Fifty? Why so many?"

Sadbh's brow wrinkled and her voice was tight. "Perhaps Padraig simply values his wife's life." Her skirts whirling up a dust storm around her ankles, she turned and stormed back to the house.

Brandubh was at a loss to explain her reaction. He glanced at his father, leaning against a fence post, whose expression of amusement was too much. Brandubh grinned.

"Did I say something wrong?"

"I hope you are more the courtly speaker when you encounter the Lady Eibhlin. There will be many interested swains when her fame spreads. A healer with a herd of her own and no family to share them? Ah, such a prize."

"So, the *Ard Ri* will have many offers to consider, will he not?" Brandubh turned to face his father. His next question was asked in deadly earnest. "Do I have your support in offering for this woman, Father? Though she is of no family, has no fortune?" He waved a hand at the cattle and smiled, "Well...."

Dougal shrugged his Italian shrug. "What did I have when your mother claimed me? Nothing but my hands to work for her and my heart to give her. Who am I to tell you not to offer for the woman you want? Your Uncle Brian will accept your offer over any other but--and I know I do not need to say it--you do not want to shame your woman by not prizing her highly enough."

Brandubh nodded. "Indeed, Father. I would offer her everything I own for her to accept me as her husband."

"As I thought. So, let us go in to our supper and see what state things are in today. If they are as when we left, you may yet have an easy conquest to make. Perhaps we can conclude this business before many of those young men hear of our Lady's talent and beauty and wealth and have you safely abed with the fair Eibhlin before they can cloud the issue." Dougal clapped Brandubh on the shoulder and they went in to supper together.

Brandubh's mind dwelled on his father's words. *Abed with the fair Eibhlin*. He offered a prayer that such would be the case.

* * * *

But it was already too late. Dougal's hall was filled to overflowing with the cream and crust of Ireland's manhood. Brandubh counted twenty men whom he knew to already be married. Yet, when presented to Eibhlin, their eyes glazed with the same lust as those younger, yet unmarried men.

And she seemed to enjoy their scabrous attention. She smiled her wide, bright smile, showing her perfect, pearly white teeth. Her sweet, rosy lips touched her chalice like a lover's mouth, and when she lowered the vessel, a glistening residue of wine remained.

Brandubh's tongue slipped out as though to lick the drops for her. Enough, he thought, pushing off the edge of the table where he'd leaned to watch her flirtations. Elbowing his way through the five-deep sea of suitors, he stood before her.

"Lady, it is time to enter for our supper. Will you allow me to escort you?" Brandubh offered his arm.

She accepted with a bright smile. "Why, Lord Brandubh, I'd heard you had returned. I'm sorry you haven't found your lost horses."

Brandubh dropped his arm, right on top of the head of an old lecher who bowed too near her bosom, attempting to gain her attention.

"Thank you, my Lady. I will find them soon."

"Your mother told me you were off as soon as you replenished your supplies and obtained fresh mounts." Her eyes flashed to the side at an admirer who was sidling too close. He noted her quick step away from the leech.

Brandubh smiled and shoved a young cockerel out of his way, moving closer to her. "I hadn't thought to leave again so soon, Lady."

Dougal, passing by, froze in his tracks.

"Did I not say that earlier, Father?" Brandubh asked, hoping Dougal was not in one of his teasing moods.

"Och, aye, he did, Lady. His first intention was to seek your company," Dougal replied with a bow to Eibhlin before proceeding to his place at the front of the hall.

"Indeed?" Eibhlin narrowed a skeptical eye.

Brandubh turned back to Eibhlin. "Shall we, Lady? Oh, my apologies, Fergus," he said to the skinny lad who yet attempted to come between him and Eibhlin.

"But, Lord Brandubh, the Lady has accepted my company for the meal."

Brandubh turned his entire intimidating height on the diminutive Fergus. "Really?"

"Yes," Fergus squeaked. With a cough to clear his throat, he added, "the Lady and I have kept company for several days and find we are very compatible."

Eibhlin's face displayed her disbelief.

"You're foxed, Fergus. I was here first. She'll come with me," one voice shouted behind them.

"No, with me," declared another.

Suddenly, a cacophony of requests, demands, and claims for her company sprang up around them.

Eibhlin looked up at Brandubh, clearly unsure of the way to proceed. Looking to him, he thought with a self-satisfied surge of male pride. He offered his arm again.

"My lady mother awaits us. May I?"

With no further hesitation, though she was urged by the slavering pack to choose another, she lay her fingers on his forearm and allowed him to escort her. It was a small victory. Brandubh realized he knew things about her that these others seeking her company did not--chiefly that she did not intend to remain.

It was time to convince her of the contentment to be found here.

"You are especially lovely tonight, Eibhlin," he whispered, his lips close to her ear, and was pleased by the light rosy blush which crept up her cheeks.

"You are very kind, Lord Brandubh."

Her voice was formally cool, but he caught the twitch at the corners of her mouth. The wench was toying with him.

"Is there no other lady you would rather dine with? I am certain I could find some poor substitute for your company, should you desire to be elsewhere." Her eyes flashed, just barely, to the crowd of cow-eyed fools that dogged their steps.

Brandubh nearly stopped their progress to bellow a dispersal to the rabble. "*Is* there any other lady here tonight? I see only you."

She smiled. "Such pretty words."

Yes, they were, but he admitted to himself they were from his heart, for she was the only woman he saw.

She was beautiful, tall and full of figure. Such a lovely armful with eyes of stormy blue-gray. And how those eyes could flash. As his own body began to warm from her proximity, he doubted very much fifty head of cattle had caused the frenzy around the fair Eibhlin.

* * * *

Painfully aware of him, Eibhlin tried to eat without letting on how he affected her. Flirting was one thing, but to let her emotions get tangled up in it was not only foolish, but dangerous.

"Apple, my Lady?" Brandubh efficiently cut the fruit into pieces and offered her a slice.

Eibhlin opened her mouth to accept it before realizing how intimate a gesture it was. Her lips brushed the tips of his fingers, bringing a seductive smile to his lips.

What the hell? she thought. Was she ever going to have such a man want her again? Would it be so bad if she....

Taking a slice of the fruit from his hand, she held it to his lips, allowing him to return her caress.

Dougal stifled a chuckle under a cough and clapped his hands together. "Let us have some real entertainment. Teague!"

A cheer accompanied the call for the poet. Teague, a gaunt man wearing the six colors allowed his rank, came to sit by the harp Eibhlin had played earlier and, just as she had been taught, closed his eyes before laying his hands on the strings.

Brandubh filled the chalice they'd shared during dinner and offered it to her. She took it from his hand and drank the rich Italian wine. Her head started to spin and she leaned back against Brandubh's wide shoulder and closed her eyes.

He rested his cheek against her hair and sighed. Eibhlin couldn't help the smile that grew on her face. It would be so easy, she thought, listening to Teague playing God's own music on his harp, so easy to stay here with Brandubh, so easy to fall in love with him, so easy to get used to having him in her bed every night.

Brandubh reached around her and took her hand.

Teague began his song, from an old tale she knew well. She rested against Brandubh's solid shoulder and just listened as Teague sang in a sharp, clear tenor.

"The fair Etain, wife of Midir, loved and was loved.
But evil Fuamnach, first of Midir's affection,
Sorceress, she cast a spell to take Etain from her lover.
Changed to the likeness of a butterfly, Etain flew away.
Midir caught her and in the nights enjoyed her love.
Until Fuamnach with a wind blew the butterfly into a river
Where she was consumed by a great fish...."

Brandubh held her hand, gently running his thumb over the back of it. It was a familiar, sweet gesture.

I want him, she thought. *I will have him once before I leave.* A silent giggle shook her. Maybe more than once.

He stirred behind her. Turning, she saw he examined her with that raised eyebrow she loved so much.

"Do you find something amusing, my Lady?"

Eibhlin had to smile. "Yes, my Lord." She squeezed his fingers and rested against him again, returning her attention to Teague. He was getting to the good part.

"Eochy, King of Tara won Etain and married her.
In his pride, Eochy allowed a stranger to trick him.
The stranger bested him at chess and claimed as his prize
A kiss from the beautiful Etain.
Once held within his arms, her eyes opened and she saw
The one true love of her life.
In his arms, she rose with him and returned to his land.
Wretched Eochy, left with empty bed and impotent cursing."

Laughter and applause greeted the ending.

"Well sung."

"Aye."

"*Bravo*." This was from Dougal, of course.

Teague only tipped his head in acceptance of the accolades which trained bards took as their due. Eibhlin smiled at the cool look of pleasure on his face. She wondered if he was as calm inside as he looked outwardly. Her father had sweated every performance, while her mother.... Seemingly of their own accord, her eyes scanned over the crowd, falling on the disapproving face of Moira ni Conor.

Even the wine couldn't keep the chill from ruining her mood.

"What is amiss?" he asked as her shoulders tensed and she removed her fingers from his.

"Nothing," she answered, too quickly, she realized. "I'm afraid I've had too much wine and I'm giddy. Perhaps I should retire. Good night, Lord Dougal, Lady Sadbh." Eibhlin rose and as quietly as possible, made her way out of the great hall to her chamber.

As she climbed the stone staircase, she knew what it was that had driven her from Brandubh's arms--guilt, pure and simple, knowing that Brandubh had jilted Moira's sister for her. Yet she also knew that if he came to her tonight, she'd not refuse him.

* * * *

During supper, three men had come asking about the healer woman with the cattle. Dougal had heard them all out, glancing at Eibhlin and Brandubh and trying to hide his amusement.

After the entertainment was complete, he'd called Brandubh to join him in a walk and abandoned all pretense of serious consideration. In fact, he was near weeping from laughter.

"God's teeth, Brandubh. I had not known such specimens were allowed to live past birth. That Fergus barely comes to her bosoms." Dougal added with a wink, "Perhaps that's as good, though. It does bring to mind some interesting pictures."

"Father, I do not wish to contemplate any of your sordid imaginings."

Dougal might find enormous hilarity in the situation, but Brandubh's humor wasn't getting any better. He wondered, not for the first time, if all Italians had as strange a sense of humor as Dougal.

"Mother of God," he cursed and kicked at a pile of dung left by her herd in the courtyard.

Dougal's whoop of mirth taunted him to patricide.

"Now, son," Dougal gasped as he wiped his eyes with the back of his hand, "this only means you'll have to come up with more than three cows. If it comes to a bidding war, you could be in trouble. One of Dallas' men who rode with us left as soon as the story was told. Dallas is just rid of a wife and is looking in earnest for another. Of course, his favored method of courtship is abduction."

"I'll kill him if he tries it, Dougal."

"Indeed," Dougal tried to say without a snicker. "Forgive me, my son. I know my humor strikes you as inappropriate sometimes. Here, sit." He indicated a low wooden bench by the stable wall.

Brandubh sat as ordered, though he would have selected a different place. The smell of cattle in the small pen assaulted his nostrils. Her cattle.

"Here is what you must do, Brandubh. You must make sure she will choose you. Brian will not marry her to a man she does not desire, does that man offer a thousand head. If she says she wants you, Brian will give her to you."

The crunch of footsteps alerted them to the approach of one of Eibhlin's swains--the scrawny, thin, short, undernourished and under-developed Fergus.

"Excuse me, Lord Dougal?"

Dougal stood and faced the young man.

"I am Fergus mac Arlyn. I would talk to you of the Lady under your protection."

Brandubh stood. "The Lady is already spoken for." He turned to Dougal. "The *Ard Ri* knows of my intentions. He may take that as an offer for as many head as he cares to name."

Dougal smirked. "I think you are being hasty, Brandubh. Lord Fergus, please accept my apology for my son. He is smitten with the lovely Lady and has as much as made his offer for her. If it doesn't work out...."

"Father." The ground-out warning only served to set Dougal laughing again.

"...I will send word to you and your father."

Fergus took one more look in Brandubh's direction and beat a hasty retreat.

Watching young Fergus' retreating backside, Brandubh said, "I offer fifty head, Father. Will you take her the offer?"

"Aye, son. I will." Dougal lay his hand on Brandubh's shoulder and squeezed. "I'm off to bed, now, however. Your lady has invented a delightful hot drink for the morning and I have asked her to share it with me. I shall present your offer when she appears amenable."

Brandubh nodded and watched his father head off to his bed. Faced with an empty bed of his own, Brandubh wondered if perhaps a gentler variation of Dallas' wife-catching strategy might not be in order.

Chapter Twelve

Eibhlin tossed onto her left side, after spending no more than two minutes on her right. Restlessness was nothing new to her, especially since meeting Brandubh. Nighttime now brought not rest, but only the reminder of her loneliness.

Part of her hoped fervently he would come, prayed that he would ignore her apparent rejection of him at the dinner table. The rest of her was sensible enough to want him to stay away. Better to avoid becoming more attracted to him, than having to deal with the broken heart that would follow having to leave him.

A gentle tap at her door demanded her attention.

"Yes," she answered.

The door opened and Brandubh entered. He pushed it shut behind him and crossed the room to stand by the fireplace.

"What are you doing here, Brandubh?"

She already knew the answer. He unpinned the brooch that held his mantle over his shoulder. The long garment fell to the floor. The rhythm of her heart quickened as he loosened his belt and let it join the discarded mantle.

"Will you tell me to leave, Lady?"

She didn't need to think about that one.

"No." She was as certain of this as anything before in her life. "I want you to stay."

He smiled and sat in the chair by the fireplace, where he started unlacing his leggings.

"Why?" he asked, looked down at the laces.

She watched his long fingers move slowly over the ties.

And she wanted them on her.

Throwing back the covers, Eibhlin got out of bed wearing only a thin linen shift. Brandubh glanced up, his eyes mapping her every feature and in his eyes she could see the desire that had brought him to her tonight. She owed him nothing but the truth, the acknowledgment that she wanted him as much.

Crossing the small room she knelt before him and began to unlace the other leg.

"Because you are the most beautiful man I've ever seen and I want you."

"Is there no other reason?" His voice, normally deep and rumbling, was even more so, as though this question were too serious for any less imperious tone. "Is it just the lust of the body you seek to quench?"

She met his gaze. "There can be nothing more, Brandubh. You know I can't stay."

"I will try to persuade you otherwise."

His form of persuasion would be devastating to her resolve. But this was what she'd hoped for, wished for.

"Fair enough," she said as she stood, accepting his challenge.

Brandubh took her arms and pulled her to sit astride his lap. In the firelight, his face glowed a burnished gold. His eyes, black and hot, traveled over her face while his hands moved steadily and intoxicatingly over the bare skin of her arms.

"I would have you to wife, Eibhlin. I would give you my children."

Her heart leapt with that promise. Children would be important to this man. There would be lots of children.

Brandubh brushed his lips across the linen-covered tips of her breasts, already full and heavy and straining against her shift. Her nipples tightened and hardened under his caress. Spreading both hands against her back, he pressed her closer and took one sensitive crest into his mouth, rasping his tongue across the nipple through the thin linen.

Shocks of delight shot through her. She wrapped her hands around his neck and rocked with involuntary rhythms against him, arching her back, offering him more.

"Sweet lady." He nipped at the pebbled tip, then gave equal attention to the other. His large hands easily palmed her bottom, squeezing and kneading, holding her closer, where her movements could more perfectly fit him. He was hard and huge against her softer flesh.

Eibhlin felt the liquid response of her body preparing itself to receive him. She combed her fingers through the silken ebony strands of his hair, tenderly stroking the white marking. She pressed her lips to the top of his head while his lips sought more of her flesh.

His fingers, starting at her knees, moved along her thighs, pushing her shift up to her waist. He sat up and pulled his tunic with one hand. Eibhlin felt another rush when his swollen flesh stood hard against her belly.

Brandubh set his hands on her cheeks and brought her mouth to his, taking her breath in a kiss of possession and need. His tongue plundered, demanding, urging, pleading. Her head became light from the lack of air, yet she couldn't pull away. She even moaned a complaint when he broke his lips from hers to pull her shift off over her head, only to return to take her mouth again.

Even with the fireplace crackling behind her, Eibhlin felt a chill at her sudden nakedness. But his hands caressed her, stroking up and down her sides, her back, her thighs, and soon, she was too hot to notice the temperature of the room.

Brandubh's lips marked his claimed territory with wet kisses --mouth, nose, eyes, ears, cheeks. His thorough planting of his seal on her took in everywhere his mouth could reach. Where his mouth was unable to go, his hands went.

Eibhlin could feel the pulse that pounded through the hard flesh pressing against her. She wanted to take him inside her. Stretching upwards, she meant to sit up and....

"Not yet, my Lady."

His mouth returned to hers and his long arms wrapped around her, pulling her flush against him, reminding her that he still wore his tunic.

"Off," she whispered against his lips.

"No," he replied, his arms tightening around her.

"Take it off," she repeated, tearing with furious impotence at his clothes.

"Oh," he chuckled into her mouth. "Certainly, my Lady." He tugged at it. "Damn. I am sitting on my tunic."

He stood up, holding her with one arm.

"Oh." Eibhlin wrapped her legs around his waist. Realizing it for the juvenile gesture it was, she passed her hands down his arm, testing the bunched muscles that held her.

With a self-satisfied smile, Brandubh knelt, laying her carefully on his mantle that lay on the floor before the fire. The scent of the new rushes, the lavender and anise and coriander, rushed up and flooded her. Mixing in was Brandubh's scent, the scent of leather and horses and smoke and man. Her lungs craved more. She inhaled him.

On his knees before her, he raised the tunic and pulled it over his head.

And Eibhlin forgot to breathe.

He was indeed beautiful. Defined muscle stretched across the broadest chest she'd ever seen. All that power was covered by olive-toned sun-bronzed skin. His long black hair fell over his shoulders and tickled her nose as he came to cover her with that perfect body.

And he was so warm. If only she could take him inside herself, she knew she'd never be cold again.

She opened for him, allowing him access to any part of her that he wanted. And he wanted it all. His mouth teased her breasts to pouty need, then abandoned them to travel to her belly, dipping his tongue into her navel, swirling it and making her giggle.

"Stop that," she said.

He knew she didn't mean it. Eibhlin could tell by the way he looked up and smiled. Then he lowered his head again toward the juncture of her thighs.

Eibhlin put her hands on his head to pull him away.

"Brandubh, no. Please, I don't think....."

Brandubh said nothing, but only gently captured her hands and held them on the floor out of his way. Then he took possession of her in ways she'd only heard of, dreamed of, and in the taking, he stole from her every bit of inhibition. His lips caressed. His tongue laved. His teeth nipped the tiny bundle of nerves nestled between her thighs, bringing her off the floor.

Deep within, she felt her muscles contracting with the instinctive need to hold. Then her eyes squeezed shut and she only felt. Her body rose to meet his questing mouth, opening wider for him to take what he wanted.

"Brandubh, please, please," she cried, wanting him to be inside her.

He moved up, his body brushing hers, teasing her to greater want, and kissed her, his lips warm and wet. She tasted the essence of herself clinging to his mouth, wondering why she'd ever thought of denying him, and herself, such a wonder.

Like a protective shelter he came over her and she gave way, allowing him entry. Her body was well prepared for him. He fit her like a sword fit its sheath.

"My God in Heaven, Brandubh."

"Aye, my Lady, aye." His rough whisper was all the answer she got.

She couldn't believe the depth of their joining. He filled her entirely, his searing heat scorching through her, hotter than the fire blazing only inches away.

Eibhlin gave herself the freedom to take him, as he'd taken her. Her hands moved over the taut skin of his back, glistening now with a sheen of sweat. He moved within her with a rhythm as old as the earth. She rose to meet him, their eyes locked together in the dying firelight, promises they didn't even hear being made between their two souls.

Brandubh's powerful body pulsed above her, within her, driving her, further, faster, toward the mindless joy that lay just beyond....

Did he feel it too? she wondered, just as the wave crested over her. She clutched his shoulders and the part of him she held deep inside herself and she could think no more.

As Brandubh let himself go, he whispered, "Eibhlin."

Sudden unplanned tears filled her eyes and trickled down her cheeks. Brandubh caught one on the tip of his tongue and wet her lips with it. Eibhlin's heart ached with awe that she was capable, after all, of the ecstasy of lovemaking that she'd never experienced before, that no one had ever been unselfish enough to share with her.

And she knew she was dangerously close to saying the words that she dared not say, words that would make leaving him impossible.

She settled for something else, which was, while close to the truth, not what her soul yearned to say.

"Thank you, my Raven," she whispered before drifting into a satisfied sleep.

* * * *

Brandubh lay her in her bed and stretched out beside her. The old ropes complained under his weight, but were sturdy enough. Eibhlin turned into his arms and snuggled against him, trusting as a child.

It was done. Now, she was his and there would be no other offers. He ought to be ashamed he had taken her in this way, but what was between them was as strong as the tides, as certain as eternity. If she remained, it would be with him, as his wife.

"Brandubh." Her sleepy whisper warned him that she did not sleep as he had thought. "Thank you."

"It is I who should thank you, my Lady."

"No, you gave me a wonderful gift." Eibhlin nuzzled his neck and stroked his chest. "You made me feel beautiful. I never felt beautiful before."

"What is, is. You are beautiful."

She shook her head and smiled sadly. "I'm not."

He wondered what sort of place it was where such a woman was not hailed as the great beauty.

"Why do you not think so?" He raised her hand to his lips and kissed each fingertip.

Eibhlin sighed, her sadness scoring his heart.

"My husband didn't think I was beautiful. He chased after other women."

"He was a fool."

"He was very handsome."

"More than I?"

She laughed, as he'd meant her to. "No, no one is more handsome than you. He wasn't nearly as tall, nor broad, nor strong. And he didn't have dimples or burning black eyes or...."

"Enough, you will make me insufferably vainglorious. Why would this man not think you a goddess?"

"Because I'm so big and...." Her pause spoke volumes. "I'm too big," she said simply.

Brandubh had to laugh. "My Lady, it appears this puny specimen was not man enough for you. He was overcome with his own inadequacy. Did he ever make you cry when he made love to you?"

"No, Brandubh, he never did."

"There, you see?"

"He never whispered my name, either."

He raised his head to look at her. "Did I?"

Her smile told him he had indeed and it had pleased her greatly. He would have to make certain it happened often.

No burden, that, he thought, and he pulled her into his arms, intent on making her smile again.

* * * *

Dougal had only been mildly displeased when Brandubh confessed to taking the Lady Eibhlin. However, curse his perversity, he had insisted on seeing the fifty head which Brandubh would offer. It was his responsibility as the representative of the *Ard Ri*, he said. So, even though it meant two days away from Eibhlin, Brandubh dutifully went off to Lon Dubh to cull out the sufficient number.

When the fifty best he owned were gathered together, he gave the signal to the men who would help him move them to Ath Sionnain.

What a damned untimely occurrence. Why did Padraig have to be so prompt with his thanksgiving gift? Why didn't he give it to the Church instead?

"Here," he bellowed, kicking out at a heifer which had seen greener grass to the side. "Women. Always going off in the wrong direction."

His mood improved when his father's gates came into sight in early afternoon and Brandubh anticipated a bath and another night spent in Eibhlin's bed. He pushed the cattle and his men faster.

As they passed through into the courtyard, a chill streaked along his spine, as though disaster had swept its finger over his skin. He looked toward the house, his eyes drawn there by an ominous expectancy.

Sadbh stood at the window to her chamber on the second level of the big house. He saw her cast her eyes from side to side...

"Brandubh! Come quickly," his mother screamed.

Heart in his throat, Brandubh knew a fear he'd never experienced before. Sadbh did not scream. She did not shout. Her regal calm never forsook her.

Brandubh kicked his leg over his horse's back and slid to the ground. As he ran into the house, old Sean was heading up the stairs and behind him two huge men dragged a struggling Eibhlin between them.

"Let me go," she shouted at the top of her lungs. More came from her mouth, but the words were her strange other language. Brandubh knew not what she was saying, but it sounded mightily unpleasant.

When she saw him, her stormy blue-gray eyes widened.

"Brandubh," she called and stretched her hand to him.

He chased up the stairs, following them into the master's chamber. The atmosphere in the room was thick with dread.

Sadbh, hair uncombed and gown disheveled, looking so much older than he'd last seen her, tossed the burly men aside and wrenched Eibhlin by the shoulders to face her.

"Think you to poison your protector? What have you done, witch? You will tell me or I will rip you to pieces with my bare hands."

Brandubh stood in the doorway. His speech stolen by the scene playing out before him.

"Lady Sadbh, I would never harm Lord Dougal. You have to believe that."

"Why? What do we know of you? We took you into our home, showed you our hospitality, encouraged your liaison with our son. Yet here is how you would repay our kindness?"

Sadbh jerked Eibhlin and shoved her to her knees by Dougal's bedside.

It was not right that bond men should see the lady of their house like this. Brandubh turned toward his father's steward.

"Sean, take them away. I will call for you if need be."

Sean's old eyes glistened with tears. "I will kill her myself, Brandubh, does the Lord die."

"Do not worry yourself, old man." Brandubh lay his hand against the wispy white strands sticking from Sean's head. "Dougal will not die."

He couldn't die.

Closing the door behind Sean, Brandubh turned and finally fixed his eyes on his father. Then he wished he'd not seen. Dougal's chest rose and fell with painful exertions. Sweat drenched his bedclothes. His skin was a pasty gray.

He tossed in a fevered stupor, shouting words in Italian that Brandubh was glad his mother had never bothered to learn.

Then, in a jarring instant, Dougal grew calm. His eyes opened and though glazed, Brandubh thought they were peaceful. That was nearly as frightening as the sweat and tossing and delirium. The peace in his father's eyes looked accepting.

"*Cara mia*," Dougal whispered and reached for Sadbh.

"Aye, Dougal, my love." Sadbh released her hold on Eibhlin and knelt by the bed, taking his hand between hers and kissing the back of it. "I am here."

Dougal managed a weak smile before he moved his eyes and caught sight of Brandubh.

"My son." Dougal's head turned to the side and his eyes closed again.

Brandubh's own heart pounded within his chest. He couldn't bring himself to ask the question. A silence bore down on them all, eased only when Dougal's labored breathing started again.

Brandubh at last approached the bed.

"What has happened here?"

"Is it not obvious? This one has tried to kill him." Sadbh again seized Eibhlin's arm.

"That's not true!" Eibhlin tried to rise from her knees, but Sadbh's unrelenting grip on her kept her on the floor. "Brandubh, for mercy's sake, please. He has been poisoned, but I didn't do it."

"Mother," Brandubh whispered, laying a cautious hand on Sadbh's shoulder, "I believe her. She has no hatred in her for my father."

Sadbh was unmoved.

"Dougal was poisoned by a concoction from her stores," she said, her voice was hard. "Who else could do this?"

He was relieved she sounded calmer.

"Who else has access to your stores, Eibhlin?" he asked as he helped her to her feet, keeping himself between them.

Eibhlin accepted his support and leaned on him, laying her hands against his chest. The tip of her pink tongue slipped out to moisten her lips. Her eyes went back to the bed, where Dougal still labored for breath.

"Only me." Those stormy eyes shot up to meet his. "And Moira."

"Moira? Why would she be there?"

"She asked me to teach her so she could act as healer after I go. I wanted to make up to her...." Eibhlin stood for a moment in his arms, her face creased in a frown. "What has he had to drink today?" she asked.

Sadbh didn't take her eyes from Dougal.

"Only that drink of roasted rowan berries you sent him. He liked it so much," she said, her voice distant. "He became ill soon after." With a disinterested wave, she indicated the small pot on the table by the fireplace. "It is there."

Brandubh felt Eibhlin go stiff as a corpse an instant before she tore from his arms and bolted to the table. She picked up the pot and lifted the lid, then tossed the contents onto the tabletop. With one finger, she stirred the mess, staring into it like a gypsy.

"Holy Mother," she whispered. She rushed back to the bed and knelt down by Sadbh. "Lady, who brought his drink this morning?"

"One of the girls from the kitchen. She said she prepared it just as you had instructed her."

"Where did she get the berries?"

"Where do you think? From you!" Sadbh tried to rise, but the fight was quickly leaving her. She lay her head on the bed by Dougal's limp hand, her jerking shoulders the only sign of the sobs she hid in the covers.

Because his mother wept so very little, her silent tears caused Brandubh's own eyes to burn. Eibhlin rose and took hold of his tunic, urging him toward the table. She reached into the pile of boiled matter and plucked out three small, black berries.

"Nightshade," she explained, unnecessarily. He recognized it. "That's causing the hallucinations and sweats. There must also be something else, perhaps hawthorn, to account for the racing heartbeat."

Even Brandubh knew what nightshade was for. "Who would want to kill my father?"

He begged her for a name, for a person with a reason.

"I don't think it was meant for Dougal. There probably isn't enough to kill a man his size." She raised her eyes to his. "For the last two mornings, I have made him some of my morning drink. But I was called out early to tend a case of the pneumonia. I told the serving girl where to get the rowan berries and how to brew them."

The implication hit her at the same time it hit Brandubh. Her eyes widened again, this time in shock, and she started to shake.

"It was my own supply. This was meant for me." Her voice held a tone of disbelief.

With sick certainty, Brandubh realized it was true. She had been the target and she would have died. With equal certainty, he knew who had been responsible. Moira, probably abetted by Uaid. Trying to strike at him through Eibhlin. Impotent fury sliced through his gut. There was little he could do to Moira, except tell Eibhlin to stay away from her. Uaid was another matter. As soon as Dougal was out of danger, Uaid would pay for this.

Brandubh put his arms around Eibhlin, content for now to shelter her from further harm. She trembled yet, and he kissed the top of her head and tightened his embrace. She needed to have something else to think about.

"My lady, is there anything you can do for my father?"

She shook her head. "Even if Sadbh would let me near him, I'd be afraid to interfere now. I just hope his heart isn't left damaged," she whispered against his chest.

He felt his own heart tighten with dread.

Brandubh said nothing more--he only held her and let her comfort him as the hours passed and they kept their watch.

Chapter Thirteen

It was near dawn before Dougal stirred again.

Brandubh kept his vigil by the window where Eibhlin had watched him all during the night as he repeatedly raised his hand to cross himself, lips moving through memorized formulas that gave comfort and hope. She wished she could offer him more than the lukewarm solace that she *thought* Dougal would recover.

Remembering her promise to wake Sadbh when Dougal showed signs of waking, Eibhlin approached her as she slept wrapped in Dougal's mantle in his huge chair by the fire, now burned down to cinders.

"Lady. Dougal awakes," she whispered. A gentle touch on Sadbh's shoulder was all that was needed to bring her to complete wakefulness.

Sadbh said nothing to her, but jumped out of the chair. She hurried to his side and held his hand as he roused.

"*Cara mia*, why are you not still abed?"

"I have been keeping watch and praying, my love."

Dougal grinned, a poor imitation of his normal expression of mischief.

"And here I am. God would not dare disappoint you, eh?"

"Do not blaspheme, you wicked man." Sadbh smoothed back the ebony strands from his forehead. Her fingers lovingly stroked the pale skin of his face. "How do you feel this morn?"

"I am tired, but I do not feel any other effects." He glanced around. "Ah, we are not alone. Surely, that is why you have not yet joined me?" He ignored Sadbh's huffed injunction to keep his mind where it ought to be and called to Eibhlin, "Lady, come closer. I would ask you some questions."

"I have asked all that is necessary, Father." Brandubh came between them. "Eibhlin did not poison you."

"Stand aside, son. I do not blame the Lady. Clearly, this was not done by a practiced hand or I would be dead." He sighed with fatigue, then asked Brandubh, "Did you bring them?"

Confused, Eibhlin glanced at Brandubh. His expression was unrevealing. He only nodded.

"Yes, Father. When you are able, I will take you to see them." One of his eyebrows rose, like a raven's wing, and he added, "I hope they are to your standards."

"I hope so, too. It would not do to have some other, more serious, man come and take what you have claimed."

Dougal struggled to sit up. Both Sadbh and Eibhlin jumped to assist him. He shoved their hands away with a snort of temper.

"By Christ's wounds! I am not an invalid. I will mend. Now, we have business to discuss. Lady." He looked at Eibhlin and motioned her closer to the bed.

"Just one moment," Sadbh said in her most commanding tone, "I have a word or two to say about this matter now. Things are not as they were before."

"*Basta*! Enough!" Dougal's voice, if not his body, was completely sound. "I will have none of your interference."

"What? You dare speak to me in this fashion?"

"I am your husband and I will use whatever tone I deem appropriate."

Eibhlin heard a family squabble heating up. She slid toward the door.

"Hold, Lady Eibhlin. I will speak with you now." Dougal's tone brooked no argument. "Brandubh, a chair." He glanced at his wife. "I would have an ale, *cara mia*."

He waved Sadbh away to do his bidding as Eibhlin had seen Sadbh herself do many times before. The older woman shot Dougal a venomous look.

"We are not finished, Dougal."

"I hope not, my Lady. I hope not."

Dougal laughed weakly as the door slammed behind her.

"There, my son, is a *woman*. Now, let us see about getting you one as worthy."

She heard Brandubh cough to hide his chuckle and she grew increasingly uncomfortable being here alone with the two of them.

"Sit, Lady. It pains my neck to look up at you from here." A wry smile softened the order.

Brandubh set a chair behind her, pressing it against the backs of her knees. Though she would have preferred to remain standing, Eibhlin sat.

"First, my son has informed me that he has passed a night with you." Dougal's voice lacked its usual good humor and he looked more serious than she'd ever seen him.

Eibhlin's face burned. "Yes, Lord."

"According to brehon law a man may offer for a woman whom he has taken in this fashion and the marriage will be recognized as a fact."

"Marriage? Wait just a...." she sputtered. "I never agreed to anything of the kind."

Dougal just waited for her to choke to silence again. "My son has also informed me that you are a divorced woman, that your first husband was an adulterer and you exercised your right to end your marriage to him. Is this correct?"

"Yes, but...."

"Were there children of this marriage?"

"No." That hurt. *Himself* had been snipped before they were married and had never bothered to tell her. One more thing to curse the rotten no-good cheater with. He'd known how much she'd wanted children. She also was reminded of Brandubh's whispered promise that he would give her his children.

"And, is there any impediment of which you are aware which would affect any future marriage that you would make?"

"No, but...."

"*Buono*! Then I inform you that my son, Brandubh mac Dougal, offers a bride price of fifty head of cattle for the honor of your hand in marriage."

"But, Lord Dougal, I'm not.... Fifty?" Curiosity ate her innards. "Is that a lot?" she whispered to Dougal.

"Only a queen would be offered more."

In spite of her sense of outrage that a woman was equatable to cattle, she was flattered. *Fifty*. He really wanted her.

Well, she knew that. After all....

"No," she said, quickly, "I'm not staying here. I'm leaving at the next solstice. I told him that before we...."

Face blazing, she popped out of her chair and whipped around, intending to tear into Brandubh for ignoring her clearly stated intentions, but hadn't heard him come up behind her. When she turned, her breasts brushed heavily across his hard chest. His small, nearly indistinguishable smile of satisfaction and the sudden ignition of that light in his eyes were the only indications she had that he was affected by the contact.

"Eibhlin, after we have loved each other, you would still consider leaving me? You could even now be carrying my child."

That suggestion stopped her. A quick calculation relieved her mind that it probably hadn't happened. Then she heated with irritation that he would try to use such cheap emotional blackmail on her.

"Listen to me, you big gorilla...." Eibhlin ignored the confused glance Brandubh exchanged with his father and Dougal's Italian shrug. "I already told you, I don't belong here. I'm not staying here. Once the solstice comes, I'm going back to Craglea and I'm going home."

Brandubh was stubborn. "All I ask is that you consider remaining with me." He raised his hand as though to touch her.

She dodged by him to get out of his reach, and with the length of his arms, it took several steps. Nearer the escape route of the door, she turned to face him.

"Your mother thinks I tried to kill your father. Do you believe I'll be welcomed into your family now? You heard how much she hates me."

"Do you deny what we feel for each other?"

"No." That was the wrong thing to say, darn it all, but he'd forced it out of her. "What I mean is I do...."

Hold on, Evie, do you really want to tell him that you *want* him? Like he wouldn't know exactly what you mean.

"I don't belong here," she said again. It was, she thought, a final statement. She never expected it could be argued with.

"Then, why are you here?" Brandubh crossed his arms over his chest and stood, towering over her. The fact that she was nearly six feet tall herself meant that didn't happen often and she wasn't used to dealing with the sense of insignificance it created. Nor the tongue-tied awe of his magnificence, especially now that she had first-hand knowledge of just how magnificent he really was.

But she had to maintain her distance or she'd never be able to get back to her own time.

"I don't know. Maybe I'm here to fix something that went wrong. Maybe I'm here to cause something to go wrong. I don't know. I just want to go home."

Home. Did she know where that was anymore? She'd been here for only three weeks and she was already comfortable. She had satisfying work. She loved the people and the land. She had a wonderful lover.

"No, it's too risky," she said, more to herself than to the two men who'd remained silent watching her at war with herself. "No," she repeated to them. "I'm going back where I came from, where I belong."

"And if you cannot?" Dougal asked quietly.

Her blood ran cold at the possibility, even as her heart leapt that her decision would be made for her. She was already losing the battle.

"If I cannot, then I cannot. But I have to try. Until then, I can't accept any offers, Lord Dougal. It wouldn't be fair."

Without another word, she turned away from Brandubh's dark gaze and left the room.

* * * *

Brandubh's gaze followed her and he was overcome by the uneasy feeling that her intentions to leave would be stronger than his determination to make her want to stay.

"Why is she so insistent that she must leave here? She seems content, all in all," Dougal said.

"I don't know. She only says she doesn't belong here."

Dougal pursed his lips. "Does she want to leave badly enough to kill?"

Brandubh stared in disbelief. "What are you saying? You said you didn't believe she attempted to kill you."

With a noncommittal shrug, Dougal asked, "Who else, then? Clearly, I was poisoned. Who has a reason to want to kill me?"

Brandubh didn't want to go into this. For some reason, Eibhlin felt responsible for Moira and he had no desire to bring more pain on that family, since Dougal had survived. His father was lord of this place, however, and had the right to know everything that happened within his domain.

So, Brandubh sighed and gave the name.

"Moira poisoned the concoction. We believe it was meant for Eibhlin, Father, not you."

"Moira?" Dougal appeared ready to ask, "Why?", but then nodded with a sigh of understanding. "Of course. She must see Eibhlin as the reason you put Caoimhe off." Head cocked, Dougal fixed Brandubh with a look. "What do I do about this? I cannot allow such a lawlessness to go unpunished."

Brandubh took the chair Eibhlin had vacated. "Father, I would not interfere in your running of your holding. But, also would I not cause Conor more pain. The attempt was not against you, but Eibhlin. If I marry her, I can take her to Lon Dubh--away from here where she'll be safe."

"I will not force her, Brandubh. Would you have a wife against her will?"

"If it will save her life, yes. Besides, she would not resist for very long." His bravado dissipated in the face of Dougal's weak smile and he added softly, "I love her, Father."

"You would so woo the lady that she would relinquish her stated desire to return home?" Dougal grew serious. "Brandubh, you have never been away from all that is familiar--family, land, even such a simple thing as the weather that you are used to. Can you understand how love alone may not be enough? There have been times, my son, when I have longed for the warmth of Italy. It is so cold here to my Mediterranean bones, and it grows colder each year."

"Would you leave Ireland?" The idea was inconceivable to Brandubh.

"If I could have convinced your mother before you were born, we would be the Fabronis of the valley of the Po, growing grapes and making wine and fighting barbarians."

"Why have you never spoken so before, Father? Do you miss Italy so much?"

"There are times, Brandubh, when I do. The air is warm and so clean it sparkles. The sea glistens blue as sapphire. In the summer, the smell of things growing overwhelms the senses--spices and herbs and flowers and fruits ripening. Yet...."

Dougal was silent for a moment, his eyes seeing a distant land that Brandubh had only heard about.

"Yet, in Italy, I was a poor man, the son of a poor man, and destined to remain so. Ireland has given me a place and a noble wife and a fine son to carry my blood. I am a confidant of the king and an important man with great responsibilities." Dougal smiled and reached for Brandubh's hand. "Ireland is my home, my son. And I tell you, if you can give your Eibhlin so much, perhaps she will decide that her place is at your side, as I decided so many years ago to remain with your mother and become an Irishman."

Dougal rarely spoke so seriously. Squeezing his father's hand, Brandubh said, "All I can give her is myself. I will pray that is enough."

"Then I wish you luck. The lady will take much wooing to break down her will. Yet, I would give her room to think over how much she wants you. Go look for your horses and leave her to herself. Let her think it over. Her own desire will become your ally. Give it room to grow so that when you come together again, she is consumed by it."

"Woo her by leaving her alone?" Brandubh raised one eyebrow skeptically. "Will that work?"

Dougal, as proof he was feeling better, grinned. "It will as long as Fergus doesn't steal her away from you."

* * * *

Walking without thinking, she went straight to the herbroom and dropped onto one of the rough stools at the long table. Tracing the thoughtless marks in the tabletop, she tried to put off considering Dougal's question.

Returning to her own time couldn't be impossible. She'd come through. She'd pass back. All she had to do was wait.

And avoid falling in love with Brandubh, which meant staying away from him. But, after the night of passion he'd shown her, was she strong enough to keep her distance?

Yet, her lovelife was nothing compared with the specter of an attempted murderer on the loose. Standing slowly, she looked up to the shelf where she kept her private stash of roasted rowan *coffee*. Her hands trembled as she reached up for the clay jar and emptied the contents on the table.

Mixed in with the roasted and chopped rowan berries was belladonna, deadly nightshade, the dried black berries and coarsely chopped leaves easily identifiable.

Eibhlin sat for long minutes, just staring at the mess of leaves and twigs that had nearly cost Dougal his life--that *would* have cost her hers had she taken any of this mixture.

How could she have been so stupid? How could she not have become suspicious at Moira's fascination, especially upon learning that Eibhlin was the only one who drank it? At Moira's insistence, Eibhlin then showed her how to grind and brew them to make a coffee substitute that was not nearly good to the last drop, but better than nothing.

She'd shown Moira the jar where she kept the ground beans.

She'd let Moira have the run of the herbroom.

When Dougal had tried the rowan drink two days ago, he'd insisted on it instead of ale in the morning. He'd invited her to share a mug of it with him in the quiet before breakfast.

Well, at least he had, she thought with a pang. Sadbh, as protective of her family as a she-bear, probably wouldn't even let her into the house again, much less near Dougal.

...Or Brandubh.

Anger at the one who'd caused this breach from the people she'd come to love shielded her from the blast of cold from the suddenly opened door.

Moira dashed into the room and slammed the door shut. Seeing Eibhlin, she bit her bottom lip.

"Ah, Lady," Moira gasped and Eibhlin thought she heard relief in her voice. "Here you are." Moira hastened to put the length of the table between them and she glanced around, eyes flitting from shelf to shelf.

"Looking for something besides me, Moira?" Eibhlin tried to gauge her reaction. "Something like this?" She held up the crockery coffee container.

Moira's eyes widened and her mouth fell open as though to explain.

Eibhlin cut her off before she could start.

"I didn't get the chance to try your mixture. However, Dougal found it very interesting."

Hand flying to her throat, Moira choked out, "No! Oh, Sweet Jesus. Is he...?"

"He will survive."

"Thank God." Moira sank to a seat. Her breathing slowed to a near normal pace and she looked up at Eibhlin with pleading eyes. "Lady, I...."

The last thing Eibhlin wanted was some excuse for the inexcusable. "Why, Moira?"

"You have to believe me, I only wanted to frighten you so you would leave. Never did I intend to kill you. Lady, you must believe me."

"Where did you get the nightshade?"

"I cannot tell you." Moira looked away. "It doesn't matter. I put it in the container. The guilt is all mine."

Who was she protecting? Who could be important enough for Moira to take all the blame herself?

"I doubt Dougal will see matters in this way," Eibhlin said, pleased by the look of terror clouding Moira's eyes. "And I suspect he has various ways of drawing out what he needs to hear."

"Lady, please. I swear I will not repeat my folly."

"What of your accomplice? Who might be harmed by his next attempt on me?"

"He won't try again."

"Why not? How do you know?"

"I won't let him." Moira looked up at Eibhlin and met her gaze straight on. "Eibhlin, I have come to know you have a good heart and would never hurt someone knowingly. Believe me, I will not allow any harm to come to you. But, please, let it lie for now. If Dougal and Brandubh were to learn my...." She paused, as though testing the word. "Accomplice's identity, they would likely kill him. There has been enough death here."

Eibhlin pondered Moira's words. As always her heart urged trust.

"All right, Moira," she said, holding up her hand to arrest Moira's burst of gratitude. "I'm afraid it's too late to protect you, however. Brandubh already knows you had access to my stores. I doubt he's not told Dougal that."

"That's all right, as long as I am the only one held responsible." She stood, facing Eibhlin like a martyr to the stake. "Will you let me continue with you? Yet another household is showing signs of falling ill. I want to help."

Did she dare take the risk? She knew she should toss this troublemaker out on her rear, but the look of sincerity was too much to resist.

Eibhlin nodded her assent. "But one time, Moira, just one thing to make me doubt you and I'll go to Dougal and demand he make you turn over your accomplice and whip both of you in the courtyard."

"You won't regret this, Eibhlin. I swear."

Eibhlin hoped she was telling the truth. "We'd better get to work, then. It looks like we're going to be busy. Start with the meadowsweet. Chop it fine, now. It helps with fever and aches."

Without another word, Moira nodded and jumped to work, collecting a handful of the dried plant. Eibhlin watched and remembered a proverb--"Keep your friends close. Keep your enemies closer."--but she couldn't remember who'd said it. Whoever it was, she thought, was onto something. For all her pretty words about not wanting to kill, Moira still had a lot to prove. Eibhlin would make sure she didn't do any more mischief while she proved it.

Chapter Fourteen

Nature and Brandubh conspired to give her the distance she thought she wanted. He left the very morning of her refusal of his offer of marriage and spent the next three weeks in the search for his horses in the wilder northwestern plains. He hadn't even said good-bye.

That bothered her more than she wanted to admit, but she didn't have the chance to stew over it. Assisted by the bone-chilling wet of early December, pneumonia swept through Ath Sionnain. One household after another was ravaged by the fever and hacking cough and one after another they called for the healer.

Barely noticing the passage of day and night, back aching and hands cramped from chopping and straining and squeezing and spooning, Eibhlin did what she could to relieve the symptoms. Her herbroom was filled with the smells of cooking borage leaves for aches, teas of wild thyme to help clear lungs, pine oil to ease breathing.

When she could slip away to her own chamber for a few minutes, she dropped into her bed like a stone and then slept like one. These stolen moments of exhausted slumber, where she didn't even dream, were the only times that Brandubh was out of her mind. The rest of the time, as she tended the sick, Eibhlin thought of him constantly, her increasingly exhausted body yearning for the comfort of his arms. Especially this morning.

She lowered herself to the rough stool at the table. Leaning on the table, she pillowed her head on her arms and let fall the tears she'd kept dammed behind a need to be strong.

Oh, how she needed him to hold her right now.

The heavy outside door opened and closed behind her, allowing a rush of cold air that raised gooseflesh and sent a chill through her.

"What's wrong, Lady?" Moira crouched beside her. "Why do you weep?"

"Where did you come from? I want to be alone," Eibhlin snapped, swiping the tears from her cheeks. She was immediately sorry, but had no words to express it.

"Nay, Eibhlin, you do not need to be alone. Here," Moira pulled another stool beside her and lay her arm over Eibhlin's shoulders. "Now, I know 'twas a terrible thing. But the child was so weak. Is it not a mercy that her suffering is past?"

Eibhlin could only shake her head. "No. No. She might have lived in my... place. Where I come from."

"We are not in your place, Lady, wherever that is."

The commonsense of that statement struck Eibhlin right between the eyes. It was something her mother would have said.

"And we have work to do. 'Twill be better for all if we get to it." Moira rose crisply. Scooping a handful of wild thyme from the drying bin, she started chopping.

Eibhlin snuffled and swiped at her eyes with the back of her hand. And she wondered at the change in the girl's attitude. Moira's initial animosity had been replaced by wary comradeship. Eibhlin had been glad for the company. Except for the sick, she saw no one. Brandubh's absence and Sadbh's continued frostiness, though she no longer openly blamed Eibhlin for Dougal's mishap, had made Eibhlin decide to take her meals alone in the workroom or her chamber.

Only Moira had refused to leave her to her solitude.

Eibhlin had not been the only recipient of Moira's care. All through the epidemic, she had tended the sick gently and capably. Countless times Eibhlin had been jarred by childhood memories--her mother Moira offering her broth, touching her brow to check for fever, her hand lingering a moment in a loving caress.

Moira had been there when the baby took her last breath. Eibhlin had shrunk into a corner and struggled against the feeling of uselessness, unable to console the bereaved mother. Moira, barely more than a child herself, had been the one to step up and offer comforting words and a shoulder to lean on. The picture had reminded Eibhlin so strongly of the death of her brother, Conor, she'd been unable to turn away, even when the memories came too hard.

To a little girl too young to understand the finality of the death, Eibhlin hadn't then understood how much it took for her mother to stand as the bulwark against the desperate sorrow that threatened the whole family. Seamus turned for a time to the bottle to find his solace, shedding loud, pitiful tears behind the door of his den. He'd lock himself away for days at a time, only to come out and pray for forgiveness. Each time, Moira took him into her arms and forgave and let him lay his head in her lap and weep. Eibhlin never saw her mother cry for Conor, though her grief was as sharp and real as that Seamus suffered. Moira had shed her tears in private, and the child Eibhlin had wondered, who hugs Mama when she's sad?

Moira's voice brought her back to this present, sailing through the air with joyous tune that really wasn't a song, but a lilting melody she made up as she went along.

To Eibhlin, thinking of her mother as she was, the sound renewed the sense of familiarity she often felt in Moira's presence. Before she could examine it, however, the sound of hoofbeats drew her attention away to the window just in time to see Brandubh ride by.

"So, he's returned at last," Moira said, still bent over the crumbling plants.

Her voice had stopped Eibhlin in mid-step by the door and she was chagrined that, unthinking, she'd been on her way out to greet him, her need for him overriding all her intentions.

Reflected in Moira's words was renewed anger, clearly all directed toward Brandubh.

"Go to him, then, Eibhlin, but guard yourself. Do not let him hurt you as he did Caoimhe."

"What did he do to Caoimhe?" Having gotten only bits and pieces of the story, Eibhlin wanted to hear it all. No one would answer her questions. Even when they had been friendly, Sadbh had been reticent to speak of it.

For a long moment, Moira stared out the window, then at Eibhlin, obviously weighing whether or not to answer. Finally, she glanced away.

"Brandubh sent Dougal to speak to our father about Caoimhe's bride price. In truth, nothing was decided, but Caoimhe has, had, ever loved Brandubh. That he made the inquiry was enough for her to believe he wanted her, and he never disabused her of the notion. Brian called Brandubh to Kincora in the summer and when he returned, he told Caoimhe he'd changed his mind about offering for her." Moira took a deep breath and leaned on the edge of the table. "She told him she'd kill herself. He rode off without warning our father about her threat. She killed herself that very night."

Like the blows of a blacksmith's hammer, the series of events hit her. While he'd been gone to Kincora, they had met on Craglea. Their attraction had been so strong he'd come back here and broken the poor girl's heart.

"You resemble her, you know?"

Moira's words caught Eibhlin by surprise.

"How so?" she managed to ask.

"You have eyes the same color as hers, that gray-blue, and they were shaped as yours are, like almonds." Moira smiled, not entirely pleasantly. "From the neck down there is no similarity, however. Caoimhe was a girl, only sixteen, and she was late blooming. And she was tiny, not a big woman as you are."

Eibhlin felt herself shrink inside as she always did when someone mentioned her size. Her mother had always told her to stand straight, to use her height to capture the attention of men. She had gotten only the notice of *Himself*, and that had been a disaster.

This Moira appeared to enjoy underscoring Eibhlin's most appalling physical feature and, with a juvenile need to strike back, Eibhlin tried to think of some suitably awful thing to reply. Before she could form a thought, Moira took all the wind from her sails.

"Did I say something wrong?" Moira stepped closer and lay her hand on Eibhlin's upper arm. With a squeeze, so like the reassuring one her mother used, Moira said, "Surely you are not sensitive about such a wonderful gift? Do you not see the eyes that follow you through the courtyard? You could have any man you desired. 'Tis no surprise Brandubh would prefer you to a young girl."

Mercy, this was getting complicated. There were too many things twisting together. Too many emotions getting jumbled and bouncing off one another. Eibhlin put her hand to her forehead, suddenly feeling dizzy. She was just able to get away from the door as it swung open.

Brandubh swept her into his arms to keep her from falling. His eyes were filled with concern that was reflected in his voice.

"Lady, are you well?"

She didn't answer. His sudden appearance took away her calm. Her body flushed with a feverish warmth. Held secure in his strong arms, she was safe, Moira's warning banished to the furthest corner of her mind. This man could not knowingly hurt an innocent.

"Good morn, Brandubh."

Eibhlin felt his body go stiff at Moira's clipped greeting. Why would he react so strongly to her? To Caoimhe's sister?

"Good morn, Moira." He held Eibhlin to his side, his grip never slacking. "I would speak with the Lady alone."

"Of course, *Lord*," Moira answered. She made no other sign of her displeasure as she passed by them.

When the door shut behind them, Brandubh finally relaxed.

"Why is she still here?" he demanded.

"Because I need the help." The air grew thick and she had trouble taking a breath.

"My Lady, are you ill? Here, sit." He practically carried her over to the bench. Kneeling before her, he took her hand and caressed the back of it.

"I'm just tired."

"You must take care, my Lady. Your suffering would pain me as well." His black eyes fixed her in her place. "You have been avoiding me."

"You've been gone," she croaked. Her throat was so dry.

"I have been here several times, since...." He paused, his eyes flashing with still remembered fear. "Since my father's illness. Each time I have not seen you. My mother says you have been keeping to yourself."

Of course she had. She was already far too comfortable here, far too fond of the people--especially Brandubh. Even living in this time was not so difficult as she'd thought, once you got used to no running water, no indoor plumbing, no electricity, no chocolate.... No coffee.

But to him she only said, "I've been very busy, Lord Brandubh."

"Aye, we are all very thankful that you are here."

"I didn't do anything that anyone else couldn't have done."

Brandubh raised one brow. "I doubt that is true, Lady. There are some who possess some knowledge of healing, but your gift is much more. Many would have perished had you not been here to treat them."

"I wasn't able to help old Michael, nor Caitlin's baby." The sound of the young mother's wail still echoed in Eibhlin's mind.

He squeezed her hand. "You know that child was born weak. In time, she might have become stronger, but that was not to be. Old Michael had lived his life and felt no burden in leaving it."

Eibhlin knew in her heart Brandubh was giving her the truth as it existed now, in this time. Michael was near seventy, an old man. He was bowed by decades at the plow. He had held Eibhlin by his bedside and with breaths that came harder and harder as the end approached he told her about his wife who'd been dead near twenty years. Michael hadn't feared death. He'd welcomed it with opened arms.

The baby, only a week old, born too early, lungs weak, could hardly have survived pneumonia even in the twentieth century, in spite of what she'd told Moira earlier.

"It's still not easy to accept. I know so much, Brandubh, but I don't know the right things."

"It is enough for all us that you have tried."

"Does your mother think so, too? She hasn't spoken to me since that morning in Dougal's chamber when he...."

"Mother knows that was not your doing. She is stubborn and cannot easily admit to being wrong. She misses your company, however, and will approach you eventually to mend the breech between you." As though in speaking of his family he'd found the opening he'd been waiting for, Brandubh cocked his head and raised one of his raven black eyebrows. "Have you considered my offer?"

Had she thought of anything else when she'd had a spare moment?

Ever since that morning when he'd risen from her bed and left her with a gentle kiss, she'd fought against the knowledge that her heart belonged to him, preferring to think of it only a case of lust at first sight. The pull he exerted on her wasn't only sexual, though that was a large part of it and Brandubh knew it, the arrogant swine. Her heart and her soul were equally involved with her more unmentionable parts.

As much as she wanted him, though, she couldn't stay here. The possibilities for interference, for wreaking havoc with history, were too frightening. She'd read enough sci-fi novels to know what messing with history could do. She *had* to return to her own time. It *had* to be possible. She wouldn't even consider it might not be.

He waited patiently while she sat, silent, avoiding his eyes as she hadn't been able to avoid the topic. She only risked a quick glance at his face. When he saw she wasn't going to answer him, he finally spoke, his face lined with concern, and perhaps a little fear?

"The time you have declared to leave grows near. I would not keep you here against your will. Though I have kept my distance from you, Lady, you must know I desire you as I have desired no other woman before. Do you stay with me, I will honor you 'til my death with my body and my life and my fortune."

No word of love, though that pretty speech sounded really close, nearly like marriage vows. Could she love him?

Did she already?

"Have you nothing to say? Is there nothing in your heart for me, my Lady?"

My Lady. He said it with such a sense of longing, she heard the deeper emotion.

It wasn't fair to leave him thinking she felt nothing for him. Perhaps she should just tell him her fears. He'd understand why she couldn't stay. Hell, he'd probably take her to Craglea posthaste and tie her to a rock to wait for the winter solstice on her own.

"Brandubh, I'm afraid to stay. I'm from the future." She waited for some reaction and was disappointed. He remained kneeling before her like a statue, holding her hand and waiting. Feeling a bit like the lead alien from Mars in a B-movie, she tried to explain, "That day you pulled me through the barrier, was, for me, November first in the year 1998."

"I didn't pull you through. You walked through to me."

Eibhlin couldn't believe what she was hearing. He didn't argue with her declaration that she was from a time nearly a thousand years in the future.

His only problem was with who was responsible for her crossing over.

"I just said I have traveled through time."

"Aye, I heard you. Did you expect surprise?"

"Of course. I've just told you a fantastic thing, something unbelievable."

"Eibhlin, I was there. I saw the red wagon you traveled in. It was clearly not of this world. Whatever the explanation, I was certain it would be fantastic."

"Brandubh, I *know* the future. I could cause something to go wrong. Something that might affect the outcome of events a thousand years from now."

He looked unimpressed. "Could you? Why would you do that?"

"I wouldn't do it on purpose, you great idiot! It would be an accident, but it would still cause horrible things to happen."

His brow furrowed as he pondered that. "Why do you think anything you could do could change the future?"

She was speechless. Brandubh took the opportunity to continue.

"Eibhlin, history is the unfolding of God's will. Did you not learn this?" At her silence, he frowned. "Do you not believe?"

"In what?"

One eyebrow shot up in surprise. "In God, the Father. In Jesus, the Christ, our Savior. By Heaven, woman, how do they raise children where you come from?"

"I was raised very properly, thank you. My mother is very devout." She remembered sitting on her mother's knee, as Moira read her stories of the saints. "But I'm a scientist, Brandubh. I believe in what can be measured and tested."

He smiled. "And yet, you believe you are now in the past?"

Eibhlin really didn't see where this was going. She held her hands out before her. "I'm here, am I not?"

"I begin to understand your perspective, my Lady. That first day on Craglea you thought me...." His lips crooked. "An apparition? Perhaps you thought me not real?"

"I definitely thought you were not real. When you disappeared on me, I was certain of it."

"Ah, I see now. In your time, is there nothing of faith? Is there no acceptance that there are things we do not, cannot understand?"

"Of course, but we know eventually someone will find the key to understanding. We keep studying what we don't understand."

"Indeed? Well, then, since God will most likely not consent to being studied by you, let us look at this problem in another fashion." He stood and paced the room, hands clasped behind his back. "Consider this. History is also the unfolding of the will of man. Think you, Eibhlin, your interference will cause men to do other than they wish?"

Eibhlin huffed. "What a typical *macho* thing to say." Brandubh scowled as the Spanish word by way of English slipped into her perfect Irish. "You don't think a little woman could do anything to upset the plans of you great big men?"

He crossed his arms over his chest. "No, I do not. Men will do what they will. Women, too, for that matter. What I am saying is, you cannot change what is done by people with free will."

"What about my medical meddling? What if Caitlin's baby had lived?"

"The child did not live."

"What of all the people who could have died if I had not been here? What will some of them, or their descendants, do to change the way things should be?"

"Perhaps you were meant to save them."

That gave her pause.

Brandubh continued. "Let us put it to the test, then. Tell me something that will happen soon. You may make your best attempt to change it. I vow you cannot." He turned to look out the window. His back to her, he gazed across the yard. She couldn't see his face, but she could read his mood well enough. He was tense, like a bowstring about to be released. Then he gave her the one thing she couldn't resist.

"Brian plans to rout the Vikings in the east."

Her heart flipped over in her chest. It was December, 1013. On Good Friday next, Brian Boru would die in the fields of Clontarf, north of Dublin. The battle would be won, but his death would end the chance for Ireland to escape her painful destiny.

"When?" she asked, knowing the answer.

"When spring comes." He turned to her. "What will be the outcome?"

He was testing her. Testing not only if she would tell him the future, but whether her presence could change it. It might already be too late to prevent that.

"Brian's army will be victorious."

His face broke into a glorious smile.

"But he will die at Clontarf."

His face fell. She could feel his sorrow.

"Clontarf? I know of it. A fair killing field it will be," he said in a low rumble. He was silent and she saw him struggle with the news. Sighing, he asked, his eyes glistening, "How will Brian die?"

Eibhlin shook her head against the horror she had to give him. "A Viking will come upon him with an ax."

Brandubh gasped, "An ax?"

"Even as he dies, Brian will strike down the Viking. He will be taken to Armagh to be buried with his shield and sword."

"Which son will follow him as *Ard Ri*?"

"None. Three will fall at Clontarf--Murrough, Flann and Conor, and Murrough's son, Turlough."

"No," he whispered.

She was driven, like Cassandra in the myths, to tell it all.

"Teague will be King of Munster, but he's not strong enough to become *Ard Ri*. Donnough is too young and will not have following enough. Malachy of Meath will retake the title."

"Malachy?" Brandubh exploded with disbelief. "Impossible. Brian took the crown from Malachy. He was not fit to be *Ard Ri*."

"He will be again. Two O'Briens will rule as High King, but there will be none like Brian again."

Brandubh returned to her and knelt again at her feet.

"What happens then to Ireland?" he asked in a breathless whisper.

Eibhlin sighed deeply. Why tell him? What good could come from him knowing? Yet, she couldn't stop her mouth from forming the words.

"In fifty years or so, the Normans will cross the Channel and conquer Britain, the southern kingdoms, at least. Nearly one hundred years after that, the King of Leinster will be exiled by the *Ard Ri* and, for revenge, he will invite the Norman king of Britain to come to Ireland."

"The Normans?"

Eibhlin nodded again. "The descendants of Vikings who settled in the north of France. After the Normans arrive, Ireland will not be free again until near my time, nearly eight hundred years, and then it will be more English than the Ireland you now know."

Brandubh sat back on his heels. His sadness tore at her heart all the more because she'd been raised a patriot herself. Her father was a tireless supporter of Irish autonomy and a scholar of Irish history. He was eloquent on Ireland's generally unacknowledged role in saving Western Civilization from the darkness of the Middle Ages, and the effect of Irish monks re-evangelizing the European continent. In 1013, that's already history.

But--Eibhlin felt her heart race and her breathing try to keep up--the rest hadn't happened yet. Perhaps it didn't have to. Brian wasn't dead yet. He'd been known as the Charlemagne of Ireland because of his desire to forge one nation from the fractious tribes and petty kings. He sure looked to her like he had a few good years left in him. Maybe even enough to complete his vision and leave Ireland united and strong enough to survive.

The idea of changing history was no longer frightening. In fact, it had taken on an exhilarating quality.

If Brandubh was right and there was nothing she could do to change history, then she didn't need to feel compelled to leave. However, if she were to choose to stay and try to prevent the tragedy of the Irish....

Either way, she could have Brandubh.

"What are you thinking?" His voice shocked her from her concentration.

Eibhlin sat straighter, reaching for him, looking deeply into his eyes. "Brandubh, do you really believe what you told me before? That it isn't possible to change what will be?"

His face was lined with sorrow. "I fear I do, else would I take you now to Kincora where you could tell Brian your tale."

"Would he listen to me? Would he take precautions?"

"How can I know what he will do? Brian has ever been unpredictable." He shook his head and frowned. "What I would like to know is how he was caught unaware by a Viking! Their stench precedes them by a league or more."

She noted with amusement that he was speaking of an event which hadn't happened yet in the past tense.

"There is time for that. Eibhlin," he said as he laid his hands gently on her shoulders, "I have had word about the reivers who stole my horses. I am going after them but I need your pledge that you will wait for me to return, that you will not allow another to accompany you to Craglea, that if you still wish to leave, I will be the one to take you."

"If I decide to go, what will you do about what I've told you?"

"I will take your words to Brian, but I have no hope he will listen. Dying an old man in his bed has no allure for him. Falling victorious in battle would be his choice."

Her heart fell at his lack of confidence that they could change what would be.

"I will wait for you, Brandubh."

He took her hands and raised her palms to his lips. "I will pray constantly that you will decide to stay with me."

"But you would let me go?"

Brandubh nodded. "Though it might kill my soul. I would hope you would still consider my offer seriously. In any event, I wanted to leave you with this...."

Brandubh stood and pulled her to him, crushing her breasts against the rock-solid muscle of his chest. His thick mustache roughed against her skin before his lips claimed hers. She opened to him as she always did, regardless of the circumstances, regardless of her determination to do otherwise.

The entreaty of his tongue, gentle, silken, hot, gained him quick access and he took it. She could only hold onto him as he plundered, taking the taste of her with him. Eibhlin returned his sparring and moaned when he licked her lips and raised his face from hers.

His breath stirred her hair. "I will return soon, my love." He was out the door before she dropped onto the stool again.

My love. He'd said the word.

She felt the fit, that she belonged here, to him, and he to her. Or maybe it was just the heat coursing through her, the dizziness swirling through her head, the difficulty she had breathing.

The pounding beat of horses swept past the door. She wanted to throw it open and shout after him that she would be here when he returned, that she'd remain with him, marry him, bear his children, be his lady.

She jumped off the bench and reached for the doorlatch.

"Brandubh," she called out to him as she crumpled to the floor.

Chapter Fifteen

Moira passed through the opened gates and headed toward the solitary willow hugging the banks of the river. Since her mother died, Moira had found her only peace while sitting under that tree, praying or singing or playing her harp. Somehow the old tree, with its long branches hanging to the ground like thick silver tresses, seemed like a loving grandmother, enfolding Moira in a nest of peace and understanding. It was a place she'd needed more and more lately.

She'd not wanted to like Eibhlin. Everything in her had been prepared to take advantage of Eibhlin's trust, to use the medicine workroom to launch her plan of revenge against Brandubh--to deprive him of the woman he loved in Caoimhe's place.

Yet as the days passed, she'd lost most of her anger at Eibhlin. All of it now was directed toward Brandubh. But she'd even abandoned her desire to revenge herself on him because of the distress she knew Eibhlin would suffer.

Poisoning the rowan berries hadn't been her idea. Uaid had suggested that. He'd assured her the amount of nightshade he'd procured from a Viking merchant in Limerick wasn't enough to kill Eibhlin, only make her sick for a time and Brandubh would suffer just a little of what he'd caused her and Uaid and their father to suffer. Uaid hadn't known, anymore than she had, that Dougal had taken to drinking the concoction. Moira shuddered at the memory of her brother's reaction to his failure. He'd repeatedly slammed his fist into the wall and cursed God and Brandubh.

She still couldn't believe he'd actually meant to kill Eibhlin.

When their plan went awry, Moira had been greatly relieved, and not just because Dougal had survived.

Her feelings were very disturbing, for the woman Eibhlin ni Seamus had touched some part of Moira she'd never known existed. Moira had never been in love before and didn't know what it felt like, but--she finally acknowledged the truth--she loved Eibhlin.

"No!" She ran the rest of the way to the willow and dropped to the ground, wrapping her arms around her knees, underneath the protective, enfolding limbs.

Moira knew there were some people who found their pleasure with their own kind, women with women, men with men. She shivered in disgust. Surely such things were not natural since there could be no children from such a union.

"Abomination," she whispered. Yet, the thought of children brought the vision of a tall, thin girl with long brown hair and almond-shaped eyes, walking along the river with the man from Moira's dreams, who held her hand as a father would.

As soon as the vision appeared it was gone, leaving Moira more confused than ever.

"There you are."

She gulped a gasp of surprise and carefully schooled her features into a semblance of calm before she turned to face her brother.

"Good morn, Uaid. Are you back home to stay? Or will you be leaving to create more chaos soon?"

He didn't smile at her jibe. He didn't smile much at all anymore.

"Have you seen Brandubh this morning?"

"Aye. He came to bid Eibhlin goodbye. I heard he's had word of his horses."

Uaid laughed now, though Moira was chilled by the sound of it.

"He won't find much."

"What do you mean?"

Uaid sat down beside her, stretching his legs out before him. "I mean that Conchobar will be having no pleasure of Lady Deirdre."

"What have you done, Uaid? You took the cattle? You raided our chieftain?"

"I merely took a bride price for Caoimhe, what he owed for killing her. Dougal was complicitous in this as well."

Moira agreed that Brandubh, and to some extent, Dougal, were to blame, but cattle were poor compensation.

"Did you intend to take the horses as well?"

"Fit, don't you think? Brandubh has such plans for that pair. Some of my friends went out this morn to geld the stallion and cut Deirdre up for wolf bait."

"Uaid, no," she whispered.

"Oh, yes. Of course, Brandubh will find the carcass there and Conchobar will like to bleed to death before he arrives."

Moira was shocked. "Wasting such animals would be a sin. Why are you not taking your revenge on him directly?"

Once more her blood ran cold when her brother turned his eyes to hers. They were brown like hers, and until Caoimhe had killed herself, they had been warm, laughing eyes.

Now they were deader than Caoimhe was.

Her fear deepened when he spoke. His voice was empty of any emotion. "We will next kill his woman. Is that direct enough for you, Moira?"

"No! No, Uaid, you must not harm her."

"Let go of me, woman."

Moira hadn't even known she'd seized the sleeve of his tunic. She allowed him to shake her grasp loose.

"What is this whore to you?" Uaid stepped back. "It was because of her Brandubh reneged on his offer for Caoimhe."

Why did she care? What was this desperate protectiveness that had risen up, placing her between her brother and her....

Her mind wouldn't finish the thought. Such a thing was not possible. Even so, what Uaid was planning was wrong. She could not be a party to it.

"Eibhlin is not to blame. I will not allow you to kill her. Do what you will to Brandubh. Leave her alone."

Uaid appraised her with narrowed eyes. She couldn't even contemplate what he might be thinking.

"Perhaps you are right, Moira. Brandubh has the blood of our sister on his hands. I would not bear the same sin."

He gave up far too easily, she thought. For the first time in her life, she didn't believe her brother.

"I'll be getting home. I have not made my return known to Father. I will see you at the evening meal?"

"Yes, of course."

"Don't sit here long, sister." Uaid tapped her shoulder and smiled his old smile before he rose and headed toward the gates and back into the keep.

Moira rose as well and followed him. She didn't want to suspect her own flesh and blood of lying, but Uaid had not been himself. He swerved off to the left side of the main house, toward the medicine workroom and Moira followed, her belly twisting with fear.

"Out of the way, girl."

The voice came from the mounted group galloping toward her. She jumped to the side and into the bed of thyme that bordered the kitchen garden.

"Are you all right, daughter?" Her father had stopped and looked down at her. At her nod, he continued, "We are off to find the wicked demons who took Dougal's cattle and Brandubh's horses. Have you seen your brother?"

Moira nodded automatically. "He said he was going to find you to tell you of his return."

Conor huffed. "Fine thing. Tell him I ride with Brandubh, but will return in time for his tale at supper."

"What tale?" she asked.

Her father smiled. "Where the devil he's been. Then will you sing for me, my girl."

"Yes, Father." Moira's eyes followed the big man on the horse, then lighted on the man leading the group. Brandubh. The man Eibhlin loved.

What *were* these feelings? Now, the idea that any harm would befall Brandubh was nearly as terrifying as if it would happen to her own father. Or her brother. Because it would hurt Eibhlin.

Moira took a deep breath and turned to go on to the workroom. Her life had been *so* much simpler before Caoimhe killed herself. And for what? For a man who hadn't really wanted her at all. Caoimhe, as usual, hadn't thought of anyone but herself. Forgiving her younger sister for her childish selfishness had become a habit that had grown very thin.

"Moira."

She turned toward the voice.

"My son is coughing up blood and I can't find Lady Eibhlin. Will you come?"

Moira sighed. Would this illness never pass through Ath Sionnain? "Of course, Ena. Let me get some herbs and I'll be along."

She approached the workroom, her stomach twisting with warning. The door was open. Moira gingerly pushed it further and, once she was

THE RAVEN'S LADY 101

sure it was empty, stepped across the threshold. She turned her head and let herself see the whole room. Something was wrong, she told herself. The fire had burned down to near ashes. It was frigid in the wet December air and Moira especially felt it today.

She took a thick wooden paddle from the table and stirred the now cooling borage stew in the kettle hanging over the ashes. Where was Eibhlin? She wouldn't have left the door wide open, nor left the concoction cooking over an untented fire.

Her eyes moving again over the room, Moira tried to focus on what was so unsettling her senses. There was a sense of violence in this room that had not been here before. Then she saw it.

On the floor by the door, by the stool where Eibhlin had been when Moira had last seen her in Brandubh's arms, one of the ivory combs Sadbh had given Eibhlin, which she wore in her long, sable brown hair every day. A treasured possession she would never leave behind.

Moira stooped to pick it up and that was when she noticed the drops of brown on the rushes that covered the floor. Drawn to the drops by an almost unnatural need to touch, smell, taste, Moira dipped her finger. It was reddish brown, nearly dried.

She'd seen enough blood to recognize it. Eibhlin was missing and her blood stained the floor. She ran from the herbroom to find help.

* * * *

Brandubh saw the smoke from the fire before he heard the horrible screams of horses fighting. His surprise was in finding they weren't fighting each other.

"Conchobar," he whispered with relief even as he put his heels to his mount, closing the distance, but not fast enough to interfere. He was close enough to see the man with the gelding knife fall under Conchobar's iron-shod hooves. A second man ran toward the thundering, screaming stallion with a drawn sword.

An incoherent roar of rage ripped from his throat. He wouldn't get there in time. But Conchobar wasn't alone. Deirdre jerked away from the third man who was holding her bridle and joined the melee.

Brandubh lost his breath in awe at the speed she made from a dead stop. Deirdre arrived to smash the sword-wielding assailant to the ground. She then turned to face down the third man. He thought better of challenging her and left the scene on foot.

Having done all she could do, she stood back and let Conchobar get on with his business.

"Get that one running away." Brandubh pointed out the escaping thief to his friend Gadhra.

Brandubh returned his attention to the grisly scene before him. Never even in a battle with sword and ax had he seen such carnage.

Conchobar snorted and screamed and pounded the man at his feet into the ground.

Brandubh dismounted and approached the site on foot. Conchobar stood in place now, blowing as though he'd run a league in a race.

Deirdre remained at her ease behind her mate, her snowy coat matted with blood and brain.

In spite of wielding a sword in many of Brian's battles, Brandubh felt a certain unease in this atmosphere.

"Holy Mother, Brandubh." Dougal went way around the stallion, and the mess on the ground that had been a man, to Deirdre. "Here, my lady, you have been a brave Irish lass this day, no?" The mare responded to his voice by bobbing her head. Dougal laughed grimly.

In contrast to Deirdre's calm, Conchobar still shifted from one foreleg to the other, waving his head and screaming a warrior's challenge between heavy breaths. Brandubh waited until Conchobar had time to catch his scent.

"Conchobar, lad." Brandubh spoke softly and took one cautious step after another, keeping his eyes on Conchobar's face. The stallion stood still for him and dropped his head to meet Brandubh's chest in the greeting they'd shared from Conchobar's foaling. With a gentle hand, Brandubh stroked the thick neck. Then he moved easily up to take a fistful of Conchobar's mane. This was the horse's signal that he was to remain still for an examination. If the dead man on the ground had known of Conchobar's training, Conchobar would be a gelding right now and the man would be alive, waiting for Brandubh to kill him.

Now what remained was to find how much damage had been done before Conchobar had struck back.

Dread filling him, Brandubh moved his hand over the sleek hide, the withers, the back, down the heavily muscled flanks. He reached underneath to check the belly, and slid his hand further back toward Conchobar's genitals.

He had only an instant's warning before Conchobar stretched out and a torrent of urine spattered on the ground--and on the smashed body of the man Conchobar had killed.

"Oh, Conchobar," Dougal scolded, "haven't you insulted the wee lad enough? Do you have to piss on him, too?"

The men in the party laughed with undisguised appreciation at Dougal's wit. They had all seen the knife in the corpse's hand. Conchobar had fought for his ballocks, as any man among them would have done.

Brandubh only shared a satisfied smile with Dougal before he went around an raised Conchobar's thick black tail. And sighed a sigh of relief. He'd been afraid the vermin had managed to do the job after all.

"Is all well, son?" Dougal asked.

"Aye, Father, our Conchobar is whole." Brandubh slapped the huge flanks and once more passed his hand along the other side, just to make sure.

Indeed, in the fading light of the winter afternoon, the black stallion appeared in good condition, even with his ebony breast flecked with foam and blood and human flesh.

"You'll have to destroy that animal, Brandubh." Conor mac Turlough spoke, real regret in his voice. "Pity though it is."

"Why, Conor? He was but defending himself."

"Aye, but how will the people feel about having a killer horse among them?"

"He will be at Lon Dubh, Conor. Everyone there knows him." Brandubh raised his hand to cut off Conor's next words. "There will be no more talk of destroying him."

Gadhra came up with his prisoner, shoving him to the ground in the middle of the gathering of men. It appeared Gadhra had begun the interrogation already, if the cuts and freshly missing teeth and purpling bruises were any indication.

"Tell him," Gadhra growled, punctuated by a kick.

"Go to hell."

Again Gadhra applied his foot to the prisoner's side.

With three steps, Brandubh stood over the man. He grabbed a handful of the miscreant's hair and jerked his head back. Leaning over, Brandubh glared into the man's eyes.

"Who are you? What were you doing with these horses?"

With a stubborn unfocused gaze, the man remained silent.

"I know him, Brandubh," Conor volunteered, his voice heavy. "He is a friend of Uaid's from Ossory."

Uaid. The ripple of whispered speculation spreading across the small band of men rattled Brandubh as much as knowing one of his kinsmen had done this thing.

But not so much as wondering what he might do when he found out this plan hadn't worked. Where might a man bent on revenge seek his next target? He'd wanted to kill the soul of Brandubh's dreams for his future. What would be more important to him than these horses?

"Eibhlin." The name came from him on a whispered breath.

Brandubh stooped before the man, releasing his hair, seizing him by the throat instead.

"Where is Uaid now?" Brandubh asked, terrified that he already knew the answer.

"He is at Ath Sionnain," the man answered with what breath he could force past Brandubh's squeezing fingers. "He wanted to see his father and sister."

Brandubh released the man's throat with a savage jerk and turned on his heel, heading for Conchobar. The stallion stood quietly as Brandubh leapt onto his back.

"Brandubh, where are you going?" Dougal asked as he came beside the stallion. "Wait and let us get your saddle and bridle.

"There is no time, Father," Brandubh replied and, grabbing two handfuls of mane, he yanked the stallion around in the direction of Ath Sionnain.

"Come, lad, take me to her." Brandubh ground his heels into Conchobar's side and braced himself for the explosion of power.

Deirdre snorted and was behind them, pulling along the hapless man who'd tried to stop her. Brandubh glanced back to make sure he was all right.

That was the only time he took his eyes off their path as they crossed field and meadow and stream, straight back to Ath Sionnain and Eibhlin.

Chapter Sixteen

The ghostly white Deirdre arrived first, unencumbered by the weight of a rider. The sound of her hooves alerted the guard and, recognizing her, they opened the gates. Right behind her, Brandubh rode Conchobar into Ath Sionnain like an angel of death. The dark blue of his mantle and Conchobar's hell-black hide, with its gristly decoration of the blood and gore, visible even in the dim torchlight, set the right tone of netherworldly retribution.

Grown men shrank against the stone walls of the big house. Women bit their knuckles to hold back screams of terror. Children hid their faces in their mothers' skirts. Even when they recognized the rider as their chieftain and lady's son, a man most of them had known and loved since his birth, Brandubh's face, frozen with rage, lined with anxiety--though it was not interpreted as such--discouraged any attempt at greeting.

Throwing his right leg over Conchobar's head just as the horse came to a stop at the steps of the house, Brandubh slid to the ground. As soon as his feet hit the ground, his relentless strides took him up the steps and into the great hall. He plowed through the crowd waiting for their supper. The tables had been prepared but no food would be coming out of the steaming kitchen until his father's return or his mother's decision not to wait for him.

But Brandubh was not seeking food.

"Uaid mac Conor! Show yourself to me. We will have this out between us."

His bellowed challenge silenced the hall. Every head turned toward him.

Brandubh scanned the crowd, his eyes searching each face for the features of the man who had become his enemy. A growl of rage rumbled from Brandubh's chest as he located Uaid, lounging against the wall across the open hall, a smirk curving his lips.

Shoving bodies aside in his haste, Brandubh saw a path clear before him as the bodies voluntarily vacated, rather than being lifted and flung through the air. Eyes fixed on Uaid, Brandubh raised the end of the last obstacle between them--a twenty-foot long trestle table, built of solid oak--and tossed it like a stalk of grass.

Uaid's eyes flickered from the overturned table and back to Brandubh.

"What is wrong? Angry, Brandubh? You should not be surprised. I told you I would hurt you."

"What makes you think I'm hurt, Uaid? Cattle are easily replaced. My horses are outside."

Uaid smiled. "That explains the blood on you mantle. I've never tasted horsemeat, though 'tis said the Vikings relish it."

Brandubh was grateful to God that he had not yet put hands on Uaid. Killing a man in his father's house was not something he really wanted to do. Yet had he Uaid within his grasp, the worthless dog would be dead already. He took a deep breath to gain enough calm so he could speak.

"The blood on my mantle, Uaid, is not horse's blood, but a man's blood. Perhaps you would like to go out to the place where you had your friends readying to castrate Conchobar? You can see what is left of them. The other my friend Gadhra is dealing with. While, you," Brandubh growled as he pressed closer, "are mine."

"Brandubh, I will not have fighting in my house." Sadbh had appeared just beyond Uaid's shoulder. "I require your presence in your father's chamber."

"Mother, I would have this done, once and for all."

"Now, Brandubh."

Uaid smirked. "Best do as Mommy says, little boy."

Brandubh took one step forward.

"Brandubh!" Dougal's voice came from the doorway, rattling the cups on the tables. Brandubh heard his father's footsteps approaching, then felt the steadying hand settle on his shoulder.

The urge to shake it off and rip Uaid's head from his neck nearly overwhelmed him. Instead of giving into the full measure of his anger, he merely turned and stalked toward the stairs.

"Uaid," Dougal said, "do not leave Ath Sionnain. You and I have unfinished business."

Uaid watched with some distress as his chieftain followed Brandubh out of the hall. Dougal had never been the target of any of his actions against Brandubh, not the cattle raid nor the poisoned rowan beans nor the destruction of the horses. Brandubh, and the whore who warmed his bed, had been his objective.

A low-burning rage grew in Uaid that none of his revenges had stuck. So far, Brandubh had escaped each one. But at last, he had stumbled upon one which would destroy Brandubh more completely than death.

All that remained was to get out to the stable and get a couple of horses before Dougal's injunction reached the stable boys. Turning to make his exit, Uaid froze in his tracks as Sadbh cast her icy-blue eyes on him. He felt her disapproval and was sorry. She'd been kind to him and his sisters after their mother had died. He'd never held it against the Lady she had not supported Caoimhe's desire for Brandubh. Truly, he had agreed Caoimhe wasn't meant for that huge clumsy lout.

"Uaid," the Lady said, her voice, as ever, low and even. "For your father's sake, you may sit at my table, though you have brought shame on his name. But I warn you to stay away from Brandubh. He could easily kill you tonight and no one would be able to stop him. I would not have him bear the guilt for murder. 'Tis enough he feels for your sister, though he had no hand in her death."

Uaid didn't agree. Caoimhe's death had been all Brandubh's doing.

"The rest I leave to Dougal." Sadbh raised her hand to get the attention of the serving women. "You may serve now. Would you take our places at the head table, Lord Fergus?" Before she went up the great stone stairway, Sadbh cast Uaid a glance that he thought was full of sadness.

Feeling sorry for me, Lady? Save it for your own household, he thought as he slipped out the side door. He wondered if they'd discovered the big whore was missing yet?

* * * *

Dougal pushed Brandubh through the door to his chamber and they both stopped short to find Moira sitting there by the fire.

"Moira, what do you here?"

"Lady Sadbh bid me wait, Lord. There is trouble with Eibhlin."

"What trouble?" Brandubh's demand came out on a roar. "Where is she?"

"She is missing." Moira's voice was soft and full of fear. "You have to find her, Brandubh."

"What are you talking about, Moira?" Brandubh forced down his growing dread.

"I believe Uaid has taken her. After I left you with her in the herbroom, I went down to the river for a short breath of air. Uaid came to me there and admitted he'd raided your cattle and the horses." She looked up and faced Dougal. "It was Uaid who purchased the nightshade and bid me put it into Eibhlin's drink mixture. I swear to you, Dougal, neither of us knew you also drank it."

Dougal grunted. "We have him, then. What else did he say to make you think he holds enmity against Eibhlin?"

Twisting her mantle, Moira looked near tears. "Uaid has become, well, somewhat mad, I fear. He has threatened Eibhlin, in order to punish Brandubh. I told him I wouldn't allow it, but I do not believe he was much impressed."

"What did he threaten to do?" Brandubh's voice was frozen by the rage threatening to boil over onto the tiny woman who sat before him.

Moira obviously recognized the look. She gulped and cleared her throat.

"He plans on killing her." She threw herself on her knees before him and grabbed his hand. "Brandubh, I know he's taken her and you must find her and keep her safe. If it comes to killing him, you must not hesitate."

"I will not hesitate," he said, knowing it was true, and turned on his heel, nearly colliding with Dougal as he left the room. It was difficult to trust Moira. She'd made her own promises of making him pay for Caoimhe, but whatever game she was playing, he believed her about Uaid's plans for Eibhlin. It reflected his own fears too perfectly not to be true.

"Brandubh, here," Sadbh called to him from the passageway leading to the kitchen. "Come, girl. Do not be such a goose."

She came toward him pulling a young girl of about twelve. The girl actually shook with her fear and Brandubh knew he must look in a killing rage to instill such terror in the child. Yet he could not smooth the fearful scowl from his face.

"Now, tell him what you saw."

The girl's eyes widened like a doe facing the hunter.

Sadbh shook the girl's shoulders. "Speak, and quickly, before I give you cause for your trembling."

"It was Uaid mac Conor, sir. He took one of the Lady's tapestries from the herbroom."

"A tapestry?"

Her head bobbed on her thin neck. "Yes, sir. It was rolled and it looked to me like there was something inside it. He had it slung over his shoulder."

"Brandubh, there were no tapestries in the herbroom," Sadbh said.

"Where did he go, child?" Brandubh asked, struggling to put some kindness into his voice. He knew there was nothing to be gained by terrifying the girl.

"I do not know, sir."

"When was this?"

"Before we started serving the evening meal. I came looking for the Lady straight away."

"All right, child. You may go to your supper, now." Sadbh released the girl's wrist.

"Thank you, Lady." The girl fled the hall.

Brandubh felt his mother's eyes on him. "I am going after her, Mother."

He turned on his heel and stalked out the house to the stable. The boys there were only a bit more helpful. Uaid had taken two horses--one for him and one for the rolled-up tapestry.

"God damn him to Hell!" Brandubh roared. "Saddle Conchobar."

The single lad who remained to receive this thundered command plastered himself against the wall. "Conchobar took a stone and has a sore foot, Brandubh."

Brandubh smashed his fist against the wall right beside the boy's head. In a terrifyingly calm voice, he said, "Then get me another. One that can run."

The boy ducked under Brandubh's throbbing arm and scooted off to do his bidding. And he moved quickly. Brandubh was already mounted by the time Dougal caught up to him.

"Son, wait. I will go with you."

"I cannot wait, Father. He has her."

Putting his heels to the horse's sides, he tore through the gates, cursing the darkness that made tracking nearly impossible. Uaid's general direction was clear, however, and Brandubh followed it across the Shannon and into the kingdom of Connaught.

"What is he going to do with her in Connaught?"

The possibilities chilled him through.

The tracks turned south, following the river to its entry into Lough Derg. With no choice, Brandubh followed, riding into the darkness.

No stars lit the way as they reached the foothills of the mountains marking the border between Munster and Connaught. Brandubh breathed easier as he entered his own province again, but his relief was short-lived. He had pushed his horse to exhaustion and as they started to meet rocky ground, the animal stumbled, tossing Brandubh over his head.

Only by anticipating the fall and rolling in the wet grass did Brandubh manage to avoid breaking his own neck. The horse regained his footing and returned, at a walk, to Brandubh, shaking his head and snorting his disapproval.

Sitting on his arse on the cold ground, Brandubh was filled with shame. He rested his elbows on his raised knees and nodded in agreement with the horse's assessment.

"Aye, lad, you are right. 'Twas my fault."

The cold rage was gone now, replaced by his heart's demand to remount and ride the animal to its death if it would get him to Eibhlin. He reluctantly agreed with the argument his head offered. Without a horse, he would never get to her.

Gazing around him, feeling the cold of the bleak autumn twilight seep into his bones, Brandubh knew such would be his life if she were taken from him.

Yet, he couldn't give up all hope. Brandubh felt himself drawn forward, pulled on, and filled with the certainty she was in front of him--somewhere.

"Come, lad, let us walk awhile." He got off the ground and took the rein hanging from the horse's bridle. With the mountains on his right hand and the Lough on his left, he tried to decide which way to go.

West. The word came from the air.

He turned and started walking toward the west, toward the sea, not knowing really why he did so.

Once before he had walked alone toward the west, toward the sea, though he had not known it then. One fine morning many years ago, Brandubh had saddled his glorious Ruari and followed Dougal, sure he was heading into a fine adventure.

But there had been no adventure.

For years afterward, Brandubh was haunted by the memories of that night. He would be shaken from sleep, body wet with sweat, heart pounding, teeth clenched against cries of horror. His head filled with the sickening sounds of ravenous growling, fangs sinking in and ripping flesh. Ruari's screams mingling with his own. Of endless tunnels leading only to death.

He thought about it all now, as he walked on. That day had formed him, more than the example of his father, or his mother's lessons, or the priest's exhortation.

THE RAVEN'S LADY

Never again, he had sworn.

Taking up a sword as soon as he could lift it, he had become a warrior to equal even Brian Boru.

She would not be harmed by the wolf Uaid mac Conor. She was his for all time. It was his task to protect her.

He continued west, toward the sea. He walked on, knowing that this way lay the Burren, the land of rocks and endless caverns and nothing much green except the mosses which thrived on the unforgiving ground. He walked on, in spite of the knot of terror that still lived in his belly at the thought of those caves. He walked on, because he could feel her presence more strongly with every step.

He walked until he could walk no further, stopping by a tree he nearly walked into, that he could barely make out in the dark. The gurgle of water told him he was near a stream.

"Come, lad," he whispered to the horse. "We will rest here."

He let the reins drag the ground. The saddle and blanket he left in place to provide some covering and warmth. The animal needed food and water and rest. For himself, Brandubh knew he'd never sleep tonight.

Settling on the damp ground in the lee of the tree, Brandubh pulled his mantle tight. He barely felt the cold or the wind whipping his hair around his face.

He closed his eyes, remembering the feeling of Eibhlin's fingers, combing through the strands, her tender caress raising desire and stirring his blood. Even now he yearned for her, the warmth of her body, the taste of her lips. The sweet agony of having possessed her once made the imaginings too painful to bear.

Yet, he allowed her memory to warm him as he sat under the tree and waited for daylight.

* * * *

Eibhlin awoke on her belly, head hanging down and barely able to breathe. Her head throbbed like a metronome, beating out a perfect four-four time. Every one of her limbs was held fast and she felt like she was wrapped like a sausage. The thundering of hooves and the steady rocking motion revealed her mode of transportation, but she couldn't see and had no way of telling if it was night or day. What had happened? She remembered Brandubh leaving then nothing more. How long had she been out?

The sound of the horses' hooves was different. Instead of the muffled pounding on the green turf near Ath Sionnain, each step rang off stones. Had he taken her to town? No, they were moving too fast to be in a town big enough to have paved or cobbled streets. If they were in the mountains, they would be climbing and the horses would not likely be moving this fast.

The Burren.

"God help me."

Bears had gone extinct in the caves underneath the moon-like surface of the barren, stony plain in the far west of Munster. On one trip there, her mother had insisted they go on a tour of a cave that had been discovered in the nineteen forties. Eibhlin had cried and put up such a fuss her father had finally given in and they'd passed it up. She'd always wondered why her mother had been so insistent.

What she would give to go back to fix her error. At least she'd have an idea of what she was facing.

"Whoa." A man's voice reassured her even as she shrank from it. At least he hadn't killed her outright. What else he might have planned for her, she didn't even want to think about. The rasping sound of a knife cutting through leather warned her a second before she slid off the horse's back and flopped down on her own.

Inconsiderate lout, she fumed silently. Still unable to move, she had to wait until he freed her, rolling her out of the heavy cloth wrapping.

Well, I finally know what time it is.

She squinted against a bright December sun at what looked like its high point in the sky. Noon, then. Looking away from the glare, she glimpsed the dark blue and green of the tapestry that Uaid had used to wrap her in.

"Sadbh will have your head for this." Her vision was a bit fuzzy and she struggled to focus on the figure of her abductor. "Who are you?"

"Uaid mac Conor."

"Mac Conor? You're Moira's brother?" My uncle, she thought, wondering how much family devotion he would feel toward her if she told him who she was. One look at his grim face and she decided she wouldn't try that tack.

"That's right." He grabbed her under her armpit and pulled her to stand on her feet. Still tingling from the long ride, her legs at first refused to hold her, but Uaid gave her support until the pinpricks of circulation returned to a full flow.

"Come, we do not have much time."

"Time for what?"

"Until Brandubh comes. I am certain he will follow."

"So am I." Why didn't she sound more convincing?

"He'll have some difficulty over the rocky ground," Uaid said, "but he's too good a tracker not to find you, eventually. Right now though, if I know Brandubh, he is in one of his rages and will not see much of anything. When he finally does find you, the rats in the cave will not have left much."

"Rats!" She shivered. "I know why you're doing this. It's because of your sister, Caoimhe, isn't it? What good will it do? Will it bring her back?"

"No. But I have sworn to revenge Caoimhe and I will. Here we are."

She looked where he was looking. Two large vertical slabs held up an even larger one horizontally. Underneath the overhang was an opening about the size of a manhole.

"A dolmen." She whispered it and a frisson of fear skittered down her back.

"Yes, indeed. The entrance to a burial catacomb, I believe. Might as well leave you somewhere where you won't have to be moved to be buried. Eh?" He smiled merrily, as though he'd just told a grand joke. "After you."

"I'm not going down there."

"Yes, you are." To prove his point, he shoved her and she slid, pretty as you please, down the hole and into the underground warrens.

Immediately, panic seized her. She struggled to control herself, thinking of Brandubh.

I'm still alive. And Brandubh is coming.

She heard the slightly anxious tone of her thoughts, and knew if she'd spoken them aloud, her voice would have been pitched higher and the words would have tumbled one over the other, her fear and growing hysteria more than evident. She would choke to death on them before giving Uaid the enjoyment of seeing her break like that.

"How do you like the accommodations, Lady? Certainly not a guesting house or what you might be accustomed to wherever it is you come from, but we poor Irish must do with what we have."

A rising bile of fear threatened to put her on her knees in the corner, but she fought it down. In her best Moira voice, she asked, "No bed, Uaid? Poor inn it is, in truth. Perhaps we should try the next one?"

As soon as the words were out of her mouth, she could have bitten her foolish tongue off. Uaid gazed at her, his face hidden in the sun's glare as it reflected through the single entry to the surface. His eyes, though, burned with an unholy light.

"Do you seek a bed, Lady? Will not any surface do where you can hit your back and spread you legs?" The savagery of his voice tore through her like talons. "How often does Brandubh taste you? Would you give your favors to any well-formed man?" He came closer, leaning toward her until his breath burned her face. "My spear is as sharp as my sword. Would you care to try it?"

"Go to hell."

His face, only a whisper away, came closer. She wanted to spit into it, but her mouth was as dry as the ground above her head. The best she was able to do was stand her ground.

"I probably will, Lady," he finally said in answer to her invitation. "My place was prepared the day my sister died."

"Why? Did you kill her?"

Eibhlin never would figure out where that question came from, but it was the one that loosed Uaid's rage on her.

"How did you know? How?" He grabbed for her arms.

She stumbled away from him and hugged the wall, too terrified to utter a word.

Silence surrounded them. He leaned against the opposite wall and stared at her, through her. After long seconds, he finally spoke, his voice distant and low.

"It was an accident. She was mumbling nonsense about Brandubh and how he would be sorry when she was gone. She had her eating knife out and was toying with it. I got tired of listening to her prattle and thought I'd teach her a lesson. So, I went up to her...."

He pulled his knife from his belt and approached, touching the razor-sharp tip to Eibhlin's breast, apparently thinking to show her, and she would have moved farther away if there had been anywhere to go.

"I took her hand and showed her where to push. She struggled with me, weeping that I did not understand how much she hurt." He gasped a sob and pushed the knife, nicking her flesh. A small red stream seeped through her gown and billowed on her dress. "I told her to push and get it over with. She jerked away from me and lost her balance. She fell into the knife."

Eibhlin closed her eyes in sorrow. All this pain, all this anger and rage over a stupid thing like this.

"Uaid, it wasn't Brandubh's fault. Why blame him for it?"

"Brandubh would have married her if not for you. Now, my only living sister has turned away from me. Because of you. You've spun some spell over her and she won't help me attain my revenge."

"What are you going to do with me?" She hadn't really decided she wanted to know.

"I'm going to close up the cave and leave you here."

On the one hand, that wasn't such a bad plan from her point of view. She'd have a chance, at least. On the other, what if Brandubh didn't find her in time? Dying in a cave was not in the top one hundred ways she would choose to meet her Maker.

"That's enough talk. Turn around."

She wasn't keen on turning her back on her new-found uncle.

"Why?" she asked, hating the quiver in her voice.

"I'm just going to tie you up. Don't worry, my dear, I will leave it loose enough that you can free yourself from them, but I need to have some time to finish your prison." He pulled out a leather thong. "Now, be a good girl and turn around."

"Why don't you just kill me and be done with it?" She turned as he ordered her.

"I will if you really want me to," he said as he wrapped the thong loosely around her overlapped wrists, his eyes on hers. "No? Willing to take your chances and wager your life that your Brandubh will arrive to rescue you? That's a brave girl. Even though I doubt you'll last very long. If the rats don't decide you're too sweet a piece to pass up, perhaps the bears will wake up for a taste."

"What bears? There are no bears in Ireland."

"Really?" Uaid's voice dripped sarcasm. "What's that?"

He pointed toward the end of the corridor, dimly lit by the late afternoon sun pouring through the opening of the cave. Eibhlin sucked in a breath as she made out the form of a large brown bear peacefully sleeping.

"Don't make too much noise, now. They are very cross when they first wake up." Uaid shoved her against the damp wall of the cave and pushed her down on the ground. "You just sit there and start working on your bonds. And remember...." He laid a finger against his lips and smiled before he turned and climbed out.

"Uaid," she called, in a harsh whisper, her rising panic clear to her own ears as she watched him pass across the opening only to return in a few moments with a rope which he looped around one of the dolmen's vertical supports. She heard the jingle of tack as he mounted his horse and the ringing of iron shoes against the rocky ground. She watched as the support fell outward, allowing the huge horizontal slab to fall across the opening, the clash of stone against stone ringing like a funeral knell, leaving only a sliver of sunlight to relieve the darkness.

Eibhlin struggled with the scream rising in the back of her throat.

Chapter Seventeen

Brandubh was ready to kill. If he found Uaid now, there would be no pause, no thought. Even though he was as angry at himself as he was at Uaid.

As soon as the sun had risen, he had mounted his rested horse and started west again. He felt Eibhlin so strongly, he was sure she was just a short distance ahead of him.

But when he'd seen no tracks, he'd turned around, retracing his path all the way back to Lough Derg until he recovered the trail. Each step, every sign that he'd wasted precious time following nothing more than a feeling, enraged him even more.

Here it was after mid-day and he was only now....

"Hold, boy." Brandubh reined in his mount and sat, shaking his head in amazement. There, on the banks of a small stream were two sets of hoofprints, heading west. He followed them and soon saw a third set--the prints of his own horse, left last night when he'd followed his heart and passed the night under the tree right in front of him. Was it possible he'd not been wrong, only too early?

Brushing aside the disbelief, for it didn't matter now, he dismounted and knelt to examine the prints, clear in the moist ground here by the river. They weren't fresh, but Brandubh knew they had not been here this morning. Once again he felt her calling him. This time he allowed the connection and followed.

* * * *

Eibhlin fell against the damp wall, her raw throat refusing to make another sound. Then she remembered her ursine roomie at the end of the corridor and struggled to calm herself.

"Stupid, stupid, Evie. Shut up and keep your head. Don't wake up the damned bear."

Her heart thumped with terror as she glanced toward the bear, fully expecting him to be lumbering her way. He lay in the same place, still napping. How had the lug managed to keep snoring through the racket of the stones falling and her own hysterical screaming?

She decided she didn't care. It was enough he was still asleep. She worked on getting herself under control.

"You're not a child that's afraid of the dark. As long as that bear stays asleep, there won't be anything big enough to kill you. Okay, so maybe the fleas on the rats will be carrying the plague. Don't worry about that now."

The first thing was to free her hands, so she raised her wrists to her teeth and started on the leather thong. The knot was tied firmly, but she quickly tugged it loose.

"Okay, that's good. Now, try to dig yourself out." Forcing herself to coolly appraise her situation, Eibhlin examined the opening to the cave. She could get her arm through the gap in the stones, but couldn't budge them a single millimeter.

"Maybe I can loosen the soil around them and they'll fall in." Not allowing herself to wonder how she would get out of the way she went to work, scratching at the unforgiving stone.

She gave up after a long time of digging, when her fingertips were raw and bleeding. Then she started coughing and her chest tightened.

"Oh, no." Laying her hand against her forehead, she felt the heat building, her body marshaling its strength to fight. Here, alone, she could only think that this cave would serve as her tomb.

"Brandubh, where are you?" she whispered between coughs. She slid down the wall to sit on the cold floor and lay her head on her knees, trying to fight her despair. "Uaid was sure Brandubh will be able to find me. He just banked on the rats or the bear getting me before then."

At that very instant, something firm, yet soft and yielding passed by her foot. Pushing against the floor, she shot straight up. Perfectly still, she could hear the scurrying of thousands of tiny feet.

She closed her eyes, and in a rough whisper, she prayed, "Please God, please don't let me die here. Please send Brandubh to me."

She swore she wouldn't cry--useless, pointless waste of energy--still she felt the fat tears plop onto her cheeks and roll down her face. How had she ever gotten into this? Rolling her head back and forth against the wall, she wondered why she'd come back to the Crag that day, nearly one thousand years from now. Instead of going to the rental car counter, why hadn't she kept walking to the international terminal and gotten on her plane?

The one that crashed and all the people died? That the one you mean?

A laugh escaped her. She could wake up from this nightmare and look out her window and see the Lusitania at the bottom of the ocean. What a scream! If she'd not been completely alone in the cave, she'd have been embarrassed at the scene she was making.

But hell, there was no one around except Smoky snoozing down the hall.

THE RAVEN'S LADY

"If you make a complete fool of yourself and there's no one around to hear it, are you really crazy?"

Another barking mixture of laughter and coughing ground from her sore throat. After a minute, her laughter slowed to a growly giggle.

"I think I liked me better when I was screaming. At least that was a sane response."

Suddenly, she was aware of the haunting sound of a harp ringing through the cave along with a wailing voice. Eibhlin followed the sound, hoping to find another exit. Her fingers slipped along the walls toward the sound. A faint light danced on the walls like a mummer drawing her to the party.

The music, the wailing, was dirgelike, funereal. She continued along the tunnel toward the sound. A shiver, in spite of her fever, rippled along her spine. Such underground passages had been used as burial chambers by the earliest inhabitants of Ireland. That's all this is, she reassured herself, relieved to have located help so soon.

The music was stronger, the wailing more pronounced, the light brighter. The tunnel she traveled opened suddenly into a room. There were signs on the walls that the cave had been widened here--along with the marks of chisels were the typical Celtic decorations of circles and connecting curves. Eibhlin focused on the carvings and didn't see the low-hanging rock simulating the top of the doorway. At least not until she slammed into it.

"Ow!" She straightened carefully, testing the height of the ceiling in this part of the cave, gingerly touching the already puffy spot on her forehead. "Watch where you're walking, Evie." Barely able to stand to her full height, she looked around the room.

She had indeed happened upon a funeral.

Arrayed around a bier were more than a dozen people, dressed in finery to put Brian's court to shame. The colors, even in the weak torchlight, were dazzling--blood reds, emerald greens, the deepest royal blues. Shimmering threads of gold were woven into many of the cloaks and the headdresses of the ladies. Fingers bore heavy rings of gold and silver. No one turned her way, though they must have heard her entry.

Her head pounding, suddenly burning with a fever, Eibhlin only noted not one of these heads reached her waist.

"Fairies," she whispered. She'd have thought they'd be smaller. Like Tinkerbell. A giggle escaped her.

"Shhh." One of the mourners hissed a warning to her.

Never feeling more conspicuously tall, Eibhlin started to back out of the cave. She only made it to the over-short doorway and banged her head again.

"Ow!"

"Shhhhh!" Now every head had turned, admonishing her to silence.

The music and the wailing song droned on. Eibhlin, with nowhere else to go, sat on the floor and waited, simply glad to be in the light again.

She watched as they carefully pulled a snow-white mantle around the body of the deceased. Six of the little men raised it up and carried it with respectful gentleness to a niche in the wall. The tiny body fit just right.

All the mourners stood back, their heads bowed, their small hands folded before them. Eibhlin stared at them. Their fingers were short and stubby and their heads seemed much too large for their tiny bodies. But her head hurt too much to worry about it. Besides, she was delighted with actually seeing real Irish fairies in their natural habitat.

"Oh, aren't they cute?" she said out loud.

"Can you not show some respect, big woman?"

"I'm sorry."

"You should be."

One of the men came over to her. He studied her face.

"You are ill." His face suddenly lined with concern.

Eibhlin nodded. She didn't have the breath for more.

"Come, child." He took her hand. Several of his fellows lent their brawn to helping her from the floor.

As soon as she got to her feet, her head started to spin. Her stomach threatened to heave what little bit she still had in it. Then the blackness came upon her again.

* * * *

The feeling got stronger the longer he rode. Eibhlin was here, somewhere. The dead rocky plain of the Burren stretched before him, but even the bleakness did nothing to lessen his hope that he would find her here.

His mount was tiring. Truth, he had again ridden the poor beast harder than he should have. Yet, he could not slow. Brandubh's mind was focused on her, on finding her, protecting her. His eyes wandered right and left over the bleak landscape. The emptiness could easily dispirit him. How could anything live here in this place? Where could she be that she would not be exposed to the wind that whipped off the ocean straight across the endless plain?

He felt the hairs on his arms and the back of his neck raise before he heard the reason--the high-pitched wail washing over the land like a thundercloud.

An otherworldly voice singing a lament for the dead.

The *ban-sidhe*.

The horse skittered to a stop, refusing to go further. Brandubh couldn't bring himself to push the animal. He dismounted and stepped around to the horse's head.

"There, lad, there," he cooed, stroking the length of the animal's face. "I would that you had Conchobar's heart, but I cannot blame you for your lack. Come, then. Let us walk."

He took the reins and walked on, urging the horse to follow. Though his blood chilled, he strode on toward the source of the sound, shoving from his mind the fear that the wail was for Eibhlin.

Uaid wouldn't have hurt her, he thought, not even able to form the thought that Uaid had indeed done more than simply hurt her.

THE RAVEN'S LADY

The pile of stone slabs caught his eye. Piled in such a deliberate manner, it could not be natural. Wondering what was hiding under the cairn, he dropped the reins and knelt down. He noted no sign of weathering and knew it was freshly built.

Then he heard the wail, coming from underneath these stones. Heart pounding, he shoved the top slab. Muscles stretching to the limit, teeth grinding, Brandubh managed to move the stone just enough to reveal an opening in the ground barely wide enough for a man. Brandubh knew of caves in the Burren. Some were rumored to run for many leagues under the surface. In such places, it was said the *Danaan* buried their dead.

With a flush of fear, Brandubh drew his sword and squeezed through the mouth of the cave, before he could change his mind. The ceiling forced him to bend low and his eyes strained in the dim light. Besides the wail that echoed down one direction, he also heard a sound like a man snoring from the other. He squinted in that direction and stopped breathing.

"God's teeth, a bear." What in Patrick's name was a bear doing here? He hadn't heard talk of live bears being seen in Ireland since he was a small boy. This one was surely enough alive if his rafter-rattling wheezing was any indication. The sound reminded Brandubh of the noise his friend Gadhra made after too much wine. Better to let sleeping bears lie, Brandubh thought and he turned toward the sound of wailing, which increased in volume as he went on through the narrowed corridors. Just missing the low overhanging entryway, he bent down and stepped into a larger room.

"Holy Mother," he whispered. "Fairies?"

"Such some consider us." One small man stepped up to Brandubh while the rest of the party continued their mourning. "Why are all you big people barging in here today of all days?"

Brandubh glanced from side-to-side, then he saw the freshly laid-out corpse. "I apologize, sir. I am Brandubh mac Dougal."

The small round face lit with a smile.

"Ah, young Brandubh. Do you not remember me, boy?" The little man grabbed a handful of cloak and pulled Brandubh double. "We seem to ever meet in caves. I am Anluan mac Eachan. My people pulled you out of a cave when you were but a tot. No bigger than I." Anluan gazed up and down Brandubh's body. "You've grown some," he added simply.

Brandubh had to smile. "Anluan? Yes, I remember well you finding me in a cave much like this one. I do not believe I ever thanked you for your kindness."

"You were a frightened child. Your father was most effusive in his gratitude."

A moan caught Brandubh's attention and he turned.

"Eibhlin." He went to her, kneeling on the dirt floor where she lay, so pale, her chest laboring for breath.

"Your lady?" The little man lay his hand on Brandubh's shoulder.

Brandubh could only nod as he started to lift her from the floor.

"Hold, young Brandubh." Anluan knelt beside him. "We have given the lady medicines which will help her breathe more easily. Give her time to gather some strength. Has Dougal found a new healer for Ath Sionnain?"

"Lady Eibhlin has been acting as healer. 'Tis the reason for her illness now."

"How came the lady to be here?"

Brandubh pondered that question, while he took stock of her condition. "She was brought here to die, I suspect."

"Indeed? She is not that ill." Anluan grunted.

"Perhaps the bear at the other end of the corridor was meant to finish the job."

Anluan didn't look worried. "I doubt that old one wakes anytime soon. We gave him enough sleeping potion to keep a man your size asleep for a year." He looked around. "We are finished here, Brandubh mac Dougal. Let us help you carry your lady to the surface and get you on your way."

The little people carried her out. Brandubh, bent double to pass through the cramped corridors, had all he could do to keep himself from giving in to his anxiety of being trapped again, as he had been on that ill-fated bear hunting trip.

Anluan's wise eyes measured Brandubh. "I have heard it said Brandubh mac Dougal of the tribe Dal Cais asks help from no man."

The walls were closing in and the ceiling dropped before his eyes. Brandubh gasped breath enough to answer.

"Helplessness is intolerable to me, Anluan. Had I been able to take care of myself before, I would not have been in the cave where you found me."

"On with you," Anluan laughed. "You were but a small child. You did well to escape the wolves."

Noticing how Anluan strolled, utterly unaffected by the close walls and the low ceiling, Brandubh concluded the idea the tunnel could collapse on his head apparently did not affect him. Brandubh wished he could be so calm.

"I know how you dread these places. Yet you came down here." Anluan tipped his head toward Eibhlin. "For her?"

"She is my wife."

"Ah. Your love for her is great, I see."

Brandubh glanced down at the little man. "She is my wife," he repeated, unwilling to put more into words.

The light at the end of the tunnel beckoned and he restrained himself from running for it. Once out in the air, even the biting winter air whipping across the Burren, he gulped at it like a fish on a river bank.

Anluan directed his men to lay Eibhlin on the ground, which they did with tender respect. They then arrayed themselves around her to form a human windbreak.

"Find your horse, Brandubh mac Dougal. We will keep watch over your lady."

Brandubh quickly did that and once mounted, he reached down to take Eibhlin from the arms of the small men who had helped him recover her from the tomb.

"Give my regards to your father and your lady mother, Brandubh."

"I will, Anluan mac Eachan." He reached down to grasp the little man's wrist. "Thank you for your help. I will not forget you again. If I can ever help you, call on me." He pulled his horse around and kicked him to a run in the direction of Ath Sionnain.

On the wind, Brandubh heard the voice of Anluan mac Eachan. "Take care of your lady, Brandubh."

Chapter Eighteen

Brandubh kicked the horse to greater speed. He knew he should slow down. He knew the animal could take no more.

The horse coughed and shuddered in mid-stride. Brandubh heard the poor beast's heart burst and then felt the animal stumble. He leapt from the saddle barely in time to keep himself and Eibhlin from being crushed under the weight of the dying animal.

Brandubh took the fall on his back, cushioning her from the impact as much as he could. She didn't even moan. He'd wrapped his mantle around them both to share his warmth, but she didn't need it. Her face was flushed from the fever he could feel roiling through the thick wool of her gown. Her gurgling breaths had him aching to breathe for her.

They were still some hour's hard ride from Ath Sionnain.

And now they were afoot. He glanced over at the willing mount who had carried them both this far and tried to not curse him for having no more to give.

There was nothing else to do, he decided. He stood with her in his arms and he started walking.

* * * *

"Dougal, your son is approaching."

At the summons from one of his men, Dougal jumped from his chair by the fire in the great hall and ran out the door and down the steps. He didn't stop until he reached the main gate. Throwing off the bar, he pulled the fifteen-foot high structure open with his own hands.

"Brandubh," he called out.

"Father, help me." Brandubh stumbled. Dougal could just make out the length of his burden, the care with which Brandubh bore it.

Then it hit him that Brandubh, who never asked for help, had asked for help.

"Yes, son, I'm coming." Dougal ran out to meet him and took Eibhlin from Brandubh's exhausted arms. "You men, come out and help my son."

Gadhra was the first there and Brandubh leaned on him.

"Brandubh, where have you been? Where's your horse, man?"

"I killed him."

Dougal and Gadhra exchanged glances over Brandubh's head, glances of disbelief.

"What do you mean, you killed him, son?"

"I ran him into the ground. His heart burst under me." A sob exploded from Brandubh's chest. "I had to get her home."

"Aye, son. I will take her in to your mother." Dougal roared for his wife as he crossed the fenced yard.

Brandubh leaned on Gadhra's sturdy shoulder. In a whisper that was barely audible, he said, "Take me in, my friend, so I may be with her."

* * * *

Moira heard the ado and came out of the herbroom, just in time to see Dougal carrying Eibhlin toward the house. She ran toward him.

"I do not think my son will want you near her, Moira," Dougal said, not unkindly, though he didn't break his stride as he approached the steps.

"Who else is going to treat her? I will be up as soon as I have gathered some things from the herbroom."

She didn't wait for approval or permission, but turned and rushed back to the place where she'd come to know Eibhlin. Where she'd grown to love her and from where she would fight heaven and hell for her life.

Moira grabbed a glass jar containing freshly chopped borage and a vial of pine oil, then looked around the room.

"What else has Eibhlin been giving the sick? For the lungs, she said. Oh, why didn't I listen better?" Moira wrapped the medicines in a linen towel.

I'm coming, my dear one, she thought, not even wondering why she did.

* * * *

Eibhlin was hot. She was burning. Her chest hurt and she could barely breathe. She feared she was dying.

"Mama," she called, "Mama, where are you?"

"Here, dear one."

"Mama."

"You're going to be fine. I need you to tell me, dear one, what do I give you for the congestion in your lungs?"

That's a strange question for Mama to ask, Eibhlin thought. Mama never needed to ask questions. Mama knew everything. But, just in case she was being tested, she answered. "Wild thyme, Mama."

"That's right. Thank you, dear one. Go to sleep. I will be here with you."

Mama was speaking Irish, just like she did when she was worried. Why is Mama worried? Oh, it must be Conor. He must be worse, Eibhlin thought sadly. "I'm sorry, Mama. I wish I could help."

"Don't worry, dear one. Just get well for me."

THE RAVEN'S LADY

Eibhlin opened her eyes and smiled when she saw her mother's face floating before her. "I will, Mama." Then, a dark face surrounded by silky black hair came clear from the mists clouding her mind. "Mama, is Brandubh all right?"

"Yes, my dear. He is resting and having a meal."

If she'd had more strength she'd have asked why her mother sounded so sad. Maybe she'd ask later. Right now she was so tired.

* * * *

The smoky blue almond-shaped eyes closed and a weak smile curved Eibhlin's lips.

"Mama." Her voice was that of a child, soft and trusting.

Mama?

Moira could not comprehend such a thing. Eibhlin was in a fevered delirium. Perhaps Moira reminded her of her mother. Yet, though she tried to make sensible explanations, her heart sighed with relief. The nagging sense of recognition, the sympathy and concern she felt for Eibhlin, even as she'd conspired with Uaid against her, now made some sense. Nastier speculations could thankfully be put to rest.

There was no time for such musings now, however. Eibhlin's lungs were horribly congested and she would die if she wasn't treated soon. Moira reached for her shawl, intending to run to the workroom for the herbs she needed.

The regal figure standing just inside the door stopped her dead.

"Lady," she gasped, slapping her hand over her mouth. Moira hadn't heard Sadbh had come into the room.

"Moira," Sadbh said, more question than address. "I came as soon as Brandubh consented to rest and give us room to work. How is Eibhlin?"

"I believe she will survive, Lady." She must survive, Moira added silently.

"Did she truly call you her mother?"

"She is in a delirium. She thinks I am her mother."

"And you were acting like her mother." The Lady tipped her head, her wise icy eyes looking deep into Moira's soul. "Why? I could see more than kindness in your treatment of her, Moira. Do you feel the attachment of a mother for her child?"

"I cannot explain what I feel, Lady."

Sadbh shook her head in wonder and strolled over to the bed. "She does resemble your family, your mother in particular. Though her height is not from any of your people."

The shock of having her thoughts spoken aloud ripped a heated path along her nerves, followed by a cooling fear.

"Lady, please, do not speculate on these things. I would not care to have to explain this to the priest."

"Nor would I, Moira, nor would I. However," she raised that eyebrow, "I would say her father is a grand specimen of manhood."

Moira glanced back at the sleeping figure of her daughter. With a sudden flush of excitement, Moira thought of the man in her dreams, the man who'd held the little girl's hand in her vision by the river, certain he was the man who had fathered this child of her.

"Where were you going?" Sadbh asked, bringing her back with a shameful jerk to needful things. Time was too precious to waste lusting after an unknown man.

"For wild thyme. She needs it for the congestion."

"I will go." Sadbh took Moira's hand and patted it gently. "You stay with her. 'Tis best with a delirium to have a familiar person tending the patient."

"Thank you, Lady. I did not want to leave her. The thyme is in a linen pouch on the table. If you will bring it, we can keep it hot in here for her."

Sadbh nodded and left.

Moira took a seat by Eibhlin's bed, and for the rest of the afternoon and into the evening battled the fever. Spooning borage brew down her throat. Rubbing pine oil on her chest to keep her lungs as open as possible. Sponging her limbs with tepid water.

And waiting.

* * * *

Brandubh dreamed of bears and little people and screaming horses. Then he dreamed of Eibhlin, pale and weak, then rosy and plump, naked in his arms, riding him like a stallion.

He woke up in a sweat, fully aroused, supremely frustrated and deeply ashamed. Pushing himself from his bed, he draped his mantle around his shoulders. He had to see her, reassure himself that she lived still, that he had not killed her with his mad ride.

He'd let his fear take hold. The horse need not have been ridden to death, he thought. They would have arrived in better time if he'd been less afraid.

Yet, the fear of losing her had eaten all his reason like moths in a trunk. He'd only thought of her, of getting her back where she could be cared for. He'd prayed, begged for her life. He'd bargained with God, offering his own life, his possessions, his good name, everything, if only she lived.

And he'd hated the helplessness of it all. What good was his strength, his prowess with a sword, his way with a horse, now? The gift she needed was the one she herself had, the gift of healing. Of this Brandubh knew nothing and so could be of no use in a sickroom.

Yet, he left his room and made his way down the dimly lit corridor of his father's house to her chamber. He didn't knock, standing at the unlatched door, afraid of what he would find. What if he were too late? With fingers unaccustomed to trembling, though they did now, he pushed the portal open and slowly entered her room.

Moira sat by the bedside, spooning something down Eibhlin's throat. She was singing, too, her wonderful voice caressing and soothing. He just stood in the doorway for a moment in fascination of the gentle ministration, like a mother caring for a child.

Yet, Moira was the child, well, at least she was some years younger than Eibhlin.

"Oh, Brandubh," Moira said from her chair by the bed. "'Tis good you are here. She will be glad to see you. Come." Moira had risen and was pulling him by his hand to the bed as she spoke. "Here, sit. I will get you a cup of something hot to drink."

He obeyed, still somewhat uncertain of whether to be concerned Moira was here or relieved that she was.

"Mama." The voice, so weak, so clouded by congestion, pierced him to the heart.

"Yes, dear one," Moira hurried over and laid her palm on Eibhlin's forehead. "I am here. As is your Brandubh."

Brandubh spared only a moment's surprise at Moira's comment before her was caught up in the fragile smile Eibhlin offered at the mention of his name. The sight was worth any torment.

"Brandubh." Her whisper trailed off as though all strength had been spent.

He took her hand, pressing his lips to the back. So hot she was, and he could *feel* her weakness. "Aye, my Lady, I am here."

She only smiled and closed her eyes again.

"Eibhlin," he called, his whisper grating and harsh. He feared she had slipped away from him.

"She will survive, Brandubh. Already she is greatly improved."

"This is improved?" To his eyes, Eibhlin was in need of a priest, though he would have killed any other who'd suggested it.

"Listen to her breathing. It is nearly cleared completely. Her fever is much less and she is not delirious with it." Moira filled a cup with the potion she tended. "She will recover." Her voice was steady and he made her conviction his own.

She brought the warm cup and pressed it into Brandubh's hands. "Drink this. It is soothing."

He sniffed the hot liquid. A tangy, sweet scent wafted up his nose, relaxing him. He sipped and sat back in the chair, never taking his eyes from her face.

"Moira, what is this that she calls you *Mama*?"

"Eibhlin is my daughter."

He gaped, his drink forgotten. "That is impossible. She won't be born for centuries after you are dust."

He bit his tongue at revealing Eibhlin's secret. Yet, Moira showed no surprise. Her confident facade never wavered.

"I do not know how it is to be. But I know it must be." She shrugged. "Besides, how foolish is it to call something impossible after what you have already seen?"

Brandubh was struck dumb. She was right. Eibhlin had told him her story, her future, and he'd believed her without reservation. Could Moira's claim be any more unbelievable?

He watched her bring a bowl to the bed. "Brandubh, hold her up so I can spoon this down."

"What is it?" he asked as he slipped his arm underneath Eibhlin and raised her up.

"Thyme, to clear her lungs. I hope I haven't made it too strong."

Eibhlin, only half conscious, swallowed the sweet-smelling liquid as Moira tenderly tipped the large spoon to her lips. When she'd taken her dosage, Moira signaled Brandubh to lay her back down. Removing his arm from around her shoulders, he ran his fingers through her hair, arranging it to splay around her head on the pillow in a dark halo.

The silence grew around them until Moira spoke. "I am giving my daughter's life into your hands, Brandubh mac Dougal. She was brought here for you."

He'd wondered how much she actually knew about Eibhlin's coming here. "How do you know these things?"

"In her delirium she relived the experience on Craglea and I heard it all. Though I could not understand everything she said, I gathered enough. From these words I came to believe our relationship."

"She will tell you I forced her to come to me."

Moira laughed. "I have heard the truth from her own lips. She wants you." She laid her hand on Brandubh's shoulder and gazed steadily into his eyes. "I know not what fate has brought us to this point, Brandubh. But I feel I must give her into your hands," she repeated the charge, "and I know you will care for her with your life."

Brandubh returned Moira's regard. This girl had changed much in the last two months. He covered her hand with his own.

"I will, Moira. You have my word."

Moira nodded, the agreement made. "Sit with her awhile. I need some air."

The door closed quietly behind her. Brandubh sat in silence, sipping the drink and studying his lady, lying so still and pale.

The strangeness of these last weeks made anything credible, he thought, sliding his chair closer to the bed. Briefly, his reason gave a rebirth to his suspicion of Moira's motives, yet he had never seen a mother tend a child more tenderly. Moira *believed* Eibhlin was her child, whether it was the truth or not, and had given him the responsibility for her. It was a charge he would gladly accept. He took Eibhlin's hand and settled down to keep his watch over her.

Chapter Nineteen

The smell of citrus wafted through the air, tingling her nose. A warmth surrounded her, comforting, soothing. Eibhlin opened her eyes. Several seconds passed before she realized where she was.

The lingering lemony scent of wild thyme reminded her of the hours of endless coughing and swallowing spoonfuls of herbal preparations. The bodice of her linen shift reeked with the residue of pine oil. Just the hint of the smell of cucumbers brought the memory of drinking borage.

She'd gone and caught pneumonia. Served me right, she thought, getting all worn down. Well, if her nose was right, someone had taken good care of her. Then she wondered how long she'd been sick. The answer to that question was partly answered by her muscles' complaint when she attempted to move.

"Ow." The groan escaped her. Deciding to take it easy, she experimented with her toes first, stretching them out and bending her foot. The muscles of her legs seemed to have been spared the stiffness that weighed down her arms and upper body. "At least they still work."

She raised her left hand, only to jerk back from the hairy unknown thing lying beside her.

"What the...." Eibhlin raised her head from the down pillow to see what was sharing her bed. With a sigh of relief, she trailed her fingers through the silken ebony strands of Brandubh's hair that spread around his head as it rested on his bended arm.

"Brandubh." My Raven, she added silently. His presence in her chamber gave her only a moment's pause. Ever since this adventure had begun, he had been the one certainty.

He breathed in a sleepy rhythm. She allowed herself to enjoy the comfortable intimacy, stroking his hair, then his olive-toned cheek, on down the thick column of his neck. Sensitive fingertips gently pressed the steady coursing of his blood. She drank in the sight of him. Studying him so closely, she could tell the instant he started to wake. His breath came a little faster and one corner of his mouth curved. He turned his head to graze his lips across her fingers.

"You are awake, my Lady."

How she loved him calling her that. "Have I been sleeping long?"

"Five days."

"Five days?" She jerked up, immediately regretting such a sudden move.

"Rest, Lady. You are still weak."

"I'm not so weak. Who is taking care of the sick?"

"Your mother."

Eibhlin snapped her head around. "My mother? What do you mean by that?" Wispy memories of her mother's face floating over her in her fever came to her.

"Moira." His black eyes fastened on her. "She is, is she not?"

She stared into his eyes, trying to stay calm. There was no reason to let her own fantasies become communal. "That's not possible, Brandubh. My mother won't be born for almost a thousand years."

"Neither will you. Yet here you are." He took her hand, his long fingers rubbing along hers. "Moira was here every hour--spooning that brew down your throat, cooling your body from the fever. She only left you for necessities." Brandubh pressed her fingers, one by one, to his lips. "Do you remember what happened? How you came to be in the cave?"

"Cave?"

"I found you in a cave on the Burren. You were sharing it with a bear and a tribe of little people burying their dead queen."

"A bear? Little people?" She gave him a narrowed look. He had to be pulling her leg. Surely she'd remember a bear in a cave. And yet his expression was perfectly serious and some tickle of memory told her he wasn't teasing. "I'm sorry, Brandubh. The last thing I can remember is talking to you in the herbroom."

"You don't remember who took you to the cave?" He raised her hand to his lips and brushed his lips across the palm. His breath burned hot on her skin. Those black eyes never wavered from hers, even as he made her heart beat faster as he made love to her hand. He seemed to expect an answer to his question, but she could think of none.

"No." Her fascination with his mouth reminded her of her last truly clear memory--his departure and the kiss that had left her head reeling. It also reminded her of her decision to remain here with him in spite of the dangers. Now she didn't know if she'd come to that decision because she'd already been delirious with fever or if he'd actually convinced her of her impotence in the face of Man's free will or God's plan or Fate or whatever it was that ruled destiny.

Too dangerous a subject right now, she thought, and turned the conversation to a more mundane subject. "Did you find your horses?"

A tired smile accompanied by a nod replaced the worried frown. "They are well and I believe Deirdre is in foal."

"How wonderful. I'd like to see them."

"So you shall." He held her gaze. "The solstice is less than two weeks away. With the weather being so poor, I was thinking perhaps you would delay your departure until at least Beltain."

The look of hopefulness on his face pleased her greatly. Would she even be able to leave him? The void he would leave in her life would be unbearable.

"Actually, Brandubh, I've thought about your offer."

He sat up straighter and his grip on her hand neared painful, but he said nothing.

What could a minor chieftain's wife do in the wilds of western Ireland to change the history of the rest of the world?

"I accept."

"Really? You would choose to remain with me?"

Eibhlin nodded, never feeling more certain of any decision in her life.

Brandubh narrowed his eyes. "What of your concerns?"

She met his gaze. "I'm willing to take the chance I may cause a rip in the space-time continuum and the resulting destruction of the entire Universe."

That was quite a mouthful in Irish and her effort was lost on Brandubh who obviously didn't get the joke. Oh, well, she thought with an inner groan, maybe the thought of the extermination of all reality wasn't all that funny. But then, Ireland's future wasn't a barrel of laughs either. If she *could* change things, would it be so bad?

And why couldn't she settle on a decision and be easy with it?

"No," she said aloud, waving away Brandubh's unasked question. "What I mean is, the chance for good is worth the risk. And who's to say the new reality won't be better than the old one?"

One of those cynical eyebrows flew up. "Still, my Lady, I would you keep your expectations low. Men..."

"Yes, yes," Eibhlin interrupted, "free will and all that. Fine. But I am going to talk to Brian. And you, husband-to-be, are going to take me."

That brought his glorious smile. "Indeed and none other. In fact, t'would be best, I think, to marry first--so there will be no cause for scandal."

Eibhlin's skeptical huff slipped between her teeth. "Simply an excuse to have the wedding night as soon as possible?"

The infinitely expressive brows raised with lascivious meaning. "We had our wedding night already, my Lady. I am certain you recall that," he added with arrogant conviction.

A smile curved her lips and mischief made her say, "Perhaps you ought to remind me. It seems to have slipped my mind."

"As you wish, my Lady." He vacated his chair and sat by her on the bed. Wrapping her in one strong arm, with gentle fingers, he tipped her face up to his. Her heart beat faster as he lowered his lips to brush across hers. He was about to take possession of his lady when the door opened.

"What is going on here?"

Moira stood in the doorway, one arm full of clean linen and what appeared to be clean clothes for Eibhlin, the other carrying a covered tray.

"What goes on here?" she repeated.

Brandubh turned for a second to answer her. "Eibhlin ni Seamus has agreed to my offer of fifty head of cattle to become my wife." His mouth returned to Eibhlin's. She was helpless to stop him.

"*Fifty?*" Moira's mouth had dropped open.

Raising his lips from their plundering, Brandubh brushed Moira's amazement aside. "A pittance for such a treasure, do you not agree?"

Eibhlin leaned against him and gasped a deep breath.

"Indeed." Moira regarded the two of them on the bed and her smile slowly grew. "You are content, Eibhlin?"

"Yes, I am content."

"Good." Brandubh squeezed her shoulder and bounced off the bed, his great bulk causing the poor ropes to groan under the strain. "I will call Dougal's brehon to write the contract. In fact, Moira, if you are not uncomfortable with this, I will make the offer to Conor."

"Yes, Brandubh. I have spoken with my father and he understands."

"Conor? Why?" Eibhlin asked even as she realized what Brandubh was about to say.

"Because he is your nearest living male relative." Brandubh dropped a peck on the top of her head and with a nod to Moira, left them alone.

This was getting too weird. Yet they acted so nonchalant, so blasé.

Didn't *anything* throw these people or did they accept everything as normal? "Moira, I don't have any living relatives here."

Moira came to stand by the bed. "Eibhlin, I know who you are. I *know* you."

I will know you, no matter when we might see each other again.

"You called out to me in your delirium, dear one."

What she had felt, what she had *known* all along fell into place like a great gaping hole in a jigsaw puzzle suddenly filling in and providing the whole picture.

With a gasp, Eibhlin whispered, "Mama," and stretched out her arms.

Moira came to the bed and wrapped her in a tight embrace.

"There, there, dear one. Why do you weep?"

"You said you would know me. *Dear one* is what you always called me." Eibhlin squeezed. "I was so afraid I wouldn't see you again."

"When did I say that?"

"I called you and Dad right after I saw Brandubh for the first time on Craglea."

"Called?"

How to explain to an eleventh-century woman a twentieth- century device?

"Your father," Moira said, her voice flat and Eibhlin couldn't tell if she was asking a question.

Moira dropped on the bed. "What is he like?" That one question set loose a torrent of girlish enthusiasm. "Where will I find him? How long before...."

"Wait, wait," Eibhlin said, squeezing her mother again with a laugh. "I'm not sure I should tell you anything. What if I say something that changes the way you feel about him?"

"Tell me this? Am I content?"

Eibhlin couldn't stop the smile she saw reflected in Moira's eyes.

"Very. My father loves you with his whole soul." Once started, she found she couldn't stop. "You have so much in common. He is a musician, a singer with a wonderful voice. The two of you make your livings singing."

Moira's eyes opened wide. "We are bards?"

"Well, I suppose it's the same thing. You'll travel a lot and do concerts... ah, appear before large crowds and sing."

"Me?" An indrawn gasp of awe followed the single word.

Eibhlin nodded.

Moira popped off the bed and went across the room to retrieve the tray. "Here, you have to eat something, but between bites, tell me everything."

"I can't do that," Eibhlin said, reaching greedily for the crusty bread on the wooden tray.

Moira jerked the tray out of her reach. "Indeed you will, my Lady."

Eibhlin couldn't help it. This exact scene had played so many times in the Fitzgerald household that her delighted laughter was impossible to restrain.

THE RAVEN'S LADY

"What's so funny?" Moira tried to keep a straight face, but she was only a girl and too starved for gladness to remain glum. Soon, she had stretched out on the foot of the bed, giggling right along with Eibhlin in helpless glee.

"I've missed you, Mama."

Moira wiped away a tear of hilarity and patted Eibhlin's hand. "Here, eat. We can talk of this later." She sobered and got off the bed. Taking a post at the small fireplace, she stared into the flames for a moment before speaking. "I suppose I will be leaving here at some time. Will I ever return?"

Thick slice of brown bread halfway to her mouth, Eibhlin froze. That was a question she didn't know the answer to.

"I don't know, Mama. But I don't think you ever regretted going."

Moira turned. "I don't think you will either."

Eibhlin was certain she was right. Except for missing her parents, she would never regret remaining with Brandubh.

* * * *

"No!"

Conor mac Turlough turned a weary eye on his son.

"Uaid, be silent. Moira has already told me of this. She believes it to be true. How else do you explain Brandubh's story?"

"It is a lie, that simple. He found the big whore at Kincora, probably one of Brian's cast-offs, and brought her here to replace Caoimhe. He had to come up with some reason for his action."

"Take care, Uaid. 'Tis for your father's and your sister's sakes alone that I do not take my just revenge out of your hide." Brandubh stood stiffly at the fireplace. Bad enough to accept that he was marrying into this family after everything, but Uaid's slanders nearly had him reaching for his sword. "Lady Eibhlin is my chosen bride and I will not accept such words about her. And even though she does not have memory of it, I know you took her off and left her to die in that cave. If I could prove it I would kill you where you stand."

"*Lady*? Where does she come by such title? She is no more than my sister, if this fantastic story be true."

"She is *my* Lady. That suffices."

Conor nodded approvingly. "Think on it, Uaid. Does not Eibhlin look so much like your own mother as to bring tears? My Nara was not such a tall woman, but as striking."

"Conor, I came to speak for myself this time, so there would be no misunderstanding. The cattle I offer are only for Eibhlin. If you desire more, a price for losing Caoimhe, name it. I will pay. Though it can never be enough...."

"Brandubh," Conor interrupted, "I hold you no more responsible for Caoimhe than I hold myself. We accept your offer of fifty head and wish you happy."

Brandubh stepped forward and seized Conor's forearm in a show of friendship. "Thank you, Conor."

With an oath, Uaid stormed out the door.

The men stood in silence for a moment.

"Conor, I am sorry for all this."

"As am I. Let us hope for better."

"Indeed."

Calling for his servant girl to bring them ale, Conor motioned Brandubh to a chair. Brandubh took it, glad to renew his friendship with Conor, but his mind kept wandering to the big house and the woman who would soon be his forever.

* * * *

By the early afternoon, Eibhlin had finally figured out what she was going to find most difficult to do without in this place.

Something to read. A newspaper, a magazine, a cereal box--anything. Dougal had some volumes of the classics, Pliny, Augustine, Aristotle in translation, selections from the gospels, but nothing resembling a library. Brian apparently had quite a collection. Naturally, everything was in Latin, Irish not yet being a literary language. That wasn't so bad. Eibhlin's Latin was passably good. After all Linneas and all the great scientists had written in Latin until the late eighteenth century. But they were at Kincora and she was here.

When she'd complained of boredom, Moira had dropped a load of clothing on her that all needed some kind of minor repair. Boredom never seemed to be a problem for her mother or Sadbh. There was always work enough for idle hands. But Eibhlin's level of desperation was evident in the fact that she'd actually sat by the fireplace this morning and gotten halfway through the pile by the afternoon. Now her fingers ached and she'd decided she needed to rest.

She didn't bother to remove her heavy woolen gown before she stretched out on the bed and closed her eyes, ready to sleep.

The door creaked and heavy footsteps crossed the room toward the bed. She smiled, thinking Brandubh had come to wake her for dinner, and waited for the touch of his hand to grab him and greet him properly.

The mattress gave way under the weight of a man, though it seemed not so much as it had earlier. She was aware that he bent over her, closer, closer--something didn't smell right.

He didn't smell right. There was no hint of horse. Brandubh always saw to his horses in the morning and the evening. Mixed with his own scent, it was a perfume she recognized.

Who is this? she thought just as the cold blade, not Brandubh's warm touch, slid under her chin.

"So, you are the woman who is worth fifty head of cattle?"

Eibhlin didn't recognize the voice. "Who are you?"

"You do not remember me even after the pleasant time we spent together on the Burren?"

For a moment, she was again in the cave, with only a sliver of light connecting her to the outside world, though the rest of the memory fought recall.

THE RAVEN'S LADY

"The Burren. The cave," she whispered.

"Yes," he said. "Though at the time we didn't realize we were related. I am your uncle Uaid, my dear." He laughed harshly in her ear. "You are my sister's child, are you not? Not that I believe it--women appearing from thin air. Only a fool would be taken in by such a tale. Have you nothing to say, Puss?"

His somewhat belligerent tone as well as the knife at her throat conspired to hold her temper in check while she tried to remember what Oprah had said about getting oneself out of a situation like this. First, be calm.

"What do you want from me?" Good, her voice had been strong and only wavered once.

Uaid loosened his hold on her. "Not much. Only your life."

So much for calm. Remarkably, her strength returned ten fold and she pushed him off and scurried to the other side of the bed, rolling to her feet.

"Leave my room, now, or I'll scream. Brandubh will...."

"Brandubh is well on the other side of the keep, Lady. He will not hear you. Unless you want to be the cause for much destruction, you will come quietly."

"Quietly? To die? I don't think so." A quick glance around revealed little she might use as a weapon. Everything was too heavy for her to raise. Even now, she could feel her shot of adrenaline wearing off and the heaviness coming across her chest again. A coughing fit was on its way.

She glanced over at the door. Uaid had left it partially open.

His eyes moved with hers. "Do not consider it. I will kill you if you try."

Other options were few, though, and the hallway beyond that door was her only hope for getting help. Fixing in her mind the location of the door, she turned her full attention on Uaid, watching his eyes. He was, likewise, watching hers, his instinct as a fighter serving him well. She wasn't likely to outrun him, so her effort had to be unexpected enough to give her time to pull the door open and scream to rouse an alarm.

But would she be alive when it was over? Stall him.

"Why are you so set on my death?"

"I explained all this to you in the cave. You for my sister."

Simple enough.

Uaid took one step to the side, his intent obvious. Only two more steps would put him between her and the door.

"How will you escape after you kill me?"

"I don't necessarily need to escape. I need only be elsewhere when your body is found."

Quiet footsteps were their only warning before the door was pushed open. Eibhlin didn't dare take her eyes off Uaid to see who it was who came in.

"Uaid, what are you doing here? Get out now, before I call Brandubh," Moira said, her voice sharp and angry.

"Mama," Eibhlin cried in relief, taking a step toward her.

"Stop," Uaid warned, brandishing his dagger at them both. "Moira, you have come at a most inopportune time."

"Put that away."

"I will sheathe it in her breast."

"Uaid, please." Moira came into the room and closed the door. "There, now, we can talk about this. You must realize, I'll never let you do this."

He laughed and it was a harsh, bitter sound. "I'll do as I please, sister. And I think I'll start with you, traitor."

He lunged at Moira, catching her arm. She grabbed his wrist and shoved it toward his face. The unexpected strength of her action had Uaid dodging his own knife. Eibhlin jumped over the bed to help her mother just as Uaid wrenched his hand free from Moira's grip and swept it back. The dagger's glinting edge warned her. She automatically jerked out of the way. In her weakened condition, that was enough to throw her off-balance. She crashed against the heavy wooden bedframe. Falling to her knees in a daze, she grabbed both sides of her pounding head to hold it together.

Uaid, now with only one woman to fight, was more than equal to the task. He seized both Moira's slender wrists in one big hand and held her. She struggled like a cat, kicking and shrieking. Eibhlin prayed someone would hear the commotion.

As though running in slow motion, Uaid drew back his fist and cold-cocked Moira, releasing her to drop like a corpse on the floor.

"Mama." Ignoring her aching head, Eibhlin leapt to the floor and moved toward Moira's still body.

A booted foot landed on her outstretched right hand. Something cracked and a pain shot straight up her arm. A scream tore from her throat, ringing off the stone walls.

Uaid grabbed a handful of hair and pulled her to her feet.

"Now, for you, my Lady."

Fear dissolved. She spit in his face.

"Don't you ever call me that."

Nonchalantly, as though he had all the time in the world, Uaid swiped at the foamy trickle sliding down his cheek.

"Why don't we go somewhere more private, where we won't be so likely to be disturbed?"

He seized her arm and twisted her around. She spied the door and decided to run.

Then stars flashed before her eyes and everything went dark.

Chapter Twenty

Brandubh returned to Eibhlin's room, the warm congratulations of his

THE RAVEN'S LADY

parents still ringing in his ears. His life was finally settling down to the rightful path--wife, children, a future for his tribe.

The absence of voices in the room led him to believe she was sleeping and he slowly pushed open the heavy oak door. His eyes lit upon her bed, thinking to see her where he'd left her, safe and warm and waiting for his touch.

"Eibhlin," he called out to the room he now saw to be empty as he entered and looked around.

A cold uncertainty surrounded him. She was gone. Then his attention turned toward the moaning form on the floor.

"Moira? God's bones, girl. What happened to you?" He knelt beside her and gently helped her to sit up. "Where is Eibhlin?"

Moira ground out a curse fit for a warrior between teeth clenched against the pain her head must be causing her. Her chin was bruised and her cheek swollen.

"Uaid has her, Brandubh. I tried to stop him, but he has gone mad."

"Where did he take her?" When she leaned her head back and bit her bottom lip, Brandubh clutched her shoulders and shook her to extract an answer. "Where, Moira?"

"I don't know. I don't know. He means to kill her, if he hasn't already. And I wasn't able to stop him." Moira dissolved in tears and grabbed his tunic. "Go after her. Find her before...."

Brandubh helped her to her feet and settled her in the chair by the fireplace.

"I'll find her, Moira."

He saw reflected in her eyes the fear he felt. He might already be too late. Would Uaid waste time in finishing what he'd started, especially after failing so many times in his quest for revenge?

The fact that it wasn't likely had Brandubh striding toward the stables with no thought in his mind besides finding a horse, riding out and picking up their tracks and following them. He didn't allow himself to ponder what might await him at the end of that trail.

Through the great house he went, moving with inexorable steps toward the front door and the direction of the stables. He was halfway across the courtyard when he heard Moira calling him from the wide stone steps of the entryway.

"Brandubh, wait."

He turned and saw her coming in his direction struggling with the weight of his long sword.

"Do not forget this." She held the heavy weapon out to him like an offering.

"Moira," he whispered, wondering if she really knew what she was urging him to do, though he needed no urging.

"Use it if you must to bring her home, Brandubh." She gulped a breath, to stop the tears, he knew. "If she is dead, kill him for me."

If she is dead.... The words had been spoken aloud and given power. They produced a fear that nearly unmanned him, nearly had him falling to his knees in the dirt, keening with grief as though he held her body in his arms. The only thing that kept him on his feet was the iron grip of Moira's hand on his. He summoned strength from her touch and nodded, taking the weapon and strapping it on.

"I will kill him, Moira."

"If needs be," she replied and returned his nod, stepping away from him.

Dougal came running from the house, followed by Sadbh.

"Where do you go, Brandubh?" his father asked, voice quiet.

"To find my wife," Brandubh replied and continued to the stables, the heavy scabbard slapping his thigh with every step. Inside the dark building, he found more proof of Uaid's madness.

One of the stable lads lay crumpled in the corner of a stall, face gray and cold as stone. The spreading red stain on his rough linen shirt told the tale of his end at the point of Uaid's dagger.

"Aw, Gillie," Dougal whispered over Brandubh's shoulder as he knelt by the dead boy's side. His voice was grating when he said, "Bring him to me, Brandubh."

Brandubh could no more promise such a thing than he could promise to bring home a fairy. He knew already how this night would end. Uaid, or Brandubh himself, would never return to Ath Sionnain again.

"No." Rage, raw and chilling, had Brandubh wasting no more time with talk.

Dougal sighed and stepped out of the way, not even offering to accompany him on his journey. Gadhra, perhaps who knew Brandubh best, simply leaned against the wall of the barn and watched him approach the stall where Conchobar waited, head up, ears perked as the sound of Brandubh's footsteps rang through the building.

"Come, lad. My lady awaits my presence."

As though he understood the importance of speed, Conchobar stood quietly to be saddled, his normal fractiousness held in check. The muscles under the sleek black coat twitched in anticipation. Brandubh promised himself, this time, Uaid would not escape.

Mind blank, nerves steady, Brandubh walked out of the stable with Conchobar close behind. Deirdre neighed a greeting to her mate from the paddock next to the stable. Conchobar tossed his head and blew out a reply.

"My regards to your lady, Brandubh," Gadhra called out. "If you are not back by morning, I will be following. Any bit of business left undone will be finished by my hand."

"Thank you, my friend." Brandubh lay his hand on Gadhra's shoulder. "Brother, if I do not return, I give my lady into your keeping. She will want to go to Craglea on Midwinter morn. You will see her safely there for me?"

Gadhra nodded. "I will, brother."

Brandubh turned from his friend and vaulted into the saddle. A gentle kick to Conchobar's sides sent the horse exploding with a blast of power

THE RAVEN'S LADY

and speed straight for the open gate.

The trail was clear. Where it wasn't, Uaid had left signs for Brandubh to follow. Here or there, a shred of linen--from a woman's shift, Brandubh noted with cold fury--just to keep him on their track. So, Brandubh thought, Uaid wants me to follow. He wants to have a chance at me.

"Let it be so," he said aloud. Conchobar's ears pitched backward at the words, but his relentless stride never slackened.

* * * *

I really used to like horses, Eibhlin thought, once again belly-down over a saddle. Uaid really had no imagination in planning an escape.

"Nearly, there, niece," Uaid shouted above the pounding of the horse's hooves.

She struggled to look ahead, not sure she wanted to see. The last outing her Uncle Uaid had taken her on had been less than enjoyable. What entertainment might he have planned this time?

Uaid slowed the horse and let him walk into the courtyard of an impressive stone keep. Once within the walls, he dismounted and with one hand on the waist of her gown, he pulled Eibhlin somewhat less elegantly from her perch.

"Didn't we already do this?" she asked.

Uaid chuckled. "Yes, Puss, but I didn't finish what I'd started. I aim to correct that oversight this time. Come, my Lady."

He said it to aggravate her, she could see it in his eyes. The name, the same name by which Brandubh called her, coming from Uaid's lips made her feel cheap, dirty.

She hesitated too long and he took a handful of her bodice and dragged her after him into the building nestled within the walls of their sanctuary.

"Now, will you sit? I have stocked our little love nest with some wine and a bit of food to refresh ourselves while we await Brandubh's arrival."

Uaid took a flint and quickly kindled a fire in the long-cold brazier by the entry, then lit a few candles. Once the room was bathed in light, Eibhlin gazed around her in wonder at the fading beauty of the building. Shadows on the walls marked the places where paintings had once hung. Empty niches cried out for their stone figures, now gone. The windows far up along the top of the wall were cross-shaped and all around the cornices were religious etchings, Bible verses in Latin.

"Here, Puss. Drink some wine. I stole it from Dougal's cellar. He does serve fine drink."

Eibhlin took the cup from his hand, glancing inside for a tell-tale sign of powder. Raising the cup to her lips, she reluctantly sipped. There was no bitterness or other taste that would hint of poison.

Uaid laughed at her caution. "Poison really is not my way, Puss. I would much rather use a blade. More manly, you know."

"What is this place, Uncle?" She tried to maintain an appearance of fearlessness. If he wanted her scared, he'd have to try harder. Damned if she'd give him her fear as a free gift.

He drank deeply of the same wine he'd given her. "An abbey. The brothers abandoned it years ago for a bigger site nearer Kincora. At the time the Vikings from Limerick came up the Shannon and raided it regular as the seasons. The good brothers decided they would be safer where Brian could protect them. It's one of the ways the *Ard Ri* buys favor from the Church."

She could see now they were in the monastery's living quarters. Chambers lined the walls on both sides, their heavy wooden doors sitting open. Behind Uaid's shoulder, an opened door showed the way to a set of stairs. Probably the bell tower, she thought, wondering if that might not be an avenue of escape.

Glancing behind him, obviously curious about what held her attention, Uaid half-smiled and strolled over to the door as though he had all the time in the world. He gently closed the door and slid the rusty bolt.

"Let's not make it too easy, shall we, Puss?"

"Please stop calling me that."

His smile spread to fullness and he drained his cup. "I think I will decide what to call you or not." Eyes narrowing, he set his cup on the table by the door. With one hand, he tenderly stroked his abdomen, then lower. A sharply sucked breath made his intent clear.

"I see why Brandubh finds you desirable, my dear. Since we have some time, perhaps we can find a way to pass it?" His hand caressed his aroused flesh, clearly outlined against his tunic.

"No way, buddy." She realized too late she'd spoken in English. Well, the hell with him. Let him wonder what she'd said. He'd get the point soon enough that she's never submit to him. Of course, the look in his eyes gave every evidence that he would be equally content to rape her.

He must have seen the thought on her face, for he confirmed it. "Yes, Puss, I'll enjoy it more if you fight me."

So, she thought, not able to form a word, she could lie like a stone and let this man--her uncle, for crying out loud--take what he wanted, or she could fight and give him a *really* good time.

"And I want you to notice, Puss, I picked a religious house, so there will be no fairies to save you this time." In spite of his jocular tone, Uaid's brown eyes burned as he advanced on her. "It's time we got better acquainted, don't you think?"

Eibhlin matched his steps, going backward, keeping her distance as long as she had room to move. When her back hit the wall, Uaid's smile spread in an unholy wreath across his face.

Too fast for her to avoid the clutching grasp of his hand, Uaid seized her mantle and pulled her closer. The blade of his dagger came up under her chin, tickling her tender skin. Their eyes, on a level, held together.

"So easy. With a sharp blade, do you know how easy it is to pierce human flesh?" He pressed the tip of the dagger against the underside of her chin. "In battle, a longsword can cleave a grown man into two pieces. It's all the stink of blood and bowels. No glory in it that I could ever see."

Her stomach churned at the picture, but she held her face steady, her eyes on his. "Then why do you do it?"

THE RAVEN'S LADY

"I am an Irishman. We are made for two things--fucking and fighting. Have you naught heard the old tales?" He laughed out loud. "Your Brandubh, there, is a lad for certain. He's bedded most of the women in Ath Sionnain and many at Kincora, including, it has been rumored, the old King's former wife. That old witch had an eye for firm male flesh and Brandubh had to have come under her notice. As for fighting, there's no man I would rather be beside on a battlefield." Something like real admiration tinted his words. "A madness comes o'er him, you see. He cannot hear nor speak. He can only kill. That sword of his sings pretty as it hands out death."

"Are you looking forward to hearing it sing for you, Uaid?"

He actually laughed. "I'm not going to die tonight, Puss. You are."

"Brandubh will kill you slowly if you kill me, Uaid."

"Oh, Puss, I'm not going to kill you. Brandubh is."

"What? You're crazy."

"Am I? I tell you, once the madness is upon him, if he were to come upon his own mother in the dark, his sword would do the work it was made for. He will kill you before he knows it is you. Then when he has regained his reason and sees what he's done, he'll be ready to die and I will kill him." Uaid's expression softened. "Then perhaps I can rest again."

It all came back to her in a rush of memory--his confession in the cave, the tragic death of Caoimhe at her own brother's hand.

Eibhlin knew it was insane to goad him, but she couldn't help herself. "You can't fight him man-to-man, so you have to weaken him, break him so he'll tip his head back and let you slice it off."

"That's right, Puss. There's not much sense in revenge that costs one his own life, is there?"

"All because you got angry at a spoiled, headstrong girl, all because of a stupid accident?"

Uaid pressed the point of the dagger harder, piercing the delicate flesh underneath her jaw. Eibhlin bit back the gasp of pain.

"Go ahead, Uaid. Push."

A flash of humor passed over his dead eyes. "Maybe you are Moira's daughter. God knows you have her sharp tongue."

"What's to make me cooperate with you in this insanity? Why would I wait for him to hack me to pieces? What's to keep me from shouting out to him, warning him?"

The sound of hoofbeats clattering across the courtyard cut off any explanation of Uaid's plans.

"He's here. Come, Puss. Let's welcome your lover." Uaid yanked on her arm, forcing her to stand and shoved her ahead of him. "Just to make sure you don't interfere, though...." He set his dagger between his teeth and yanked her hands behind her and tied them with a piece of leather he pulled from his belt.

The huge, oak door of the abbey slammed against the wall.

"Brandubh."

Chapter Twenty-one

Brandubh waited for some sign of Uaid before he set a foot inside the abbey but he waited in vain. Drawing his sword, he took deliberate steps through the door, listening for any sound of warning. The shuffle of feet as an assailant took a better position. The unintentional clank of a sword against a wall or door or table. The unnatural silence of ambush.

"Eibhlin." His shout echoed through the abandoned building. "Where are you?" Silently, he begged God for mercy, for some sign that he wasn't too late.

"Brandubh." Her voice sounded strained. "Uaid is here. He means to kill you."

"I will welcome his attempt, my Lady."

"Will you be serious?"

"I have never been more serious." He followed the sound of her voice. "Keep calling, Eibhlin, so that I may find you."

"Why did you come anyway?"

Brandubh smiled at her irritation, even as the fear it masked stuck his gut like a dagger.

"He would have gotten tired of this and nobody would be getting hurt," she shouted.

"Except for you."

"Brandubh, please go. I don't want you to die because of me. Please, don't get yourself killed."

"Why, Eibhlin?" Brandubh called back to her. "Why do you care?"

"Because, I love you."

"Nice touch, Puss," Uaid said.

Brandubh grimaced at the cynical comment.

"Then you understand why I must, my Lady." He sucked in a deep breath. "Uaid. You son of a dog, you jackal, you coward. You wizened excuse for a man. You have my woman and I will kill to have her back. You may as well face me and die like a man. What say you, Uaid?"

The silence coming from the end of the dark hall seeped into Brandubh's bones like the cold mist on the bog. Every urge was to charge forward, to take her from Uaid's filthy hands.

Yet, he waited.

"All right," Uaid shouted. "You want to fight. We shall."

Is that not what we are here for? Brandubh wondered with a flash of irritation.

Out of the shadows of the end of the hall, he saw her. Her hands were tied behind her back, Uaid's razor-sharp blade dancing against her tender neck, the sight threatening to trigger the blood lust. Already, the blindness and deafness and desire to destroy began to cloud Brandubh's mind. He struggled against it. Such madness was good only for battle, where everyone was a warrior and in the fight because of desire or duty. It was his Irish legacy, and Brian, who also suffered--or was blessed--with the madness, had taught him the ways to restrain it, lest he kill without meaning to.

Tonight, he meant to. But his control was even more important, least the wrong person die. Much as it would satisfy him to cut Uaid into tiny pieces, Eibhlin was too much in the way for him to give rein to the desire.

She came closer, her spine as straight as a queen's. Right behind her, almost hidden behind her impressive height, was Uaid.

Hiding behind a woman, Brandubh thought with a mental smirk.

Once within blade-range, Uaid lunged, going over Eibhlin's back. Brandubh stood his ground.

"Brandubh!" she screamed, as the tip of Uaid's blade carved a clean swath through Brandubh's tunic. A bright red line appeared on his chest to mark Uaid's path.

The pain was minimal. One part of his mind marveled that the madness hadn't taken hold of him--the first cut was usually all it took for him to be consumed. The sword continued its path and rang against the stones of the wall, sending sparks flying.

Uaid's eyes were filled for once with uncertainty.

He'd expected the rage to take hold and now that it hasn't, he's not sure what to do, Brandubh thought, everything clear to him as it had never been.

Uaid pushed Eibhlin toward Brandubh and charged. Brandubh stepped aside and allowed her to fall to the floor behind him. Then he took his place in front of her and let his sword sing through the air.

"Stay behind me, Eibhlin."

Uaid, a good fighter, was even better because he had nothing to lose. His attack was disciplined, yet Brandubh felt the strength of desperation behind every blow as their swords clashed and crashed together.

"Aha, the Raven is clipped," Uaid crowed as his blade sliced through the skin of Brandubh's forearm.

Brandubh bit back the pain and raised his sword to parry another strike heading for his neck.

Eibhlin's choked scream distracted him enough that Uaid's blade slid off Brandubh's and only his torque prevented the glancing blow from becoming luckily lethal.

Brandubh realized too late he was allowing Uaid to back him into a corner.

"Stay here, Eibhlin," he shouted over his shoulder even as he lunged toward Uaid, his weight carrying the smaller man several paces.

Breaking off the fight, Uaid backed away, then turned and ran toward an opened door. Brandubh started after him.

"Wait, Brandubh, wait." Eibhlin grabbed his tunic. "Don't follow him, for God's sake. Let him go. Let's leave while we have the chance."

"No." He shook off her hand and went toward the door where Uaid had disappeared.

She ran ahead and slammed the door shut, throwing the bolt.

"There. He's trapped. Let's go."

"Get out of the way, Eibhlin. I will kill him this night."

"No, Brandubh. You can't. What will my mother say? What will Conor say?"

"Your mother brought me my sword before I left Ath Sionnain."

Her eyes clouded with disbelief.

He shoved her aside and opened the door.

"Stay here. If he should escape, lock yourself in one of the chambers. My friend, Gadhra, will come for you. He will take you to Craglea on Midwinter Day."

"No," she shouted and grabbed at his sleeve, but he was already halfway up the steps.

His footsteps sounded hollow as he made his way up the tower. "Uaid. I come. Are you ready to die?"

Laughter bounced off the walls and down the stairway.

"Stick your head up here, Brandubh. I will shave your neck for you." He made a sound that did indeed sound like a head being separated from its neck.

The stairs led straight up to the floor of the belfry. It was a most vulnerable position. Brandubh leaned against the wall and considered.

"Oh, come on, Brandubh. I will let you get up here before I kill you."

He laughed without humor. "Uaid, you truly are mad if you think I am going to trust anything you say."

Uaid's face appeared in the opening over his head. It was difficult to read the expression, there was so much anger and hatred mixed in with the love of a good fight. "Come, Brandubh," he said as he backed away from the entry.

"All right, Uaid," he said and finished climbing the steps to the belfry. Uaid stayed in sight the whole time, but as soon as Brandubh had both feet on the floor, he charged, sword in a high two-handed grip.

It was a clumsy move, one which Brandubh easily parried. Too easy, Brandubh thought with a growing sense of unease. He had to attack, this was going on too long. Holding his blade level, Brandubh kept his eyes locked with Uaid's and closed the distance between them. When he was within range, Brandubh would cut him in twain.

Uaid charged him again.

The clanging of steel on steel rang through the belfry like the long silent bells. Their blades slid along one another to the hilts and Uaid grabbed Brandubh's wrist and shoved.

Brandubh muffled a curse as he fell against the huge bell and nearly followed his blade down the shaft where it clattered to the stone floor below. Arms flailing, he wrapped them around the bell and held on until he felt firm footing again.

"Farewell, Brandubh. Your lady awaits my attention."

Brandubh's eyes found Uaid, in the stairway, trapdoor over his head.

With a salute of his sword, Uaid let the door fall shut and Brandubh heard the sickening sound of the sliding of a bolt. He was trapped.

* * * *

The ringing and clanging of swords echoed through the abbey. Eibhlin had followed Brandubh to the door, but now she backed away from the terrible sounds of mortal combat and leaned against the opposite wall. The cold stones chilled her through, leaving a heavy emptiness in her stomach. What if Brandubh were killed?

No, she shouted silently at herself. Don't even think it. It isn't possible Uaid could kill him. She slid down to sit on the freezing flagstone floor and prayed as she hadn't for years, calling on saints not yet born to protect Brandubh and bring him down to her whole.

The thud of something very big against the huge bell and Brandubh's bellowed curse made her jump from the floor and run across the hall just as a sword--Brandubh's sword--hit the floor under the bell's pull-rope. Stopping at the threshold, she was afraid to call out to him. If he didn't answer....

Again, Eibhlin shoved her fears behind her.

"Brandubh," she shouted as she placed her foot on the first step.

A muffled voice drifted down to her at the bottom of the stairs, but strain as she might she wasn't able to make out the words. She took the second step, refusing to consider how foolhardy her actions were. What did she hope to accomplish up there, besides getting in the way? She knew perfectly well it had been her distracting him that had gotten Brandubh cut so badly. Hell, she'd almost cost him his life when Uaid nearly decapitated him right in front of her.

Those thoughts wouldn't leave her alone. What if Uaid killed him?

Rage was supposed to be cold, she thought, but it ran like a fire through her veins at the thought of Brandubh falling to the likes of Uaid mac Conor. She'd kill the bastard herself, she promised and started running up the stairway.

The thud of the trapdoor followed by the grinding slide of the bolt brought her up short. It was a good thing, too.

A blade touched her nose. With a quirking smile, Uaid stepped down toward her, forcing her to retreat.

"Where are you going, Puss?" Uaid set the tip of his bloodied sword against her throat, stroking her pulse with the cold steel. "Your blood is racing. Were you thinking to take part in the battle?" He laughed. "Would you like to be the great queen, Maeve of Connaught, riding chariots and wielding a spear like a man?"

"What did you do to Brandubh?" Eibhlin stepped up, meaning to push past him and open the belfry door.

Uaid stopped her with a caress of the sword. "Ah, here, Puss. Brandubh is not seriously injured. Yet. He is merely confined so as not to disturb us."

The sword moved up her cheek. Uaid raised a hank of her hair and pushed it back, then rested the razor edge on the top of her ear. She could feel the bite of the blade into the tender skin.

"You are much prettier with two ears, Puss, so do not move too much. Now, let's go down, shall we?"

"Uaid!" Brandubh's booming voice rattled the walls and dust sprinkled onto their heads as his huge fists pounded on the floor above them. Eibhlin jerked her head up toward the sound.

"Ow," she yelped as Uaid's blade nicked her. Gingerly touching the cut, wincing at the sting and the sticky wetness, she glared at Uaid. "Be careful with that thing."

Uaid only looked amused. "Down."

"Uaid," Brandubh roared on the other side of the trap, punctuating his threats with another gigantic bash against the floor. "Touch her and you will not be fit for the dogs when I am finished with you."

"Join us when you can, Brandubh. We will wait for you down here, where I can entertain your woman properly. Do not make too much noise, will you?"

"Uaid!" Brandubh roared, his pounding fists raining dust on them.

One hand clamped on her upper arm, Uaid passed her on the stairway, then dragged her down behind him.

"What now, Uncle? Are you going to kill me?"

His pace unimpeded by her question, he laughed and answered. "I think I made myself very clear, Puss. You and I are going to engage in a wee bit of fornication. Once I have taken you, I will have won, don't you see? Even if he kills me, I will have taken you from him." He stopped and threw her against the wall. His eyes narrowed and his lips drew tight in a grin. "Here is as good a place as any."

In an instant, he grabbed her shoulders and pushed her to the floor. He stood over her, feet spread apart, sword in his hand.

Before she could react, Uaid slipped the sword under her gown to the juncture of her legs. With one lightning flick of his wrist, her skirt had been laid open like the belly of a fish. The tip of the sword moved up, coming to rest at the pulse in her throat. Uaid used the toe of his boot to scoot her shift up, his eyes taking in every inch of her exposed legs. Leer firmly set, he dropped the sword by his feet and grabbed the two pieces of her gown, jerking them apart, all the way to her neck.

"Ah, my, my. What a sweet morsel you are."

Eibhlin kicked at him and rolled over, pulling her rent gown together. "Don't you put your hands on me. I'll kill you myself."

Laughter mocked her threat. Uaid reached down to twist his fingers into her hair. As he pulled Eibhlin felt each strand strain against her scalp. Gritting her teeth, she followed his silent direction and got to her feet. The discomfort was forgotten with the shock of Uaid's roughened, bloodied hands snatching the neck of her gown and shift, yanking the garments down both shoulders, trapping her arms, exposing her breasts for his examination.

Humiliation washed over her when he trapped her against the wall with his body, rubbing himself against her like a stag in rut. He laid his hands over her breasts, kneading them, teasing her nipples.

Eibhlin closed her eyes against it all, hiding behind the self-induced darkness. All the while, his hands played with her.

"Please, don't." Eibhlin's eyes flew open as she heard her own voice. Uaid's enjoyment of her mortification was displayed on his face.

Damn it all. I will *not* beg him.

She straightened her spine and gazed directly at Uaid, eye to eye.

"Whatever you might do, you won't win. Brandubh would never cast me aside."

A flash of what might be admiration warmed his eyes, just for a moment before he regained his sneer.

"I have always wanted to do this on Holy Ground. What do you think of that, Puss?"

That *Puss* business was getting really old, she fumed silently, nursing her temper and trying to free her hands. The idea that her own uncle was going to rape her in an abandoned abbey was really too sick for words. Wrenching her shoulders back, she tried to get away from his groping hands.

"I can't say I think much of it, Uncle. Why don't we play Parcheesi instead?"

Uaid paused in his kneading to give her a baffled look, but Eibhlin was damned if she was going to explain Parcheesi to him.

"I won't submit to you, Uaid. You'll have to use that sword."

An ugly smile curved Uaid's lips. "Oh, I will use a sword, Puss, and you will love it."

He captured her chin and pushed head her back against the wall. She saw it coming and refused to let her panic rise to cloud her reason.

I can stand this, she thought. As long as Brandubh doesn't die.

Uaid's mouth came hard on hers, grinding, hurting. Eibhlin wouldn't open her lips to him. She would resist, not giving an inch nor taking any insult she could return.

"Come on, Puss. Why do you not simply enjoy what can be between us?"

His gentle plea confused her, putting her off-stride so she couldn't recover in time to stop his next assault. Tongue plunging, one hand bruising her breast and the other holding her head still, his weight keeping her in place, Uaid simply overpowered her.

Her anger rose again as she felt him grind his erection against her thigh. She struggled against the heavy woolen manacles that had been her gown, shifting it upward to free her hands. All those self-defense courses hadn't been a total waste, she thought as she grabbed Uaid by the balls and twisted.

Uaid's howl ripped through the empty building, echoing off the walls, answering from one end of the hall to the other. When he released her to apply both hands to protect his manhood, she ducked underneath his arm and ran inside the nearest chamber, slamming the thick oak door and pushing the bolt closed.

Above the thudding of her heart, she heard the ring of metal against the walls. She slipped open the peephole and glanced out. Uaid stalked the hallway, his steps still unsteady, his eyes darting from one wall to the other.

"All right, Puss. You want to play dirty, I can do that, too. When I find you, there will not be any kissy-kissy. It will be as rough as I can make it."

He would. She could hear the finality in his voice.

"He cannot save you, Puss. You are done. Give yourself up and I will make it quick."

Uaid came alongside the cell where Eibhlin hid. She eased away from the peephole and stood behind the door. She checked her breathing and made not a sound.

The doorlatch rattled as he tried it. "So, here you are." The thick planks of the door bowed when Uaid slammed against it. The bolt bent, just a little, and she knew with a shock of fear it would not hold for long.

Where the hell was Brandubh? What was taking him so long getting down from that belfry? It wasn't credible to her that he couldn't, that he wouldn't, arrive in time to save her from Uaid's threats.

Then it hit her. Brandubh's raging threats and the thundering blows of his fists on the trapdoor had stopped.

* * * *

Brandubh shoved himself from the floor, cursing the day of Uaid's birth and praying that today was the day the worthless crowbait was destined to die.

"I have to get out of here," he said aloud. "She is down there with him, alone." He convinced himself it was not the old fear crowding into his mind, the fear of weakness and impotence.

Brandubh stalked around the belfry, approaching the open windows where the peeling of the bells had called the faithful to worship, counted off the hours, mourned loss. The sheer drop of perhaps fifty cubits discouraged any ideas of escape in this direction.

"Damn." He whirled on his heel and looked around for another possibility.

He thought of the sword, lying on the floor below the bell.

Again the frustration overtook him and he began pacing in the dark. So great was his anger that he did not look at the floor as he passed by the great bell. It wasn't until his right foot found no floor under it that he realized his mistake.

"God's Blood!" he cursed as he shifted his weight but fell anyway. His arse hit the floor and he hugged the damned bell once more to keep from falling to his death through the opening under it.

He pushed against the bell and swung his leg back up onto the floor of the belfry. As he did so, he noticed the pull of something wrapped around his ankle.

"What is this?" He bent toward his foot, fingers out. "A rope. How convenient." He whispered a prayer of thanks as his questing hand touched the twisted flax fibers used to ring the bell from the floor below. Standing, he traced the rope to the arm which tipped the bell to make it ring.

He pulled the rope up and wrapped a good length around the beam from which the bell was suspended, tying a good strong knot and dropping it back down. In the darkness, he couldn't tell if it reached the floor.

I suppose I will find out soon, he thought. With a yank on the rope to test its strength, Brandubh stepped off into the opening, easing by the bell to avoid sending Uaid a warning. He wrapped his feet around the rope and started down.

He was halfway down when the roar of a wounded beast ripped through the abbey. Brandubh stopped, hanging on the rope, listening to the commotion from below. The scurry of a hunted animal seeking cover was followed by the hunter, clanging his weapon on the walls to terrify and intimidate.

When Uaid's voice echoed through the hall, with its threats of rape and murder, Brandubh loosened the hold of his feet on the rope and let his hands slacken. The rope cut into his palms and burned the insides of his thighs as he descended.

In the dark, he couldn't see the floor and, unprepared, hit the cold stones in a heap.

Brandubh shook his stinging hands, then picked up his sword and cut strips from his tunic. Grateful for the pain that would keep him focused on the job at hand, he wrapped the strips around his palms. It wouldn't do to have his sword slip from bloody hands when he was ready to deal the death stroke.

Hefting his sword, he entered the hall where now he could hear the thud of a man's body connecting with the thick planks of a chamber door.

She was behind a door. She was safe.

Brandubh felt the madness rise again, blinding, deafening, urging him toward his prey. No longer needing to control himself, he raised his voice and let it ring off the stones.

"Eibhlin, stay behind that door until this is done."

* * * *

"Finally," Eibhlin whispered in relief, hearing Brandubh's voice. "Where the hell have you been?" she shouted at him through the door.

The door bowed inward once more. An uneasy silence followed, broken only by the sounds of shuffling feet and the song of metal slashing through the air. Eibhlin jerked open the peephole, frantically searching the hallway.

"Brandubh, I don't want you killing anybody."

He didn't answer her. She pushed at the bolt. "Damn it, what's wrong with this thing?" She shoved against it with all her strength, still it wouldn't budge.

The first clang of swords startled her. It had been so quiet until then.

Feeling somehow she'd be better off not to, still Eibhlin shoved open the peephole and peered out.

And caught her breath. Her stomach turned. If she hadn't heard his voice before, she would never have known him. Brandubh's face was transformed into a mask of unnatural fury. His eyes appeared unseeing, though the onyx darkness flashed with fire. He wielded his sword with one hand, toying with his victim.

For victim Uaid was. Even with both hands wrapped around the hilt of his own weapon, he couldn't parry Brandubh's slicing blade. No words passed between them as Brandubh cut into Uaid's flesh, again and again, with the precision of a surgeon opening up a patient for life-saving surgery.

But the result of these incisions would be only death.

"Brandubh, stop!" Eibhlin pounded on the door. "Don't do this."

Her begging didn't affect him that she could see.

With the back of his huge hand, an insulting blow, Brandubh sent Uaid flying across the hallway. Then leveling his sword, Brandubh slowly pursued his prey for the final killing stroke.

Eibhlin held her breath.

"Brandubh. Don't do this."

The eyes that turned to her were not Brandubh's eyes. They were the blood-crazed eyes of a killer. The eyes of a man who would do murder or die trying.

Something inside her died a little. The gentleness with which he'd loved her, the tenderness he'd shown her while she was sick, the love he had for his mother and father, for his horses, and for her--all seemed a dim memory now. This hulk of a man, this warrior, this killer, wasn't the man she wanted to have children with.

That thought choked her.

Uaid's head passed by her door. "Come, Brandubh. Shall you see what I've done to her? I took her while you were stuck in that belfry. She was sweet as a partridge, tender as a lamb."

Brandubh didn't answer his taunt. That frightened her more than the thought he might kill her uncle before her eyes. Turning to face the retreating Uaid, Brandubh held his sword level. Then he closed his eyes and took a deep breath.

Eibhlin imitated him. He was coming to his senses. She had reached him.

"He can't beat you, Brandubh. There's no honor in killing him. Take him back and let the judges deal with him. Let Dougal make an example of him, Brandubh. Please, don't murder him."

His eyes met hers. She held his gaze, begging him not to give in to the murderer lurking behind his rage. His shoulders drooped as he relaxed the monstrous tension that filled his whole body.

"Aye, my Lady," he said, his voice raw and rusty as a tool left out in the rain. "As you command." He lowered the tip of his sword toward the floor.

"Thank you," Eibhlin offered to God as she melted against the rough wood door.

Her relief was short-lived.

"You think to take me back to die a coward's death?" Uaid shouted. Eibhlin looked out in time to see Uaid pull his dagger and raise his sword. "I never thought to see you take orders from a woman, Brandubh."

"Don't listen, Brandubh. He's just trying to make you kill him. He knows it would come between us."

"I know, my Lady, now that the rage has left me. I am not a boy to be fooled by such a trick. I will not kill him unless he insists upon it."

That didn't reassure her. "Please." She knew she was becoming redundant.

"Yes, Puss, plead with him. He's a beast, is he not? You saw before, the lust for blood on his face. When he is in such a state, he drinks blood, did you know?"

For just a moment, she believed it, especially when Brandubh didn't bother to deny it.

"Are you so anxious to go to Hell, Uaid?" Brandubh asked, the calmness in his voice surprising her.

Uaid stood defiant. "I prefer death and damnation to seeing you live."

Such hatred was unfathomable to her. She had nothing else to say. Someone was going to die here tonight, she realized with clarity. To these men, dying in battle was the most honorable way to pass to the other world. But she couldn't condone it. Death had never been anything to her but an enemy to be thwarted.

Brandubh caught her eye. If she'd ever hoped to be telepathic, it was now. Her heart cried out for him to put aside the sword, to take her home. His face told her that he could not.

He sighed and looked away. "Come, Uaid. Take my head, if you can."

Uaid's thin smile showed his acceptance of the challenge. "It is well."

Sword and knife ready, Uaid charged forward, into the face of death. Though it should have been easy to close the peephole, Eibhlin felt compelled to stand there and watch, time slowing to a crawl, while Uaid covered the little distance between him and Brandubh. Every event was crystal, every motion distinct.

Brandubh stood unmoving, calm. His eyes never wavered from Uaid's. Uaid's sword flashed upward toward Brandubh's neck. The blow was easily parried with a dropped stroke as Brandubh forced Uaid down. The glint of metal warned Eibhlin only an instant before Uaid's dagger closed on its target--Brandubh's ribs.

Her cry of warning died in her throat as Brandubh caught Uaid's wrist. Almost as though filling the void, Uaid roared and twisted out of Brandubh's hold. Sword again raised, for Brandubh hadn't disarmed him, Uaid swept the blade up and then down on a sure killing path. Brandubh ducked under the blade and brought his own sword up. Once on its way, it sliced through Uaid's arm like butter.

Eibhlin spun away from the sight and covered her mouth to stifle the scream that came from her soul.

"Oh, my God, my God, my God," she chanted. Eyes closed, she leaned against the door, hoping the nauseous rippling in her stomach would die... calm quickly.

"Take my head, Brandubh." Uaid's pinched request brought her to her senses, but she refused to look, terrified that Brandubh would actually comply.

"No." Brandubh answered as she heard him kick Uaid's blades away. One, the dagger, slid across the floor with a clean metal-on-stone sound. Then a muffled *clank* hit the far wall, making her wonder if Uaid's sword remained clenched in his lifeless hand.

"Oh," she murmured, again closing her hand over her mouth to quiet her quivering stomach.

This kind of thing never happened in Oregon. Her sudden choice to remain now made no sense at all.

Brandubh knocked on the door. "Open the door, Eibhlin. We're going home."

Home. Did she even know where that was anymore?

Hadn't she asked herself that question before?

"I can't. Uaid bent the bolt when he tried to break it down."

"Move away, then."

Clutching the remnants of her gown around her, she did as he ordered, not even sure now she *wanted* him to get her out.

The door fell inward, hinges torn from the doorjamb. He stood in the doorway, swordless at last, covered in his own blood and Uaid's. A spray had covered the whole left side of his face, probably from the big artery in Uaid's arm when he'd....

"Come," he said, offering her his less-bloody hand.

The same hand that had coaxed her to such joy now appalled her. Eibhlin forced her way by him, disgusted by the feeling, the smell, the sight of him.

"My Lady," Brandubh whispered as she passed.

Eibhlin stopped. The words came from her in a rush, unbidden, unintended, but still she found she meant them.

"Don't call me that ever again. I will not be your lady. I will not stay here with you. I will leave here if it kills me."

"Eibhlin."

Her heart broke at the sound in his voice. She had to explain to him and she would, when she herself understood what had happened. She spared a look at Uaid, lying on the floor, his life pooling around him.

"I wish you a long existence in Hell, Uaid. You deserve all the torments Satan can devise for what you've done."

"My lady," he replied weakly with a courtly gesture of his remaining hand.

She headed toward the courtyard. The smell of death was too strong in here and she needed some air or she would suffocate.

Brandubh followed her into the entryway, seizing her arm and turning her around.

"Eibhlin, you cannot mean what you are saying. I will not believe you would leave me. Not now."

"Believe it, Brandubh. Believe it. *Especially* now. You almost cut him into shark chum right before my very eyes. You would still do it."

"Yes," Brandubh nodded, after a momentary look of perplexity. "If he survives, do you think he will give up on his revenge? He can hire men who would do things to you that you cannot even imagine." He nodded again, more forcefully this time. "I would kill for you."

"I didn't see anything going on out here for me, Brandubh. I saw a blood-crazed animal and I was disgusted by it."

That wasn't true, it wasn't fair, and Eibhlin knew it. Looking into his eyes, she could see the pain her words had caused and she turned away from him. He had feared for her, he had followed her, alone, to risk his own life to save hers.

She knew he needed to be strong, able to protect what was his. If not for him she'd be dead already. Hadn't she even threatened to kill Uaid herself? But, there was a lot of difference between threats and actually picking up a sword to do the job.

No, she couldn't get past the horror of it all, the cruel agony of life in this time. She'd been right in the first place. She didn't belong here. She was the product of a more civilized, less breathtakingly barbaric time.

"Take me back, Brandubh. Now."

His eyes went dull. "As you wish, my Lady. I will get my horse." With one glance to see that Uaid was still lying defeated on the floor, Brandubh went out into the cold night.

Eibhlin couldn't bear to watch him and turned back toward the hallway just in time to see Uaid, bloody stump hanging by his right side, grab Brandubh's sword from the floor and stumble toward her.

"One last try, eh, Puss?"

So amazed that he had the strength to get up, much less walk with a huge sword in his hand, Eibhlin couldn't make a sound. Uaid took another step and raised the weapon over his head. When it landed the stroke would cut her in two. She could only watch the blade as it swept back in preparation for the final blow.

A whistle passed by her ear and a look of disbelief appeared on Uaid's face. A patch of red spread across his saffron tunic from the middle of his chest. In the center, like the stamen of a flower, was the hilt of a dagger.

No, no, no. The words formed on Uaid's lips, but she heard no sound as he fell at her feet, sword clanging against the stones of the floor.

Eibhlin backed away from the body of her mother's brother and turned to run out into the cleansing air. Her feet froze when she saw Brandubh standing in the doorway.

They faced each other, eyes locked together. Eibhlin felt her emotions close up shop, inundated, overcome, exhausted.

Finally, Brandubh broke the spell. He yanked off his mantle and swept it around her shoulders, pulling it tight and daring her with a look to shake it off. "You are not attired decently." Standing aside, he waved his hand toward the open door. "Come, my Lady. Let us go."

Chapter Twenty-two

Brandubh put her on Conchobar and mounted behind her. He reached for the reins, using the action as an excuse to hug her to him. She didn't resist, but held herself as stiff as a statue. Not a word passed her lips.

Yet had her eyes spoken loudly enough, Brandubh thought while he held her, allowing Conchobar to take them both home. December's cold wind whipped across the plain, slapping his hair around his face and stinging his eyes, yet it was as nothing compared to the sting of her expression at the abbey.

His actions, spurred by fear for her, had so disgusted her that she was now loath to touch him. There was more. Sadness, a sense of loss. Conchobar's long strides, even carrying the two of them, ate up the miles while Brandubh tried to think of some way to heal the breach between them. Too soon, they reached gates of Ath Sionnain, with nothing said.

He brought Conchobar to a stop before the stone steps of his father's house.

"Take me to Conor's." Her first words since leaving the abbey were colder than the drops of rain that pelted him and soaked him to the skin.

"You will remain here."

"I will not. Conor is my nearest male kin and I will accept his protection and none other." Her voice had not risen with the heat of her words, but remained as even and unfeeling as before.

"Nay, Eibhlin. Brian put you under Dougal's protection and there you shall stay." Brandubh tossed his leg over the saddle and dismounted.

Before he could help her down, Eibhlin seized the reins and jerked Conchobar's head around, kicking his sides. The powerful haunches bunched and exploded in a burst, all but unseating her.

It is a good thing Conchobar is fatigued, Brandubh thought as he whistled a signal for the animal to return. This Conchobar did, in spite of the heartless wrenching he endured from Eibhlin's attempts to turn him again. The big black trotted back to Brandubh, coming to a stop before him. Brandubh took the reins from her hands.

"Here, my Lady. I will not allow you to harm Conchobar's mouth with your careless sawing." He set his hands around her waist to take her down.

The impact of her foot with his armpit caught him by surprise. He seized her ankle and pulled her from the saddle, catching her against his chest.

"Woman, are you mad?"

"Mad! You have the gall to ask me if I am mad? You cut a human being to pieces and now you act as though nothing happened. Me mad?" The explosion nearly blew him down and he released her, letting her stand on the muddy ground.

She leaned against Conchobar, looking so tired, so shaken. He wanted to carry her in and lay with her in a clean bed and wrap her in his arms. He wanted to sleep with her curled alongside him, her head pillowed on his shoulder, her warm breath brushing across his chest.

In truth, the day's events had not been easier on him than on her. True, killing in battle was nothing new, but Uaid had been a kinsman, nearly a brother. Killing him had not been easy, even with so clear a choice.

Now, they were both tired and wet and in no condition to discuss this matter. He knew he should let her go to Conor's.

Yet, he heard himself arguing with her.

"Listen well, my Lady. Uaid mac Conor was after my head. You heard him." His words were true, but they rang hollow in his ears. What must they sound like to her?

"He could never have killed you." After the words left her lips, her eyes widened. "What I mean is, he wasn't strong enough to kill you... I mean, he...."

Had that been a compliment? Having no response, he remained silent. She babbled on.

"You could have restrained him and brought him back."

"Do you understand our ways so little?"

"I am not stupid, Brandubh."

Her shoulders stooped under the burden of holding herself up. She was exhausted and here he was arguing with her. Yet he could not stop trying to defend what he'd done.

"He would have been humiliated. This way, at least, he died with some honor." He would never forget if he lived to be one hundred, the sight of Uaid coming at her with a broadsword. She apparently had, though. "Perhaps I should remind you that I saved your life when I killed Uaid."

"Nonsense. He wasn't going to kill me."

Surely, she *was* mad to say that.

"Eibhlin, he had a blade raised over your head." Ruthlessly, Brandubh snatched his mantle from her shoulders, revealing the rent garment she held together in a futile attempt to cover herself.

"I suppose this was simply an accident. His blade slipped, did it? And this, Eibhlin." He grabbed the neck of his tunic and ripped it down to his belly. Her anguished gasp was satisfying. Glancing down, he saw the gash across his chest had crusted over but was still red and slightly puffy around the edges. The raindrops dripped scarlet over his exposed skin.

"And this." He tore the sleeve down his arm to reveal the wound in his forearm still oozing. "It was a pleasure outing, was it? Mayhap I should apologize, Lady, for killing you uncle while he was trying to kill us both."

"Brandubh, let her come in and warm herself."

His mother's voice drifted from the open doorway of the house. He glanced back at her where she stood in the doorway, Moira at her shoulder.

"The lady may do as she wishes, Mother. I must see to my horse." Brandubh turned on his heel and started for the stables, Conchobar following behind like a dog.

* * * *

Pushing away the truth of his words, Eibhlin watched him go, heart empty, soul aching. Yet she couldn't call him back, haunted as she was by the too-fresh image of the man she loved hacking and slashing another man to ribbons.

"Come, dear one," Moira whispered as she laid a mantle across Eibhlin's shoulders and guided her like a hen one of her chicks through the wide front doors. "Let me get you a warm bath. You are chilled through."

"Yes, indeed. Come, Eibhlin." Sadbh preceded them inside and clapped her hands, bringing a gaggle of women to do her bidding while they got an eyeful to speculate on later in the kitchen. "Hot water and a tub in the Lady's chamber right away." The women scurried away, their whispers rippling through the great hall.

Eibhlin refused to listen. It didn't matter. She'd ask Dougal to take her to Kincora. The solstice was only days away.

"Just a few days longer," she whispered. Just a few days before she could be in civilization again.

"What did you say, dear one?" Moira's arm tightened around Eibhlin's waist.

"Nothing," she lied.

Though her eyes wrinkled with concern, Moira said nothing more, but only opened the latch to Eibhlin's chamber and pushed open the door, allowing Eibhlin to go in first.

The rushes have been changed, she thought, sniffing the fresh application of lavender and thyme. The bed looked so inviting that she headed for it.

"No, no, you will have a warm bath first to take the chill off." Moira bustled about, gathering clean underlinen and a fresh woolen gown. Sadbh rushed in with a pair of thick woolen stockings.

"Here, Moira, make her put these on."

"Thank you, Lady." Moira took them and laid them on the bed. "Come, Eibhlin, let's get those wet clothes off."

Eibhlin could almost hear the thread snap inside her head. "I can undress myself. I can take a bath by myself. I can take care of myself. I only want to sleep now. So, please, leave my chamber." She turned her back on them, hoping the gesture of dismissal would work.

"Excuse me, my fine lady," Moira said, "I do not know what has happened this night, mayhap I do not wish to learn, but I do know you will chill if you do not get warm. Now, get in this chair and sit by the fire until your bath arrives."

Glancing at her mother, Eibhlin saw a girl of only eighteen, but she remembered well that there would be no getting around her without a tremendous battle of wills.

For which Eibhlin was just too tired.

After she'd sat in the chair as instructed, Moira knelt by her side. With a gentle hand, she brushed aside Eibhlin's windblown, tangled hair. "Tomorrow, dear one. Tomorrow, you will tell me all. Until then, you will let me take care of you."

"All right, Mama."

Moira and Sadbh helped her out of her sodden clothes and wrapped her like a mummy in a heated linen cloth. A delicious warmth seeped around her to replace the chill she'd almost gotten used to.

Sadbh answered the knock at the door. "Bring it here by the fire." With the characteristic wave of her hand, she showed the two servants where to place the empty oak tub. A maid followed with another length of linen with which she lined the inside. Then the procession of water bearers came, each carrying two large buckets of steaming water.

The whole process was ridiculous, Eibhlin thought as she watched. You should be able to twist open a tap and get all the hot water you wanted. Suddenly, she missed it all so much. Her mother--her real mother, not this child--her father, her work. The dreams she'd had of finding cures for dread, killer diseases that snuffed out lives before they'd been lived. Coffee. Chocolate. Take-out Chinese.

Silly, stupid things like old movies and frilly panties. A place where men didn't go around hacking each other to pieces.

A gasp exploded from Eibhlin's throat. The blood, the severed arm, the whole ghastly scene reappeared on her closed eyelids like a movie flickering on a screen before her in Dolby stereo. She remembered the sound of Brandubh's sword cutting through Uaid's flesh--a soppy, slightly rasping sound--and the crunch of bone breaking under the force of the blade.

"What is it, dear one? Why do you weep?"

Eibhlin could only shake her head.

"Moira, let her be tonight," Sadbh counseled. "She needs to soak and sleep. Tomorrow will be soon enough for her to talk."

Moira didn't take her eyes off Eibhlin's face. "Come. Into your bath now."

Eibhlin didn't even feel the two women take the linen wrapping from her body, nor did she remember being helped into the tub. Nor did she remember laying her head back against the pillow thoughtfully placed behind her and falling asleep.

Nor did she remember saying, "Mama, put a compress of St. John's wort on Brandubh's wounds, please."

* * * *

Brandubh poured grain into Conchobar's feed bin and watched the stallion dig his muzzle into the food.

"You did well, Conchobar."

The horse raised his head at the sound of his master's voice. Freshly brushed and cooled, with food for his belly and Deirdre in the stall next to him, her sides not even bowed yet with the foal she carried, Conchobar was content.

Such contentment evaded Brandubh. He'd done the best he could. He'd gone after her and saved her from a madman.

"Now she calls me a barbarian!"

Conchobar snapped his head up, his look rebuking Brandubh for disturbing his meal.

"I do not know what she expects of me, Conchobar." He twirled a stalk of grass between his fingers. "I should have known this would be her reaction. She has ever thought me a mindless warrior."

"Does he ever answer you, son?" Dougal entered the stable and leaned against Conchobar's stall, ignoring Brandubh's sigh.

He'd wanted to put off seeing his father. When the particulars of the night's activities were known, Uaid's father would have to be told. That was a visit that Brandubh could not face tonight. At least not without a full measure of ale.

"Here, *paisano*," Dougal said as he reached over and grabbed Conchobar's forelock, pulling the horse's muzzle from the grainbox. Conchobar puffed a greeting and nuzzled Dougal's cheek. Out of the silence came Dougal's next words. "Did you kill him, son?"

Brandubh detected no condemnation in the tone of Dougal's question.

"Yes, Father. I did."

Dougal nodded and with a sigh said, "I feared it would be so. Tell me."

Brandubh told him. After the tale was done, Dougal's brow furrowed. "Did he hurt Eibhlin?"

"No. He threatened to, but he did not."

"You are certain? Your mother tells me the Lady's clothing was torn from her body. Mayhap some of her reaction is due to being violated."

The idea had Brandubh ready to spill Uaid's blood again. "He did not touch her in that fashion."

"Then why does she act so strangely?"

"We are savages, Father. Barbarians who fight for sport, kill for fun." His anger cooled a bit. Clearly the scene had been terrible. He could understand how she could be upset by it.

He was upset by it.

"She saw him die. I do not believe she has ever seen anyone die like that before."

"You saved her life, Brandubh. Uaid would have killed her. He was mad."

"I know that, Father, but rather than have her look at me with eyes filled with disgust, I would that I had died there."

Dougal seized him by the shoulders and jerked him around.

"Never again say such a thing in my presence." Eyes glazed with the tears he would not shed, he growled to clear his throat, then squeezed Brandubh's shoulders before releasing his grip. "Mayhap your lady is suffering from shock. When she has had time to reflect, she will see that you had no choice. Tomorrow, we will go to Conor together. For now, your mother has ordered a bath for you and there is great commotion among the women as to who will assist you." Dougal wiggled his eyebrows.

"Can you never be serious, Dougal?"

"Only when absolutely necessary, son." He smiled and passed his hand fondly down the back of Brandubh's head as he used to when Brandubh was a boy. "Don't be long. Your mother needs to get a look at you." Giving Conchobar one last fond smack on the neck, Dougal left them alone.

Brandubh watched him go, the giant of a man he loved above all others. Dougal had once had the answer to any problem. Brandubh wished life were that simple again.

Having no better plans, he followed his father's order and returned to the house. After dismissing the gaggle of helpful women, he stripped off his torn clothing and sank into the hot water.

Surrounded by warmth, the fire crackling in the fireplace, newly spread rushes scenting the air, Brandubh tried to think through his situation. His efforts lasted only a few minutes before he drifted into a dream of his night in Eibhlin's bed. The room's scents faded, replaced by hers. Every detail played out in his mind, evoking every reaction. He could taste her again. Her skin was smooth and soft against his.

His body ached for her.

"Brandubh, do you mind if I come in?" Moira's voice came to him from the door.

Jerking from his dream, he sprang forward, splashing cooling water over the sides of the tub. Of all the times....

"I'm in my bath, Moira."

"Of course. I brought something for your wounds."

He couldn't remember being this uncomfortable before.

"That is generous of you, Moira. Considering...." What did one say in such a situation?

Moira pushed open the door. "No, let's not talk about it. Eibhlin, actually, asked me to look after you."

"She did?" He was surprised.

A slight smile curved Moira's lips. "She was practically asleep, but she did say it. Come along, get out and wrap up so I can take care of you and get to my own bed before daybreak." She handed him a long length of linen. "Don't be shy, Brandubh. It isn't as though I don't have a brother...."

Her stricken countenance cut a fresh wound across Brandubh's heart. "I am sorry, Moira."

She waved her hand. "I am the one who is sorry. Much of his guilt is mine as well." She again held out the linen.

"Thank you, Moira."

"Tis I who should thank you. You saved her life."

Their eyes met, forgiveness and acceptance offered and received. Moira averted her eyes as he took the linen and rose from the tub, carefully wrapping the length around his waist before stepping out onto the rushes. Taking a chair by the fire, he watched Moira pour a reddish oil onto a clean cloth.

She worked silently, first on his arm, gently covering the gash with the treated cloth and wrapping it. Then she moved to his chest.

"Did you learn this from Eibhlin?" He pointed to the oil. "The herbs and such?"

"Yes. She knows so much," Moira answered, her voice filled with pride. She motioned him forward and began wrapping a long swath of cloth around him to hold the compress in place. "I imagine you'd rather Eibhlin be doing this."

Brandubh smiled. "Why would you think that?"

Moira's expression was canny. "Why indeed?"

"I am certain my company would not be congenial to her right now."

"She did seem rather upset with you."

Such an understatement, he thought. "She said she will return to her own place."

"Did she mean it? How could her feelings change so quickly?"

He felt his smile fade. "She had just seen.... She claims her place is more civilized than this. I fear I killed her feelings for me when I killed Uaid." As the words left his mouth Brandubh could have cut his own throat.

Moira smiled a sad, forgiving smile. "My father does not know?"

"Not yet. I could not go to him tonight, Moira."

"I understand. 'Twill not be an easy thing. Uaid has brought much shame on my family." She tied the cloth around Brandubh's chest and sat back on her heels. "As have I."

"As have I," Brandubh answered. "And it appears my punishment will be to lose what I had hoped to gain."

"Eibhlin. You love her, then?"

"Do you have to ask? I thought it was more than obvious."

Moira sat before the fire and crossed her legs underneath her gown. "Perhaps to those who see the look in your eyes when you think no one is watching. I can tell you that she loves you. I would have her happy, Brandubh, and I do not believe she belongs in that place she left behind. She belongs here, with you. Why else is she here if not to be with you?"

"Perhaps there are many reasons." He stopped before he said more. The future was a dangerous thing, even if a man believed it was immutable.

"Think of the way she blended in here so easily, as if she'd been born here. Besides, think of the good she can do, Brandubh, with her skills." Moira fixed him with knowing eyes. "Think of the sons she will give you."

He repaid her with a narrowed stare. "Are we not getting ahead of ourselves, my Lady Matchmaker? You saw for yourself how things are. How can I change her mind when she is so determined to leave me as soon as she can get herself to Craglea?"

Moira smiled, the sunshine of her countenance a reminder of Eibhlin's. "That, my Lord, is your problem. Eibhlin has told me I will meet her father on Beltain of my eighteenth year. I will convince her to stay to help me prepare. You will have four months to convince me you will care for my daughter and make her happy or I will take her with me."

These strange goings-on left him at a disadvantage. Why did women always seem to understand the rules, leaving men to play along with them or not at all?

He did know he didn't like being dictated to by this slip of a girl.

"Your ultimatum is unnecessary. I promised her I would take her to Craglea if that is her wish."

"Good." Moira rose from her seat and brushed her skirts. "In the meantime, perhaps you can show her why she should want to stay. Mayhap offer to let her civilize you."

He raised his eyebrow. "That could get a man killed."

Moira laughed. "Then make her love you so thoroughly that she could not think of leaving you. Four months, Brandubh. Make the most of it," she said as she picked up her things and left the room.

Brandubh sat for a long time, staring into the flames.

Make her love me? She'd said she did. He knew she did. She wanted to stay, but thought him and his world too barbaric for her.

She'd been afraid to stay for fear of changing the future.

He'd overcome that objection.

Could he overcome this one?

Then he thought of his life, his real life and how little of it she knew. His course was clear. All he needed was a little time.

Chapter Twenty-three

The next morning, rested but restless, Eibhlin faced the gauntlet of curious stares and straightened her spine. No one would see how she hurt. As she headed for the lord's table to put her request to Dougal, her heart fussed and fumed with her stubborn determination to go to Craglea and leave this place.

"There you are," Moira appeared at her elbow and linked her arm through Eibhlin's. "Come, sit with me, so we may talk."

Eibhlin glanced at Moira's face. "Sounds like you have something in particular to discuss."

"Indeed," Moira said, sliding onto a bench at a table near the lord's table. She applied her attention to pouring cups of ale for them both. "I had a talk with Brandubh last night. His wounds are clean and bandaged."

Moira looked aside at her as she cut some bread from the warm, crusty loaf in front of her. Clearly, she wanted to gauge Eibhlin's reaction to her mention of Brandubh.

"I'm glad he will recover," Eibhlin said as she took a seat beside her and tried not to look concerned about Brandubh's health. Unwilling to give her any more, Eibhlin said nothing else. "Is that what was so important?"

"No," Moira said, laying bread and cheese on the napkin before Eibhlin. "Actually, I wanted to discuss you and Brandubh. Did you really tell him you were intending to leave as soon as you could get to the Crag? In spite of giving him your word."

"What does that mean?"

"You accepted his offer. He has already given Father possession of the cattle."

"He got ahead of himself, then, didn't he?"

"Eibhlin, he risked his life to save you."

"That's ridiculous. Uaid wasn't man enough to take Brandubh. Oh, Mama, I'm sorry. I...."

"Dear one, Uaid, my brother, was not the man who stole you away. Ever since Caoimhe took her own life.... Well, it is all over now, is it not?"

Eibhlin saw the wound that would never be completely healed, but threads of recollection had woven together until she had the whole of the cloth. Now she would give what salve she could for this one hurt.

"Mama, in the cave, Uaid told me things, things I had forgotten, with the fever and all. Anyway, Mama, he was with Caoimhe when she died." Eibhlin related the story of the accident that had taken Caoimhe's life and Uaid's part in it. "He was mad from the guilt, I think."

"Then, it wasn't suicide." Moira's eyes glistened with grateful tears. "Thank sweet Jesus," she groaned and laid her head on her arm. "Father will be so relieved. We can move her."

"Move her?"

Moira sat up and wiped the trailing tears from her eyes.

"We couldn't bury her in hallowed ground, because we thought she had taken her own life. But, if it was an accident, we can bury her properly. Oh, thank God. And thank you, dear one, for telling me this. Though I am so sorry of the circumstances." Moira shook her head. "It has been such a terrible time for everybody. So many things said and done that cannot be taken back."

"Do you think we will ever get over it, Mama?"

"I hope so, Eibhlin, I truly hope so."

They sat in silence for a few moments, sipping ale and nibbling at their food. Then Moira turned to Eibhlin.

"Ah, we must deal with the present. What of your promise to marry Brandubh?"

"What of it? Conor will have to give back the cattle. He can have mine. I won't be needing them."

Moira nodded. "I see. What are your plans?"

"I'll ask Dougal to take me to Kincora as soon as possible. I want to be there on the solstice if I can."

"Oh." Moira's voice was small. Eibhlin knew that tone.

"What's wrong?"

"Nothing, I suppose. Well, there is only four months until Beltain. I was hoping that you would consent to remain to help me prepare for my own journey. Things will be so strange. How can I go with no idea of what I will find?"

"Mama, don't worry. Dad will be there to take care of you."

Moira blushed prettily. "Yes. And I will be able to communicate since the language has not changed."

Eibhlin set her cup down. "Actually, Mama, nobody much speaks Irish. You taught me how to speak it. And you also got me interested in plants and you taught me how to play the harp."

"I did?"

"I mean, you will."

Moira's eyes grew large and round. "My, this is strange, is it not?" She recovered quickly, as Eibhlin had seen her do many times when she saw the way to get what she wanted. Patting Eibhlin's hand, she said, "But you see? I prepared you. Now, you are here to prepare me. That must explain your being here. That is, if we disregard the possibility that you came here to be with Brandubh."

"Mama," Eibhlin said, "please don't make more of this than there is to be made. I fell through a rip in some kind of... I don't know, a separation between where I was and where I am. There is no eternal matchmaking service pairing up people."

"Too bad. I would prefer to know someone is directing this thing." Moira nibbled her cheese. "You still have not answered my question."

At the same instant that Eibhlin was trying to remember what question Moira was talking about, Brandubh entered the hall to a wave of appreciative whispers sweeping along as he made his way to the front of the hall. Eibhlin, in spite of her efforts, found herself looking too, appreciating his masculine beauty.

But Brandubh was different today. The fine woolen tunic had been replaced by heavy linen. His long legs were enclosed in leather breeches and laced boots, Viking style. Gone was the golden warrior's torque he had worn every day she'd known him and his hair was pulled back and tied with a leather thong. No sword hung at his plain belt. His only weapon was the small knife he used at meals.

He walked differently, too. There was a leisure in his step she'd not seen before.

"My Lady," he said with a nod as he passed her.

Eibhlin raised her eyebrows when the smell hit her. He always had the scent of the fields about him, the pleasant man and horse smell that she associated with him. This morning, though, he must have done more than pet and feed them.

"Is there some problem?" he asked.

"No," she replied, raising her napkin to her nose.

"Do I offend you, my Lady? Perhaps I should take my meal in the barn with the horses."

"That is not for me to say. If your mother permits you at her table...."

One cheek dimpled and his eyes shone. "Thank you." He took a step toward the head table. "Oh, by the way, I have had word from Lon Dubh. We have need of a healer's gifts. Would you be willing to go there for a day or two to treat some minor sicknesses?"

Moira turned a hopeful eye to Eibhlin.

"What a wonderful idea! Then you would have another reason to stay than just because of me...."

The martyr complex must be part of being a mother. It must be caused by the hormonal changes in the woman's body when she carries a child. Of course, Moira hadn't carried a child yet.

"All right, Mother. I'll stay until Beltain."

Moira smiled as though canary feathers were caught in her teeth.

Well, Eibhlin fumed silently, what else could I do? Moira is only eighteen and there's so much I can help her understand, so her new life will be easier to adjust to. It's only four more months, after all. What's four months in a whole lifetime?

"And my request, my Lady? May I have the pleasure of your company at Lon Dubh?"

Brandubh waited for her answer. Eibhlin realized with a start his earthy scent suddenly wasn't all that unpleasant.

"All right, Lord Brandubh. I will be glad to help out."

"Good," he said, smile breaking out fully. "We will leave after the meal." With a bow, he went on to his own breakfast.

Eibhlin noted with a secret smile Sadbh had raised her own napkin to her lips. Dougal had the ghost of a smile on his lips. Yet even with the smell of the stables about him, Brandubh was the most desirable man she had ever laid eyes on. In spite of everything, she still wanted him.

Her heart fussed some more. Her mind urged it to shut up.

* * * *

Brandubh watched her from the corner of his eye as he tore a hunk of bread. He did not even look up as his mother came to sit beside him. Dougal, perpetual smirk of amusement fixed on his face, sidled closer--to listen, Brandubh was sure.

"Are you mad, Brandubh, to come in stinking like a herdsman?" Sadbh whispered in an outraged hiss.

Brandubh chewed his cheese and bread. "I am a herdsman, Mother."

"What about her?"

"What about her? She has rejected me. Besides, I have business to attend to and cannot sit around mooning like a lovesick boy."

"Perhaps that is exactly what you should do."

Brandubh turned and winked. Confusion flitted across Sadbh's face, quickly replaced by understanding and a small smile. When he continued, Brandubh carefully allowed his voice to carry to the table where Eibhlin sat with Moira.

"Mother, my place is at Lon Dubh. I have played the warrior long enough."

Aha, he thought triumphantly as Eibhlin's eyes jumped up to meet his. He bit off some cheese and sat back.

"So, what will you do when Brian calls you again?" Dougal asked. Brandubh couldn't miss the glint in his father's eyes and the way he raised the volume of his voice just enough to reach Eibhlin's ears. "He will need you if he presses his campaign against the Vikings."

The bolt found its mark. Her blue-gray eyes clouded with sorrow. Brandubh, too, felt the shaft of Dougal's words, unintended as they were, straight through the heart. The campaign that would cost Ireland its king, he thought. What could he say? She had to know.

"If the *Ard Ri* calls, Father, I will obey, of course." He did not have to dissemble in the least to appear unhappy about the prospect of returning to battle.

Dougal nodded, approval in his manner. "Of course." He drained he cup. His voice somewhat lowered, he added, "Before you go, Brandubh, we must go to Conor. I sent men to the abbey to recover Uaid's body."

Brandubh could only nod. He owed Conor a face-to-face meeting and an explanation. He knew it was the right thing to do, yet the food on his tongue suddenly tasted like straw and he swallowed with no enthusiasm.

His eyes met Eibhlin's again. There was a difference, a softness, a tenderness for him that had been missing last night. Perhaps his strategy would work, after all.

Dougal rose and, his wife at his side, left Brandubh staring at Eibhlin. "Come along when you are finished. They should be back by now."

Brandubh nodded in assent, eyes still locked with Eibhlin's smoky ones.

If only I could read her heart, he thought. If he could be certain that there was real love for him there, that deep inside her woman's heart she wanted him, there would be no limit to the labors he would perform for her. If only he could erase the memory of those hours in the abbey, where he'd lost her.

He tipped back his cup, draining the warm, yeasty ale. Then he faced up to his duty and got up to go to Conor. He stopped at Moira's side.

"I go with Dougal to tell Conor of Uaid, Moira. Would you want to go with us?"

She nodded. "Come, dear one," she said to Eibhlin. "It is time you made the formal acquaintance of your grandfather."

Eibhlin appeared loath to go, but without a word, rose and proceeded Moira down the middle aisle of the hall. Brandubh stepped ahead to catch up with her.

"My Lady, it is not necessary for you to do this."

"No, I have to. I've waited too long to go to him."

Dougal and Sadbh were already at Conor's small house inside the compound. When Brandubh appeared, his father waved him forward and knocked on the door.

Conor opened it himself and just stared at Dougal for a moment. Then he stepped back and pulled the door wider.

"Enter my home, my Lord."

"Thank you, Conor."

The party entered the squat, round building. A fire burned in the hearth and a serving girl stirred the pot that bubbled over it.

Brandubh saw his mother glance at it, but she said nothing.

Conor motioned his guests to sit by the fire and waved the girl away.

"To what do I owe this visit, Dougal?"

Dougal sat forward and rested his elbows on his knees. Clasping his large hands together, he spoke so softly Brandubh had to strain to hear.

"Conor, my old friend, my brother, I fear I bring you grievous news."

"My son is dead." Conor's voice was devoid of any life.

"Conor," Brandubh knelt before him. "Conor, Uaid died by my hand. We will have the judges set the blood price and I will pay it." He laid his hand on Conor's knee, nearly drawing away from the frailty he felt there.

"What price can return my son to me? Or my daughter?"

A knife could not have wounded Brandubh more deeply.

"Father, Brandubh is not to blame for what has happened to our family. Caoimhe's death was an accident. Uaid felt responsible and in the madness caused by his guilt, he transferred the fault to Brandubh."

Conor waved Moira aside. "Speak not to me of these things. I cannot bear it."

"But, Father, I have to tell you so you will understand and forgive."

"How can I forgive? Uaid has brought shame and disgrace to my name. Caoimhe took her life and banished her own soul to hell."

"No, Conor," Eibhlin joined Brandubh on her knees before him. "She didn't. Her death was an accident. Uaid wasn't responsible for what happened either, but the guilt drove him mad. He told me everything when he...." She stopped. Brandubh could see the battle going on inside her. Her words would hurt Conor anew and she did not wish to speak them.

"Tell him, Eibhlin," Moira commanded. "Tell him what my brother did to you."

Eibhlin looked at her mother. Then she glanced into Brandubh's eyes and he tried to give her the resolve to continue.

"He took me to a cave in the Burren and left me there to die. Then he took me to the abandoned abbey and intended to rape me and force Brandubh to kill him." She sat back on her heels. "Conor, I am so sorry."

The old eyes closed and tears squeezed from behind the lids.

"He wasn't well, Conor. He was sick."

Conor only stared into the flames.

"Father, we have to go on. I have brought you your granddaughter."

At the old man's nod, Eibhlin asked, "Do you believe this is possible?"

"I do not know. Anything, I suppose, is possible. Yet, it matters not to me. My children are dead. If your tale is true, will I not also lose my Moira? Then will I have nothing."

Sadbh choked back a sob. Moira's eyes glazed with tears. Eibhlin had no words to console the grieving man.

"Whatever power brought you here, child," Conor said to her, laying his hand over hers on his knee, "has played an awful game with my family. Were it not for the beauty of your face and the purity of your eyes, I would think you an agent of the evil one, to do this. Yet, do I see my own Nara there." He squeezed her hand. "You are, I think, as much a pawn as the rest of us. As for the blood price, Brandubh, I will not seek it. I do not believe I would live to see it paid."

"Nay, old friend, speak not so," Dougal begged him. "How can I go on without my right hand?"

Conor smiled. Wrinkles spread from his tired eyes. "Your right hand has ever been your son, Dougal. I merely held his place until he was of age to assume it. I have always envied you your Brandubh. Perhaps I held him up as the model for Uaid too often. Perhaps I wished aloud too many times for his blood to join to mine and sowed thoughts of marriage in Caoimhe's head." He smiled. "It is truly said that a man should be careful of what he wishes for." He looked at Eibhlin. "How could I have thought to have my wish come true in this way?"

"Father, please do not...."

A hacking fit caught Conor and wracked him. He held a linen square to his mouth. When he drew it away, there was blood on it. Eibhlin grabbed his hand.

"How long has this been going on? Why didn't you tell someone?" She moved to rise.

"Nay!" Conor's voice was strong, in spite of the lack of breath in his lungs. "Do not bother yourself, child," he said, more kindly. "I have been ill for sometime now. It has gotten worse with the weather and I will not see the spring. Dougal." He reached for Dougal's hand.

"Aye, my brother."

"I wish to be buried by Uaid and Caoimhe. Will you have her moved to hallowed ground for me?"

Dougal nodded. "But you have many more years...."

Conor laughed, setting off another spate of coughs. "Humor me, my friend. We have seen many excellent fights together. This one I must face alone." An attempt to get a deep breath caused a hack or two. "Please, I am tired. Let me rest now."

His old eyes settled on Eibhlin, still kneeling at his feet. "Will you come to see an old man, child? Come tell me of this strange place you come from. Tell me how my Moira turns out?"

"Of course, Grandfather."

With a weak smile and a nod, he accepted her. "I look forward to it." He settled back in his chair and closed his eyes.

Brandubh rose and helped Eibhlin to her feet. She pulled away and crossed the room, where she stood with her back to him, her hands covering her face. Moira dropped onto the bench at the table by the hearth. She gazed with undisguised pain at her father's ravaged face. It was as though he'd aged decades since they'd come in. Sadbh stood by the fire, stirring the unattended pot.

Only Dougal sat where he had been, his face reflecting the pain of his friend's losses and griefs. Brandubh leaned against a post and sighed. What could he have done differently? So many times he'd asked himself that question. Still he had no answer.

Eibhlin came back to the old man and lay her hand on his shoulder. "I will be back soon, Grandfather."

Conor nodded weakly.

She turned away and went to the door. Brandubh followed her out into the windy day. Only Dougal remained to keep watch for the time being.

"Brandubh, I can't leave him now."

He nodded, understanding. "Take care of him, Eibhlin. He is my father's dearest friend after my mother." He turned, and left her there by Conor's doorway, feeling somehow he'd lost a battle.

Eibhlin watched him go, mantle flowing behind him in the gusty wind like a pair of wings.

"Why did you not tell Conor you were leaving?" Moira asked as she came out of her father's house.

"Because it won't make any difference to him. He will be dead long before that."

"Is there nothing we can do?"

"Not when the patient has no desire to live."

Moira let out a gasped sigh. "Oh, sweet Jesus, how did our lives come to such a pass?"

"I came." Eibhlin ignored Moira's attempt to soothe her and pulled her cloak tighter before she headed to the only place where she had some control--the herbroom. She took down all her bottles and jars and sachets. Sitting at the marred table, she started cataloguing them. Then she arranged them by action, seeking the ones that would provide the best treatment for the pneumonia that had filled Conor's lungs, sapping his strength and taking his life. Perhaps if he thought he had some hope of recovery, he would fight.

But what could she give him to fix his broken heart? He'd given up because of the bitter disappointments of his children and the sure knowledge, personified in Eibhlin--more guilt--that he was about to lose his only remaining child. What did he have to live for?

Still, bound to the old man by ties stronger than familiarity, since she couldn't give him ease for his mind and spirit, she searched for something that would give his body ease from the racking coughs. She was grateful that Moira hadn't followed her. She needed solitude to deal with her guilt and grief.

Maybe Moira needed time herself because it was some hours later before the door to the herbroom opened and Moira entered on a breath of cold air.

"Hello, dear one. Do you need help?"

Eibhlin looked up from the mortar where she ground dried comfrey roots. "I'm just trying to keep busy doing something useful. This will help Conor's lungs."

Moira nodded. "Will you take it to him?"

"Of course." Leaning her weight onto the pestle, she finished powdering the comfrey. "How is he?"

"Resting. I tried to get him to explain how he kept this from me for all this time." She looked to her toes. "Then I remembered I have not been spending a great deal of time with him of late."

"We'll take care of him and make him comfortable. Maybe we can convince him that we need him around and he'll fight to stay alive."

"Can one really fight such a sickness?"

Another Conor flashed into Eibhlin's mind. If a ten-year-old boy could fight for life beyond what the doctors predicted, then an old war-horse like Conor mac Turlough should be able to. She wouldn't let him go until he forced her to.

To her mother, not knowing what she should reveal about the Conor-to-be, Eibhlin only said, "Everyone can fight."

Moira nodded. "I bring you a message as well. Brandubh rode out for Lon Dubh. He left his regrets for not coming to see you first." She laid her mantle across the back of the chair and sat down, putting her hands to work picking dried leaves off the stalks of comfrey. "Eibhlin, I am so sorry for all the pain that lies between you and Brandubh because of what has happened."

Eibhlin didn't know what to answer. "It's all behind us, Mama. There's nothing that can be done about the past."

"You are right, of course." Moira looked up. "I still wonder, though, why you are here? Can it be simply to help me? Could it not be that you are meant to be here?"

"I don't know." She took the ground comfrey and funneled it into a small clay jar, using the task to give her time to think. It was clear what Moira wanted her to believe--that she had been brought here to fulfill her destiny as the wife of Brandubh mac Dougal.

"When Brandubh returns, will you still go with him to Lon Dubh?" Moira asked.

"I promised I would. I suppose I ought to keep my word. Though now, I want to stay with Conor for as long as I can."

"Brandubh will understand, dear one."

Eibhlin knew he would. He'd asked her, after all to look after Conor. "And afterwards...." She could tell she didn't need to elaborate. Moira understood her meaning. "If there's time before Beltain, I'll go with him for a few days. Lon Dubh isn't far from here, is it?"

"Oh, no, barely more than a half-day's ride."

"Have you ever been there?" Eibhlin found herself curious about the place that was Brandubh's and that she had never seen. "He once said he'd like me to see it."

"I have never been there, but my father says that when Brandubh took it over it was not more than a collection of huts inside an earthwork. It is barely more than an outpost, you see. Brandubh keeps some horses and cattle out there, but rarely does he stay there. As the only son, he will most likely be selected by the tribe to be chieftain at Ath Sionnain when Dougal is gone."

"Where is it?"

"It sits on the east bank of the Shannon, where Connaught, Meath, and Munster come together."

Eibhlin figured for a moment how it all fit together. "It's rather exposed, isn't it?"

"Thinking like a soldier, Eibhlin?" Moira asked with a smile. "It is, and that is one reason Brian gave it to Brandubh to hold."

"One reason?"

"It was also reward for service."

Ah, she thought, for fighting. And killing.

"You'll see it when you go there. Father says it is in a very pretty place, next to the river like it is. Even prettier than Ath Sionnain, though I cannot give credence to that."

Moira had never been to a place that was probably less than fifty miles from home. What a shock she was in for when she got to modern times, Eibhlin thought, where fifty miles was nothing. What she'd give to see her mother's reaction to the trip to California.

Then she thought about her own trip back to the future. Back to the pollution, the crowds, the crime....

Her heart and mind warred constantly inside her. One of them had better get the upper hand and settle this thing. She was tired of the headache it was causing her.

Chapter Twenty-four

"Ah, my Nara in those days was tall, though not near as tall as you, with hair the color of a seal's coat. She was as wild as the deer, she was." Conor winked at Eibhlin as they sat snug inside his small house, while the wind roared its empty threats, beating impotently against the tightly shuttered windows. "My blood was near to boiling all the day, just thinking of her."

His laughter turned to a spasm of coughing. Eibhlin left her chair as she had too many times over the last days, raising him from the pillows that propped him up, helping him lean over the crock that he spat into, wiping his chin when it was all over. Settling him back down, she kissed his forehead.

"Thank you, my dove." He reached for her hand. "You give this old man better care than an angel."

"I'm just being selfish. I want to hear more about your Nara." Eibhlin pulled her chair closer so she could keep her hand in his. "She was beautiful, was she?"

Never having this side of her family to connect to, Eibhlin felt the empty space in her heart fill with memories of lives long over.

"I saw her by the Little Brosna one lovely morning. My father sent me to borrow one of her father's bulls. Put ideas into my head, I will admit."

"Conor! Shame on you talking to your granddaughter about such things."

"Ah, get on with you, girl. You and young Brandubh will be sowing the seeds soon, do not say me nay." Conor leaned his head back and closed his eyes. "Fine man, he is, too. He will get strong children from you. He will do right by you, Evie."

Eibhlin couldn't bring herself to tell Conor it was not to be. She let him muse on about children who would never exist, a life that was impossible.

Yet the longer he talked, the stronger the images became--children, faceless, yet her heart told her they were hers.

Hers and Brandubh's.

"Are you listening, Evie?" Conor croaked. "I was telling you about how I stole Nara away from her old papa."

"Stole her?"

"Aye. The old wolf would not agree to a bride price. He wanted more than I could pay. Nara, though, she was a canny one. She met me one evening and before I knew what had happened, she had me on my horse and her in front of me and off we rode for Clonmacnois." He chuckled. Eibhlin could see he was struggling to stave off another coughing fit. "We stopped a bit shy, though. Nara jumped down and pulled me after her. Soon, we were...." His face blossomed red as he realized what he was about to say. "Well, her father was pleased to accept a price after that night."

"Rascal." She couldn't help smiling. "Does Mama know that story?"

"Nay. It is our little secret." He winked at her just as the door opened.

Moira came in from the blustery outside and stopped in her tracks as her sharp eyes took in the cozy scene.

"What did I interrupt? There is scheming going on here." She shook the snow off her cloak and hung it on the peg behind the door before coming toward the fire. "My, it is so cold out there. Snow up to your knees nearly." She dropped a kiss on Conor's head. "Good day, Father. And to you, daughter."

"Good day, pet." Conor reached for her hand. "Our Evie has been telling me bedtime stories. Quite the bard, she is. Though I vow she has been embellishing upon the tales."

Moira sat on the floor by her father's bedside. When their gazes met over Conor's head, Eibhlin wished she could give some sign that he was getting better, but Moira couldn't be fooled. So, they sat together, the three of them, looking at the play of the flames on the hearth.

Somehow, they all knew the end was just waiting.

Conor drew a labored breath. "Evie, tell me again, how you came to be here."

Her story of the curtain on the Crag had become his favorite, even more than the story of Nuada of the Silver Hand. It was, after all, a very Irish tale so the strangeness hadn't fazed him in the least. So, she told him again, taking care to add details that were absolute nonsense, but made the story much better. Conor laughed gently, coughed much, and enjoyed it thoroughly.

"So, Conor mac Turlough, think you that I come from the *Danaan*?"

"Truly you must, my beauty. But we won't be telling anybody of your tale. And we for certain will keep it from the priests." He shook his head. "Shame it is, taking perfectly good Irishmen and turning them into, well, I don't know, but it seems to me an Irishman who does not believe in the faerie realm can not be much of an Irishman, no?" He laughed and coughed some more at his joke.

Eibhlin helped him hold a linen cloth to his mouth and Moira ladled a cup of comfrey and borage from the kettle Eibhlin kept hot on the fire. Eibhlin stepped back and straightened her spine, easing away the tension and stiffness while Moira helped Conor drink.

Her own lungs hurting for him, Eibhlin listened to his labored breathing and had to stop herself from trying to breathe for him. She tried to keep any concern from her face as she helped him get comfortable on the piles of pillows at his back.

Conor lay quietly, gathering his strength. Then his face became wrinkled with the effort of forming words. "You say my Moira will have to go?"

Eibhlin sat down on the bed beside him. Moira joined them on the other side. Exchanging glances over the sick man, they each saw the fear in each other's eyes.

"Yes, Grandfather. On Beltain next."

Conor nodded. "Oh, well, I suppose she would be leaving my house some day, Evie." He took Moira's hand and squeezed it. "Will she be happy with this man?"

"Yes, Grandfather."

He nodded again. "Then I can let her go. And I will have you and your little ones to keep me company. Yours and Brandubh's."

Moira looked at Eibhlin. Do we tell him? her expression asked. But Eibhlin couldn't tell him that there would be no little ones.

"Of course, Conor. You will dandle them and their children on your knees."

Conor smiled, his leathery face crinkling like parchment. It looked fragile enough to fall to dust.

"Good. Boys, Evie. Lots of boys. Ireland will need good, strong men to run the damned Northmen off our shores." Another coughing fit overtook him and he drifted off to sleep.

Eibhlin sat with him, Moira on the other side, taking turns holding his hand and singing to him. Smiles flitted across his face as he dreamed.

Eibhlin could tell when his dreams were of things recent. The names of

THE RAVEN'S LADY

Uaid and Caoimhe spilled from his lips as tears spilled from his eyes. Finally, he spoke the name of his long-loved Nara, weakly reaching upwards.

His eyes opened for a second, clear and free of pain and sickness. Harboring a senseless hope that his fever had broken and the pneumonia wouldn't take him, Eibhlin leaned over him to hear the words that came from his dried, blistered lips.

But there was no air to carry them.

"Conor. Conor, don't." Eibhlin sat back in her chair and closed her eyes over the pooled tears.

The two of them sat in stunned silence while the wind buffeted the house.

"Mama, I'm sorry."

"For what, dear one? You did all you could." Moira was up in a moment and came to her. She knelt and wrapped her arms around Eibhlin.

The winter-muffled afternoon passed slowly as they shared their grief.

* * * *

Conor was buried two days later. Dougal wept openly during the Mass while Sadbh stood by his side, arms around his waist, sharing her own tears. All during the service, Eibhlin felt her eyes drawn to Brandubh, only to find that his were on her.

Guilt rushed through her that at her grandfather's funeral she should be staring at her one-time lover. Surely her face must show what was going on in her heart. Yet...

She stole another glance at Brandubh. His face wasn't distorted with lust. Rather, it was filled with tenderness, as though he would offer her comfort. His strong arms to hold her, the gentle touch of his hands, the glancing caress of his lips against her hair. He would whisper to her that she had done all she could, that she had made Conor happy in his last days, that she had helped him find some peace with what God had been pleased to give him as his burden.

Eibhlin felt her resolve to duck across that curtain come Beltain wavering as those beautiful black eyes gazed at her, the message as clear as though he shouted it across the crowded chapel.

Let me hold you, my Lady. Let me love you.

She tried to summon up the vision of the other Brandubh, the one she could never love, as he had been in the abbey that night, but that cold-eyed killing machine somehow eluded her. Not that it mattered. She was going back where she belonged.

Even with her mind made up, even with every good reason to go back to what was familiar, turning away from him to face the front was the hardest thing she'd ever done. It took everything she had to shove away the yearning of her heart to run to him.

* * * *

Watching her at dinner, Brandubh felt as helpless as he ever had.

You are so unhappy, my Lady. If only I could take you in my arms and hold you and shelter you from all the pain.

Yet he knew it was not possible. She was a strong woman who would face whatever came, not eager, perhaps, but able to shoulder the burden. She would accept no man to take care of her. She would have to be his partner.

That thought brought a smile to his lips. What could a man accomplish with such a woman as his partner?

He rose and took up his cup, all too aware that every eye was on him. Ignoring them, he went down to the table in the first rank before the lord's table where she sat with Moira.

"My ladies, may I?"

"Indeed, Brandubh, please," Moira spoke quickly.

Murmurs whipped through the crowd like a fire in the summertime.

"I am very sorry about Conor, Moira. He was my friend and I am missing him."

"Thank you, Brandubh. You were as a son to him."

This was spoken without any ironical twist to it and Brandubh wanted to believe it was spoken in truth.

"Thank you. Moira, I have consulted with the judges and the blood price for Uaid has been set...."

Moira shook her head. "This is not necessary. Uaid brought his death on himself."

"But, Moira, the law...."

Again she interrupted him, this time with a smile. "Very soon, Brandubh, there will be none of Conor's line left. Who will take the cattle? Leave them in the tribe. That will be sufficient."

At this reminder that he had very little time to win Eibhlin back, Brandubh turned toward her. "And you, my Lady? Are you well?"

"Yes, Brandubh, I am."

Her eyes gave the lie to her words. They were open, yet he could not see into her soul as he had once been able to.

"Do you remember my request, my Lady?" She appeared confused, so he refreshed her memory. "You were coming to Lon Dubh to tend my people?"

"Oh, yes. Do you still need me?"

Indeed, he thought, but he said, "Things are not at a critical stage, yet I would have you come. If you can do aught for them, I would appreciate your efforts."

Her eyes narrowed at his words. "That's all? Just see to your people?"

"Well, if you had the time to teach some things to one of the women, so we may tend to our own henceforth, but yes, what else could there be?"

He tried to keep his face passive.

"I mean, you won't try to convince me to stay and marry you?"

"You have given me your answer, my Lady. I will not force my attentions on any woman." He let the pause hang before adding, "No matter what my own desires are."

Her expression fascinated him. Was she glad he was not intending to pursue her? Or was she glad he had mentioned that his own desires would have him do otherwise?

Whatever, he knew he had finally touched something. That was a beginning, at any rate.

"I suppose I can come along with you. When do we leave?"

"I must return on the morrow. There is much to be done 'ere the foals start dropping."

"Foals? You mean baby horses?" she asked, her eyes wide with wonder.

His smile spread, unbidden. "Yes, my Lady, baby horses. Raising horses is what I do, after all." He drained his cup. "Is tomorrow morning too soon?"

"Not at all," Moira answered for her. "I can look after things here for the few days you will be gone."

"Mother," Eibhlin whispered, yet he could hear her clearly. "Don't you think you should come along with me?"

"Why?"

"As a," she paused, waving her hands. "I can't think of the word. You know, so people won't think...."

"Think what? And what of it? You're leaving here in just a few more months. What does it matter what any of them think?"

Eibhlin's brow furrowed, but Brandubh could see she had no answer to that. She took a deep breath and turned a look on him as though he were a wolf on the prowl.

"All right. I'll be ready tomorrow morning."

Excellent, he thought, barely restraining he sense of triumph. His voice sounded calm to his own ears, though, when he spoke.

"Thank you, my Lady. My people will be grateful for your care." He raised her hand and waited for her to pull it away. When she didn't, he pressed his lips to her smooth skin, gently tracing the delicate bones beneath. "Until tomorrow morning, my Lady."

As soon as he was away from her table, the women gathered around him, inviting him with smiles and pouts and suggestive words. He ached to know her reaction, yet not for all the realm of the *Danaan* would he turn to see.

* * * *

Oh, wouldn't he just love to see how this is eating at me? she fumed, trying to keep the expression of sublime disgust off her face.

"What is amiss, dear one?"

Moira's face was altogether too innocent.

"Nothing." Even as she said the word, Eibhlin felt her eyes narrow and her mouth tighten when the lovely daughter of one of Dougal's guests brushed another aside and plastered herself along the length of Brandubh's leg. She didn't trust herself to say a word, so she kept it shut.

"Such a lovely girl," Moira mused. "Don't you think? She must be no more than, what would you say, Lady?"

Eibhlin glanced up in horror to see Sadbh had joined them, cup in hand.

They were going to gang up on her, she was certain.

"I believe she has seen only fifteen summers," Sadbh finally answered.

"Fifteen!" Eibhlin quickly clamped her mouth shut. "Where is her father?"

Sadbh laughed softly. "He probably sent her over to charm Brandubh."

"She's just a child."

"I was but fifteen when Brandubh was *born*, Eibhlin. Besides," Sadbh's expressive eyebrow rose, "it appears she has the situation well in hand."

Indeed she did, Eibhlin noticed with more simmering irritation. The little tramp had gotten Brandubh on a chair and was sitting at his feet, stroking his leg as though he belonged to her. She looked like a wolfhound sitting there, her hair hanging all over her shoulders and down to cover her thighs.

Wait a minute, Eibhlin shook herself from the inside. What are you getting all upset over?

Don't be stupid. You know exactly what you're getting all upset over. That adolescent tart has her mitts on your man.

And he doesn't appear to mind at all.

"I think I'll go to bed now."

Sadbh sat up quickly. "The entertainment has not begun yet."

Oh, yes, it has, Eibhlin thought sourly.

"I'm tired, Lady. And Brandubh wants to go back to Lon Dubh tomorrow. I promised I would go and give out some medicaments to his people."

"You're going to Lon Dubh? Wonderful." Sadbh sipped her ale. "I mean, your care will be welcomed."

"I'm sure. Well, I'm going to get some rest. Excuse me."

Eibhlin had to walk right by him to get out. So she straightened her spine and passed by, only slowing down to give him a glance designed to tell him exactly what she thought about his cradle-robbing.

* * * *

The child at his feet was becoming annoying, he thought, yet from here by the fire, he could see Eibhlin's face and she was greatly vexed. At least she looked vexed.

And jealous.

That made him sit still, enduring the pawing of the girl who was more knowledgeable than she ought be.

When Eibhlin passed by, he kept his eyes fixed to hers, not letting her go. She slowed just a bit as she came even with his chair and glanced down at the girl on the floor.

Well, well, my Lord, her look said, taking in children now?

Not if you are available, my Lady, he replied, his eyes doing the talking for him.

She could see it, he knew she could. There was the satisfied knowledge in her eyes that he was hers for the asking.

So, she still wanted him. That was a start. Now if he could persuade her to ask. He only had four months.

It would be enough, he promised himself.

Chapter Twenty-five

"Ah, my Lady. I trust you had a restful night?"

Brandubh stood with two horses, looking delicious enough to eat whole and gloriously rested. She wondered if he'd rested alone.

None of your business, Evie.

"Yes, Lord Brandubh. I slept like a baby, thank you."

"A baby?" His too-devastating smile momentarily blinded her, producing as riotous a reaction in her as his touch ever had. "Come, let me introduce you to Deirdre."

She had heard of the wondrous Deirdre, Conchobar's mate.

"This is the horse that stomped a man into the ground?"

His smile disappeared. "She was defending her mate. Human women should be so faithful."

The sudden change in his demeanor startled her and she stumbled around trying to get a sentence together. "I only meant she's so beautiful, so delicate...."

His warm fingers closed around hers. "Beauty does not indicate a lack of courage, nor is a delicate frame necessarily a weak one." He squeezed her hand up to the point of pain, showing her what he meant. "Shall we go?"

"You're going to let me ride her?"

"Do you wish another mount?"

"No, no. I just thought you never let anyone ride these two. I've never seen anyone ride Deirdre. Besides, isn't she pregnant?"

He nodded. "Yes. But she is growing fat in the stables. The lads pamper her and do no job at all working her. She needs some exercise."

"But should I ride her? I...."

"My Lady, Deirdre is a horse. It is her place in life to carry a rider. Do you want to ride her?"

Eibhlin had never even seen an animal like Deirdre. So sleek, so finely boned, with eyes so full of intelligence, she could swear words would come pouring from between the velvety lips.

"I'd love to, if you're sure it won't hurt her baby."

Brandubh made a sound very like the snort of one of his horses.

"If she is that feeble, I had better find out, eh?" He stroked the snowy white neck. Deirdre tossed her head, then brushed her nose against Brandubh's cheek. "However, I am not so poor a judge, am I, my Lady Deirdre?"

A ripple of jealousy coursed through her at his words.

Come on, Evie, she scolded herself. Jealous of a horse now?

Brandubh put his hands around her waist and lifted her to Deirdre's back as though she weighed no more than a child. His fingers lingered for a moment, then he thoughtfully pulled the hem of her gown down to cover her legs and arranged her mantle as well.

"It would not do to have men distracted from their work by such a lovely sight, would it? There could be terrible accidents," he said with a flirting wink.

She had to smile, enjoying the easier feeling between them, reminiscent of their earlier relationship.

"Is it such a danger, my Lord?"

"Oh, indeed. One look and the smith might hammer off his own thumb. Or perhaps the tanner's knife would slip...." He frowned as though picturing the carnage.

He went around to Conchobar's left side and mounted with a completely masculine grace. Simply watching him was a treat. She would miss that.

"Shall we, my Lady?" He turned Conchobar and Deirdre followed with very little direction from Eibhlin. "We will take our time. The day is good for a long, slow ride."

Sounded like a great idea to her. More time to be with him, to enjoy him before she had to go.

As they left the security of Ath Sionnain, she wondered what it was that was different. She pondered what it was as they rode along the Shannon. When it came to her, it shook her assumptions to their bedrock.

"Brandubh, you're not wearing a sword."

"Of course not. We are on Dal Cais land and it is not all that far to Lon Dubh."

"But you always wear one."

"No. Not always."

"What about the Vikings?"

"It is only the Dublin Vikings we are at war with and that only since Brian sent his contentious wife back to her son's care. The Limerick Lochlanders are our allies now, and they have no reason to break the peace. After all, they profit from the *Pax Hibernius* as we all do."

The Latin flowing so easily from his lips threw her. He apparently didn't notice.

"You have heard the tale, have you not?"

"Tell me," she answered automatically with the response to the bard's opening question.

"There was a young woman of unsurpassed beauty, the daughter of a great chieftain of Dalriada in Ulster. His tribe held the land up near the place where great Fionn mac Cumail built his causeway to Scota. The farthest place on Ireland it is and a cold and harsh place to live."

He glanced over at her as they plodded along.

"I have heard that it is so," she replied.

"But this Ulster princess could find no fit man to wed in that bitter place and decided she would travel all Ireland to find a husband worthy of her. She packed a single bag and left her father's house the next morning."

"All alone?" Eibhlin asked, as an audience would fill the pause of the poet.

"Wait and see," the bard Brandubh answered. "So, our princess traveled by foot, day after day, passing her nights under the hospitable protection of Irish households the length of the island. By day, she walked, greeted by all with respect and honor. She wore a gown of pure white satin and a golden girdle the width of my hand." He held up the specimen to astound his listener with the enormity of the thing. "Protecting her swan-white neck was a torque, cunningly woven of a thousand golden threads. Her hair was braided and secured at the ends with hollow balls of silver. Her cloak was in four colors, as befit her station, and fashioned of the finest wool, secured with a brooch of enameled bronze, inlaid with precious stones."

Eibhlin sighed, right on cue.

Brandubh smiled. "She traveled for many days, without guards. Without weapons. Without fear. Yet throughout the length of Brian's Ireland, no man molested her."

This was the end of the tale as it was normally told, but her bard wasn't finished.

"She searched and searched, yet found no fit men in Ulidia. Nor in Oriel. Nor in Brefni. Nor in Connaught. Nor in Meath. In Leinster, she found no men at all."

Their laughter mingled together in the cold air, while Brandubh continued around his chuckles. "Nor in any of the Viking cities, did she find a man worthy of her."

"Oh, how sad."

"But then," he raised his hand in a dramatic gesture, "she came to the kingdom of Munster. And our princess scolded herself for a fool for wasting all that time. Indeed our High King himself is a Munsterman. Where else would a woman looking for a man go?"

Eibhlin tried in vain to hide her smile at the arrogance.

"When finally she came to the fine land of Munster, she cast her eyes about for a husband to warm her bed."

"Did she find none to suit her?"

Brandubh cut her a look. "Indeed. There were so many she could not decide. In despair, she sat on a rock at a crossroads near Lismore. There she sits still, but even as she settles on one man, another Munsterman struts by like the very cock of the morning and she must begin her deliberation anew."

Eibhlin laughed out loud. "Mayhap she would do better to return to Ulster?"

Brandubh nodded in mock sympathy. "Aye, poor lass would have an easier time choosing, for certain. Yet, when the suggestion is made, she weeps at the thought of leaving our green hills to return to a place even the great Fionn built a road into the sea to escape."

"Oh, Brandubh, what a tale," she laughed. Without even thinking, she dropped her reins on Deirdre's neck and applauded. "Teague had better watch out or you'll take his job."

"No, my Lady," he replied with a smile. "I prefer my own occupation."

Like a wash of cold water, her mood soured. "Soldiering?"

He turned to her with a frown of his own. "I told you, I raise horses."

"But didn't you get your holding as a reward for service?"

"Eibhlin," he said, and she knew he was serious because he hardly ever called her by her name otherwise. "For as long as I have known you, you have assumed that I am a warrior and nothing else. Yet you are an intelligent woman and you must know you must reevaluate your assumptions in the face of contradictory evidence. I will not apologize for serving my king. He is the head of my tribe, my province, my country. When Brian calls on me, I will go. And yes, he has rewarded me for many things. For fighting for him. For providing him with the best horses on this island. Yet, Lon Dubh was not a reward. I hold the northern border of Munster against the Meathmen and Connaught. Brian is not fool enough to believe that a screaming rock is enough to make ambitious men accept he is true High King."

Eibhlin's heart puttered. "The Stone of Fal screamed for him? Really?" Of course, she'd heard the legends of Brian's coronation, but was it possible....

Brandubh nodded. "I was there at Tara. I heard it."

A chill crept along her spine at his words and the tone of reverence with which he spoke them.

He grew quiet, his irritation mellowed. "Eibhlin, I am an Irishman. I can be nothing else. I suppose our ways and our lives seem harsh to you. If so, I cannot blame you for wanting to return to your gentler world. But we are not total barbarians and I cannot believe people have changed so much in one thousand years."

His words silenced her while she tried to remember what it was that made the twentieth century so much more morally superior to this one.

"Do not men contend with each other in your time? Is there no struggle for land or wealth or women?"

Her annoyance at her sex being lumped in with possessions must have shown in her eyes.

"Ah, so men do not vie with each other for a woman's favor? Truly, then, this time you come from is a more civilized age."

"Go on, laugh. I already told you what the difference is. In my time men don't hack each other to bits."

"Is the method of struggle so much the matter?"

"It was awful to see that, Brandubh. The tearing and slicing and the blood...."

"Yes. The blood." He turned his eyes forward. "'Tis the blood that makes killing a thing to be avoided."

Eibhlin turned toward him, seeing an expression of regret and remorse on his handsome face.

"Did your history tell you of the madness of the Celtic warrior?" he asked. "I have seen Brian and my father caught up in it and it is a terrible thing to behold. I have been told that I myself experience it."

He slowed Conchobar to a stop. Deirdre matched the pace and stopped when her mate did. Brandubh turned and leaned on the saddle's pommel, his eyes catching and holding Eibhlin's.

"I have created mayhem on the battlefield that I cannot remember, my Lady. I have been told that I have ripped men's heads from their bodies with these hands." As he held them up for her to see, his voice cracked. He breathed deeply. "Yet, the greatest joy for me is to use these hands to pull a new foal from his mother's body and wipe him clean. Or," he raised his hand and gently pushed a wayward strand of her hair from her face, "to bring pleasure to you." The backs of his fingers trailed across her cheek.

"The madness keeps me alive in battle, Eibhlin, for without it I would not be able to kill."

He turned his eyes back to the road and Conchobar, receiving a silent sign only he and his master knew, started walking again. Deirdre, obedient girl that she was, kept pace with him.

Eibhlin let the horse just follow. Her mind was too full.

...*Without it I would not be able to kill.*

Though she didn't want to continue the conversation, she said, "Uaid told me about the madness. He said you would have killed me, too."

Brandubh didn't answer the implied charge.

"Would you, Brandubh? Could you have killed me?"

There it was, she thought, the fear she had pushed aside for so many days. The fear that had plagued her since the poisonous words had left Uaid's lips.

"What else did he say?"

"That you would kill your own mother when you were taken in the madness. Are you so blinded by the rage that you could do such a thing?"

A deep breath later, Brandubh said, "I do not know, my Lady. Truly, I do not know."

They rode in silence beside the quiet Shannon, each deep in private thoughts.

After a time, Brandubh started pointing out every point of interest along the way. Occasionally he asked what something would be like in her time, but he would stop her.

"I will be dust long before that happens. It would probably be better if you do not tell me anymore."

But the next sacred rowan or crossroads or fairy mound or Druid well would appear in the road and he would ask again for its future after telling her the significance of the site.

So, the ride was hardly boring, and she saw more of the countryside than she would ever see again.

In the late afternoon, they crested a rise and she found herself looking down into a shallow valley that lay blanketed in snow, with the Shannon running cold and clear in between.

"There it is, my Lady. Lon Dubh."

The round houses of the tenants lay out beyond the main compound which was circumscribed by an earthwork. The big house in the middle was constructed not of stone, but of wattle. Though not nearly as grand as Ath Sionnain's main house, it was big enough to house quite a family. Fresh thatch covered the roof and limewater gleamed on the walls. It shone in the sun like a freshly scrubbed face. The usual secondary buildings, workrooms, stable, barn for cattle, lined the inside of the protective embankment.

"Do you like my home, my Lady?" Brandubh's voice carried a note of concern.

She loved it. "Yes, Brandubh, I like it very much."

His smile was her reward.

"Come, then. I am anxious to show it to you."

As they came closer to Lon Dubh, she noticed something that she had not thought to see. Women, young and old, scurried around the grounds, carrying baskets or buckets from the well or barn, or arms full of fresh rushes.

"Brandubh," she began carefully, "I seem to remember that Brian said there were no women out here."

"Did he say that?" Brandubh seemed to look away as though avoiding the conversation. "I believe he said there were no ladies out here." He glanced over at her, and extended his hand, palm up, to direct her attention back to the women. "Clearly, my Lady, there *are* women. Just no ladies." At her silence, he turned and expanded his answer. "There are serving women. Wives and daughters of the herdsmen and farmers." With a wave of his hand, he finished. "Women."

They rode along for awhile.

"In fact," he said, as though there had been no break in the conversation, "perhaps you can find one of them who would be able to learn something of healing while you are here."

"Now that you mention it, you did suggest the possibility last night."

"I did?"

"Yes. Though I can see how you might have forgotten talking to me altogether when Lolita started climbing all over you."

"Who? I do not know a Lolita."

Of course, he didn't get it. "I meant that little girl."

He smirked at her. "Little girl? My mother was no older than she when I was *born*."

"So she informed me. In that exact tone, too. Stop it."

His deep laugh irked her.

"You have told me you do not want me. So, what vexes you about my seeing other women?"

"You can see whatever women you set your eyes upon. I don't care."

"I was actually talking about bedding other women."

"You didn't!" Eibhlin jerked poor Deirdre's bridle and whipped around. "Brandubh, tell me you didn't touch that child."

"No, I did not. However, she was most insistent in her interest in being touched."

Eibhlin snorted. "Arrogant, pompous...."

Brandubh ignored her and frowned. "She did appear a strong girl. And I am thirty. It is time to marry and settle down. Since it appears you have set your mind to leaving... well, 'twill make my mother happy."

"You don't think this juvenile attempt at manipulation will change my mind, do you?"

"I am not attempting such. I was merely musing. I have responsibilities to my tribe. I would marry to please my mother and father also. They have a wish to see grandchildren 'ere they are too old to enjoy them. For that it seems I must look elsewhere since I cannot have what I desire."

There was no mistaking what he desired. He was looking at her that way again, the way he did when he was about to wrap her in his arms and consume her body and soul.

Why was *she* trying to pretend she didn't care?

"Is your mind truly set, my Lady?"

Eibhlin couldn't answer for she didn't know what to answer.

They rode into the gates and a crowd assembled around them.

"Brandubh, welcome home." The speaker was a man, older than Brandubh, short and stocky, with the white-blond hair and blue eyes of the Northmen. "'Tis good to see you. Is this the lady?"

"Indeed, Hauk." Brandubh dismounted and came around to Deirdre's left side and set his hands at Eibhlin's waist, lifting her off and lowering her very tenderly to the ground.

Eibhlin felt every pair of eyes that gazed at her, some with the good-natured envy of women who knew the man they admired was out of reach, others shooting fire at the interloper.

"Eibhlin ni Seamus, this is my steward, Hauk Ingvarson."

A Viking as a steward? She managed to keep her mouth shut and smile.

"An honor, Lady. Brandubh tells me that you are a healer. Odin knows we will welcome your talents."

"Ah, Hauk," Brandubh shook his head in a warning. "The, ah, *arrangement* never materialized."

Hauk's mouth fell open. "It.... You mean, you.... And the lady.... But, my Lord, you took fifty head of cattle...."

A gasp of disbelief blew around her like the winds of a cyclone.

"Fifty!"

"God's teeth! No woman is worth fifty head of cattle!"

Heads were shaking all around them.

Brandubh glared at his steward. "Thank you, Hauk, for discussing *my*," he yelled the word for the benefit of all the mutterers, "business for the entire tribe to hear."

Hauk was only momentarily abashed. "If you are not married, my Lord, why does the Lady come here?"

Eibhlin stood by in silence.

"The lady will only be with us for a short time to treat what sicknesses there are and to perhaps impart some of her knowledge to one of the women."

"How will she do that if she cannot speak?"

A plump woman in a very tight gown, came forward to stand way too close to Brandubh. Her manner spoke of a woman who knew she was attractive to men. Eibhlin looked her over. The woman's dull brown hair hadn't seen a brush for a long time, or else she had just gotten out of bed. Her clothes were stained. Her face was dirty.

Yet, there was something about her, almost a scent, like an animal in heat. Yes, Eibhlin understood, a man who needed a woman would recognize a willing bed partner in this one.

"I can speak very well when I have something to say," Eibhlin said, letting all her irritation pour out in her words.

The woman's eyes widened and she smiled derisively. "So, she does have a tongue."

"Paili," Brandubh said, though he made no move to step away from the woman, "mind your own tongue."

She gazed up at Brandubh. "Aye, my Lord. Now that you have returned, I will have plenty to keep me busy and my tongue will not be so idle." Her eyes made any further analysis of the situation unnecessary.

"Paili," he said, his tone warning. "Show the Lady to her chamber so she may refresh herself."

Are you nuts? Eibhlin wanted to shout. Putting her in this woman's charge was like asking Ivana Trump to mix Marla Maples a martini. Poisoning was a definite possibility.

"Of course, my Lord." Paili trailed a hand down his arm, slowly, possessively.

Slut. Tramp.

"This way, Lady. We will make you most comfortable for your short stay."

"Thank you, Paili." Eibhlin let her go first, as a servant should when leading the way. "My Lord Brandubh," she said with exaggerated courtesy and formality. "I will see you at dinner?"

"Of course, my Lady."

Were those black eyes laughing at her? Eibhlin felt her brow lift in irritation, and forced it back down. She turned and followed Paili.

Chapter Twenty-six

Brandubh stood by Conchobar and watched Eibhlin's face reflect her emotions. The force of her jealousy when she realized that Paili had been his lover was very satisfying.

He compared them. Paili's hips swayed with provocative invitation which he was not yet sure was unintentional. 'Twas certainly not the

THE RAVEN'S LADY

unconscious motion with which Eibhlin moved. Paili was half a head shorter than Eibhlin and the fullness of her figure, while attractive to him--at least it had been--was not the equal to Eibhlin's lush beauty.

"Brandubh, why did you really bring her here?" Hauk, standing at his shoulder, asked.

"Hauk, I dare not tell you the whole of the story. But I have until Beltain to make her change her mind and marry me. I shall give it my most sincere effort."

Hauk laughed. "If I were after making a woman love me, Lord, I certainly would not put her in the care of Paili. She has her own designs on you and will not be your ally in this."

"No, I suppose she will not." Brandubh joined Hauk in his amusement. "Then, she may be my ally whether she desires to be or not. I do not think she will be able to avoid it. She has already helped more than she knows."

A deep chuckle rumbled from Hauk's chest. "I would be grateful if you would make sure that I can see her face when you thank her for her assistance in keeping your lady by your side."

Brandubh lay his arm around Hauk's shoulders and handed him the reins to the horses. "If she does not put a knife in my heart, Hauk, I will. Take care of the horses, will you, my friend? I wish to go in to wash off the dust of the road before the meal. I also do not want them alone for too long."

Hauk's amused snort followed him as he took the steps into the house.

* * * *

"Here we are," Paili pushed open the door and walked into the room.

Eibhlin had to duck under the doorframe to enter. She stood up and her jaw dropped open.

It was tiny. There were no windows. There was no fireplace.

There was no bed.

In the corner were piles of wool and tanned hides and a few bolts of finer material.

"This is a storage room."

"Yes." Paili appeared unconcerned.

"Am I supposed to sleep here?"

"The wool will make an excellent bed."

Eibhlin chewed on the inside of her bottom lip, considering.

"I will not stay here."

"Who are you to spit on hospitality?"

"This is hospitality?" Eibhlin laughed. "Listen to me, you short, pudgy slut, I know exactly what's going on here. You're angry at me about Brandubh. Well, you needn't fear. If he wants you, he can have you. I'm here to treat sicknesses. That's all. But, I will not stay in this room. Now, you march your wide-bottomed rump out of here and find me a proper room. If there is one."

A middle-aged woman poked her head into the doorway.

"What goes here?"

"Ita, this woman refuses the hospitality of our lord."

Eibhlin recognized the name. Sadbh had said that Brandubh's housekeeper was called Ita. Approaching the older woman, she said, "Ita, is it? Hello, I am Eibhlin ni Seamus."

"Lady Eibhlin? Oh," Ita smiled and wiped her hands on the rough apron covering her gown. "I am so happy you have finally come to us. We have had much word from Ath Sionnain about you. Och," she shook her head, "such goings on, with Uaid mac Conor and all. But here you are now."

"She is not married to him, Ita. She is only here to work."

Ita looked shocked. "Work? We thought...."

"Brandubh asked me to come see to your sicknesses."

Recovering, Ita said, "Oh, that is good. There are some who have been down with the sickness in their chests for weeks. Nothing I have prepared for them has helped much. Will this be your workroom, then?"

"I believe Paili was suggesting this would be my chamber."

"Paili!"

"There are no others."

"You know full well that Brandubh ordered his own to be made ready for Lady Eibhlin."

Paili sputtered. "But, where will he sleep?"

"You stupid girl. What Brandubh does is his business and you are not to bother yourself about it. Now, get out of the way. No, get to the kitchen and get yourself to some useful work other than reaching above your station." Ita took Paili by the ear and pulled her to the door, tossing her into the hallway.

"I never intended to be any trouble," Eibhlin said.

"Tosh, Lady, you are not the trouble. She is fortunate Brandubh did not hear her. He took her in, though she was turned out by her own parents. Come, I will see you comfortable."

"Ita, I wonder, too, where is Brandubh planning on sleeping?"

Ita turned to her. "I did not ask him. However, I am certain he will find some place." Ita didn't speak unkindly, but Eibhlin still felt the rebuke.

She followed the older woman back toward the front of the house to the large chamber off the main hall.

It was Brandubh's. She could feel him there. It was warm and clean and comfortable.

"Your bath will be along as soon as I can hurry up the gossips in my kitchen."

"Thank you, Ita."

Ita smiled as she closed the door.

Eibhlin gazed around the room where Brandubh slept here at Lon Dubh. She'd never seen his chamber at Ath Sionnain and there was a sense of new discovery here.

On a small table by the fireplace, where a merry fire crackled, strips of leather were braided together, the beginnings of a bridle recognizable. A tiny set of horseshoes lay on the hearth, two-by-two. She knelt down and tried to pick one up, but found it was nailed to the floor.

"They were Ruari's."

She turned quickly toward the sound of his voice.

"He was my first pony." A smile, sad and at the same time fond, quirked the corner of his mouth. "It is a sentimental bit of nonsense, but...."

"No," she averred quickly, "it's a sweet gesture." She ran her finger along the shoe. "I suppose he's...."

"I lost him when I was ten." He crossed the room and knelt beside her. With the tip of his finger he, too, traced the band of iron. "I disobeyed my mother and it cost Ruari his life."

And still he hurt, she thought.

"What happened?"

"Dougal got word a bear had been seen emerging from one of the caves. He gathered a band of men to ride to the wild west of Thomond to see this marvel. I begged to be allowed to go along, but Mother forbade it. She feared greatly for me then, as she probably still does. I pretended obedience, but as soon as her back was turned, I saddled Ruari and followed after my father.

"I lost sight of them quickly, for they were men mounted on horses and I was a boy on a small pony." Brandubh sat on the floor and stared at the horseshoes. "I had heard them planning and I knew they were going south around the Lough, past Kincora, then turning west. I knew the way well, so Ruari and I continued. Oh, I was certain I would catch up with them. My Ruari was a fine pony.

"It was the first time I ever saw the Burren, Eibhlin. And me with no food, no water, no weapon. The wolves came as soon as the sun set." He said it so calmly. "I could only watch while they tore him to pieces."

"Oh, Brandubh," she said, sympathetic tears welling in her eyes.

"The blood, Eibhlin. The growls, the sound of flesh being torn from bone. Ruari's screams...." He finally turned to her and she could see his exquisite eyes shining with the pain of the memory. "Strange, is it not, after the things I have seen, the things I have done.... I still have terrible dreams about it."

A heavy silence sat around them while Brandubh hung his head and she saw a solitary tear course its way down his lean cheek.

"I hid in the caverns. And I watched. When I could watch no more, I ran into the dark where I could see nothing, hear nothing. My incompetence was such that I soon got lost."

"Brandubh, ten-year-old boys are not known for their competence. Grown men would get lost in those caves."

"I suppose," he said, no great fervor in his agreement. Turning to her, tear-tracks still visible, he continued. "That day had formed me, Eibhlin. I am the man I am because of the disobedience of that ten-year-old boy."

His lips barely curved in what, she supposed, was meant to be a smile. It didn't reach his eyes.

"I probably should have tried to explain this to you sooner, my Lady.

That day, I swore I would never again be weak and at the mercy of the strong. Never again would I be helpless. Never again would someone I love be torn from me and hurt."

His eyes met hers.

Do you love me, Brandubh? she asked silently, unable to phrase the question aloud. He had never exactly said the words, but there had been so many times--she recalled each one--when he had said something so close....

"Do you find the room comfortable?"

His question, so far off the subject, threw her.

"Yes, well, I only just...." She stumbled. "Actually, Brandubh, I don't want to put you out of your bed."

"I will find a bed somewhere."

"I'm sure you will." She hadn't meant for her voice to be that sharp.

A chuckle escaped his lips as the door opened behind him.

"Ah, Brandubh, here you are. We have a bath waiting for you in Hauk's chamber. Out, wi' you now." Ita shooed him toward the door. "Here, girls, bring it in."

"It seems I must leave you in Ita's capable hands, my Lady. I will see you at dinner." He evaded Ita's capable hands which were aiming at shoving him no less ignobly than she had Paili early. "I go, woman, I go. Why do I put up with such treatment?"

Ita whacked his rear as though he were a naughty child.

"Because I remember you before you had all the women in Munster pantin' after you. Get on."

Brandubh laughed and bent to kiss the old woman's cheek. "If I cannot have you, Ita, my plump pigeon, I will have to seek elsewhere."

"I would not have you, half-breed whelp." She slammed the door in his grinning face.

Eibhlin could see the relationship that allowed a servant to treat her master so. "Were you his nurse?"

"Only after his mother weaned him. Sadbh allowed no one near the child until she was heavy with another." Ita smiled and raised the first steaming bucket of water, dumping it into the oak tub. "Here, Lady, do you need assistance out of your clothing? I fear we have so little cause to tend ladies that our skills are somewhat rusty."

"No, I can manage." Eibhlin pulled her gown over her head. "He loves you as a mother."

"I suppose he does, or nearly so, for none can take his own mother's place. They are very close the three of them." Ita poured the second, third, fourth buckets into the tub. "He should have been sent to foster with one of Brian's sons, but Sadbh could not part with him. Well, especially after her little girls all died so young. It is a wonder he turned out to be so fine a man with his mother hovering over him like a hen." Ita turned a canny eye to Eibhlin. "Why will you not marry him?"

Eibhlin chuckled nervously. "I am only traveling here. Soon, I will return home."

"Your water is ready, Lady." Ita sat on the stool by the fireplace, apparently intending to stay for a talk.

The two of them stared at each other. Neither budged.

All right, then, Eibhlin thought and, shedding her shift, stepped into the tub.

Ita tossed her a bar of scented soap.

Holding it to her nose, Eibhlin sniffed. "Ah, bayberry. Very nice."

Ita's approving nod was the only acknowledgment she got.

"Are you going to sit there and watch me bathe or talk to me?"

"I would talk if you give me leave."

"You don't need to ask me permission to speak, Ita."

Indeed, Ita got right to what was on her mind.

"He loves you."

"How do you know that?" Eibhlin soaped her face and arms, trying to hide how the subject affected her.

"He took fifty cows from here to pay your bride price. Nobody gets fifty cows, Lady. Only the magnificent Gormlaith who was for a time the wife of the High King got so much." Ita sat back, lacing her fingers together over her paunch. "And he has taken no woman to his bed since the summer."

"His mother told me the same thing. Do the two of you really think he has had no one?"

"Has he had you?"

A blush crept up from Eibhlin's belly to the top of her head. "Once."

"It is enough. You accepted his offer. You shared your body with him. It is done."

"No, Ita, it is not done. I told you, I'm only passing through." Eibhlin was still burning from the sight of Paili hanging on Brandubh's arm and knowing that the woman had been in his bed. "Let Paili comfort poor, lonely Brandubh."

"Phhht. Paili has as much chance of getting into Brandubh's bed as Hauk does."

Eibhlin had to laugh.

Ita pursed her lips. "You would be a fit wife for him, I think." She peeked into the water. "Healthy children would come from you. That is what is needed here. Many healthy children to carry this blood into the future." She rose with a grunt from the stool. "If you require no further assistance, I will be getting supper ready. My Lady."

Sitting in the cooling water, Eibhlin thought about it. Time had put some of her fears and shocks into perspective. She still wanted him. His life here at Lon Dubh was, on the surface, anyway, peaceful. A gentleman horsebreeder. That was much more soothing to a potential wife than marrying a homicidal maniac.

"Not fair, Evie."

She leaned back in the tub and pondered. And pondered.

And did it some more.

* * * *

Brandubh watched her enter the hall for supper. Ah, he could watch her forever.

She smiled at him. Her pleasure in seeing him was real.

Good, Eibhlin. You are weakening, are you not?

"My Lady, I am pleased you are joining me."

"Thank you, my Lord." She accepted his hand and let him guide her to the chair beside his own.

Someday here at Lon Dubh, and later at Ath Sionnain, she would rule as his lady.

"Ita," he said, "you may begin. I hope you are hungry, my Lady. Ita has prepared quite a large meal."

He served her himself, taking the meat and cutting the best parts for her. Carefully, he selected vegetables and bread and put it on the trencher before her.

Things were actually going quite well. She was amusing, laughing at the jokes that were being bandied about the hall, charming his men and their women. He could see she felt comfortable.

When the maids came to refill the ale, the show began.

One clumsy girl bumped into Eibhlin, slamming her into the edge of the table.

"Oh, please, excuse me, lady."

Paili. He might have guessed. What was Ita thinking letting her come near Eibhlin? He was not exactly sure what to do. In his father's household, this kind of thing did not happen.

A gentle hand on his arm, Eibhlin's hand, stopped him from taking some action.

"That's all right, Paili. Do be more careful, though." Eibhlin's gaze locked with Paili's. "You would not want to disturb Lord Brandubh's meal."

"No, Lady. More ale?" The pitcher was held up over Eibhlin's head.

The room stopped breathing, each person waiting for the outcome of this quiet battle.

Eibhlin had been taking lessons from Mother, Brandubh thought. Her left eyebrow raised like a bird's wing. Her eyes were as cold as the Lough in January. Not one muscle of her face so much as twitched.

"No." The word was precisely spoken. "Thank you."

The unspoken message was clear. Pour one drop of that on me and I will slap your face off your head.

She was magnificent.

Brandubh knew enough about women not to interfere. He took up his cup and sipped his ale.

"Put the pitcher here on the table, Paili. I will take care of anything Brandubh needs." Eibhlin spoke as to a dull child and took the pitcher from Paili's hands. "That will be all, Paili." Turning to Brandubh, she said, "Here, my Lord, let me refill that for you."

"Thank you, my Lady."

Task done, she set the pitcher on the table before her.

"Brandubh, I need a place, a small room, perhaps, to use as an herbroom. I think the storage room back by the kitchen would be ideal. Do you suppose Ita could have someone," she glanced behind her at the still frozen Paili, "clean it for me?"

"Indeed, my Lady. Your desires are my own." He glanced down at the first table. "Ita, will you see to it?"

Ita could not answer. Her shoulders shook with unrestrained amusement.

"It will have to be done well, Ita." Eibhlin's voice rang with the authority of the lady of the house. "Medicines cannot be kept in a filthy place."

Accepting Eibhlin's right to issue instructions, Ita nodded, still smiling. "I will see to it, my Lady."

"Thank you." To the general audience, Eibhlin announced, "I will begin tomorrow. Anyone who needs care may come to me here in the hall until the room is prepared."

This was proceeding better than he'd dared hope.

Brandubh turned to his hall. "Who will give us a tale tonight?"

* * * *

Watching Paili slink away, completely undone by Brandubh's indifference, Eibhlin sat at his side, greatly relieved her strategy had worked so well. She had established her place.

Now what?

She glanced at Brandubh as he listened to the unschooled, yet wonderful, voice of his head herdsman telling the beginning chapter of the Cattle Raid of Cooley.

His black hair shone and his olive skin glowed in the rushlight. The fine lines of his face could have been sculpted by the greatest of the Italian masters.

She loved him.

That was no surprise. From the first she'd known it. And it had been so long since they had loved each other, body to body.

She raised her hand to sweep back his hair.

He turned to her. When his eyes met hers, the agreement was made. While she was here, she would be his lady. When it was time to go to Kincora... and Craglea....

Well, she would ford that river when the time came.

"Well done, Murchad, well done." The hall broke into applause. Eibhlin joined in though she hadn't heard a word. Brandubh reached for the pitcher and refilled her cup.

"Do you want to go on alone? Or shall we go together?"

His voice was low, his words for her ears alone.

Do you want to let everyone know we will be together tonight?

She realized she didn't care whether they knew or not.

"I will wait for you, my Lord."

Brandubh nodded, understanding. "I believe I am ready for my bed. Come." He rose and took her hand.

Eibhlin followed willingly. Maybe if he asked her again. If he still wanted to marry her and asked her again. After all, the cattle....

They slept in his bed, on a mattress he told her was new. It smelled new. The covering was new. The ropes were even new, he said. He'd had it done when he thought they were getting married.

Now, she'd gotten used to it. It was probably the most comfortable bed she'd ever slept in. Of course, she'd been sharing it with the most beautiful man in the world for two months.

January was gone. February was waning. March would soon be upon them. Word had gone back to Ath Sionnain that the lady's skills were more sorely needed than at first expected and so her stay was extended.

A reply from Dougal, filled with his bizarre humor, gave his agreement. He was, after all, responsible to Brian for her safety. His admonition to Brandubh to not take too much of the lady's healing made her smile.

Now, sitting at the kitchen table, preparing oils, she had nearly convinced herself that she would propose to him if he didn't do it himself, and soon.

She was startled by the outside door flying open. Brandubh stepped inside with the cold air, his face grim.

"Eibhlin, Brian has called me to Kincora."

A cold weight dropped into the pit of her stomach. "It has begun?"

"Brian raised the siege of Dublin at Christmas. Instead of taking the peace, Maelmordha and Sitric have forged alliances with Northmen from all over the isles. A host gathers even now in the east."

"Clontarf?"

He nodded.

"Will you go?"

He was silent for a long time. "If he asks me, I will go."

A large, cold fist closed over her heart. He will die, she heard her frightened soul cry.

Brandubh came to kneel by her side.

"Will you come to Kincora, Eibhlin? It is time to tell him of the future. Perhaps we can convince him to remain behind and leave the fighting to the rest of us."

He took her hands between his. They were cold and Eibhlin switched with him, warming his huge hands between her much smaller ones.

"Do you believe he will?" she asked.

Brandubh's eyes averted from hers.

"I do not know. I fear he will jump on a horse and run toward it. He is almost like a Northman in his desire to die in battle. Yet, he also loves Ireland. He has always done what he thinks is best for her."

There was no decision to make.

"I'll pack my things."

As she passed him, he gently seized her elbow. "When is the battle?"

"Good Friday. I don't know the date."

Brandubh considered. "It will be April twenty-third. That will give me a week to return before Beltain." He glanced into her eyes and didn't need to add the words--*if I survive*. "I will return and take you and Moira to the Crag if I am able."

He still thought she wanted to go to the Crag, even after.... She nodded, then pulled away and ran from him before her tears betrayed her.

Chapter Twenty-seven

"Here I am, Uncle." Brandubh waited for Brian to raise his eyes from the book he held on his lap.

"Ah, boy, good for you to wait upon me."

Brandubh smiled. "Come, now, Brian, I've been waiting for three days to get the chance to speak with you. You summoned me two weeks ago, just as I was about to have Conchobar cover that roan mare you gave me last year. He was somewhat chagrined at being interrupted."

"I imagine," Brian answered, his blue eyes glittering with humor.

So, Brandubh thought, he is in a good mood. Brian had been apt to melancholia of late. Too much time alone.

"How is our lady, Eibhlin ni Seamus?" he asked, all indications of innocence wasted on Brandubh. He knew this old lion far too well.

"She is here, Uncle. And well, if my eyes are any judge."

Brian laughed. "Have you persuaded the lady to marry you?"

"Have you been talking to Dougal again? You know he is highly unreliable."

"Such impudence. Where is your respect for your father, Brandubh?"

"I respect him, Uncle, above all others. I love him above all other men, but he is my father. If I do not see his faults, who will?"

"Your mother keeps a book, I understand."

"I believe she must," Brandubh replied with a laugh.

Brian sobered and poured them each a cup of wine before he got to the point Brandubh had dreaded. Handing Brandubh the cup, he sighed.

"I need your sword, boyo."

Brandubh shut his eyes, forcing down the anger behind the words he swallowed.

"Uncle, I have served you for more years...."

One hand, palm up, silenced Brandubh.

"We have taken the campaign to the east, Brandubh, to Leinster, to Maelmordha. I should be there now." Brian's eyes clouded as he mentioned the name of his former near-brother. "He has enlisted the assistance of Sitric Silkbeard, and God alone knows what other packs of Viking dogs. The word is Sitric has offered his mother to the man who kills me. Quite a tangled family feud, is it not?"

Brian looked up, his smile empty of his earlier humor.

Brandubh tried to hide his pity. He wondered if anyone else knew how much Brian had loved the wife he had put off for the good of Ireland. The wife now being offered as the reward for his death.

"Well," the old man said, "all that remains is to ensure that Gormlaith remains unmarried, eh? And that means I need every strong arm I can get. I need men I can trust, Brandubh. There are too many...." He didn't need to finish the sentence.

In the silence that followed, Brandubh considered his options. Perhaps now was the time....

"I will go if you agree to remain here."

Brian dropped his mouth open in astonishment. "No. Why would I remain behind?"

"You are seventy-two, Uncle."

"That is none of your affair, puppy."

Brandubh chuckled out loud. "Uncle, I am thirty years old. Hardly a puppy. But I will not risk my life just to watch you go out and get yourself murdered."

"I am the match...."

"Brian, I am not saying you are not. But more important than a warrior, you are the...." Brandubh groped for the right word. "The rallying point. You are our standard. Without you, Ireland dies."

He stopped suddenly, perilously close to telling Brian about Eibhlin's prediction.

"What do you mean, Ireland dies?" The canny blue eyes searched Brandubh's face.

"I only mean you have brought us this far. You have united the whole of Ireland under one king. You have ensured a long period of peace. If Sitric's prize is sufficient to inspire the effort, you will not be safe."

"What man in a battle is safe, Brandubh?"

Brian was clearly offended that his ability to defend himself was being questioned. But at the bottom of the kettle was only one question. He got back to it.

"What I do is my concern. I have asked for your sword. I do not wish to command it."

"Would you command it?" Brandubh asked, holding Brian's gaze, prepared to refuse.

But Brian was the *Ard Ri*. He was Brian Boru. Brandubh had known few men who would not obey when called to his side.

"I will not command you, boy. But I need you."

The old lion had not lost his power. Brandubh felt it pulling at him as surely as the silken threads of the siren's song called sailors to their deaths. He silently whispered a prayer that this call would not have a similar end.

"My sword is yours, Uncle."

Brian's smile, so rarely given, was the reward Brandubh could never refuse. All his life, only Dougal had held a higher place in Brandubh's affection than Uncle Brian. Brian had treated Brandubh as his own, often taking him along on trips, then on battles, and now it was happening again.

Brian set his hands on the sides of Brandubh's face and gazed on him. So many times, they had stood thus, and Brandubh had always wondered what was on the old man's mind. This time he finally found out.

"I always wanted to tell you, Brandubh, how proud Mahon... your grandfather would have been of you." Brian laughed. "He probably would have even forgiven Dougal for being Italian once he held you in his arms."

As they shared a laugh, Brandubh was struck by the thought that at Lon Dubh or Ath Sionnain, there was naught he could do to prevent Brian's death. The only place anything could be done was at the battle, at Clontarf.

Perhaps, Brandubh thought, he could even take his king's place, if whatever gods who ruled such things demanded blood. It would be a sacrifice worth making if the terrible darkness of Eibhlin's prophecy could be averted.

* * * *

Eibhlin studied him as he moved through the crowd of men, stopping here and there to talk and laugh at some joke.

Well, she thought miserably, at least he seems to be in a better mood.

She couldn't say much for her own. Their too-few weeks of near perfect bliss at Lon Dubh had come to an end with Brian's summons. It was as though Brandubh had expected his return to Brian's service would revive her stupid rejection of him as nothing more than a killer and he decided to reject her first.

Their ride down to Kincora--in his haste he hadn't even stopped at his father's house to join Dougal's party--had been tense, with the long silences broken only by terse questions about what was about to happen. When her answers had been non-existent or inadequate, Brandubh had bitten back the angry words she could see forming on his lips.

Every bit of closeness they'd shared was gone and Eibhlin blamed herself. If she'd just not been so quick to throw aside what he'd offered her. If only she'd thought about him instead of the single incident at the abbey.

If only....

Now, if only he would look at her like he used to, call her *my Lady* with the same fervor in the depths of his black eyes. If only he would come to her bed and let her show him how much she loved him.

One of the younger ladies of Brian's household sidled up to Brandubh, laying her hand on his arm. Her eyes could be read across the room as they flashed in neon-clarity the invitation to enjoy her favors later on.

But it was Brandubh's reaction that really burned Eibhlin.

Lowering his lips to the woman's ear, he whispered something that made her giggle like a simpleton.

"Well, well. What is he up to? And so openly, too."

Eibhlin acknowledged Sadbh, wondering how she could materialize like that from the air?

"It looks like he's fishing." Eibhlin's voice sounded bitter to her own ears. She could only imagine what it must sound like to Sadbh. "I suppose he must like pushy women."

"You mean, forward?" Sadbh asked. "No, but he does like a woman who decides what she wants then sticks to it."

"Is that directed at me?"

Sadbh shrugged. "You must admit, Eibhlin, you have not been exceeding constant in your desires."

"Lady, I have been exceptionally constant, considering everyone in the kingdom of Munster has been harping at me to marry Brandubh. I told you from the beginning I couldn't stay here."

"You told Brandubh you would marry him."

"I was sick. He'd saved my life. I was grateful."

"Hah!" Sadbh burst out laughing. "Grateful?"

"It's not funny, Sadbh. Really, your sense of humor is getting as weird as Dougal's."

Sadbh laughed harder, Eibhlin's jab bouncing off. "Why do you not admit what you feel? It is clear as the waters of a mountain stream."

The woman courting Brandubh slipped her arm into the crook of his elbow. Her mouth never stopped moving and he attended her as though she were the most fascinating creature on earth.

Eibhlin rolled her eyes just as he raised his to glance at her. Knowingly, he passed his gaze up and down Eibhlin's body, then stood slightly back from his willing companion, as though comparing the two.

"The swine," Sadbh muttered, shaking her head. "'Twould serve him right if you turned your attention elsewhere."

"Where else could I go from that?" Eibhlin asked, her eyes feasting on him, her body still reeling from his visual caress.

"Ireland is chock-a-block with handsome men."

"Not like him." Eibhlin sighed. "Anyway, he hasn't asked me again. He doesn't want me anymore, at least not to marry."

"Ah, so that is the way the wind blows." Sadbh crossed her arms and fixed Eibhlin with a steely gaze. "He will not ask you again. You will have to make the first move."

"I'm not very good at chess, Sadbh. I never learned how to play the game."

"This is no game, Eibhlin. However, there is one way to check that king with your opening move."

In spite of herself, Eibhlin asked, "How?"

"Go to your chamber. I will order a bath for you and a new gown. Then come out for the evening meal prepared to wed, if," she added with her exquisitely raised auburn eyebrow, "that is what you have finally settled upon." Sadbh's icy blue eyes softened and she asked, "Do you love him, Eibhlin? Can you see yourself in any other man's arms?"

"No. I can't."

"Then you must offer for him."

THE RAVEN'S LADY

"What?"

"I will explain when it is time. Do you accept?"

Eibhlin studied him, still paying gallant attention to the young woman. Yes, a voice deep inside cried out to her. Yes.

I've got to think about this, one more time, she thought. To Sadbh, she said, "For now, I'll accept the bath."

Sadbh's laughter followed her from the hall. Eibhlin didn't look to see if Brandubh's eyes did as well.

* * * *

What in the world is Mother up to over there? Brandubh asked himself, while trying to pay attention to the woman hanging all over his arm. Once again, he felt as though women were moving around a gaming board and he, a simple-minded man, could only watch and try to discern the game before he was mated.

Mated?

Eibhlin said something to Sadbh and stalked out of the hall in the direction of the sleeping chambers.

"Oh, no, Mother," he whispered, unaware he'd spoken the words aloud until the woman on his arm--he'd forgotten her name--tightened her grip.

"What is wrong, Lord Brandubh? Are you displeased by something?" Her empty face waited for his answer.

"No, my lady, nothing at all. However, I do now remember some business with my mother which I dare not let linger. As much as I regret having to leave your pleasant company...." He raised her hand and barely brushed her fingers with his lips. "Please excuse me."

"Will I see you later?" she asked, her voice much too loud and causing many heads to turn.

"I do not believe so, lady."

He made a courtly bow to the lady and turned his attention to his mother. Sadbh, cool as ever, stood her ground, half-smile playing on her lips.

"Mother," he said by way of greeting, kissing her offered cheek.

"Brandubh, my son, how nice of you to finally find time to speak to your mother. Have you informed you father of your continued good health? We feared for you when we heard naught for so many days."

"You need not fear that I will die from lack of attention."

"On the contrary," Sadbh said, swallowing her laughter, "I see you are well-tended. Though not by the right woman."

"The right woman will leave me soon."

"Yet, you took her to Lon Dubh. Did nothing transpire there?"

He could not keep the smile from his lips. Sadbh saw it.

"So, our lady is no longer pure?"

"She is as pure as when she came to me."

"That is an uncharitable thing to say, Brandubh."

"I do not mean it to be, Mother. I mean only that I have not dishonored her. She is, in my heart, my wife. My body, does she want it, is hers. I use hers as she offers it to me."

He felt Sadbh's eyes on his face. "Does she know you love her so?" When he did not--could not--answer that question, she asked another. "Have you told her?"

"I have not said the words. She knows how I feel."

Sadbh rolled her eyes. "God's Bones, Brandubh!" Heads turned again. "She sees you with another woman draped over your arm and you make no move to disengage yourself. You do not press your suit, but you take her when she wants you. She is *confused*, you great fool! And I fear we have done naught but add to her confusion." Sadbh tossed her hands up. "I do not know why I continue to help you."

"Because you want to see your grandchildren," Brandubh whispered into her ear.

A smile crept across her face. "That must be it. So, when will you offer for her again?"

"I will not. I have told you this. She must make the choice freely to come to me."

"For Heaven's sake, Brandubh. A woman wants to know she is desired. Needed. Wanted. She does not want you to act as though you could live as well without her." Shaking her head, she said, "Once again, you foolish men show you do not know what is good for you."

She started off. Brandubh caught her elbow gently and turned her.

"Mother," he said, his voice as stern as it had ever been with his mother. "I would not have you interfere with her decision."

Sadbh raised her eyebrow, her indignation palpable.

"When have I ever interfered in your life?" she asked, a frown forming on her face as she turned and walked away, motioning for her maid to follow her.

He could only watch her stride out of the hall with a purpose that would have terrified a lesser man. Whatever his mother had planned, Brandubh thought, he doubted it would be entirely comfortable for him. When Moira joined her on the way up the staircase, he was certain.

Yet if she had made up her mind to interfere, he knew from long experience he was incapable of stopping her. And, he thought, suddenly encouraged, if she were on her way to Eibhlin, there was a plan afoot. Sadbh's plans seldom went awry.

His amused chuckle rumbling from his chest, Brandubh went to find Dougal and one of Brian's judges, just in case there was a marriage contract to write tonight. She would not get away again.

* * * *

Eibhlin had endured a couple of hours of Sadbh's maid and Sadbh and Moira and young Blanaid who had tended Eibhlin during her first visit to Kincora--was it already over four months ago? When they were finished, though, she had to admit she looked pretty good.

"Oh, dear one," Moira whispered.

Eibhlin saw the glistening tears of pride and joy in her mother's eyes. It reminded her of the night she'd gone on her first prom date.

Why did I have to think of that? Eibhlin moaned silently. A disaster, that's what it had been. Jeremy Terwilliger had been the only boy to ask her. Pressured by her friends, she accepted, against her better judgment. On prom night, she'd sat at Moira's vanity table and allowed her mother to transform her from ugly duckling into homely emu.

Moira's collection of Max Factor cosmetics couldn't change the immutable. Eibhlin was still too tall and too awkward and too *unusual* looking. Jeremy arrived late enough to give her time to concoct reasons. He didn't want to go with her. He died in a terrible accident on the way over. When he finally did arrive, her relief at not being stood up made her goofy and clumsy.

Now, she was being dolled up to make a man want to marry her. Really, she thought, how could he? Not only did he have every woman in the whole of Ireland after him, she'd turned him down. Oh, sure, he was more than willing when she let her hunger and thirst for him show, but there probably wasn't a man alive who would turn down any woman when she was offering free sex.

"Are you listening to me, Eibhlin?" Sadbh said, bending down and staring right in her eyes.

"I'm sorry, Sadbh."

"Is this what you want, Eibhlin?"

She'd just spent an entire afternoon in a tub of water, thinking, weighing, pondering. Brandubh had brought her to Kincora to give her the chance to change history. He wasn't afraid of that. Why should she be?

Point one down.

Next, this time, this place, was so different from the world she had grown up in.

The world in which she had always felt like a badly cut pair of blue jeans, she reminded herself. From her first contact with Brandubh on Craglea, she had felt the fit of this place. Was that why the curtain had appeared to her? She'd finally showed up *where* she belonged. The curtain gave her the chance to be *when* she belonged. Could she live here for the rest of her life?

Eibhlin shut up her brain, listening for the small voice that was her heart's.

Yes, it said softly, gently. No ruckus needed to get the point across.

Point two down.

Last. Brandubh.

"Sadbh, does he want me?"

The cool Sadbh grabbed handfuls of her own hair and pulled, then twisted on one heel and paced by the bed. "I am surrounded by fools! Does no one know what they want anymore?" she shouted to the walls.

"Lady, let me," Moira said in a whisper, her hand on Sadbh's arm. She faced Eibhlin, smile barely restrained. "Eibhlin, Lady Sadbh is, well, impatient. Not only with you, but with Brandubh as well. You see, dear one, he will not offer for you again, though he wants you. He insists that you must make the choice. So, you see, if you want him, you will have to offer for him."

"Sadbh has already told me that. But what do I have to offer? My cattle?"

"No." Sadbh, calm now, knelt before Eibhlin. "All you need do is offer him water to wash his hands. It is an old custom, but he will recognize it. Like as not, he will haul you before a judge to solemnize the contracts before supper." She glanced toward heaven, "I hope. It must be done before an assembly. Normally a feast would be arranged for an unmarried daughter. And he must accept the basin from your hands."

"Lady, will the priests protest?" Moira asked, uncertainly.

"I hardly care, Moira, if I can get that son of mine married and settled. Now," she said, turning back to Eibhlin, "do you want to do this?"

"Yes." Eibhlin nodded emphatically. She did want it.

Sadbh's smile opened like a ray of the sun on the surface of the lake. "Thank you, my dear," she said, her voice cracking as she wrapped her arms around Eibhlin and pulled her close. "Now, I must go and prepare. I will inform Dougal so he can keep Brandubh close by." Before the words were all out of her mouth, Sadbh was out the door in a blur of dark blue and gold.

"Are you content, dear one?"

"I really am. Finally."

Moira beamed as brightly as Sadbh had. "Good. I will be more easy about leaving you in his care." Taking both Eibhlin's hands, she pulled her to her feet. "Come, my Lady Eibhlin, we go to meet your husband."

My husband, Eibhlin thought, following Moira's youthful exuberance out the door. My husband.

Yes. Yes, her heart answered.

"Ready?" Moira asked, just outside the hall.

Eibhlin nodded.

They crossed through the doorway. The first person she saw was Brandubh. He lounged against a table, holding a cup loosely in his hand. His eyes were far away, and she wondered what he was looking at.

Then he turned and looked at her.

* * * *

She stood on the steps leading into Brian's great hall looking like a princess of the *Danaan*, even Dana herself. Holding herself so straight and proud, the smile on her beautiful face gentle and full of....

Was that what love looked like? He had seen desire, anger, fear. Disgust, even. This expression was indeed more than any of those. And it was directed at him.

The sounds of the crowd faded in his ears to the buzzing of a gnat. His eyes could only see her.

Descending the steps, she went to the table where basins waited for the diners to wash and dipped her hands. With maddening deliberation, she dried her fingertips on a length of linen that she then threaded through her belt. Raising the ewer, she filled a basin, glancing at him as the water flowed. When the basin was half-full, she set the ewer back down and

THE RAVEN'S LADY

picked up the basin, turning toward him.

Some snippet of a thought raced through his brain as he tried to think of why this was especially significant.

What is it? What does it mean? She's bringing me water to wash my hands in front of....

His breath caught in his throat.

She was making her choice. Before witnesses.

Brandubh caught sight of his mother and Moira waiting behind her.

What was he supposed to do? He had no thought but that she had chosen him. She wanted to marry him. She would stay.

But what was he supposed to do? She came closer, basin before her.

He glanced at Sadbh.

Take it. The words formed silently on her lips.

Of course, accept what she offered. He cursed himself for a fool and blessed his mother for her interference.

The roomful of people was silent, except for the whispers as explanations were offered to those who did not understand what was happening.

Eibhlin stopped before him, holding the basin out in front of her.

"My Lord?" she asked. Her eyes spoke promises such as he could not contemplate right now.

"Thank you, my Lady," he said, voice cracking on the words. He laid his hands over hers on the basin, accepting her gift.

"Well, finally," Dougal said, none too quietly.

The swell of cheers and congratulations drowned out her voice, yet he heard her.

"Finally," Eibhlin echoed.

"Finally," Brandubh added as an amen.

He stood, looking into her eyes, his hands on hers, until Dougal came over.

"Son," he whispered for all to hear, "shall I summon the *brehon*?"

"Um?" Brandubh asked.

"The *brehon*, son. The judge, so that you may marry this woman and take her to bed and we might get our dinner tonight?"

A roar of laughter swept over the hall.

The blush crept up Eibhlin's cheeks. What a picture she makes, Brandubh thought before answering his father.

"Please, Father, do that." He took the basin and set it down on the table behind him and used it as it was intended. When he had washed his hands he turned to her, wet hands hanging in the air. "My Lady?"

She calmly pulled the linen from her belt and dried his hands. "May the thing be done so soon, my Lord?" she asked, as though asking about the weather.

"It must be done and quickly, my Lady, for I will not risk losing you now."

The light in her eyes grew brighter and he knew he had finally said something right.

* * * *

Dinner continued without them. And the fast was broken the next day without them. And the mid-day meal did not see them.

At about None, Brandubh raised his head from the pillow and groaned.

"I will die 'ere I leave this bed," he whispered into her hair. "I may die in this bed," he added, laughing weakly.

"We'll both die if we don't get some food soon," Eibhlin giggled. She slapped her hand over her mouth. "Oh my God, I giggled. I don't believe it." She smacked his stone-hard shoulder. "You made me giggle."

"Is this a bad thing?" Brandubh's chuckle mocked her. "I would have you laugh always, my Lady."

"Oh, you are so sweet," she said and grabbed his hand and bestowed kisses all over it, palm, back, each finger. Then she let it fall over her breast.

"Are you content, my Lady?" Brandubh asked, turning onto his side. His hand, so big and warm and strong rested on her hip, fitting from the notch of her waist to the top of the curve.

"Aye, my Lord, I am content," she said, hearing the purr in her own voice. Geez, first giggling, now purring. Where will it end? Her hand moved--of its own volition, she would swear--to his cheek. Her fingers desired to comb through his silky black hair and she allowed them to go. Her palm ached to caress the back of his neck and while it was there, her lips asked if it would pull his mouth over to hers.

"Ah, yes, my thoughts exactly," he murmured when her hand did the favor for her lips and she hadn't even thought anything at all.

Except that she loved him.

Had he seen it in her eyes? He smiled at her, a secret lover's smile that said everything and nothing.

"Come, we are wasting good daylight, wife." Effortlessly, he rolled over her, covering her, his weight pressing her into the mattress, a comforting burden.

Her every sense fastened on him. The tickle of his hair falling into her face, across her neck. The moisture of his lips and tongue on her breasts. The taste of his skin against her mouth, the salty flavor she could not remember from anywhere else. His whispered words of desire and need. The rasping sound of his breath as his heart beat faster and faster against hers, fairly shaking her with its pounding.

She couldn't touch enough of him and her hands raced to pull him closer, hold him tighter.

Brandubh ran his hands down her thighs and behind her knees, bringing them up around his waist. His entry was quick and he filled her so completely her body arched in pure animal satisfaction.

So right, so right, her heart sang. How could you have thought to deprive us of this?

The rest of her joined in, cheering her final decision to take what God, surely, had offered.

Chapter Twenty-eight

She lay in his arms, his body warm and hard against her softer one.

"I spoke with Brian." His voice was nearly too quiet to hear. "He has commanded me to come with him on his campaign."

"No." The word slipped out. "We've only just married. He can't take you away from me now."

"Eibhlin, I do not wish to go. In truth, I have had enough, but Brian needs me, he needs every sword arm he can get. If I do not go, there will be others who will stay home."

"The Irish will win, Brandubh. You don't need to be there."

His hand stroked her arm, his warmth seeping through to her bones.

"I have wondered if perhaps there is not something to your original fears. If I could prevent Brian's death...."

"Do you think it's possible? Before...."

"I know what I said before. But without him, Ireland will die. If there is any chance...." He pulled back and looked into her eyes. "Perhaps that is why you are here, to prevent this from happening." He settled back against the pillows and tightened his arm around her. "The Ireland I want for my descendants is not one torn by constant conflict. I want peace and quiet and a green place to raise my horses. And our children."

"That's all I want, too." And she realized it was true.

She'd done the best she could and left behind her some successes, but even before she'd crossed that curtain, she'd felt an emptiness and longing for the truly lasting things. She wanted children, Brandubh's children.

Now, even that modest dream was in jeopardy.

"If I can watch over him," Brandubh went on, "bring him back alive, he will have time to prepare Ireland for the future." He closed his eyes. "If I fail, if he dies anyway, we will be no worse off than we..." He glanced down at her, a wry, sad smile on his face. "We will be no worse off than we are going to be."

Eibhlin couldn't, even for his sake, return that smile.

"When will you leave?" She feared the answer.

"Tomorrow at dawn."

Eibhlin shivered and Brandubh's arms tightened around her even more. She felt her ribs bowing under the pressure. More, she could feel the desperation of his need for her. Her own was no less urgent.

"We have so little time, my Lady," he said in the instant it took him to turn with her in his arms, placing her firmly underneath his body.

She eagerly accepted his kisses, straining to get closer--inside him if she could have--and share his very soul.

"My Lady," he whispered against her cheek, his lips grazing her skin down to her neck. "If I do not return...."

"No, no. Don't." Eibhlin grabbed his head and brought his lips to hers, silencing him.

Brandubh raised himself away from her. "Eibhlin, please. If I do not return, do not remain here out of some sense of duty to me. If you wish to return to your own time...."

She wrapped her arms around his strong neck and pulled him back down, hiding her face against him.

"Please, don't," she whimpered, heart breaking at the thought. "Don't make me promise something like that." Drawing his mouth to hers, she kissed him with everything that was overflowing her heart.

"Just love me, Brandubh. Leave the rest," she whispered against his lips.

* * * *

Every eye was on them as Brandubh led his wife into Brian's hall for the evening meal. He glanced over at her, pleased by the rosy glow in her cheeks, the way she held her head up high, allowing her height to impress. Never had he felt so proud of another person.

Indeed, every eye was on her. The assembled provincial kings and tribal chieftains preparing for the war that seemed imminent followed her with lust-filled gazes.

"They are so eager to fight," she whispered to him.

"Yes, they are, my Lady."

"Is there no other way?"

"Not now."

"Come, pup, bring that lovely lady of yours up here and join us." Brian was standing by his chair at the table. "I hope you are content with your state, Lady. Our Brandubh appears so."

"Mind reader, Uncle?" Brandubh asked as he helped Eibhlin step up onto the dais.

"I do not need to be a mind reader, boyo."

"I understand you will take my husband from me, Lord, even before I have a chance to become tired of him."

Dougal laughed. "Daughter, how could you threaten the boy that way?"

"I never discount any possibility, Father," Eibhlin replied. "Though I admit with his breeding, it is extremely unlikely that I will tire of him before he is, oh, eighty years old?"

Brian chuckled. "So much as that? God willing, I shall never attain such a degree of decrepitude."

"You would deprive us of your company, Uncle?" Sadbh asked. "Sounds rather selfish to me."

"Ah, my love," Brian answered fondly, "there are few people I will miss more than you when I at last leave this vale. However...." He raised his cup and sipped. When he replaced it on the table, his eyes had become clouded. "When a man's time has passed, a graceful exit may be desired without being selfish."

"Nay, Uncle," Sadbh said, laying her hand on Brian's arm. "Your time will never pass."

"Would you condemn me to immortality?" he asked with a smile.

"I would have you always as you are, for I am selfish enough to wish never to be without you."

He raised her hand to his lips and kissed it. "Ah, Sadbh, you are as loving as your father." Brian brushed her cheek with the backs of his fingers. "Do you remember him, child? You resemble him a great deal, though I believe you have your mother's temper."

Sadbh smiled. "I fear I remember little of him, Uncle."

"Indeed, you were young, just a babe, when he was murdered. I begged him not to go, you know."

Brandubh saw the tears form in Brian's eyes. Only mention of Mahon was able to touch him so deeply.

"I begged him to let me go with him at least. He refused. It was as though he knew what was coming and welcomed it." Brian closed his eyes and, with a voice roughened by sorrow, he asked, "Has it really been so long?"

The grief was as strong as ever, Brandubh thought.

A silence fell around the table, though the hum of amiable conversation buzzed around them from the other diners.

"Ho, Brian," came a voice from the floor, "will we go off to kill the Vikings with no entertainment?"

Brian smiled, rousing from his melancholy memories. "Very right, Owen, indeed. What shall we have?"

"We need stories of the old heroes."

"Aye. Where's MacLiag? Get the bard out here, Brian."

"Inspire us, poet!"

MacLiag, preening in his six-colored robe, assumed his place at the corner of the dais where the king sat. He wrapped his fingers around the front edges of his robe and, with serious eyes, gazed out upon his audience, waiting for silence.

Turning to bow to his king, and receiving a nod in return, MacLiag faced outward into the hall and opened his mouth. The crowd as one being breathed a sigh of expectation as he uttered the first words of the tale he had selected.

"In the days long ago, when Conchobar sat upon the throne of Ulster, a lord of that province called Bricciu of the Poisoned Tongue made a feast. He invited Conchobar and all the greatest among the fighting men of Eriu. His purpose was not to provide hospitable entertainment, but that by them he would be entertained. For you see, Bricciu deserved his name."

The audience, though each could have told the story, sat up.

"The poisoned-tongued Bricciu set the warriors to contending among themselves which was the champion of the whole land...."

The warriors assembled under this roof attended the poet's words as he wove them a picture of a heady time. The story of the Demon Knight's Challenge was one of Brandubh's favorites and he sat back to listen, pulling Eibhlin closer.

"To decide between the mighty warriors, a demon called Dreadful *was summoned forth. He proposed a test of courage."*

"Fighting and fucking," Eibhlin said under her breath.

Brandubh was not certain he had heard her correctly. "What did you say?"

Eibhlin huffed. "Uaid said the Irish were good only for fucking and fighting. Looking at this bunch, I believe it."

Brandubh wiped the smile that threatened to break out over his face at her words. He could see she was in no mood for levity. "Do not be so harsh in your judgments, my love. These men go to die on the morrow."

As soon as the words left his mouth, he would that he could have them back. He set his hand on her arm to comfort her from the reminder of his departure with this bunch of fucking fighters. "Eibhlin."

She shook his hand from her arm and sat stiffly between him and Brian. Brian noted her sudden change.

"My lady, are you well?" he asked in a whisper.

"No, Lord. You are sending my husband to die. How can I be well?"

Brian sat up, his eyes narrowed on her. If she noticed, she ignored his censure.

MacLiag continued, unaware of the silent battle going on behind him.

"Cuchulain was proclaimed Champion of Ireland and her boldest man." He folded his arms across his ample chest and bowed to the cheers.

Brandubh watched her eyes pass over the audience, then up to Brian. Then she turned and examined Brandubh himself, as though looking for the sign that he, too, had been seized by the need to spill other men's blood.

MacLiag had retired to his chair to have a drink of Brian's fine Italian wine. The audience clamored for more.

Eibhlin was up and around the table before he could stop her. She took the bard's place before the dais and stood, waiting. Every tongue fell silent and every eye froze on her.

"Men of Ireland, though I be no poet, I have a tale to tell you...." she began.

Brian sat up, leaning on his elbows on the table.

"It is the tale of the greatest of all the High Kings of memory. No myth is he. No tale from the misty times of ages past. He is not the creation of an ollav poet, nor romantic boy."

She paused, waiting for her audience to catch up with her. In her bearing and her voice, Brandubh saw a bard, a teller of tales.

"My tale is the tale of Brian mac Cennedi, Boru, King of all kings."

An awed whisper rippled through the hall.

"Brian was a small child, the youngest of twelve. His spindly legs and freckled face gave only his mother pleasure."

Even Brian smiled.

"Yet even this small child grew. And grew...." She gazed upon the king and raised an eyebrow. "And grew...." She paused again, waiting for the laughter to die down. "Until he was the tallest man in Eriu, a beautiful young man who made the hearts of young women flutter like birds. Aye, he had no equal."

Her face became serious. "And, he lived many years, king of Thomond, then King of Munster. When the time came to bring his strong hand to ruling all of Ireland, he stepped upon the Stone of Fal and the very rock itself proclaimed him to be the one true *Ard Ri*, the King of all kings." She raised her arm and swept her pointed finger over all the assembled. "Is there one here who will deny my words?"

Her finger stopped in mid-air, pointing at Malachy, king of Meath, the bandy-legged man whom Brian supplanted as High King. He gave her no answer.

Eibhlin took a deep breath and turned to look at Brandubh. He knew before she opened her mouth what she was going to do. He only hoped the priests had already retired for the night. She would surely be charged with fortune-telling if they found out about this.

"The stone sang for him. Is there one here worthy to take the title from him? Can he not, even now, best most of you with sword or ax? Who can forget the great battles of his youth, when he set the Vikings of Limerick to rout? Or when the petty kings from the north...."

No, Eibhlin, do not do this, Brandubh begged her silently.

"Took arms against him. Yet did he defeat them all." She turned back to her audience. "And, yet will he be best remembered for victories yet to come. Stand with him, Men of Ireland, that you, too, will be remembered with honor by bards yet unborn. Know that before the next High Holy Day, Ireland will fight for her life. Brian Boru will lead his great army against the Northmen and their Leinster puppets."

Her deep breath gave her audience time to catch theirs.

"I have not seen Cuchulain. I have not seen Nuada of the Silver Hand. I have not seen Conchobar or Maeve or Finn. But, I have seen Brian mac Cennedi. I have seen Brian Boru. I have seen the Champion of Ireland and her boldest man."

She closed her eyes and bowed her head, ever so slightly.

The hall sat in silence. For a beat of time, nothing, no one, not so much as a hair on a dog's hide moved.

It began, one or two voices from the back at first, then picked up and multiplied and carried forward.

"*Boru. Boru. Boru....*"

Just as they did in battle, chanting the name of the man they would die for, they did now. In battle the sound was enough to strike fear into the hearts of Boru's foes. Now it was softly said, prayerfully spoken.

Brandubh rose, taking up the chant. Out of the corner of his eye, he saw Dougal had done likewise.

Brian stood up, his expression one of pure love. From every corner of the hall they came forward--the men who chanted his name, the common soldiers and junior officers in Brian's army. They lined up in front of their king, once more offering their swords, their lives, their honor to Brian and to Ireland.

Down at the tables, sitting in stony silence were the old men, men with ambitions of their own. Men that Brian held in check by his own determination to keep Ireland whole and strong and able to withstand what was bound to happen when he was gone.

Brandubh looked at those ambitious faces. They were easy to spot. They had been impressed by Eibhlin's call, but their hearts remained untouched.

She knew it too, he could see from the slump of her shoulders and the sadness in her eyes that she knew she had not changed anything.

* * * *

Eibhlin stood at the door of the king's chamber, heart pounding.

"Go in, Lady. The king awaits." The steward who had brought her to Brian turned and departed.

Drawing a deep, calming breath, she laid her hand against the door.

"Come, Lady," Brian's deep voice rumbled at her.

"You called me, my Lord?" she asked, trying to hide her trepidation.

"Aye, I did." Brian lounged in his chair, elbows resting on the arms. Steepling his long fingers before his face, he studied her. "Tell me, lady, is there no end to your talents? What other hidden gifts may we expect you to display? Do you also stitch a pretty line? Perhaps you write poetry."

One coppery eyebrow rose. The ghost of a smile played upon his full lips.

"My parents were bards, troubadours. I suppose I inherited some of their talent."

"Sit, please. I would speak with you about one thing you said." He waited for her to take the chair across from him at the fireplace. "Tell me again, this tale of Brian Boru, who will be remembered best for victories yet to come. A fascinating thing, to ponder one's future, is it not?" He sat up and rested his elbows on his knees. Clasping his large hands together, he said, "Tell me, Lady. How come you to know of things yet to come?"

"I don't know, Lord," she stuttered.

"Call me Brian, Eibhlin." His voice was low, gentle, persuasive. "Please tell me about what will come."

"No."

"Please." It wasn't the command of a king. It was a plea.

"I can't, Brian. How can it help? What if I tell you something that makes you change the way you will conduct the campaign?"

"You do know how it will turn out, don't you?"

Eibhlin was aghast she'd given away as much as she had.

"Brian, don't ask me. Please don't ask me."

"Will I die?"

Her answer was loud and clear. She could see in his eyes that he'd seen in hers the truth that he would not return.

"You can't go, Brian. You must stay here, out of danger."

"I have never stood back to send men to die in my place. I will not stay behind."

"At least don't go into the battle yourself. You are needed if Ireland...."

He raised his eyes to hers. "What? Brandubh also spoke of Ireland when he begged me to remain behind. Tell me all." The king's voice commanded her. He glanced away for an instant. "I am sorry, my dear. I have been a king for a long time. I am used to giving a command and having my will fulfilled." He reached over and took her hand. "Please. I have to know. We will defeat the Northmen?"

She nodded.

"What else, then? I will die." He said it as a fact which he accepted. "What then?"

He loved Ireland as he had never loved a woman. Perhaps that is where she should concentrate her effort to convince him.

"When you die," she began shakily, "the squabbling and tribal wars will start again. Bandits and thieves will haunt the roads. The conquerors will come again and this time they won't be happy just mixing with the Irish as the Vikings have done. These conquerors will destroy Ireland, Brian, because we won't be strong enough to defeat them."

Brian sat back in his chair, his face etched by lines suddenly deeper and more prominent.

"I had thought perhaps that would be the case. Yet, what can I do? The battle is joined, and not by my will. I would have my land in peace, Eibhlin. There is nothing more important than Ireland."

"If you die before Ireland is truly united behind one king, she will only survive in myths and legends."

Brian smiled. "Then that will have to be enough. Especially if such poets as you create them. Here, Lady, is the harp among your undiscovered talents?"

She could only nod.

"Go there, child," he said, pointing to the small harp on the hearth. "Play for me, will you? I need to think and the music soothes me and clears my mind."

"I will play for you, of course, my Lord," she smiled, "if you will play for me."

He nodded and leaned back, eyes closing.

Eibhlin left the chair and knelt by the harp. She played a tune that wouldn't be written for seven hundred years, one of O'Carolan's. Then Brian joined her on the floor and played for her. Then she played another, one of Moira's future compositions. They exchanged tunes for hours, their mutual admiration outlasting the fire.

Finally, Brian stretched from the enchantment of being, for a short while, a poet, not a king.

"I fear, my dear, my old bones require some rest." He took her hand and raised it to his lips. "Thank you, my Lady, for passing the evening with me. I have rarely spent such an enjoyable time with such a beautiful woman."

Eibhlin narrowed her eyes in cynical disbelief.

Brian laughed, the rich tone bouncing off the walls.

"Believe it or not, my Lady, it is the truth. I do envy Brandubh. It is too bad I do not haunt Craglea as I used to, for it would have been I who found you." His eyes held hers. "And I would not be sending you back to him now."

He rose, amazingly lithe for a seventy-two year old man, and offered her a hand up. "Come, Eibhlin. Go warm your husband's bed. Get with child tonight...." Brian kissed her hand. "If it be a male child, name him for me."

She could only nod obediently. The words she would say caught in her throat and her heart clutched with premature grief. Reaching up, she lay her hand around his neck and pulled him down to brush her lips against his.

"Good night, Uncle," she whispered, squeezing his hand and turning to go.

"Eibhlin," Brian called as she opened the door. "Wait."

He came to her, bearing a bundle. "Take it. I will not be able to take it with me."

She pulled the linen back and saw the small harp she had just played. "Oh, Brian, I couldn't...."

"If I return, I will reclaim it. If I do not, it would please me to know you are enjoying it."

"But your own children...."

"If it relieves your mind, Eibhlin, I have already given one to MacLiag. None of my children has demonstrated the talent," he added sadly.

Eibhlin held the harp to her breast. "Thank you, Brian. I will treasure it all my life."

"Play it and think of me."

The tears flowed and she threw her arms around him, unable to speak.

He squeezed her and released her. Pulling the door open, he shooed her out. "Go. Young Brandubh will comfort you much better than I. Go, now. You keep this old man from his bed."

This time, it was Brian who gently shut the door in her face.

Hugging the harp to her breast, she stumbled along the corridor toward the chamber she shared with Brandubh, her tears blinding her.

* * * *

He heard her footsteps, hurried, stumbling, but he stayed in bed. The door opened and she entered the room, carrying a linen-wrapped bundle against her breast. Soundlessly closing the door, she turned and leaned against it, her eyes finding his and holding his gaze, sharing her misery.

"He wouldn't listen, Brandubh."

Of course he had not, Brandubh thought. There was nothing Brian had hoped for more than dying on the field.

"Damn him!" Eibhlin lay her bundle on the chair and pulled her gown over her head.

Brandubh watched her take her anger out on her clothing, snatching the gown off and tossing it across the room in a ball. He smiled reluctantly at her fury.

"What are you grinning at, you mindless ass?" she huffed, crossing the room to sit on the edge of the bed. "The whole damned family is deranged," she muttered. "And I married into it! I can't believe it."

Unable to restrain himself any longer, Brandubh sat up and lay one hand on her shoulder. The muscles bunched underneath the satin of her skin. He ran his fingers along the length of her arm, pausing in the fold of her elbow to tickle.

"Stop it. I'm not in the mood."

"In the mood for what?" he asked as he brought his lips to the back of her neck.

"For this." Her words were put to the lie by the way she leaned her head forward to let him have more of her neck to nuzzle. "He wants to die."

"Yes." Brandubh half-expected her to jump away at his easy agreement. Yet she only sat still. When she finally spoke, her words came out on a shaky whisper.

"Why, Brandubh? How can he *want* to die? If he goes, Ireland...."

He raised his mouth from her neck and lay down, resting his head on one hand. The other stroked her back.

"My Lady, he is a soldier. He has seen his friends get wrinkled and flabby, their muscles wither away, their eyes grow pale. Old age is the only thing he fears."

"But...," she started, turning to him.

He raised a finger to lay against her lips. "There is nothing more to say to him. Besides, what could he do that he has not already done? He has brought Ireland peace, prosperity. He treats the provincial kings with respect and honor. Yet those fools care nothing for uniting Ireland to keep her safe from the hungry wolves that would cross the sea and devour her. They care only for their own petty ambitions. They will never accept the idea of an O Brian dynasty. Every *Ard Ri* has to earn the right, either by warfare or through politics. That is the Irish way."

She lay down across his belly, her head hanging over his side. "It seems so pointless, then."

"Why so?" He stroked her forehead and combed her hair with his fingers. "You said we would win."

"Yes, but don't you remember? The Northmen who settled in...." Her forehead wrinkled as though she were trying to remember something. "Gaul?"

"Normandy?" he offered.

"Yes. Of course, that is what they're calling it now."

Brandubh laughed. She slapped at his face with a lazy backhand.

"Anyway," she continued, "they are the people who will come to conquer Ireland."

He thought about what she had already told him and chuckled with Irish appreciation of the irony.

"Indeed, my Lady. We go on the morrow to kill the Northmen and drive them from our shores. Yet they will return and prevail after all. So, what do we do about it?"

Silence greeted his question. What could two people do in the face of such a prospect?

"We can live," Eibhlin said as she sat up and looked down at him. "Brian gave me a royal command, husband, to make a boy-child this night and name him *Brian*."

Brandubh considered the idea. Kingdoms, nations, rulers, came and went. Whole civilizations rose and fell. Yet, through it all there was this one constant.

"I do not know, wife, if I am capable of fathering a child worthy of such a fine name. Ummm, Brian mac Brandubh." He narrowed his eyes at her. "Would you like to try?"

A smile blossomed across her face. "I think it would be treasonous to ignore a direct command, don't you?"

"Absolutely. We must obey our king." He reached for her. She came eagerly. Gently, anxious that his actions spoke the words that were too difficult to say, especially tonight, he slipped her shift up and over her head, then pulled her naked body on top of his own. "Come, my Lady, let us make me a son."

Chapter Twenty-nine

April 23, 1014--Good Friday

The killing madness cooled as the number of Vikings before him diminished. As he regained his senses, Brandubh felt his stomach churn at the stench of the blood and the bowels of the dead. His brain recoiled from the screams of the dying and mutilated. His eyes cleared and he watched the bearded, fur-clad Northmen, most capped with the horned helms, retreating toward their ships riding the tide at the mouth of the Liffey.

Brandubh lowered his sword and slackened the grip on the hilt of his dagger. His shield had been discarded somewhere along the way. Turning one way, then the other, he realized he had no idea how long he'd been fighting, nor where he even was.

To regain his bearings, he looked about for Brian's tent standing in the protection of the trees. At least they had kept Brian out of the battle. Perhaps the worst of Eibhlin's prophecy could be averted, then.

He wandered through the litter of dismembered bodies and gore, trying to see nothing for now.

The roar of attack warned him an instant before he saw the glint of the lunging spear. Only years of training made his weary body side-step the strike and bring up his sword into his attacker's boneless belly. The man was dead before he hit the ground. Brandubh watched the Viking go down.

"Enjoy Valhalla, my friend," he whispered and wondered how many others he had prepared for the Valkyries today. Raising the sword, he saw the blood coating the blade, that of his fresh kill and the crusty remains of earlier ones. He pulled the tail of his tunic and used it to wipe his blade as clean as he could.

It would take much scrubbing to clean it all off.

The melee was beyond him now. It continued down by the river and Brandubh thought with disgust he recognized the squat figure of Malachy, king of Meath, pulling his sword from the neck of a dead man.

Now, he decides to join in, Brandubh thought. Malachy's Meathmen had sat atop the nearby hill and watched most of the fight. He'd held them back--Brandubh had heard that there had been a disagreement between Malachy and Brian at the last moment before the battle was joined. Maybe it was for the best, though. The Meathmen were fresh, hungry for blood.

For himself, Brandubh never wanted to hold a sword in his hand again.

He wandered through the field, trying to find his father. They had been back-to-back at first, until their rages overtook them and they became blind to anything but the enemy.

A slight figure flew down the hill toward the dispersing armies. Brandubh stared at the boy, Brian's personal attendant.

"Boy, where do you go?"

"To see the battle, Brandubh."

"And where is Brian?"

"In his tent." The boy pointed toward it.

At that moment, six Dal Cais warriors passed by, swords at the ready, headed for the fight.

"Where the hell are you going?" Brandubh grabbed the nearest one and pulled him aside. "Are you mad? Who is left with the *Ard Ri*?"

The man appeared dazed. "I don't know, Brandubh."

"Who is left with him?" Brandubh grabbed the boy and yanked him off the ground so he could bellow directly into the beardless face.

"No one, Brandubh. He bid us leave him and join the battle."

"What!" Brandubh's roar reverberated off the rocks and the ground and the trunks of the trees. "Have you all gone mad? Don't you know why he remained behind?"

Of course they didn't know. How could they know that Brian was destined to die this day? Now, instead of being surrounded by trusted guards in his tent, he was alone with every Viking and traitorous Irishman on this field sniffing for his blood.

"We will go back, Brandubh," one of the guards offered, looking longingly toward the waning fight.

"No. I have had my belly full of fighting. Go on. I will go to him."

They grinned and took off, their voices loud with the name of their king.

"*Boru!*"

Brandubh glanced at the boy. "Go on. Stay out of the way of danger, though."

The boy's face split in a smile. "Thank you, Brandubh. I will return before dark."

Brandubh turned and headed toward the tent. Finally, he sheathed the sword that had been in his hand all day. His fingers were stiffened into a near circle. They wouldn't relax until sometime tomorrow, he knew.

Clenching and working frozen joints, he walked on, his mind on his aching hand. Out of the corner of his eye, he glimpsed a shadow moving through the trees. Too far to make out the identity, there was no mistaking the destination.

Brandubh broke into a run for Brian's tent.

There was the shadow again, sneaking like a weasel through the brush. A Viking, he thought, catching the setting sun's glint off the ax the man carried strapped to his back.

"Sweet Jesus." Brandubh ran on, grateful for the spurt of energy. At the first sounds of metal on metal he looked around for help. He was too far away. He wouldn't get there in time.

"God's blood, it's just as she said." A Viking came up behind him and killed him with an ax.

"No!" Brandubh struggled up the hill, knowing he was already too late. A man screamed in pain--surely not Brian, he thought. Wood splintered under an ax-blow. A sword sang through the air.

Brandubh closed the distance to the tent, his lungs burning, his muscles crying for rest. The tent flap was open and he could see inside. He drew his sword and trotted forward, yet he could have been slogging through mud for all the progress he made. The tent seemed to get further away instead of closer.

Time slowed to a crawl.

"Brian, I'm coming," he shouted.

But Brian showed no signs of hearing him and Brandubh watched helplessly as the old king fought his last.

A grim grin on his face, Brian swung his sword. The Viking roared in anger when the blade bit into his upper leg. The blade cut into the big bone and the sound of the crunch echoed off the leather walls. Brian pulled on the hilt, struggling with the sword as he was covered by the Northman's spurting blood.

At that moment, the dying Viking raised his mighty ax, nearly as a reflex. There was no mind guiding it.

"*Brian!*"

Brian bent to pull at his blade, finally freeing it. Then he looked up.

Into the edge of the falling ax.

Brandubh stopped. He felt his mouth drop open.

It was over.

He hit the dirt on his knees at the entrance to Brian's tent.

Inside, Brian mac Cennedi, *Ard Ri*, lay dead next to his murderer. Even from here, Brandubh could see the peace which had settled upon Brian's

# THE RAVEN'S LADY

face.

From the marshes, the howl rose on the wind. The *ban-sidhe* wailed for Brian Boru.

* * * *

The sun was setting behind her, but Eibhlin's eyes were on the east. Somewhere on the other side of this island, a battle was being fought--perhaps it was already over by now--one of those pivotal things historians would argue about for centuries to come.

Did the men on the field even think of that? Or did every battle seem pivotal to those who felt the sting of the blade and seeping of their blood as they faded to death?

It was Good Friday evening, a time of dying and grieving and Eibhlin walked the palisade, praying for the souls of the dead and the health of the living. Sadbh had been with her for most of the day. Though she had not taken her mother-in-law into her confidence about the outcome, Sadbh was sensitive enough to know that Eibhlin knew more than she said. All during the day, Sadbh had looked over at her, and the question, though unasked, had been plain on her face.

Will our men return?

Eibhlin couldn't have answered for she didn't know.

Finally, Sadbh had gone to the chapel.

Maybe I ought to join her, Eibhlin thought. At least praying was something. All I'm really doing is waiting.

Like she'd been doing for more than five weeks. Yet what more was there to do?

She carefully descended the narrow stairway and crossed the courtyard. All around was a hush, an expectation, a sense of apprehension. Then the howling wind rushed around the buildings, raising the fine hairs on the back of her neck.

As though the wind had been the breath of a mourner, there came a wail, an unearthly cry of despair and loss. The chapel door slammed open against the inside wall and Sadbh stood, arms bracing against the doorframe, flickering light outlining her body.

Eibhlin could see in her eyes the near hysterical fear she only just kept at bay.

"The *ban-sidhe*," Sadbh cried out. "Dougal! *Brandubh*!"

Eibhlin set her hands against the older woman's cold cheeks.

"Sadbh, the wail is for Brian. He is dead."

Sadbh turned eyes of ice blue, now cold with fear, on her.

"How do you know?"

"I just know. Come," she said as she took Sadbh's hands and pulled her out of the chapel. "Let's go get roaring drunk, Lady. There is little else to be done until we hear some word. I think I prefer to face the next couple of days completely insensate."

Her mother-in-law didn't laugh at the joke.

"I hate myself when I get like this," Sadbh whispered. "I despise being so weak."

To tell the truth, Eibhlin had worried about her since the army had left. Over the weeks, Sadbh had been less and less her usual self. Still, Eibhlin attempted to reassure her.

"You worry about your husband and your son. There's nothing weak in that," Eibhlin reminded her.

Sadbh shook her head. "No, it is more than that. I have this unnatural fear for Brandubh. He is my only child, Eibhlin. The only one who survived, that is. I have always felt my lack in not giving my husband more children."

"Does Dougal feel deprived? In my opinion, Brandubh is enough, son or husband, for anybody."

Sadbh finally smiled, though weakly. "Dougal would never say he was displeased, no. But I see in him the same fear for this only child of ours." She shook her head. "How he can go off and watch Brandubh with sword in hand, fighting for his very life, and not go mad...." Stopping in her tracks, she pulled Eibhlin around to face her. Her eyes bore a more terrifying light, one of desperation. "What if he is dead? There will be naught of him left."

Eibhlin smiled and took Sadbh's hand, laying it against her belly. "Nay, lady."

The icy blue softened as Eibhlin's meaning sank in. She wrapped Eibhlin in a hug and wept softly into her hair.

"Thank God. And thank you, my dear." Sadbh suddenly stood back. "My goodness. Look at me, weeping on you when you need to be resting. Come, now." At last the fear had been put aside and Sadbh had a mission again.

Eibhlin let herself be pulled inside, fed, bathed, wrapped, kept company, knowing there would be times in the future when she would weep herself dry with joy for such attention. She let Sadbh have her way to keep their minds off the fates of their husbands, so they could both stay sane.

* * * *

Nine long shields had been lashed together to accommodate Brian's body. He lay there even now, looking as much a king in death as he had in life. They had managed to keep the priests away from him, thank God, while they had washed his wounds and put a clean tunic on him. Now, except that he lay far too still, he didn't look dead.

Brandubh stared, the pain sharp, the guilt heavy.

I should have been quicker. I should have been here, by his side all the time. The battle didn't need one more warrior. I had known what was really at stake today and I let myself get caught up in the fighting.

Eibhlin was right, he thought in his misery. *I am nothing more than a killer.*

"What is going on here?"

Brandubh looked up. One of the priests paced before the fire, arms waving, brown robe flapping like the wings of a troubled chicken.

"I will not permit this pagan heresy."

Cian, Brian's near son, the husband of his second daughter, entered the firelight.

"Quiet, priest. You will get your chance at Armagh. Here, he is still ours and we will tend him as befits an Irish king."

Cian elbowed the priest aside. The cleric shuffled further away to avoid Cian's burden--he carried in each hand the head of one of the Irish dead. Brandubh watched the care with which Cian and the others arranged the heads of the dead around Brian, facing out, their lifeless eyes on the horizon.

He would love this, Brandubh thought, knowing that Brian was more Irish prince than Christian king. Not that he trafficked with the Druids, but he respected all the old ways.

"*Il Papa* would spit holy water if he could see this," Dougal said *sottovoce*.

Brandubh felt the snort stirring and didn't try to hold it down. Of course, heads turned at his sniffling, choking, finally, outright laughter as he thought of the Pope's reaction. Yes, he probably would spit, though Brandubh doubted that it would be holy water. Probably more likely he would piss in rage.

He howled even louder, evoking a glance of concern from even Dougal.

"Nothing, Father. I was just thinking...," he tried to explain. Again, a convulsion of mirth had him leaning against the tree in helplessness.

"Brandubh," Dougal said, uncertainly, seizing Brandubh's shoulder.

Brandubh took a deep breath and regained control of himself.

"I'm fine." He chuckled, even while the grief still hurt.

Dougal nodded. "I will not be going to Armagh, Brandubh. There are too many wounded and not enough able-bodied men to see them home." With a dismissive toss of his head toward Malachy, he said, "Let the *Ard Ri* there see Brian's body safely to the dirt where he has wished him for years. They don't need me."

This last was said in a rather loud voice.

Malachy turned toward Dougal. "What say you, Italian?"

"I said, you wanted him dead. Now he is. You bury him. I will take his army home." Dougal turned to leave the scene.

"Dougal, or whatever you name is, do not turn your back on me."

"You are not my king, Meathman."

"But I will be again."

"When that time comes, I shall be at Tara to hear the Stone shout for you as it did for Brian. If it does, I shall agree you are my king. Until that time...." Dougal tipped Malachy a mocking bow and turned his back again.

Brandubh stepped between them.

"Nay, Malachy." Brandubh whispered down into the man's face as he grabbed Malachy's hand, already on the hilt of his sword. "No more killing today."

Leaving Malachy in silent rage, Brandubh caught up with Dougal and lay his arm around Dougal's shoulders. His voice lowered for his father's ears alone, he said, "I will ride ahead to Kincora and return with help. I do not expect we will get any from the people of the kingdoms between here and Munster."

"I agree. However, I would have you ride with me, Brandubh. Such a large contingent will attract attention and few are in shape for fighting."

"I have to get back by Beltain, Dougal. You know that."

"Aye, boy, I know. Yet every man here wants to see his woman."

Brandubh sputtered. "There is more than just wanting to see her. I told her if I did not return she was to go back to her own place. If I don't arrive before Beltain, she may be gone."

"Then we will send ahead to Kincora the message that we have won,"-- how hollow that sounded--"and that we are returning." Dougal waved to a boy, not yet shaving, who ran up to them at once. "Rory, get a sound horse and hie you back to Kincora ahead of us. Carry this message to my wife...."

The boy listened, his intelligent eyes shining as he absorbed his instructions. Brandubh envied him his charge. He would be at Kincora in two days, surely no more than three.

Brandubh raised his head and whistled. Conchobar came trotting from the trees, tender blades of grass sticking from between his lips. If he couldn't go himself, Brandubh would make sure the boy arrived with his message.

Rory's eyes got big as Brandubh handed over the reins.

"Here, lad, take Conchobar. Stay in Meath until you get to Munster and watch your back. If you are set upon, give Conchobar his head and hold on. He will get you out of trouble."

"Aye, Brandubh. Thank you. I will care for him well."

Brandubh held Conchobar's head, allowing the boy to mount.

The stallion jittered, uneasy to have this mite on his back instead of Brandubh's bulk. He twisted his head to focus one big brown eye on Brandubh.

"Be gentle, Conchobar. Take him home to Kincora."

Conchobar stilled at Brandubh's voice. He lowered his head and nudged Brandubh in the middle of the chest.

"Aye, lad. I know," Brandubh said, stroking the huge hell-black head.

Rory had a good seat, Brandubh noted, and good hands, too.

"Rory, when you arrive and you've delivered the message Dougal has given you, find my lady and tell her I am well and I am returning, though it will be later than we had agreed upon."

"Aye, Lord. I will."

With a smile of pure joy, Rory turned Conchobar toward the west and gave him his head. Conchobar, rested and fed and ready for an adventure, bunched his heavy flanks and exploded like a bolt from a bow. Rory was with him from the first and Brandubh smiled. To be so young, so easily pleased.

Watching Conchobar grow smaller in the distance, Brandubh prayed his message would reach his wife in time. On the salty breeze coming off the sea behind his back, he sent her a silent apology.

I failed you, my Lady. I failed you and he is dead.

A heavy push from the back roused him. Turning, he felt his eyes cloud with grief. Brian's horse stood there, head hanging.

"Ah, Lugh," he grated in a whisper, laying his forehead against the thick cream-colored neck. "Do you miss him already?" Brandubh stroked the wide white blaze in the middle of the animal's head, thinking of the day twelve years ago when he'd presented the young colt to Brian. That was the day Brian had become the *Ard Ri*. Brandubh had been little more than a boy.

"Take him, Brandubh. It is right that you should have him."

Brandubh raised his head. Cian stood beside him, stroking Lugh's shoulder.

"His sons will want him."

Cian seemed to consider this. "Then ride him home and give him to Teigue. Of course, we could take him to Armagh and bury him with Brian."

Brandubh turned his shocked face toward Cian, who only smiled. "Old Celt practice, bury the prince's horse with the prince."

"I never heard of that one."

Cian pointed toward the pasty-faced clerics who were still tut-tut-ing the collection of detached heads attending their dead king. "Do you think they know that? Mayhap I should suggest it."

"Cian, your sense of humor is more bizarre than Dougal's."

Cian pasted an outraged expression over his face. "Is that even possible?"

Brandubh finally laughed. "No. I suppose not."

"Take him, Brandubh." Cian slapped Brandubh's shoulder and walked off. "We go to take Dublin now," he said as he walked off, reminding Brandubh the fighting wasn't over yet.

But it is for me. At least for now, Brandubh thought.

"Come, Lugh, we go to Kincora."

Chapter Thirty

April 30, 1014--Kincora

The deep peal of the abbey's bells announced one of the hours. Eibhlin noted the sound but could not remember which it might be. For seven nights and days she had paced the rampart of Kincora's high palisaded wall, her eyes searching the eastern horizon for some sign of Brandubh's return.

He's alive, a small voice assured her. Just wait and believe. For a week they'd waited for word from Clontarf, but there had been none.

Uncertainty made it difficult to hear the sure faith of her heart.

"Ho. A horse," the guard shouted. "A black."

"Who is it? Can you see?" she asked, peering into the darkness, straining to make out the approaching figure.

"Well, my Lady, it looks like Brandubh mac Dougal's horse, that Conchobar."

"Conchobar. Thank God." A swell of relief surged through her. She turned to the guard. "Go, quickly. Tell Lady Sadbh."

Eibhlin would have gone herself, but she couldn't take her eyes from Conchobar once she'd made him out. He paused to crop a blade of grass, as though glad to get back to decent food. Eibhlin became irritated with him, letting Conchobar dally like that.

"Come on, Brandubh, come on," she whispered.

But when Conchobar trotted toward the gate that had been opened for him, Eibhlin saw he was riderless. Her shoulders fell under the weight of the realization.

"No," she breathed, "No."

She leaned against the wall, fighting with the surety her husband was dead. How long she stood there, she didn't know. A gentle hand on her shoulder shook her from her torpor.

"Is it?..." Sadbh stood beside her. "The guard told me Conchobar...."

Eibhlin could only nod.

"Brandubh?..."

The nod became a shake. "No. Conchobar arrived alone."

Sadbh's mouth opened but no sound came out, for a moment, then her cry flew out on the wind.

"No, no, not my son. Not my son." Sadbh's shoulders convulsed with her grief as she wept.

"Stop it!" Eibhlin grabbed her husband's mother and shook her. "He's not dead."

"His horse would never return without him."

That bit of logic hit drove her to her knees on the walkway and she leaned against the wall, her own cry joining with Sadbh's in a melody of heartache.

The women who loved Brandubh mac Dougal held each other and wept together.

Even as she wept, Eibhlin thought of his words.

If I die at Clontarf, you should return to your own place. Then she thought of the secret she held sleeping even now within her body and wondered if she could dare the trip through the shimmering barrier without destroying the only part of Brandubh she had left.

* * * *

May 1, 1014--near Cashel in Munster

The silent stone walls of Cashel kept the watch in the early morning as the broken of Brian's great army roused for another day's travel home. Brandubh gazed up at that fortress where his grandfather, Mahon mac Cennedi, had ruled as King of Munster.

THE RAVEN'S LADY

Mahon died at the hand of traitors, lured by promises of peace and the Church's protection. Brandubh had heard Brian's version of the story often enough. Brian had been bitter, even after all these years, that Mahon had ignored sensible--that is, Brian's--counsel. Brandubh had always understood Brian was more angry that his adored brother had proved to be no more than a mere man, a man who could be struck down by the puny mortals around him.

He understood now better than ever. His eyes teared anew with the sting of grief.

"How could you die, Brian?" Brandubh tried wiping away his anger along with the tear that rolled from his eye. All was done now. The power of the Northmen destroyed. Ireland was free.

For now.

"Are you ready to get under way, son?" Dougal asked in his rumbling morning voice.

"Aye, I am anxious. When do we make Kincora?"

Dougal glanced up at the sky. "If we have fair weather, I think sometime day after tomorrow. We have pushed the wounded too hard. I do wish Rory would return with some help." He set his hand on Brandubh's shoulder. "We could use your lady's skills right now. Some of the men may not make it all the way back to Kincora without some care."

"It is Beltain, Dougal."

Dougal heard his fear. "She will be there, Brandubh. Rory and Conchobar have arrived by now. She knows you are returning to her. I'm grateful that you stayed with us instead of going to Armagh."

"Would Brian have left them?"

Dougal laughed. "That depends. Not for a woman, but should there be something needful for Ireland, he would have ridden off without a backward glance." His laughter faded, replaced by a deep sigh. "Ah, I miss him. It hardly seems possible he is truly gone."

Brandubh let his father grieve for a moment, then slapped him on the shoulder.

"Come, Dougal. Our women await."

"Impudent puppy. I shall inform your mother of your insolence." Dougal grinned. "But not before I have made my own greetings."

He wrapped his arm around Brandubh's shoulders and they walked back toward the camp to see to preparations for moving. They had little, so it was quickly done. Mounted on Brian's war horse, Brandubh rode up and down the lines, making sure no one was left behind, keeping his eyes on the horizon for the predators sure to come out of the woods now that Brian was dead.

There had been signs along the way--burned houses and dead animals. And dead men. And women. And children.

After all the blood and the broken bodies at Clontarf, it would seem the shattered body of a child would evoke nothing more than notice, but Brandubh's eyes had burned and his stomach had tightened at the sight.

When he'd turned away, he'd seen the signs of tears trickling into beards smeared with Viking blood on faces old before their time.

"Sweet Jesus." He heard that name invoked more than once. Some heathen voice in him asked where sweet Jesus was for all this to happen to men who called on His name?

He brought himself back to today and rode on, keeping his eyes on the far away line where sky met earth. Dougal galloped up to his side and laid his hand on Brandubh's arm.

"Look there. Isn't that?...."

Brandubh followed Dougal's motion to a yellow-brown lump on the side of the road. Reining in his mount, he gazed in disbelief at the body of a boy, his chin not yet shadowed by a whisker.

"Rory," Brandubh whispered. The boy who had taken off on Conchobar to get to Kincora in good time with the news of Clontarf.

To tell Eibhlin that he lived and was returning.

He dismounted and knelt by the body. At first he feared Conchobar had killed the boy, then saw the real cause of death.

A plain dagger protruded from the lifeless neck.

"Thieves. So much for our message. Or for getting wagons for moving the wounded." He spoke softly, for Dougal's ears only. Scanning the area, he looked for sign of Conchobar, but the rains had erased any trace of hoofprints. Had the thieves killed the poor boy for the horse?

He stood and whistled and waited, but the echo of Conchobar's hoofbeats did not come to him on the morning breeze.

"Where did he go, do you think?" Dougal asked, clearly his thoughts the same as Brandubh's.

"Home. Kincora, since that is where we last were."

"Holy Virgin, Brandubh. If your mother sees Conchobar come in alone, she will believe you dead and wail like the ban-sidhe until she is spent."

Of course, Dougal's first concern was for his own wife, but Brandubh had more serious concerns. Sadbh would recover from her spasm of grief once Brandubh appeared alive. Eibhlin would be deciding right this moment whether to go to Craglea to leave him forever.

"Father, I have to get to Kincora today." He leaped into the saddle and gauged the horse's stamina. "When I arrive, I will send as much assistance as I can gather."

Dougal nodded. "Go, son. We are in Munster now and as safe as men ever are. Tell your mother I am well and on my way."

Brandubh nodded his thanks for his father's understanding and kicked Lugh to a run.

* * * *

Moira had paced by the window all morning, gazing at Craglea. She was as bad as a kid. Are we there yet? When, when, when? Eibhlin could practically hear the questions. Yet, she couldn't begrudge Moira her excitement. Today really *was* the first day of the rest of her life.

And mine.

She didn't realize she was so self-absorbed until she felt Moira sit beside her on the couch.

"Eibhlin, are you listening?"

"I'm sorry, Mama. What is it?"

"I said I cannot leave you here alone. I will not go."

"You have to. If you don't go, what happens to me?"

Moira's eyes widened as she pondered that. "This business is very complicated, is it not?"

Yes, it certainly is, Eibhlin thought. And it gets more complicated all the time.

"Mama, I have some news. I wasn't going to tell you until Brandubh got back, but now.... Anyway, I'm pregnant."

"How wonderful," Moira said, her happiness tempered by the knowledge her daughter would raise this child alone. "You have him still, then." This last was spoken slightly like a question.

"Yes. You know, Mama, I think it's a boy." She tried to smile, but the clenching heartache stopped it.

Moira took her hand and held it. "Perhaps you can take the child to your place and raise him there," Moira said.

"I could. But...." She hadn't really thought of why she wouldn't take Brandubh's child to the twentieth century, even if she could. It was clear to her now, though. "But he couldn't be the man his father would want him to be there. Brandubh's child belongs here. I belong here, now."

It was true. Finally, she knew it for a fact.

With a heavy sigh, Moira nodded. "And I do not. Any more."

Eibhlin did manage a little grin at that. "So, you are not afraid?"

"Oh, no. What a grand adventure it is! Think on it...." Her face lit in a truly amused smile. "Why do I tell you this? Who could know better than you what an adventure this will be? No, I am not afraid, but I would like you to go with me if you will. I am not sure I would know what to look for. Will you?"

"Certainly, Mama."

"When do we go?"

Eibhlin had absolutely no idea of when they should go. Each time, she'd just been there.

An anguished wail drifted down the hallway to the solar. Sadbh's grief overflowed her and Eibhlin felt drowned by it.

"We can go now, Mama. I just need to get something."

Moira glanced toward the sound of Sadbh's cries and nodded.

* * * *

"Ho, Kincora. Open the gates for Brandubh mac Dougal."

Brandubh was surprised he could get the strength for such a shout. He rode without slowing into the courtyard and toward the stable.

"Brandubh! Brandubh, by the bones of Christ, boy, we thought you dead." The stableman, long in Brian's employ, took the reins of the spent horse. Lines appeared in the old face and his stroked the horse's face tenderly. "Our lord Brian?" the old man asked quietly.

Brandubh lay his hand on Leary's shoulder. "He's gone. They've taken him to Armagh for burying in the great church there as befits the true *Ard Ri*. He died a warrior's death, Leary, and I believe he was glad to do it."

Leary nodded. "'Tis well, then."

"Leary, is my horse here?"

"He is, Brandubh. I have taken good care of him for you. Even though we thought...." Leary's faded eyes teared finally. "He came in yesterday evening, foamin' and frothed. There were signs of maltreatment, but he will be well." The old man clucked to the horse and went inside the stable.

Brandubh watched, knowing that there would be much more grief brought by his arrival this day. He turned and headed for the king's house that occupied the middle of the huge compound. The door was opened and he entered, letting his eyes adjust to the darkness.

Had no one thought to open the shutters?

He hurried along the corridor to the chamber he had shared too few nights with Eibhlin.

"My Lady," he called to the empty room as he threw open the door. "Eibhlin?"

A gasp snatched his attention away from the emptiness for a moment.

"Brandubh." His name hung on the air.

"Yes, Mother," he answered and went to take her in his arms. Sadbh clung to him, her heavy tears dampening his face.

"My sweet baby," she sang to him. "Oh, my dear, you are alive? You are well?"

"Yes, Mother, I am well."

"Dougal?" she asked, and he could hear the fear of his answer in her voice. "Where is your father?"

"Father is coming with the column of wounded, Mother. No, no...." At her muted cry, he grasped her hands between his own and for the first time noticed the signs of age. He released her grip enough to stroke her hair, once glittering copper red--he could remember playing with it and arranging it to shine just so--now the sheen was tempered by strands of white. "Father is fine. Not a scratch on him."

That was a bit of a lie, for Dougal did bear a few marks of the battle, but the relief in her eyes gave him forgiveness.

"Thank God. Oh, thank Jesus." She collapsed against him and wrapped her arms around his waist.

"Mother, where is Eibhlin?"

"She and Moira went out just a short while ago. They headed toward the Crag carrying a couple of bundles."

"Craglea? Are you certain, Mother?"

"Yes." Sadbh raised her eyes to his, realization dawning. "Brandubh, you must hurry. Go after her and show her you are alive. We had thought, when Conchobar returned without you...."

"Did she say she was leaving?"

"I have not spoken with her since this morning." She closed her eyes, clearly embarrassed by her weakness. "I retired to my room to grieve in privacy."

"It is all right, Mother, but before I attend to my own business, I have to send wagons for the wounded...."

"Where are they?"

He frowned, but answered her, "On the road to Cashel."

"How many?"

"There are fifty or more who will need serious care. Some twenty are able to walk, but are slowing the column."

"Good. Go, Brandubh, I will attend to it. Go, now before you lose her."

"But, Moth...."

Sadbh had already turned from him and was striding down the hallway toward the guard's station. Her back was straight and she stepped as quickly as he'd ever seen her. "*Go*, Brandubh."

"Yes, Mother," he said with a smile and he turned and ran from the house, not stopping until, lungs rebelling and legs weak as watered ale, he reached the foot of Craglea.

What if she were already gone?

No, don't think that. If she were gone, you would know it, feel it. No, she's still here, up there. He raised his eyes, scanning the grassy hillside. Then he saw her, Moira at her side. She carried a large bundle in her arms.

He gulped a chestful of air.

"Eibhlin!" He shouted her name with every bit of strength he had. Yet the sound only bounced off the wall of grass-covered rock and echoed around him, mocking his impotence.

She continued toward the top of the hill, where he'd found her. Where time had no meaning and she would be taken from him forever.

"Eibhlin! Wait!" Brandubh took off at a run up the hillside, urging his weary legs to get him up to her before she was gone.

* * * *

"Well, here it is." Eibhlin set her bundle on the ground and looked around. She'd never been able to see the curtain until Brandubh showed it to her and wondered if she'd see it now. What if they missed it? What if Moira didn't meet Seamus? Would Eibhlin just disappear and not be?

"What in Heaven?..."

At Moira's whispered question, she glanced over and saw Moira staring down at the lake. Kincora was gone. Slightly upriver where only the monastery had stood, was the bustling town of Killaloe.

"Careful, Mama. There it is."

Down on the Shannon, sailboats worked their way toward Limerick. Above them, a plane departed Shannon airport headed for the northeast. Eibhlin had never been one for planes, but this one looked like it had propellers.

Moira stared in open-mouthed amazement. Eibhlin laid her arm over her mother's shoulders and squeezed.

"Better get used to it, Mama. It'll only get worse."

"There are more wonderful things than that?" She pointed to the disappearing plane.

Eibhlin laughed. She wished she could see Moira's adjustment to modern life, but, there were important matters to attend to. She leaned over and picked up the bundle.

"I have a favor to ask you, Mama."

"Anything, dear one."

"Take this with you."

Moira took it and opened the linen with which it had been wrapped. "Oh, Eibhlin, where did you get it? It's beautiful."

"Brian gave it to me before he left. You'll teach me to play this. There is one other thing. When I disappear--you'll know the time--I want you to go to my house. My neighbor, Angela, has a key. This'll be in my bedroom by the gas fireplace."

"By the what?"

Eibhlin smiled. "You'll understand when it's time, Mama. Speaking of time, come, we probably don't have much more." She took Moira's hand and they walked along, stopping before a boulder.

"You know, I regret so many things about this. Leaving you and not being able to know your child." Moira laughed. "Wouldn't it be wonderful if you could leave me a message?"

"Too bad there's no postal service between here and there."

"What?"

"Nevermind," Eibhlin said as she gazed at the hedgerow running along the Crag and remembered her history. "Listen, maybe there is a way. Can you remember where we are right now?"

Moira looked around. "I think so. Why?"

"When the Northmen were going about sacking the monasteries and great houses, treasures were buried to keep them from falling into Viking hands. Sometimes they stayed buried for hundreds of years. We're going to try it. You and Dad come here. Dig among the roots of this hedge right behind this boulder. I'll bury a message for you."

Moira smiled and shook her head. "So strange."

At that moment, the air around them shimmered. A man appeared over the rise from the direction of Killaloe. He was tall, broad-shouldered, with ruddy cheeks and russet hair waving around his face.

He glanced around, as though looking for something. Then he stood straight and opened his mouth.

Eibhlin shut her eyes. The angel's music surrounded her with memory. Seamus Fitzgerald sang out, his baritone ringing over the hill. It carried like a living thing, filling the whole air. She listened to the whole song, knowing it would be the last time she would hear her father's voice.

Then it stopped and her heart felt the loss. She opened her eyes and saw Seamus looking at them.

Well, not at *them*. His eyes set on Moira and didn't move. He didn't appear to notice Eibhlin at all. Moira returned his gaze.

"It is the man from my dreams."

"Yes. That is my father. Go to him."

Seamus held out his hand. Moira stepped forward to take it. Her hand passed through the barrier setting up a shimmer, which Seamus watched dissipate in rivulets from the spot. Glancing back, Moira reached for Eibhlin.

Eibhlin stretched and laced her fingers with Moira's. At that moment, she saw Seamus' eyes widen in surprise as though she had just appeared to him.

"Goodbye, Daddy," she said--in English--unable to stop herself.

Moira's joyful smile shone like the sun. She pulled Eibhlin closer and kissed her gently on the lips. "Goodbye, dear one. Take care." Then she stepped through the barrier and collapsed into Seamus' arms as the effects of her journey overcame her.

Eibhlin had taken care to explain this part and had no fear Moira would not recover. After all, Seamus was there to look after her.

Standing alone in the light of the dying day, Eibhlin laid her hand against her belly and watched her mother and father fade from her view.

* * * *

Brandubh, exhausted, waited for the curtain to disappear. She hadn't passed through. She'd made her decision.

"Eibhlin," he called to her.

Her shoulders straightened and she turned, very slowly.

"Brandubh," her whisper floated to him on the breeze. "You're alive."

"Indeed, my Lady. I am."

She ran to him and leaped into his arms. Her lips peppered his face, landing wherever they could. She held onto him as though to let him go was death.

"Oh, my love, my love. I was so afraid. I saw your horse... and your mother said... and you didn't come back...."

Her mouth divided its time between the words and the kisses. For Brandubh's part, his mouth was devoted solely to tasting her from head to foot and every place in between.

She cried. She laughed. She sobbed. She giggled.

They stood there, clinging, touching, reveling in the feel of each other's firm flesh.

"My Lady," he whispered when kisses were no longer enough. "I would take you here, if you are willing."

Her answer was to pull him down to the ground to cover her. Neither thought of witnesses. It was Beltain after all, a time of fertility and license.

He filled her quick and hard. Too soon, she arched beneath him, her joy giving her a quick release. He emptied himself into her warm body, spent before he really had the chance to get the feel of her again.

"Don't ever leave me again, Brandubh." Her whispered command brushed across his cheek.

"Never, my Lady."

They lay on the hill, still joined by the fleshly bond which was only a reminder of the bonding of their hearts.

"I love you, Eibhlin." The words came of their own accord, unbidden.

The look in her eyes told him what it meant. "I love you, my Raven."

He found her mouth with his own. Now that the edge of his hunger was blunted, he could take his time feasting on her.

"When I saw you up here, I thought you were leaving. Why did you stay?"

"What's the matter, warrior? Are you insecure?"

"I do not understand."

"Never mind. I probably can't go back anyway. So, it's no big deal."

"You didn't even try?"

"No. The curtain was open for my mother, not me. I didn't want to go back to before I was even born."

As though bidden, the shimmering air announced the appearance of the barrier. It beckoned and danced around them, surrounding them with flashing light. It seemed stronger this time, Brandubh thought, wondering if such a thing might be somehow alive. Did Moira's passing feed it somehow? Was it looking for more?

"Oh, no." Eibhlin grabbed his arm as they rose from the ground.

He looked down at the Lough and saw the reason for her fearful tone. Kincora was gone, only tumbled stones remained. The site of the monastery was a town of some kind. The roar of some strange machine took his attention upward.

"God's bones. What is that?"

"A jumbo jet." She tightened her hold on him, her grip one of a person trying to keep from drowning. "Don't let go of me, Brandubh."

Brandubh asked the question he feared the answer to. "Is this your time?"

She nodded, but said nothing.

Stretching his hand out as he had before, he located the barrier. He still was unable to pass through, and it surrounded him, trapping him.

"Eibhlin, I want you to try to pass."

"No. What if I can't get back?"

"Do it quickly before it fades. It may never appear for us again. If you don't we will both wonder for the rest of our lives if you could have left if you'd wanted to."

"I won't wonder. I don't care. I've made up my mind."

"Then do it because I will wonder."

The shimmering curtain beckoned.

She stared into his eyes. "You really want me to try?"

"Yes, I do. I have to know, Eibhlin."

"All right. I'll do it because you want me to. Just don't let go."

"Never." He took her hand and held his breath as she stepped across the barrier.

She trembled, the nervousness traveling to him through their joined fingers. "I'm here," she said, her voice weak.

Brandubh saw the uncertainty growing in her eyes. Did she want to stay on that side?

"Should I release you?" he asked, struggling with the tremor in his voice.

"No!" She threw herself back through and into his arms.

The curtain shimmered and faded. Brandubh fell to his knees and wrapped his arms around her waist. They both gasped for breath and Brandubh could feel her heart beating wildly against his cheek. Eibhlin stroked his head, weaving her fingers through his hair as though caressing a charm.

"Thank you, my love," she said, "Thank you for making me try. Now I know I made the choice."

He suddenly realized he was weeping with relief. Eibhlin pulled back and looked at him.

"What's wrong, Brandubh? Didn't you trust me when I said I love you?" She knelt with him and held his head between her hands. With her thumbs, she smoothed away the tears that streaked his face.

"I always said I would not keep you here against your will."

"My will is to be with you."

Unable to say the words in his heart, Brandubh wrapped her in his arms and held her tight against him as the sun fell into the Great Sea.

Finally, Eibhlin tipped her face up to his.

"Come, husband. I would continue this in our chamber. I have news that will be of interest to you."

"News?"

"I will tell you when you have bathed and eaten and rested, and after you have told me everything that has happened since you left. My news is best saved to temper the taste of sadness."

Down by Lough Derg, Kincora reigned, for now. The monastery bell tolled Vespers. Clinging to each other, Brandubh mac Dougal and his wife went down Craglea for the last time.

Epilogue

November 10, 1998--Another piece of Irish history was unearthed this week. Taking its place beside the Ardagh Chalice and the Book of Kells, a small box was discovered buried on a hillside in County Clare. The style of the gold decoration dates it to the early eleventh century, but it is the contents which are most interesting.

Inside was found a splendid warrior's dagger bearing a set of names and dates--Brian (1014), Ailis (1016), Etain (1019), Mahon (1021), Cennedi (1025). Scholars are even now poring over volumes of Irish history to determine the significance of the list. Obviously, the first is a reference to the near-legendary Irish king, Brian Boru, who died in the year 1014 at the Battle of Clontarf. His seat of government has been traditionally located near the hill where the box was found.

More puzzling are the other contents. One, a note written in Irish but executed in Roman script by a feminine hand, bore the words, "Dear Mama and Dad, If you find this, know that I am fine and we have had a good life. Evie."

Five locks of hair had been meticulously tied with a piece of royal blue silk embroidered with one of the five names from the dagger. The two female names were assigned to the copper red and brown locks, while the male names--Brian, Mahon, Cennedi--were tied around tiny bundles of black hair in which white strands had been mixed.

The only other contents were a set of brass harp strings, such as were used in the tenth century.

An interesting sidenote is that this extraordinary find was made by international folk singing legends, Seamus and Moira Fitzgerald. The Fitzgeralds have been traveling in their native Ireland where their daughter, Eibhlin Fitzgerald Wilde, was last seen alive. A noted phytopharmacologist conducting research in Ireland shortly before her death, Dr. Wilde was a passenger on ill-fated Flight 902, which crashed on November 1 with the loss of all on board. Hers is the only body not yet recovered.

"Being here in Ireland is giving us a sense of peace and closure. Eibhlin will never be completely lost to us," Moira Fitzgerald said, her face serene, as she handed the box and its contents over to the curator of the National Museum in Dublin.

*The scholarly debate has already begun on everything from the derivation of the name **Evie** to the identities of the persons named on the dagger to Evie's purpose in burying a note to her parents along with what looks like locks of baby hair.*

The debate will rage for years, but for now the beautifully decorated box and its contents are on display at the National Museum in Dublin.

Printed in the United States
34287LVS00003B/67-633